KATHRYN SPRINGER
A Treasure Worth Keeping

Hidden Treasures

HARLEQUIN®LOVE INSPIRED® CLASSICS

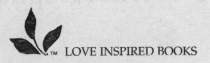 LOVE INSPIRED BOOKS

ISBN-13: 978-0-373-65164-1

A TREASURE WORTH KEEPING AND HIDDEN TREASURES
Copyright © 2013 by Harlequin Books S.A.

The publisher acknowledges the copyright holder of the individual works as follows:

A TREASURE WORTH KEEPING
Copyright © 2008 by Kathryn Springer

HIDDEN TREASURES
Copyright © 2008 by Kathryn Springer

www.Harlequin.com

Printed in U.S.A.

CONTENTS

Books by Kathryn Springer

Love Inspired

Tested by Fire
Her Christmas Wish
By Her Side
For Her Son's Love
A Treasure Worth Keeping
Hidden Treasures
Family Treasures
Jingle Bell Babies
*A Place to Call Home
*Love Finds a Home
*The Prodigal Comes Home
The Prodigal's Christmas Reunion
*Longing for Home
*The Promise of Home
The Soldier's Newfound Family
*Making His Way Home

*Mirror Lake

Love Inspired Single Title

Front Porch Princess
Hearts Evergreen
  "A Match Made
  for Christmas"
Picket Fence Promises
The Prince Charming List

KATHRYN SPRINGER

is a lifelong Wisconsin resident. Growing up in a "newspaper" family, she spent long hours as a child plunking out stories on her mother's typewriter and hasn't stopped writing since. She loves to write inspirational romance because it allows her to combine her faith in God with her love of a happy ending.

A TREASURE
WORTH KEEPING

But store up for yourselves treasures in heaven, where moth and rust do not destroy, and where thieves do not break in and steal. For where your treasure is, there your heart will be also.

—*Matthew* 6:20–21

To Linda—
A fellow traveler on the writer's journey.
I'm glad we're in this together, friend!

Prologue

"Please think about it, Evie. You're the only one of us who doesn't have—"

At the sound of a meaningful cough, Caitlin's words snapped off and Evie McBride smiled wryly.

Who doesn't have a life.

That's what Caitlin had been about to say before Meghan, "Miss Tactful," had broken into the conversation. They were talking on a three-way call, the usual method her two older sisters used to gang up on her. Sometimes advanced technology made life easier, and sometimes it was simply a pain in the neck.

"What Caitlin was going to say," Meghan continued in an annoyingly cheerful voice, "is that you're the only one whose summer schedule is...flexible."

Flexible. Nonexistent. Was there a difference? And if Evie had known how many times she'd be called upon to be *flexible* over the past few years since their father had retired, she wouldn't have chosen teaching as a career. She would have tied up her life with a neat little job that kept her working year-round, like her sisters had.

It wasn't that she minded helping out their dad. They were extremely close and she loved him to pieces. No, what drove her crazy was that Caitlin and Meghan always assumed she didn't have any plans for her summer vacation. And that just wasn't true. A neat stack of novels, the ones she hadn't had a chance to read during the school year, sat on the floor beside her bed. There was a miniature greenhouse in her backyard full of tomato seedlings waiting to be nurtured. And a gallon of paint in the hall closet, ready to transform her front door from boring beige to Tuscan yellow because she'd read somewhere that a front door should sport a friendly, welcoming color. And really, was there anything more friendly than yellow? Evie didn't think so.

"What if I have plans?" Evie asked. The sibling ambush had occurred at nine o'clock at night, interrupting her favorite educational program. There had to be some consequences for that. Unfortunately, stalling was all she could come up with.

"You do?" Meghan asked cautiously.

"What plans?" Caitlin demanded.

Now she was stuck. "Painting."

"Painting." Caitlin repeated the word like she'd never heard of the activity, and Evie could picture her rolling her baby blues at the ceiling.

"Is it something you can put off for a few weeks, Evie? Once I'm done with this photo shoot, I'll try to take some time off to help you." Meghan, bless her heart, let her keep her dignity.

Silence. Evie's cue to cave in. After all, that was her role. She sighed into the phone, knowing her sisters would accept it as the cowardly white flag of surrender that it was.

"All right. Fine. I can run Beach Glass while Dad goes on his fishing trip."

"Dad will be so happy." Caitlin's voice was as sweet as glucose syrup now that she'd gotten her way.

Evie resisted the urge to stick out her tongue at Caitlin's smiling face in the family photo on the coffee table.

"Evie, we *really* appreciate this," Meghan said. "And Dad will be thrilled. He didn't want to have to close up the store for two weeks."

"But he didn't want to ask you for help because he didn't want to take advantage of your free time," Caitlin added.

"Well, it's a good thing *you* don't have a problem with that, then, isn't it?" Evie said.

But not out loud.

What she said out loud was *good night,* allowing just a touch of weariness to creep into her voice. Hopefully enough to generate a smidgeon of guilt in her sisters' consciences. Not that it would matter when another crisis barked at the trunk of the McBride family tree. Why these crises always surfaced during the months of June, July and August, Evie didn't know.

Three years ago, Patrick McBride had officially retired from teaching and bought a small antique shop, whimsically christened Beach Glass by the previous owner. A quaint stone building, it sat comfortably on the edge of a lightly traveled road that wound along the

Lake Superior shoreline. A *very* lightly traveled road. It wasn't even paved. The first time Evie saw it, she had a strong hunch why the previous owners had practically *given* it away. They'd probably cashed the meager check in nearby Cooper's Landing on their way out of town, anxious to rejoin civilization.

Evie had spent most of that summer making the year-round cottage that had been included in the deal suitable for her father to live in. The calluses still hadn't completely disappeared.

The following summer she'd been the one drafted to spend "a few days" teaching their dad how to use a computer so he could manage all the financial records for the business. The brief computer lesson had turned into a month-long project that had ended with Patrick's mastering of the power button and not a whole lot more.

The previous summer, Caitlin's tail had gotten tied in a knot when Patrick happened to mention a woman's name *twice* during their weekly phone conversation. A Sophie Graham. Evie had flatly refused to act as the family spy. Her dad was an adult and it wasn't any of their business if he'd found a friend. Less than twenty-four hours after Evie had drawn a line in the sand over that situation, Caitlin had figured out a way to tug her over it. Beach Glass needed to be landscaped and since the only thing she and Meghan knew about plants was that the root part went into the ground, Evie was the obvious choice to spend six weeks mulching and planting flower beds.

Suspiciously, her sisters were always too busy to help out but never too busy to call and check up on her.

But Evie loved them. Even bossy, tell-it-like-it-is Caitlin. And she knew they loved her. And really, was it their fault all she could find to fill up three months of summer vacation was painting her front door, transplanting tomato plants and living vicariously through the lives of the characters in her favorite books?

Evie had missed most of her program during the kissing-up portion of the conversation so she turned off the television and closed her eyes.

I want my own story, God.

Even as the thought rushed through her mind, she treated it like the mutiny that it was.

Your own story! What are you talking about? You're a junior high science teacher. Shaping impressionable minds. It's a high calling.

Wasn't she the first teacher who'd taken the Rock of Ages Christian School to first place in the science fair competition the past few years? While all the other schools had entered working volcanoes and posters labeling the parts of a rocket, her students had brought in *inventions.* Like Micah Swivel's solar-powered toaster. And everyone knew the reason Angie Colson won the spelling bee with the word *bioluminescence* was because Evie had just finished a unit on insects. The day before, Angie had taken the chapter test and had chosen fireflies, a stellar example of bioluminescence, as the subject of her required essay. They'd shared the victory, celebrating with doughnuts and hot chocolate in the teachers' lounge.

Evie basked in the knowledge she had been loved by every seventh and eighth grader in her charge since the school had hired her. And if their test grades didn't prove their devotion, the number of cookies on her desk every morning did.

She had a story all right. It just happened to be woven into the lives of an age group most people ran, screaming, away from. She thrived between the months of August and May. The summer months made her feel restless. And lonely.

Maybe that's why she didn't fuss too much when her sisters rearranged her summer plans. It was nice to be needed. And she couldn't deny that their father, whom they affectionately referred to as the absentminded professor, needed a watchful eye.

Evie reached for the phone and pressed Speed Dial. "Hello?"

"Hi, Dad. I hear you're going fishing."

Chapter One

Sam Cutter had driven almost twelve hours when an old joke suddenly came back to him. Something about a town not being the end of the world but you could see it from there.

Now he knew that place had a name. Cooper's Landing. And it was cold. No one had warned him that winter released its grip with excruciating slowness along Lake Superior's shore. The second week of June and the buds on the trees had barely unfurled in shy, pale shades of green.

He drove slowly down the main street and pulled over next to the building that sagged tiredly on the corner. The color of the original paint on the clapboard siding was only a memory, and the shingles had loosened from the roof, curling up at the ends like the sole of a worn-out shoe. A red neon sign winked garishly in the window. Bait.

He glanced at the girl slumped against the window in the passenger seat. Her lips were moving silently, showing signs that yes, there was brain activity. Since she hadn't talked to him for the past five hours, he'd been forced to watch for obvious signs of life. They'd been few and far between. Changing the song on her iPod. The occasional piece of candy being unwrapped. A twitch of her bare toes. Well, not completely bare. One of them had a toe ring.

He touched her elbow and she flinched. Sam tried not to flinch back. Once upon a time she'd been generous with her hugs.

"Faith? I'll be right back."

She frowned and yanked out a headphone. "What?"

"We're here. I'll be right back."

She straightened, and her gaze moved from window to window. She had a front-row seat to view Cooper's Landing, and Sam expected to see some expression on her face. Shock? Terror? Instead, she shrugged and pushed the headphone back in place.

He wished he could disengage from reality and disappear into another world so easily.

The warped door of the bait shop swung open when he pushed on it, releasing an avalanche of smells. The prominent ones were fish, sauerkraut and bratwurst. Sam's eyes began to water.

"Let me guess. Cutter. You look just like your old man."

Sam saw a movement in the corner of the room just after he heard the voice. Between the heavy canvas awning shading the street side of the building and the tiny row of windows, the sunlight couldn't infiltrate the inside of the bait store. Shadows had taken over, settling into the maze of shelves. The lightbulbs flickering over his head held all the power of a votive candle.

"Sam Cutter." Sam walked toward the voice.

He heard a faint scraping noise and a man shuffled toward him out of the gloom, wiping his hands on a faded handkerchief. By the time he reached Sam, he'd stuffed it in the pocket of his coveralls and stretched out his hand.

"Rudy Dawes."

Sam shook his hand even as he silently acknowledged that a long, hot shower and half a bottle of the cologne he'd gotten for his birthday weren't going to completely strip away the bait store's unique blend of odors.

"I wasn't expecting to see you so soon. S'pose you're anxious to get a look at her." Rudy squinted up at him.

"That's why I'm here."

Rudy started to laugh but quickly broke into a dry, hacking cough. "Come on, she's outside."

Sam followed him to the back of the store, and his boot slipped on something, almost sending him into a skid that would have taken out a shelf full of fishing reels. He didn't bother to look down, not wanting to know what was filling the tread of his hiking boot. In some cases, ignorance *was* bliss.

Rudy pushed the door open, and Sam found himself standing on a rickety platform that trembled above an outcropping of rocks. At the base of the rocks, a blackened, water-stained dock stretched over the water. With one boat tied to it. Sam stared at it in disbelief as it nodded in rhythm with the waves.

"There she is. The *Natalie*. She's a beauty, ain't she?" Rudy tucked his hands in his pockets and bowed his head in respect against the crisp breeze that swept in to greet them.

"*That's* the boat?"

Faith had materialized behind them, and Sam twisted around to look at her. She'd pushed her chin into the opening of her black hooded sweatshirt but the tip of her nose was pink, kissed by the wind.

"It can't be." Sam blinked, just to be sure the faded gray boat wasn't a hallucination due to the sleepless nights he'd been having. "When I talked to Dad, he said the boat was *new*."

"He's one of them positive thinkers." Rudy grinned and spit over the side of the railing. "It was new to him when he bought it. I can tell your first mate here knows quality when she sees it."

Faith's shy smile reminded Sam of his manners.

"I'm sorry, Mr. Dawes, this is my niece, Faith Cutter. Faith, this is Mr. Dawes."

"Aw, it's just plain Rudy." He smiled at Faith, revealing a gold-capped front tooth. "Jacob said you wouldn't be here until mid-July. And he shoulda warned you we don't pack away our winter coats until then."

Sam glanced at Faith and noticed she was shivering. Instinctively, he wrapped his arm around her shoulders and pulled her into the warmth of his flannel-lined denim jacket. Instead of pulling away, as he half expected her to, she tunneled in farther. For a split second, she was six years old again, snuggled up against him with a copy of Dr. Seuss's *One Fish, Two Fish* book in one hand and a raggedy stuffed rabbit named Mr. Carrots in the other.

"Dad said the boat was available whenever I wanted to use it," Sam said distractedly. "June…worked out better for us."

"Doesn't matter to me none. I just keep an eye on it for him. Go on now. Get acquainted with her."

Faith skipped down the skeletal wooden staircase that spiraled to the water. Sam was tempted to yell at her to slow down and grab the railing, but one look at it made his back teeth snap together. It was probably safer *not* to use it.

By the time Sam hopped on board, Faith had already disappeared belowdeck. From his dad's description of the boat, Sam thought he'd be in a luxury cabin cruiser for the next few weeks. Now he simply hoped it was watertight.

"Sam!" Faith's muffled voice sounded more excited than it had in months. "You've got to see this!"

He ducked into the narrow stairwell and found her standing in the doorway of one of the cabins.

"Can I take this one?"

Sam peered in cautiously. A narrow bunk bed, a corner desk and a small table were the only furnishings in it, but even though they were old, everything was spotless. He exhaled slowly in relief.

"Sure. The desk will come in handy."

Faith rolled her eyes in typical twelve-year-old fashion. "You had to remind me."

"That was the deal. Your mom let you come with me if you kept up with your homework."

"Mom would have let me come anyway." Faith lifted her chin defiantly, but he could hear the tremor in her voice. "I heard her. She told you that I've been 'too much' for her lately."

Sam closed his eyes. He had no idea that Faith had overheard his last conversation with Rachel. "Faith, it's not you. Your mom… Things have been hard for her the past few months."

"Well, here's a news flash." Faith's eyes narrowed and suddenly she looked years older. "Things haven't been easy for me, either…."

Her voice choked on the word and Sam pulled her against him. He wasn't sure what he could say to comfort her. Not when he hadn't discovered anything to fill in the fissures in his own heart.

"I miss him." Faith clung to him.

The knot of sadness forming in Sam's throat strained for release, but he kept a tight rein on it.

"I miss him, too."

"I thought you were only staying two weeks, Evangeline."

Evie saw the mischievous gleam in her dad's eyes and handed him another duffel bag from the trunk of her car. Patrick was the only person who called her by her full name, a gift from her parents to her paternal grandmother, the first Evangeline McBride, when she was born. "A person can't be *too* prepared."

"But what is it you're preparing for, sweetheart? A tidal wave? Or maybe an asteroid?" Patrick peered in the car window at the flats of tomato plants lined up across the backseat.

Evie was used to her dad's teasing. "Don't be silly." She handed him a large sewing basket embroidered with strawberries. And a stadium umbrella. "We'd have plenty of time to get ready if one of those things was going to occur. This stuff is just for...every day."

Her dad frowned as she handed him a bag of groceries. "There *is* a grocery store in Cooper's Landing."

"Do I need to mention that the expiration date on the can of corn I bought last summer coincided with the Reagan administration?"

Patrick winked at her. "You love it here."

He was right, but Evie wasn't about to admit that to Caitlin and Meghan.

A week after school had officially closed for summer vacation she'd packed up her car, locked up the house and driven away with her traveling companions—the box of books on the passenger seat beside her.

The closer she'd gotten to the adorable stone cottage her dad now called home, the more excited she'd been. When Patrick left on his fishing trip, Evie knew she'd be perfectly content just to stretch out on the wicker chaise longue in the backyard and admire the lake from a distance. She loved watching Lake Superior change from steel-gray to vivid blue, depending on its mood. And Superior was a moody lake. The proof was in the hundreds of ships that slept below her ice-cold surface.

Evie leaned close and kissed her dad's bristly cheek. "You forgot to shave again this morning."

"I didn't forget," Patrick grumbled. "I'm retired. A man shouldn't have to shave when he's retired."

Evie looped the strap of a canvas messenger bag over her shoulder and headed toward the house. "Did you and your friend finally decide when you're leaving?"

"Day after tomorrow. Jacob's picking me up at five in the morning. And—" Patrick put up his hand to prevent her from saying what he knew was going to come next "—you don't have to get up and make oatmeal for me. The reason we're leaving so early is because it's a long drive to the lodge, and then we have to get to our campsite."

"Why don't you just stay at the lodge?" They'd had this conversation several times already, but Evie thought it worth repeating. Until she got her way. Patrick was only fifty-nine, but she didn't understand why he'd turned down a soft bed in the main lodge for a tent on a secluded island several miles away.

"Jacob's been camping for years," Patrick said. "He'll take care of me."

Evie snorted. "From what you've told me about Jacob Cutter, he's a daredevil. I don't want him to talk you into anything stupid. Or dangerous."

"You've been teaching the peer-pressure curriculum again, haven't you?"

Evie gave a weak laugh. "I'm sorry, Dad, it's just that I want you to be careful."

"Careful is my middle name."

"Stubborn is your middle name," she muttered under her breath.

The sound of tires crunching over gravel drew their attention to the vehicle creeping up the long driveway.

"Looks like you've got some customers," Evie said, watching a black pickup truck rattle into view.

"Maybe they're lost." Patrick grinned. "But I'll still try to talk them into buying a pair of seagull salt-and-pepper shakers."

Evie laughed. Beach Glass didn't have a single kitschy item like the ones he'd just described. Her dad spent the winter months combing estate sales to find rare objects—the ones that escorted his customers down memory lane. Patrick had told her more than once that everyone needed a connecting point to their past. Sometimes it was a book they remembered reading as a child or the exact twin of the pitcher their grandmother had used to pour maple syrup on their pancakes when they were growing up. Beach Glass was off the beaten path, but people still managed to find it. And when they left, it was usually as the owner of some small treasure.

"Just put that stuff by the door, Dad, and I'll take care of it in a few minutes." Evie couldn't help glancing over her shoulder at the truck idling in the tiny parking lot next to the antique shop. The tinted windows obscured the inside cab from view. She hesitated a moment but whoever was driving the pickup wasn't in a hurry to get out.

She went inside and finished unpacking her clothes, glad she'd tossed in a few sweaters. A person could never be too prepared and the breeze off the lake still had a bite.

When she peeked outside half an hour later, the truck

was gone. She poured two iced coffees and headed across the yard to the shop. More than half the furnishings in her own home were compliments of Beach Glass, and she was eager to see the latest bounty her father had added since her last visit.

"What do you mean he's staying on the boat?"

Evie paused at the sound of Patrick's agitated voice through the screen door.

"Well, that's just one of our problems…." His voice lowered, ebbing away like the tide, and then strengthened again. "He stopped by a little while ago, insisting we bring him along. No, I don't trust him any more than you do, Jacob…but Sophie—"

Evie realized she was holding her breath. She'd never heard her dad sound so stressed.

"I suppose we can delay the trip but I'm afraid if we don't go as planned, Sophie is going to get…No, go ahead. Evie might be on her way over. I'll talk to you later this evening."

It suddenly occurred to Evie that she was eavesdropping. She backed away from the door, replaying the part of the conversation she'd overheard.

The elusive Sophie Graham again.

Evie had never seen the woman, even during the reconnaissance mission Caitlin had tried to set up the previous summer. In the interest of maintaining sibling harmony, Evie *had* dropped a few subtle hints to her dad that she'd like to meet Sophie sometime, but all she could get out of him was that the mysterious Sophie wasn't in good health.

"Evie?"

She froze midstep.

Her dad may have been a bit forgetful but apparently there was nothing wrong with his hearing.

Evie winced and caught her lower lip between her teeth. All the times she'd preached to her students that honesty was the best policy came rushing back. She pressed the glasses against her cheeks to put out the fire in them. The downside of having red hair and fair skin. She couldn't hide a blush to save her life.

"I brought you a reward for working so hard," she called through the screen door.

Patrick appeared on the other side and Evie could see the furrows in his forehead, as deep as stress cracks in a wall.

"So, did you sell some of those salt shakers?" Evie asked, deliberately keeping her voice cheerful to cover up the guilt nipping at her conscience.

Patrick's mouth tightened. "No. He wasn't interested in buying anything."

"Who—"

"Let's take this out to the garden, shall we? You can enjoy the fruit of last summer's labor while you take a break. Some of the plants are already coming up, and it's going to be beautiful."

Evie handed him one of the glasses and saw his fingers tremble as he reached for it. Worry scoured the lining of her stomach.

"Dad, is everything all right?" She tried to piece together the fragments of the conversation she'd overheard. It had sounded like someone else wanted to come along on the fishing trip. But why would that upset him? And what did Sophie Graham have to do with it?

"Right as rain."

"There's nothing right about rain unless you have an umbrella," Evie said promptly. It was an old joke between them, and she relaxed when he smiled.

Maybe her concern over the fishing trip was making her read more into the conversation she'd overheard. It was possible her father was simply a little uptight because he was taking a vacation for the first time in— Evie did a quick calculation—twelve years. Not since the year her mother was killed.

Chapter Two

Evie had her alarm set for five-thirty. Not to make sure Patrick ate his oatmeal but to make sure he didn't forget anything. Else.

She pulled on her robe and slipped into the kitchen, only to discover her sneaky father had already left. The coffee was on and he'd left a note taped to the refrigerator.

I'll call you as soon as I can. Relax. Love, Dad.

Evie snatched the note off the fridge and frowned. The faint smell of bacon and eggs lingered in the air. No wonder he hadn't wanted her to get up before he left. He'd wanted to eat his artery-clogging breakfast without a witness.

And what exactly did he mean by *relax?* Was she supposed to relax because she was on summer vacation? Or was she supposed to relax while knowing her dad, who thought one pair of socks per day was sufficient, was going on a two-week fishing trip with Jacob Cutter? A former Marine. The two men had known each other only six months, and already Jacob was pushing Patrick out of his familiar routine. Evie didn't like Jacob Cutter. Her dad was a scholar, not an outdoorsman. A retired high school English teacher. What was Jacob thinking?

Her doubts about the trip had increased the evening before while Patrick packed his things. Evie had noticed an important piece of equipment missing from the gear piled by the door. When she'd called his attention to it, Patrick had laughed self-consciously and disappeared outside to rummage around in one of the outbuildings, finally returning with a fishing pole.

Shortly after watching her dad hook his thumb on one of the lures, Evie had had a burst of inspiration. She could go with them. As the cook. Keeper of the campfire. That sort of thing. When she'd brought it up to Patrick, he'd looked less than enthusiastic. In fact, he'd looked slightly offended and had reminded her that the reservations were for *two* people and they couldn't add someone else this late in the game. Which meant the owner of the black pickup truck who'd tried to coerce Patrick and Jacob into taking him along wasn't going, either.

No wonder Patrick had run out on her so early in the morning. Maybe he'd thought she'd stow away in the backseat.

Too bad she hadn't thought of that sooner.

If only her dad would have mentioned the fishing trip to *her* before he'd brought it up to Caitlin and Meghan, who'd both thought it was a great idea. Of course. They always had their passports ready to go at a moment's notice.

"Dad never does anything." Meghan had listened to her concerns and gently brushed them aside. "He loves to go to auctions and estate sales and putter in the store, but maybe he's decided he needs to expand his interests. You know, find a new hobby."

Caitlin, as usual, had been more direct. "Don't be such a worrywart, Evie. Dad wants to go fishing, not skydiving. If you see a parachute in the trunk of his car instead of a fishing pole, call me."

It was easy for her sisters to live their own lives and let their dad live his. Both of them had already moved away from home when Laura McBride had died unexpectedly. Meghan had been a freshman in an out-of-state college, and Caitlin a graduate student in France for a semester abroad. Evie had just turned fourteen and she'd been the only one left to take care of Patrick.

Lord, you'll take care of Dad, won't you? Keep him safe and comfortable, just like I would if I were with him? Don't let that reckless Jacob Cutter try to talk him into doing anything dangerous. And help him remember to change his socks if they get wet.

Patrick had always encouraged her to talk to God, her heavenly Father, as easily and naturally as she talked to him. Some people might think she was crazy to talk to God about wet socks, but Evie figured if God knew when a sparrow fell to the ground, He cared about the details of His children's lives, too. No matter how small.

She opened her eyes, ready to start the day right.

Beach Glass officially opened at ten o'clock, giving her time to weed the garden and go into town to pick up a gallon of milk and some eggs.

She'd just make sure to check the expiration date before she bought them.

Cooper's Landing was five miles from the antique shop, yet Patrick thought nothing of hopping on a rickety old bicycle and riding it into town. Evie kicked the tire with her toe, and when it wobbled back and forth like a toddler taking those first precious steps, she decided to drive her car instead.

Johnson's Market stuck to the basics—not bothering to cater to the tourists who used Cooper's Landing as a brief resting point to fill up their vehicles and stretch their legs a bit.

The sandy stretch of beach, strewn with sculptures of satin-smooth driftwood, drew Evie's attention when she stepped outside the store with her purchases. Ever since Patrick had moved to what Caitlin referred to as "the end of nowhere," Evie had been fascinated by Lake Superior. She'd grown up in a suburb of Milwaukee, where the only connection she'd had with water was the local swimming pool. But here, right in front of her eyes, the lake stretched across the horizon in variegated shades of blue. And even though today the water was a comforting shade of indigo, it could change with a turn of the wind.

A glance at her watch told her there was time for a short walk down to the dock. She tucked her groceries into the backseat of her car and headed toward the water. Picking her way down the rocky bank, Evie vaulted over a small ledge of rock and practically fell on top of someone.

"Hey!" A girl rose up from a crouched position. "What do you think you're... Oh, sorry."

"I'm the one who's sorry," Evie apologized. "I was staring at the water and didn't see you."

"That's okay." The words came out grudgingly.

She looked to be in the same age range as Evie's students, so Evie knew better than to take the edge in her tone personally. The girl hugged a sketchbook against her chest, and a metal case on the ground by her feet revealed a rainbow of oil pastels.

"You're drawing the lake? Or the boat?"

"The lake. The boat's kind of ugly."

Evie couldn't argue with that. The boat tied to the dock was as plain and drab as a cardboard box. And looked about as seaworthy.

"I admire anyone with artistic ability." Evie held out her hand. "Evangeline McBride. Science geek."

The girl's eyes met hers shyly and then she smiled. "My name's Faith. I'm a jock."

"What sport?"

Faith shrugged. "You name it."

"But Lake Superior inspired you, huh?"

"No, I'm being forced. It's art class." Faith peeked at the sketch pad and made a face. "It's terrible."

Evie knew better than to push. If Faith wanted her to take a look at her drawing, it had to be her idea.

"Okay. Tell me the truth." Faith suddenly flipped it over for Evie to see.

"It's..." Evie's voice trailed off when she saw the

gleam of humor in Faith's eyes. She'd colored the entire page blue. "You captured it perfectly, I'd say. A close-up of the water."

"*Very* close up!"

Faith giggled and Evie joined in.

"Faith!"

The voice behind them startled Evie. Her foot slipped on the rocks, sending an avalanche of stones skipping down the bank.

"Hi, Sam." Faith's giggle changed to a bored mono-tone.

Evie looked up and sucked in her breath. The man looming above them blotted out the sun. Evie could tell immediately that he and the girl were related. Both of them had silver-gray eyes and thick, shadow-dark hair. Faith's eyes were still warm with laughter, but the other pair trained on Evie were as chilly as the water.

"I'm Evie McBride." She scrambled to her feet to re-gain her dignity, but it didn't matter. She barely reached the man's broad shoulders. "Your daughter and I sort of…bumped…into each other."

Sam looked from the slender redhead to his niece in disbelief. He'd been looking for Faith for the past hour—so he could ground her for the rest of her life. He was pretty sure he had the authority. Although Faith might not agree. The truth was, they hadn't been agree-ing about much the past few days, and Sam was at the end of his rope. Moodiness he could cope with, but Faith had started to disappear whenever the opportunity pre-sented itself. Like an hour ago.

They'd been staying with Jacob, who'd left early that

morning on a fishing trip, and Sam had brought Faith into town with him while he got the *Natalie* ready to launch. This would be the first time they'd had an opportunity to take the boat out. While he'd checked the engine, his wily niece had pulled another disappearing act.

He hadn't expected to find her in the company of Patrick McBride's daughter. The uptight schoolteacher his dad had warned him about. But somehow Jacob had forgotten to mention that Evie McBride was a *beautiful* uptight schoolteacher.

And he hadn't expected to hear Faith giggling the way twelve-year-old girls were supposed to giggle. The sound had thrown him off balance. He realized he hadn't seen Faith smile or heard her laugh for a long time. Too long. Dan's accident had been like a scalpel—going in deep and removing the laughter from all of them.

"I'm Sam Cutter—"

"He's my uncle, not my dad," Faith interrupted.

Sam exhaled silently. No one knew better than he did that he couldn't fill Dan's shoes. His twin brother had been a great dad, and all Sam could be was what he'd always been—a doting uncle. But lately he found himself wondering if that was enough to keep Faith from drowning in grief. When Dan had been injured, she'd taken a leave of absence from school. Now she was so far behind, the principal had said the only way she could pass to the next grade level was by completing her homework over the summer. What bothered Sam the most was that Faith didn't seem to care.

"Cutter? Are you related to Jacob Cutter?"

"I'm his son." Sam noticed the instant change in Evie's expression.

"It's nice to meet you."

Sure it was. Jacob hadn't been kidding. Evie Mc-Bride *didn't* approve of him. He wondered why. "Dad mentioned you're minding the store while he and Patrick are fishing."

"I don't know a lot about antiques, but I do know how to dust them." She glanced down at Faith and winked.

Faith grinned back.

Maybe Ms. McBride came across as a little stuffy, but she definitely had a way with kids.

"Faith, are you ready? We should be long gone by now." Sam stared his niece down, not ready to let her off the hook for disappearing on him.

Faith shifted uncomfortably and he saw a flash of good old-fashioned guilt in her eyes. *Good.*

"Are you house-sitting for your dad?" Evie directed the question at him, her voice polite but strained.

Sam suppressed a smile. With that tone, she sounded just like a prim schoolteacher. All she needed was a pair of horn-rimmed glasses and a bun. They'd go really well with the heavy cardigan she had buttoned up to her chin and the ankle-length denim skirt.

"We're staying on the *Natalie*." Faith pointed to the boat nodding drowsily in the waves.

"You're living on *that*?"

Sam bristled at what sounded like an accusation. It scraped against the doubts he was already having about bringing Faith along. So the *Natalie* wasn't the best-looking boat in the harbor. And maybe she didn't have all the latest bells and whistles. But he'd checked her over, and she was sturdy. The engine had purred like a kitten before settling into a reliable, even hum.

"A few days on the water and a few days at the cabin." Sam lifted one eyebrow, daring her to comment.

Evie McBride's chin lifted, accepting his challenge. "I don't think—"

"You should come with us sometime," Faith broke in, leaving both adults momentarily speechless.

"That's sweet of you, Faith, but…" Evie turned and stared, almost mesmerized, at the water. "Beach Glass is going to keep me pretty busy over the next few weeks."

She was afraid of the water, Sam realized in surprise. His gaze dropped to the hem of her skirt, where the toes of a sensible pair of shoes peeked out. Not exactly the type of footwear designed for splashing in the surf. He hid another smile.

"I should get going, too. The shop opens at ten." Evie's expression softened when she looked at Faith. "Be careful when you're out on the lake."

Sam expected Faith to give Evie her signature don't-fuss-over-me-I'm-not-a-little-kid-anymore look, but his niece nodded solemnly.

"Sam knows what he's doing."

Sam's mouth dropped open at the confidence he heard in her voice. Before he had a chance to bask in the glow, she skipped down the rocks toward the dock. "I can't keep up with her."

He realized he'd said the words out loud when he felt Evie touch his arm. The warmth of her fingers soaked into his skin. When he glanced down at her, he saw a knowing look in her eyes.

"Don't try to keep up with her." Evie smiled. A genuine smile that sparkled like sunlight dancing on the water and had a curious effect on his pulse. For the first time, he noticed a dusting of cinnamon freckles on her nose. "The secret is to stay one step *ahead* of her."

On the way back to the cottage, Evie couldn't stop thinking about Faith Cutter. *And Sam.* Although she didn't want to think about him. Anyone who would take a child out in a boat on a lake as unpredictable as Superior for any length of time had to be a live-on-the-edge type of person. And in the end, that kind of person always hurt the ones closest to them, whether they meant to or not.

Just like her mother.

Growing up, Evie had loved hearing the story of her parents' romantic courtship. Her father and mother had met in the principal's office of the local high school. Patrick had been a first-year English teacher and Laura McIntyre—*Officer* Laura McIntyre—had been invited to talk to the students for career day. The principal had asked Patrick to give Laura a tour of the school before the assembly started.

They'd married six months later.

Growing up, Evie had been blissfully unaware of the dangers of her mother's career. By the time Evie was in middle school, Laura had been promoted to sergeant and spent the bulk of her time at a desk, scheduling shifts and taking complaints.

And then one day, Laura hadn't come home on time. Evie could still see the look on her father's face when the squad car pulled into the driveway and the chief of police had walked up to the front door.

Laura had been struck and killed by a drunk driver while assisting a stranded motorist.

Patrick's strong faith had never wavered, and he'd appealed to his daughters to lean on God, not blame Him for Laura's death. But in the following months as her family handled their grief in different ways, Evie had struggled with a growing realization. It wasn't God she was angry with. It was her mother, for choosing a career that had put her at risk.

Chapter Three

Evie's first customers of the day turned out to be new-lyweds who spent more time exchanging loving glances than they did browsing through the aisles.

She felt a stab of envy as she watched the young man press a lingering kiss to his bride's cheek. The young woman, who didn't look much older than Evie, blushed and halfheartedly pushed him away. Evie pretended she hadn't seen the kiss. There were times she asked God why He was waiting so long to bring her future mate into her life. She liked to think God was work-ing on a certain man's heart, making sure he was just right for her so when they met, she'd recognize him at a glance....

Sam Cutter's face flashed in her mind, and Evie fum-bled the ironstone pitcher she'd been dusting. Fortu-nately, she caught it again before it hit the ground. *Sam Cutter!* Not likely. He wasn't exactly Mr. Personable. In fact, she'd sensed he'd found her...amusing. She hadn't missed his quick, appraising glance when she'd stood up. Or the half smile on his face when his silver gaze had lingered on her wool cardigan. It *was* chilly by the shore. Not everyone had an internal thermostat that made them comfortable wearing a T-shirt on a cool day.

Which brought to mind the tanned, muscular arms his T-shirt had revealed...

"Ah, Miss?"

The bride's tentative question zapped her back to reality. *Snap out of it, Evie.*

"I'm sorry. Can I help you?"

"We'll take this." She pushed a small figurine toward Evie. A ceramic horse with one ear missing.

"Did you notice it's chipped?" Evie wanted to make sure Patrick's customers were satisfied with their purchases when they left.

The woman nodded. "I don't care. It looks just like the horse I had when I was ten. And believe it or not, half her ear was missing, too."

Her husband hovered nearby while Evie carefully wrapped the figurine in tissue paper.

"Enjoy your trip," she called after them.

The store remained quiet for the rest of the afternoon, so Evie took advantage of the time by rearranging shelves and washing the leaded-glass windows in the store.

Solitude was wonderful during the day when she could see boats out on the water and the glint of the church steeple as it winked back at the sun. But as the sun melted into the horizon and shadows began to sift through the trees and creep toward the door, Evie realized it wasn't so friendly at night. To counteract the silence, she turned on her dad's ancient record player and curled up in a chair with one of the books she'd been waiting since Christmas to read.

It was just after eight when the motion lights in the front yard came on. Evie walked over to the window and peered outside. All she could see was the outline of a shadowy figure walking up the sidewalk toward the house.

Evie's breath caught in her throat until she saw the person's face briefly illuminated in the light.

Sam Cutter.

She hurried to open the door. His clothing looked rumpled from a day out on the water, and his hair was in disarray, combed by the wind. She didn't understand why he'd come for a visit so late in the evening, unless...

"Is Dad okay? Did you hear something?"

"I imagine they're fine. I haven't heard otherwise."

Relief poured through Evie. "Then why—"

"I'm sorry. I didn't realize you'd be tucked in for the night already." The faint smile had returned.

Evie didn't like his choice of words. He made it sound as if she were a chipmunk, hiding in a hole.

"Come in." Evie stepped to the side and he stalked past her. Her traitorous nose twitched at the pleasing scent of sunshine, wind and sand that clung to his clothes. "Where's Faith?"

"I didn't leave her alone on the boat, if that's what you're thinking."

That *had* been what she was thinking, and the

warmth flooding into her cheeks gave her away. Evie ducked her head so he wouldn't notice.

"My father mentioned that you're a teacher, Miss McBride."

"Evie," she corrected, wondering where this was going. "That's right. I teach seventh- and eighth-grade science classes at a Christian school—"

"Faith needs a tutor."

The terse interruption reminded Evie of Caitlin. Her back stiffened like an irritated cat.

"A tutor." Evie repeated the words, giving herself a few extra seconds to process the unexpected statement. Was Sam simply stating a fact or asking *her* to be Faith's tutor?

"We're planning to stay in Cooper's Landing for…a while," Sam said. "We'll be out on the water most of the day, but in the evening we'll be back at the cabin. Faith needs to finish some of her classes before school starts in the fall and someone has to check her progress. Are you interested?"

Sam didn't bother to fill in the gaps. Originally, he'd planned to come to Cooper's Landing alone, but when Rachel, his sister-in-law, had found out, she'd insisted a change of scenery would be good for Faith. Sam had agreed reluctantly, not because he didn't love spending time with Faith but because he couldn't find a way through his own mixed emotions. How could he help Faith deal with something he wasn't dealing with very well himself? And then there was Faith herself. The happy-go-lucky little girl he'd spoiled since the day she was born had turned into a sullen stranger.

When Faith had laughed with Evie that morning, it had made Sam realize just how much his sweet-tempered niece had changed over the past few months. Maybe she needed someone outside the family to motivate her to get her schoolwork done. A tutor. And Evangeline Mc-Bride—with her funny wool cardigan and disapproving eyes—happened to be the perfect solution. She obviously liked kids or she wouldn't be a teacher. And maybe a woman would be able to navigate Faith's changing moods better than he could.

"I don't know." Evie perched on the edge of a leather chair and stared at him. "What exactly does Faith need help with? Did she fail a class?"

Sam walked to the window and stared outside at the darkness. "Not yet. She got…behind…a few months ago and didn't have enough time to make up the work she missed. Rachel, Faith's mother, talked to the principal and he said if she completed the work over the summer she could move on with the rest of her class."

Evie sensed there was more to the story than what he was telling her. Questions tumbled over each other in her mind. Obviously, since Faith's last name was Cutter, her mother, Rachel, must be Sam's sister-in-law. But Sam hadn't mentioned his brother—Faith's father. Several things didn't add up. If Faith needed to catch up on her schoolwork, why was she vacationing on a boat with her uncle instead of working on her classes at home with her parents? Maybe Rachel and Sam's brother had divorced.

The possibility softened Evie's initial reservations. Losing a parent under any circumstances was traumatic, especially for someone in an already vulnerable age group like Faith.

"I'll only be here for two weeks," Evie reminded him. "And I have the shop to take care of."

Sam turned to face her again. "We'll work around your schedule. What time do you close for the day?"

"Four o'clock."

Patrick lived on his pension, so Beach Glass provided a supplemental income and gave him the luxury of flexible hours. He could open the antique shop late and close early, even take a day or two off if he felt like it. And her dad had encouraged Evie to do the same if necessary.

"I don't expect you to do this out of the goodness of your heart," Sam said. "I'm willing to pay you whatever you think is fair."

Evie wasn't sure why he put her on the defensive. She was usually a very easygoing person. "It isn't about the money."

"Then what *is* it about?" He crossed his arms.

If he could be blunt, so could she. "Why can't *you* help her?"

Sam's jaw worked, and for a moment Evie didn't think he was going to answer. He thrust his hands into the front pockets of his faded blue jeans. "She… I don't think she wants anything to do with me." It was clear the admission stung.

Evie remembered the change in Faith's tone when Sam had joined them on the beach. Faith was at the age when she was beginning to assert her independence—

to try to figure out just who Faith Cutter was and how she fit into the world.

Evie knew from experience the "tweenage" years had a tendency to put unsuspecting parents into a tailspin. Especially parents who weren't expecting the radical change in their homes when formerly cheerful, compliant kids entered the hormone zone. And if there'd been some kind of upheaval in Faith's life, the fallout could be even worse.

"She's been taking off a lot lately." Sam must have read the expression on her face because he quickly amended the statement. "She's not at risk as a runaway. Eventually she comes back. She either wants attention or time alone. I'm still trying to figure that out. But today—when she was with you—it was the first time I've heard her laugh in months."

Evie's heart, which had a soft spot for kids Faith's age anyway, melted into a gooey puddle. She remembered the glimmer of humor in Faith's eyes when she'd shown Evie her drawing of Lake Superior. Maybe she'd gone through a difficult time recently, but the faint spark of life—of laughter—hadn't been extinguished. It just needed tending. Evie gave in. Not because Sam needed her but because *Faith* did.

Okay, Lord, I'm going to assume this opportunity is from you. But did you have to include Sam Cutter?

"How about two hours a day? After I close up the shop in the afternoon?"

"We'll make it work."

"I thought you were going to live on the boat for a few days at a time."

"You'll only be here two weeks, but we'll probably be here longer. There'll be plenty of chances to take the boat out."

Even though Evie had agreed to tutor Faith, she needed to cover one more base. The one that would give her a clue whether or not the next two weeks were going to be a battleground. "How does Faith feel about this? Does she know you're here?"

Silence.

Uh-oh. Evie's eyebrow lifted.

"She knows I'm here," Sam finally admitted. "She didn't seem very happy about it but then she said, and I quote, 'Whatever.'"

"That's because it was your idea. The 'Whatever' meant she's not totally against it. Which makes my job easier." Evie hid a smile at the uncertain look on Sam's face. Obviously, he had no insight into the workings of an adolescent girl's mind.

As if his internal defense radar picked up on her smile, the uncertainty in Sam's eyes faded and it was back to the business at hand. Evie wondered briefly what Sam did for a living. Even in worn blue jeans and a faded black T-shirt, he oozed confidence. She could easily imagine him in an expensive suit, making important decisions in a high-rise office building, miles above the cubicle crowd.

Sam glanced at his watch. "Can you start tomorrow? We can hammer out more of the details then. Faith is spending the evening with a friend, and I promised I wouldn't be late picking her up. Sophie's one of those peculiar people who go to bed early."

Evie ignored the unspoken words *just like you* that hung in the air between them. "Sophie Graham?"

"That's right. You know her?"

"I've never met her, but Dad has...mentioned...her once in a while."

"Sophie's place is just down the road from us. Her dog had a litter of puppies a few months ago, and that's where I usually find Faith if she's missing."

Which gave Evie the opportunity she'd been hoping for. "If you give me directions, I'll come over to your place tomorrow."

"Are you sure? I don't mind driving Faith over here."

"I'm sure." Evie didn't hesitate. Maybe to break the ice between her and Faith, they'd take a walk down the road to see those puppies. And she'd finally get the opportunity to meet Sophie Graham.

Sam waited until he heard the lock on the front door click into place before he strode back to his car.

The antique shop really was off the beaten path.

He paused, scanning the trees that formed a thick wall between Evie McBride and civilization. Her closest neighbor was two miles away. As cautious as she seemed to be, he was surprised she didn't have any trepidation about staying alone on a secluded piece of property. Not that Cooper's Landing was a hotbed of criminal activity, but with the tourist season starting, the place drew a lot of people from outside the area.

None of your business what Evie McBride thinks or doesn't think, Cutter.

All that mattered was that she'd agreed to be Faith's tutor for the next two weeks.

Faith met him at the front door of Sophie's home, a drowsy puppy cradled in her arms.

"Sophie is going to let me name this one," she whispered, her eyes sparkling with excitement.

Sophie appeared in the doorway behind his niece. She was close to his father's age but still a striking woman, her beauty enhanced by the kind of smile that lit her up from the inside out. "I hope you don't mind, Sam. That puppy is Faith's favorite, so I thought it was only right that she be the one to name him."

"I don't mind." Sam was about to reach out and ruffle Faith's hair but caught himself. The last time he'd done that, she'd shrieked and disappeared into the bathroom, emerging only after she'd washed, blow-dried and styled her hair all over again. Later that day, they'd climbed to the top of an observation deck at Miner's Castle, where the wind had given her a new hairdo that made her look as if she'd been caught in a blender. She'd laughed. Go figure.

"I can't think of a good name," Faith fretted, rubbing the puppy's silky ear.

"Give him one to live up to," Sophie suggested, resting one hand on Faith's shoulder. "How did it go with Patrick's daughter? Did she agree to it?"

"Yes." Sam didn't bother to mention the split second when it had looked as though Evie would refuse to help Faith. The split second after he'd mentioned money. She'd looked offended he'd even brought up the subject, and he wasn't sure why. He didn't expect her to give up her time for free. "She's coming over tomorrow afternoon."

"Why don't you come in for a few minutes. Faith and I made cookies and we're just finishing up the last batch."

Sophie looked so hopeful that Sam didn't have the heart to say no. She ushered them into a small living room where the sparse furnishings looked old but well cared for. His gaze zeroed in on the man sitting at a desk in the corner, hunched over a computer keyboard.

Jacob had mentioned that Sophie had a son she didn't talk about very often. And now Sam had a hunch as to why.

"Tyson, would you like something to eat?"

Tyson looked up and scowled. His thin face was streaked with acne scars. Strands of dishwater-blond hair had been pulled back into a ponytail that trailed between his shoulder blades. "I told you I'm not hungry, Mom."

"You're going to ruin your eyes staring at that screen all night," Sophie scolded lightly. "At least turn around so I can introduce you to Sam Cutter, Jacob's son."

"Hey." Tyson barely glanced at Sam.

Sam saw the hurt look on Sophie's face before she murmured an excuse and disappeared into the kitchen. Faith followed her, still cuddling the puppy.

"That's a pretty nice setup you've got," Sam said, moving closer to see what Tyson was so focused on. He found himself staring at a blank screen. Tyson had shut down whatever program he'd been working on. A red flag rose in Sam's mind, especially when he noticed Tyson's shoulders set in a tense line.

"Thanks." Tyson's eyes glittered with resentment at the disruption. He yanked a pack of cigarettes out of his shirt pocket and shook one loose from the package.

"Outside with those, Ty." Sophie returned with a plate of cookies in one hand and a pitcher of milk in the other. "You agreed not to smoke in the house."

Tyson shoved the chair away from the desk and stalked out of the room.

"I'm sorry." Pain shadowed Sophie's eyes. "Tyson just lost his job last week, so he had to move back home while he looks for another one. He just got here this morning."

Sam didn't consider losing your job an excuse to be rude, but he didn't want to say so. Sophie looked embarrassed enough. "Those cookies smell delicious. How many am I allowed to have?"

Sophie brightened. "As many as you want. I miss feeding hungry men now that Patrick and Jacob are gone. I hate to say this, but Tyson is a picky eater."

Judging from Tyson's bloodshot eyes and sunken cheeks, Sam had a strong hunch the guy preferred to drink his meals.

He took a cookie from the plate Sophie offered and hid a smile when Faith reluctantly put the puppy on the floor. With her skinned knees and her mussed-up hair, she looked twelve years old again instead of twenty. Spending the evening with Sophie had been good for her.

"Faith and Evie will get along well." Sophie smiled

at Faith as she handed her a glass of milk. "I feel like I know her already. Patrick brags about those girls of his constantly. Evie was voted Teacher of the Year last fall in their school district. According to Patrick, it was the first time a teacher at a Christian school won the award. From what Patrick says, out of the three girls he and Evie are the most alike."

Sam remembered the cardigan. *Poor guy.*

"Maybe he was referring to their adventurous streak."

Wait a second. He must have missed something. *Evie McBride? Adventurous?* Sam tried not to laugh. "I doubt it, Sophie."

And as far as Sam was concerned, a guided fishing trip at a cushy lodge didn't qualify as adventurous in his book.

"The whole trip was Patrick's idea," Sophie went on. "I only pray that Bruce Mullins can help them."

Mullins. The name sounded familiar. "Is Mullins their fishing guide?"

"He is a guide there, but he's not taking them fishing."

She'd completely lost him. "But that's why they went to the lodge. To go fishing."

"Oh, dear." Sophie bit her lip and set her glass down on the worn coffee table. "Is that what they told you?"

Every nerve ending in Sam's body sprang to attention at the odd inflection in her voice. "Dad said they were going on a two-week fishing trip at a place called Robust Lodge, which caters to retired businessmen."

"They'll probably do some fishing," she said weakly.

Sam took a deep breath. Judging from Sophie's expression, she was trying to figure out a way to explain without incriminating the two men.

"Sophie, it's all right. What's going on?"

"The whole trip is for me," she finally said. "Bruce is an old friend of your dad's, and they need his help."

"His help?"

"To find the treasure."

Chapter Four

From the roof of the cabin, Sam watched Evie get out of her car. He pushed to his feet, anchoring the hammer into a loop in the tool belt around his waist. He didn't have time to retrieve the T-shirt he'd discarded earlier in the afternoon. It lay in a damp heap near the base of the chimney, just out of reach.

Evie lifted her hands to her hair, tucking in a few strands that had dared to escape from the sedate braid. Her slender frame stiffened as Jacob's flock of guinea hens charged around the cabin to greet her. The birds were as tame as dogs but as noisy as a squadron of fighter planes.

Sam expected her to dash back to the safety of her car. To his astonishment, a smile tilted the corners of her lips as the guinea hens swarmed around her feet, looking for a treat. Jacob always kept a handful of corn kernels in his pockets, a ritual Sam hadn't realized Faith had started to copy until he'd found a layer of soggy corn in the bottom of the washing machine.

Sam yanked the handkerchief out of his back pocket and swiped it across his forehead.

What was he supposed to tell her?

He wasn't sure Evie would take the news very well that instead of fishing, their fathers had somehow gotten involved in a wild-goose chase to find a sunken treasure.

Evie took a few steps toward the cabin and spotted him on the roof. She stopped dead in her tracks, shading her eyes against the sun with her hand as she looked up at him.

"Isn't that dangerous?"

Now he was positive she wouldn't take the news well. Not if standing on the roof of a one-story building was her idea of dangerous.

Thanks for leaving me to clean up the mess, Dad.

After hearing stories about how overprotective Evie was when it came to her father, Sam could understand why Patrick hadn't told her the truth behind the trip. According to Jacob, Evie had even driven up to Cooper's Landing the previous summer, apparently suspicious of Patrick's friendship with Sophie. No wonder the poor guy had moved to Michigan's Upper Peninsula to escape her coddling.

Keeping Evie in the dark made sense, but what Sam couldn't figure out was why *his* father hadn't confided in *him*. But he had a strong hunch it had something to do with Dan's injury. As a carpenter, Jacob had spent the majority of his life after the Marines fixing things. Until he had come up against two things he couldn't fix. His wife's illness and…Dan. Now Jacob had been presented with an opportunity to help a friend and feel useful again.

Sam couldn't blame his father. Jacob coped with his feelings of helplessness one way and he had chosen another.

The conversation with Sophie the night before had been quite enlightening. And frustrating. Sam had spent half the night battling his conscience. Evie had generously agreed to help him by tutoring Faith. Didn't he owe her the truth? But if Patrick didn't want Evie to know what he was up to, was it his place to fill her in? And it wasn't as if there was any cause to worry. Jacob and Patrick were grown men, certainly capable of making their own decisions without getting flack from their adult children.

Sam had no doubt the men could handle themselves. It was adding Sophie to the mix that made the situation more difficult.

Her story wasn't his to share. She hadn't been able to provide many details because Tyson had slunk back into the living room, abruptly ending the conversation. It was obvious Sophie didn't want her son to overhear them. From the brief conversation, however, Sam had managed to put together a few of the pieces.

Sophie had been working on her family's genealogy when she was diagnosed with cancer. While searching through family archives, Sophie discovered diaries kept by her grandmother that exposed a skeleton in the Graham family closet. A scandal caused when a ship sank in Lake Superior and her great-grandfather, Matthew

Graham, apparently saved himself and a young woman's dowry. No one else had survived.

At that point, Tyson interrupted them and Sophie had quickly changed the subject.

Sam buried a sigh and dodged between the boxes of shingles scattered on the roof, pausing long enough to scoop up his shirt. By the time he reached the ladder, Evie stood below him, holding the bottom of it.

"They do make aluminum ladders nowadays, you know," she called up to him. "They don't rot. They're splinter free. And they're equipped with multiple safety features."

Sam suppressed a smile. *You've got to be kidding me.* "I'll keep that in mind."

Sam bypassed the last three rungs of the ladder and landed on his feet beside her, light as a cat.

Evie averted her gaze as he pulled the damp T-shirt over his head and rolled it down over his abdomen. As if he knew exactly why she'd looked away, his eyebrow lifted in a silent question.

Better?

He was laughing at her again. Heat coursed into Evie's cheeks and she took a step away from him, knowing her freckles had lit up like laser dots against her skin. She took a deep breath and decided to focus on the reason she was there.

"Is Faith inside?"

"I think so. She was helping me but took a break about an hour ago."

The glint in his eyes told Evie he was deliberately baiting her. She took the bait anyway.

"I don't think that's a good idea—"

The guinea hens drowned her out as they recognized Sam's voice and charged. He sank his hand into the pocket of his tattered blue jeans and retrieved a fistful of corn, tossing it on the gravel.

"Numida meleagris," Evie said without thinking.

Sam pushed his hand down his leg to wipe off the dust and looked at her. "What?"

"Numida meleagris. The Latin name for guinea fowl."

"I'll take your word for that, Miss McBride." Sam scraped a hand through his hair and ended up tousling it even more. "I should probably warn you. Faith doesn't really like science. Or math."

"She enjoys English? History?"

Sam shook his head and a few strands of dark hair flopped across his forehead. Evie resisted the urge to smooth them back into place.

"Gym class."

"She's into sports." Evie remembered that Faith had described herself as a jock the day they'd met on the beach. That didn't bother her. In a school like the one she taught in, the smaller ratio of students to teachers allowed her to focus on each individual child. Over the years, she'd found creative ways to tap into her students' natural abilities to make learning more fun.

"Don't get me wrong, she's a good student," Sam told her. "But she'd rather study basketball plays than sit down with a textbook."

"Is there anything else I should know?"

A strange expression flickered across Sam's face, but he shook his head. "I can't think of anything."

"Good, because I hate surprises."

Sam glanced at the canvas bag looped over her shoulder. "Here. Let me carry your...suitcase? You didn't have to bring your own books, you know. Faith's mother sent up an entire library."

"I've got it. And, just to set the record straight, it's a purse, not a suitcase."

"What do you have in that thing?"

"Oh, the usual stuff."

He studied the bulging bag. "Sleeping bag? Jumper cables? The kitchen sink?"

Evie saw the look on his face. "Of course not. Just the essentials." Her laptop computer. A miniature sewing kit. Tape measure. Collapsible umbrella.

"You must have been a Girl Scout."

Her eyes narrowed. Was he mocking her? "It's always good to be prepared."

The cabin door flew open, and Faith stepped onto the narrow porch. Evie guessed the reason behind the mutinous look on the young girl's face. Even though the two of them had connected over Faith's sketch of Lake Superior, Evie's role had changed. Instead of a kindred spirit, now she was the person responsible for making sure Faith kept her nose buried in the books.

Evie almost laughed. It wouldn't take long to put those fears to rest. "Hi, Faith."

"Hi." Faith studied her toes, refusing to meet Evie's eyes.

"Did you get your books out like I told you to?" Sam asked.

Faith shot him a look ripe with resentment. "Yes."

"Faith? Remember what we talked about this morning."

Judging from the edge in Sam's voice and the anger simmering in Faith's eyes, Evie doubted they'd talked at all. She guessed Sam had lectured and Faith had tuned him out.

"We don't need any books today," Evie said. "We're going on a field trip."

Sam and Faith both turned to stare at her.

"A field trip?" Sam sounded skeptical.

"For science class. We're going to study *Canis familiaris.*"

"Good. Great." Sam looked way too eager to escape. "I'm going back on the roof. I'll see you later."

"Sam?" Evie dug in her bag and pulled out a plastic bottle. "Here. Sunblock. The sun isn't as strong this late in the day, but you should still wear it. Or, ah, your shirt. That would work, too."

You aren't only a geek, Evie, you are officially their queen.

Sam stared at the bottle as if it were a live grenade and then at her. Evie braced herself, expecting to see amusement lurking in his eyes. She was used to it. Over the years her sisters had developed entire stand-up comedy routines based on her cautious ways.

We're not laughing at you, Evie. We're laughing with you.

To her amazement, Sam didn't laugh. But he did

smile. A slightly lopsided smile that lightened his eyes to silver and warmed up her insides like a Bunsen burner.

"How can I turn down…SPF 50?" he murmured.

Maybe he *was* reckless but he knew his sunscreen.

Evie waited for Faith to join her, and they started down the driveway. Faith's plodding steps conveyed her unhappiness with the situation, but Evie didn't push for conversation or attention. When Faith wanted to talk, she would.

"What did you say we're going to study?" Faith finally asked.

Evie hid a smile. *"Canis familiaris."*

Faith kicked a rock and sent it skittering down the lane. "I've never heard of that."

"It's Latin for the domestic dog," Evie said. "We're going to visit Sophie's puppies."

Faith grinned. "I think I'm going to like having you as a teacher, Miss McBride."

"This is summer school. Call me Evie."

By the time Sophie's modest, two-story house came into view several minutes later, Faith was still chattering about the puppies and how it was up to her to choose a name for her favorite.

"I've always wanted to have a dog, but Mom doesn't like it when they shed," Faith continued. "Sophie says she'll keep the one I name and I can visit it whenever I want to. That's kind of like having my own dog, isn't it?"

Evie thought it an extremely generous gesture on Sophie's part, which made her more anxious to meet the woman. And even though Faith's comment about her mother made Evie curious, she knew it wasn't the time to press Faith to talk about her family.

"There she is." Faith broke away and sprinted toward a woman kneeling in a patch of freshly turned soil. "Hi, Sophie!"

No wonder Patrick talked about her. Sophie Graham was beautiful. Blessed with classic features and smooth, porcelain skin, Sophie resembled an aging film star. Her faded housedress and scuffed gardening clogs couldn't disguise her natural grace as she rose to her feet and greeted Faith with a hug.

Faith pointed in her direction and Evie quickened her steps, hoping Sophie wouldn't mind they'd shown up without a formal invitation.

Before she could apologize, Sophie's warm smile put her at ease. "Evangeline. I'm so glad to finally meet you. Patrick talks about you and your sisters all the time."

"Dad talks about you, too," Evie said, surprised to see a hint of rose tint Sophie's cheeks.

"Can I show Evie the puppies, Sophie?"

"If we're not interrupting anything," Evie added quickly.

"Not at all. You came at just the right time. I'm ready to take a rest." Sophie swept her straw hat off and used it as a fan.

Evie's breath caught in her throat as she saw the irregular patches of silver hair on Sophie's head.

"I'm in remission, praise the Lord," Sophie said simply, and then gave Evie a mischievous wink. "Now, let's get acquainted over ice cream and puppies, shall we?"

Chapter Five

When an hour went by and Evie and Faith still hadn't returned, it occurred to Sam that his niece may have tried to sweet-talk Evie into stopping at Sophie's house.

Which meant Sophie might inadvertently reveal the real reason behind Patrick and Jacob's fishing trip.

Sam winced as the hammer missed the nail and ground the tip of his thumb against the shingle.

None of your business, he reminded himself. If Evie had a problem with her dad, she should take it up with him. Sam had his own stuff to worry about. He was one hundred percent uninvolved in the situation.

Except that Evie was Faith's tutor. And for the next few weeks, he was committed to making sure she stayed that way.

Sam sat back on his heels, trying to convince himself it wasn't necessary to look for them. Evie would be a strict teacher—the kind who wouldn't waste precious minutes of a two-hour tutoring session playing with a litter of puppies. Hopefully the reason they were late was because the search for *Canis familiaris* was taking longer than expected....

A dim memory from Biology 101 struggled to the surface. Canis. Canine. *Dog.*

Sam's shout of laughter scattered the guinea hens in the yard below.

So maybe he'd misjudged her. But he knew one thing for sure. He had to get to Sophie before Evie did.

It didn't take Evie long to understand why Faith frequently "ran away" to Sophie's house. And it wasn't just to visit the puppies or because Sophie's home, filled with simple yet comfortable furnishings, created a peaceful retreat. Sophie was the reason Faith returned. The older woman radiated a warmth and inner peace that instantly made a person feel welcome. And accepted.

"I wish I could keep all four of them," Sophie said as Faith wrestled on the braided rug with two of the more active puppies while their mother, Sadie, kept a watchful eye from her wicker basket in the corner. "A few days after my diagnosis, Sadie showed up in the yard. I knew right away she was a stray—her fur was matted, and, even pregnant, she looked like she hadn't eaten for days. I called your dad and he came over and helped me bathe her. He even offered to take her home with him, but I'd already fallen in love with her. God must have known I'd need her." Sophie smiled. "She's a very good listener."

Was Sadie the only one you fell in love with?

Evie didn't voice the question that sprang into her

mind. Whenever Sophie mentioned Patrick's name, her eyes sparkled with affection. The two of them had obviously become close. But had the friendship developed into something more?

And how would she feel if it had?

The previous summer, Evie had scolded Caitlin for her strong reaction to Patrick and Sophie's friendship. If Sophie Graham brought some happiness into their dad's life, shouldn't they be supportive?

She had to admit, though, that the possibility of making room for another person in her dad's life was a little unsettling. Especially when Evie had been the one looking out for Patrick since Laura died.

"I don't know what I'd do without Jacob and Patrick," Sophie went on. "They fuss more than they ought to, but I wouldn't be able to live out here if they didn't help me keep the place up. The Lord sent those two wonderful men. I was in the hospital with complications from pneumonia, worried I'd have to sell my house, when Patrick showed up one Sunday with a group of men from his church to read to the patients. Your father got stuck with me." Sophie chuckled at the memory.

"We had a nice chat afterward and found out that we both loved antiques. The next Sunday, he introduced me to Jacob. They brought Monopoly along and convinced me to play. I don't think I ever laughed so much in my life. By the time I came home from the hospital, they'd spruced up the place and every day one of them would stop by or call to check up on me. I think they adopted me like I was a stray—just like Sadie."

Evie hid a smile. Somehow, she doubted it was an accurate comparison!

"They were a reminder that no matter what the future holds, God's already there, preparing the way. Oh, He doesn't always smooth out the rough spots in the road ahead. Those are the places we have to exercise our spiritual muscles, you know. To build our faith, so to speak. But God always provides the strength I need to keep going."

The sincerity in the words touched Evie and explained the source of the peace in Sophie's eyes. Evie knew that the woman's deep faith, the fruit of years of walking with the Lord, was another quality Patrick would have been drawn to.

A sudden movement on the stairs caught Evie's attention. The man glowering at them over the railing looked to be only a few years older than she was, but the expression on his face made him look like a cranky toddler who'd just awakened from a nap.

"Evie, this is my son, Tyson." Sophie ignored Tyson's sullen look while she made the introductions. "Tyson, this is Evie McBride, Patrick's daughter."

"Hey." His hooded stare fixed on Evie. It reminded her of a crocodile. Cold and flat.

This was Sophie's *son?*

A shudder chased up Evie's spine, but she forced a polite smile. "It's nice to meet you, Tyson."

"Evie is taking care of Beach Glass while Patrick is away on his fishing trip," Sophie told him.

"There's not much to do around here." Tyson's gaze burrowed into her. "We should hang out sometime."

A shiver coursed through her. "I'm afraid I don't have much free time. I'll either be minding the shop or tutoring Faith."

Tyson shrugged and stomped down the rest of the stairs. "I'm going out for a while."

"Ty, where—"

The door snapped Sophie's question in half.

Evie's heart went out to her. It was hard to believe someone as rude as Tyson was Sophie's flesh and blood. With his unkempt appearance and surly attitude, Tyson didn't seem to be someone Sophie could depend on. No wonder she was so grateful for Patrick and Jacob's help.

Faith broke the awkward silence as she plopped next to Sophie on the couch, the puppy draped over her arm. It raised its head and tried to lick her cheek, igniting a fit of the giggles.

Sophie smiled but Evie didn't miss the pensive look in her eyes. Compliments of Tyson. Impulsively, Evie patted Sophie's hand before rising to her feet.

"We should go back, Faith. We still need to go over your homework for tomorrow."

"I'll have to do it on the boat. Sam promised we could spend the whole day on the water. And I get to make lunch." Faith launched to her feet and put the puppy back on the rug with his littermates.

Evie kept her expression neutral. She didn't want Faith to pick up on the fact she wasn't happy with Sam for taking her out on the boat. The thought of them at the mercy of Superior's changing moods made her uneasy.

It's not your business, Evie, and Sam Cutter would be the first person to tell you so.

"Come back soon." Sophie escorted them outside. "When I talked to Patrick this morning, he asked me if I had plans to stop by Beach Glass soon and introduce myself. I can't wait to tell him that you beat me to it."

"Dad called you? *This morning?* I thought they weren't going to be able to contact us until they got to the lodge."

Sophie looked away, flustered. "We talked only a few minutes. I think he called from a gas station and the connection wasn't very good…. Look, there's Sam."

Sure enough, Sam was striding down the driveway toward them. Seeing the uncomfortable look on Sophie's face, Evie got the impression Sam's appearance provided a welcome disruption.

She tried to squelch the tiny pinprick of hurt. Why had her dad checked in with Sophie first? It didn't make sense. Especially when Patrick knew she wanted to keep in close contact…

"Studying hard?"

The glint in Sam's eyes told Evie he was on to her.

"Don't you dare scold these sweet girls, Sam," Sophie said. "They're good company. And Sadie and the puppies love the attention."

Faith wrapped her arms around Sophie's waist and gave her a fierce hug. "We'll be back."

They said their goodbyes, and Evie and Sam fell into step together while Faith dashed ahead of them.

"*Canis familiaris,* hmm?"

Evie swallowed hard when Sam's breath stirred her hair. He was so close she could smell the pleasing blend

of shower soap and afternoon sun. And a hint of coco-
nut-scented sunscreen.

When she finally found her voice, it sounded a little
breathless even to her own ears. "I thought Faith and I
should take some time to get to know each other before
we jumped into her lessons."

Sam slanted a look at her. "I think you know her already. It didn't take you long to figure out the way to
Faith's heart is through those puppies."

Faith, several yards ahead of them, heard the word
puppies and darted back.

"I thought of a name. I'm going to call him Rocky."

"Rocky?" Sam laughed. "Like the boxer?"

Faith nodded. "I watched the movies with Dad on
cable last year. He said he liked Rocky because he never
gave up."

Sam's throat closed.

Dan was giving up. The last time Sam had seen his
brother, Dan had ordered the entire family to leave the
room. When they'd hesitated, he'd thrown a pitcher of
ice water at them. Along with a stream of angry words.

The man lying in the hospital bed had been a
stranger, not the twin brother he'd wrestled, competed
against and laughed with over the past thirty-two years.

Fortunately, Faith hadn't been there to witness her
father's rage.

Moments before, the doctor had reminded Dan how
lucky he was to be alive. But Dan had looked at him as
if he'd just been given a death sentence.

Sam couldn't blame him.

Dan had been at the height of his career and the sole supporter of the family he loved. And he'd just been told he was facing months of painful rehab with no guarantee he would ever fully regain the use of his legs.

Responding to the doctor's meaningful look, they'd left Dan alone and gathered together in the family lounge. Sam had never seen Jacob look so defeated. And he'd never felt so helpless in his life. Even when Natalie, their mother, had died, he and Dan had stuck together. Leaned on each other. Found strength in their bond as brothers.

But not this time. Nothing Sam could say or do could change the reality of the situation. And he didn't know what to do with that.

Rachel, as emotional as Dan was easygoing, had clung to him. It would have been better if she'd been able to cry. At least tears could be dried. Sam had had no idea how to comfort a heart totally emptied by grief.

He had lain in bed that night, despair lapping at the edges of his soul. He'd tried to pray, but it had felt hypocritical. He wasn't sure if God would even recognize his voice. It wasn't as if they talked on a regular basis.

A week went by and Dan had still refused to see them. Faith had started to blame "the adults" for not allowing her to visit her father. Her close relationship with her mother had deteriorated, and she'd alternated between outright defiance and long, stubborn silences.

The hospital had transferred Dan to a private care facility to start rehab, and the doctor warned them that Dan's attitude would be a pivotal part of his recovery. The hospital social worker had told them Dan was battling depression and had compassionately suggested they give him a few weeks to adjust to his new surroundings before visiting again.

Jacob had reluctantly returned to Cooper's Landing. Sam used up more vacation time and had stayed longer, watching in disbelief as Dan became verbally abusive to the nurses and refused to cooperate with his physical therapists. His bitter tirades had kept Rachel on the verge of tears.

Sam had always been able to encourage his brother. Even to bully him, if the situation called for it. But for the first time in his life, Sam had sensed his presence was causing more harm than good. The bitterness in Dan's eyes every time Sam visited had weighed him down with guilt. He was able to walk while Dan was confined to a wheelchair, and Sam couldn't find a way to break down that barrier between them.

When Rachel had overheard him talking to Jacob on the phone about taking the boat out for a few weeks, she'd begged him to take Faith along. Torn between meeting the needs of both her daughter and her husband, she'd said she needed time to concentrate on Dan and encourage his recovery.

Sam had balked. He'd wanted to be alone. His world had shrunk to the size of the hospital and he was tired of sterile white walls, the hum of machines and plastic tubing that kept a man alive but couldn't make him want to *live*. He struggled between feeling selfish for leaving Rachel alone with Dan and the overwhelming need to escape.

In the end, he'd agreed to take Faith with him.

He'd tried to talk to her about her dad but she'd refused. Somewhere along the way, Sam had become a member of the opposing team. An hour didn't go by when he didn't second-guess his decision to bring her along.

"I think Rocky is a great name. Don't you, Sam?"

With a start, Evie's voice and the touch of her hand on his arm pulled Sam out of the shadowy path his memories had lured him down. Faith hadn't voluntarily talked about Dan since they'd arrived in Cooper's Landing. She'd even rebuffed her grandfather whenever he'd tried to talk about her dad. Now, because of Evie's gentle prompt, he realized Faith was watching him, waiting patiently for his response. She wasn't just asking if he liked the name. There was another question in her eyes.

Is Dad going to be like Rocky? Or is he going to give up?

He couldn't answer her. It wasn't fair to give her false hope, yet he didn't want to be the one to crush it, either.

"I think you should take a picture of you and Rocky and send it to your dad." Evie bravely stepped into the silence.

"Really?" Faith glanced at him for affirmation. "The nurse told me the last time I called there was a bulletin board by his bed. She said Dad has my letter on it."

Sam had had no idea Faith had written to her father or called the rehab center. Guilt washed over him. He'd failed his brother and now he was failing his niece. He struggled to find his voice. "Evie's right. I think he'd like that."

"Does that mean we can study *Canis familiaris* again

tomorrow?" Faith's tentative smile was like seeing a beam of sunlight peek through the clouds.

"You'll have to discuss that with your teacher."

Faith sprinted ahead of them and Sam held his breath, expecting Evie to hit him with a hundred questions now. And she'd be within her rights. He should have been honest with her the night he'd asked her to be Faith's tutor. He'd convinced himself Evie didn't need to know their family business but the truth was, he'd always kept a tight rein on his emotions and Dan's accident had stirred them up. Brought them to the surface. Even saying his brother's name had the potential to let those feelings loose, and he couldn't risk breaking down in front of a complete stranger.

Evie didn't say a word but one look at the set of her shoulders told him everything. He should have told her there was more to Faith's discontent than homework.

"Dan was…is…a police officer, and he was injured in an…accident." It wasn't the whole truth, but Sam didn't know how else to describe what had happened. His jaw tightened. *Someone deliberately tried to kill my brother?* Too harsh. And it would only raise more questions.

"I'm sorry."

The simple words threw him off balance. He'd expected questions. Maybe even accusations. What he wasn't prepared for was the compassion he heard in Evie's voice. And it nearly undid him.

Sam retreated behind the walls he'd put up to stave off the pain of the past few months. He felt a rush of relief when the cabin came into view.

When Evie reached her car, she opened the passenger-side door and hoisted her gigantic bag inside. He caught a glimpse of a package of gum and a box of bandages.

Bitterness welled up, catching him by surprise.

So Evie McBride thought the contents of her duffel-size purse meant she was prepared for anything. It was too bad there wasn't something in it that could fix messed-up lives.

Chapter Six

I've been praying for Sam. And Faith.

The words scrolled through Evie's mind every time she woke up during the night.

In March, her father had asked her to pray for a friend and his family. He'd only shared a few details. The friend's son was a Chicago police officer who'd been shot while responding to a call. After surgery to remove a bullet near his spine, the doctors were still uncertain whether he'd ever walk again. He had a wife and twelve-year-old daughter. And a devastated twin brother.

"No one in the family is a believer, Evie," Patrick had told her. "They don't know how to comfort each other or how to *be* comforted. Instead of coming together, the family is splintering apart."

Evie had added them to her prayers even though she'd struggled with the circumstances. Another parent had chosen a dangerous profession and now a family had to suffer the consequences of that decision.

She'd had no idea the man she'd been lifting up in prayer for the past three months had been Jacob Cutter. And the child she'd asked God to comfort wasn't a nameless, faceless little girl. It was Faith. And the twin brother, Sam.

As daylight filtered through the sheer curtains, Evie gave up on sleep. She sat up in bed and wrapped her arms around her knees.

Lord, now I know why you brought me here. And why Sam asked me to tutor Faith. Give me wisdom to know how to encourage her. I wasn't much older than Faith when Mom died. I know what it's like to have your whole world turned upside down and not understand why.

Reveal yourself to them. Show them that even though the situation might seem hopeless, they can find hope in you.

Patrick had told her that none of the Cutter family were believers, but Evie had confidence God was at work. His timing was always perfect and there had to be a reason why Patrick's fishing trip and her arrival in Cooper's Landing had corresponded with Faith and Sam's trip.

Evie remembered Sam's expression when Faith had mentioned her dad. For a split second, the bleakness in Sam's eyes had reflected all the pain and anger and helplessness he felt.

Strengthen Sam, too, Lord.

Evie was closing up the shop for the day when a van pulled in and a stocky young man jumped out of the driver's seat, intercepting her on her way to the cottage.

Evie hadn't had many customers over the course of the day. If only his timing would have been better! When Patrick called, she wanted to be able to tell him she was single-handedly reducing the store's inventory. "I'm sorry. We're closed."

"Are you Evie McBride? Patrick's daughter?"

Evie paused. "Yes."

"I'm Seth. Seth Lansky? The computer tech? Mr. McBride hired me to install a new software program."

Computer tech? Evie's gaze traveled over the man's husky frame. In a flannel-lined plaid shirt and heavy boots, he looked more like pictures she'd seen of the legendary Paul Bunyan than someone who spent his days at a keyboard.

"Dad didn't mention you were coming over." Not that it was unusual for her dad to forget something. The day before he'd left, she'd caught him wandering around the house looking for his glasses. They'd been tucked in the front pocket of his shirt the whole time.

"I couldn't tell him the exact day I'd be stopping by," Seth explained. "Emergency calls get priority."

That sounded legitimate. Evie glanced over his shoulder at the vehicle parked in the driveway. It didn't have a logo painted on it but that didn't mean anything. Sleepy little Cooper's Landing wasn't exactly on the cutting edge when it came to business practices. The local post office and Ruby's Beauty Salon operated out of the same building.

"I was just about to leave for a few hours."

Seth scratched a ragged thumbnail against the stubble on his chin. "If I don't take a look at it now, I'm not sure when I can come back around. Mr. McBride seemed pretty anxious to get it taken care of. Shouldn't take very long."

Evie glanced at her watch. Four-fifteen. She was already late for her meeting with Faith.

"I suppose it's all right."

"Great." Seth flashed an engaging smile and followed her inside. Evie led the way past the kitchen to the room her dad had converted into an office when he'd moved in.

"Here you—" Evie turned the doorknob and frowned. It was locked. "That's strange. Dad never locks anything."

"There must be a key around somewhere."

"I'll look in the kitchen."

When Evie returned a few minutes later with the ring of keys she'd found hanging on a hook by sink, Seth had his back to her, talking on a cell phone.

"I'm surprised you get reception. Half the time, mine won't work."

Seth gave a visible start and snapped the phone shut. "This one didn't, either."

Evie sifted through the keys, looking for one that might fit. "You'll have your work cut out for you. Dad hates computers. The PC my sisters and I bought him a few years ago when he opened the shop is already outdated. I tried to teach him how to use it but I'm pretty sure he kept his old typewriter as a backup. Here. I think this is the right one…." Evie choked as the door to Patrick's office drifted open.

"Looks like your dad got the hang of it," Seth drawled.

"I can't believe this," Evie murmured, studying the expensive flat-screen monitor she *knew* hadn't been part of the package they'd bought for Patrick. There was also a combination printer and—Evie blinked— *fax machine?*

Seth didn't answer as he sat down at the desk and pressed the power button.

Evie lingered, still uncertain whether she should leave him alone in the house. But Faith needed her. "I'll be back in a little while."

Seth chuckled. "Don't worry about me. Like I said, this shouldn't take long."

Evie slung her bag over her shoulder and made a quick detour to the garage before leaving for her afternoon tutoring session.

When she pulled into the Cutters' driveway, she was encouraged to see Faith sitting on the step, waiting for her to arrive. And relieved they'd made it safely back to shore.

Thank you, Lord.

Instead of saying hello, Faith greeted her with a gloomy announcement. "Sam says I have to work on my math assignments first."

"Really?" Evie opened the trunk of the car. "I hate to veto your uncle, but the teacher sets the schedule. We're having gym class first."

Faith peeked into the trunk and her eyes lit up when she saw the basketball hoop. "Is that for me?"

"It's for us. I warned you I was a science geek, right? You'll have to take it easy on me until I learn the rules."

"We can mount it above the garage door. I'll get Sam." Faith bounded away before Evie could stop her.

Evie's heart gave a strange little flutter when Sam emerged from the cabin. They must have recently come off the lake because his hair curled damply at the base of his neck. His casual clothing should have looked scruffy, but Sam wore the threadbare chambray shirt and faded jeans with casual ease. He could have graced the cover of any popular boating magazine.

Once again, Evie wondered what he did for a living. He'd walked across the roof with catlike grace the day before, but his skin didn't have the weathered look of someone who worked outside all day. Although his biceps could have been honed by construction work...

"Heads up, Evie!" Faith's cheerful warning rang across the yard.

The basketball sailed toward her, and Evie instinctively lifted her hands. And missed. The force of the ball against her abdomen winded her.

"Wow." She gasped the word. "There's a lot of power in that pass."

Faith grinned. "I'll get the ladder."

Sam stared after his niece in disbelief. "Who is she and what did she do with my niece? That is *not* the girl who was on the boat with me. The girl with me today refused to talk and deliberately left out the jelly on my peanut butter and *jelly* sandwich."

Evie's soft laugh rippled through him. "You don't know how many times I've heard variations of that question at parent-teacher conferences."

The sound of her laughter never failed to surprise

Sam. It was…young. Jacob had mentioned Patrick's youngest daughter was only twenty-six, but the serious blue eyes and conservative clothing made her seem older. Most women wore hats as a fashion statement, but Sam had a hunch that Evie had chosen the wide-brimmed straw hat to protect her from the sun. Probably because she'd given *him* her sunblock. Today she'd kept the cardigan but traded in her skirt for a pair of pleated khakis. And the flat-soled leather shoes on her feet weren't exactly the kind of footwear endorsed by the NBA.

Sam nudged Evie aside as she reached into the trunk of the car and wrestled with a rusty basketball hoop. "Gym class. You do have some interesting teaching methods, Miss McBride."

"Thank you."

Sam wasn't sure it was a compliment. They had two weeks to bring Faith's grades back up. So far the only books he'd seen were the ones he'd fished out of Faith's laundry basket that morning.

"I can play basketball with her anytime—"

Evie tossed the ball to him. "Great. Let's get this net up."

Not exactly what he'd meant. "Ah, maybe I didn't mention how much homework Faith has. She took it pretty hard when her dad got hurt. She stopped caring. About school. About…everything. You've got your work cut out for you over the next two weeks. To be quite honest, I don't know if there's time for puppies and basketball."

"Those are the things Faith cares about. We're going

to *make* time for them. Everything else will fall into place. You'll see."

"You're the teacher."

Evie's chin lifted. "I'm glad we got that settled."

Sam expected Evie to sit on the sidelines. Maybe look over Faith's assignments while she had the opportunity. But no. She'd joined in the game with an enthusiasm that amazed him. The woman had two left hands and feet, but what she lacked in athletic ability she made up for in effort.

"You're going to have blisters on your blisters," Sam murmured as they crouched face-to-face in the center of the driveway in a battle for control of the ball.

Evie blew a wisp of hair out of her eyes. "Between the shin splints and the torn ligaments I won't even notice them."

Sam couldn't prevent the rusty bark of laughter that rolled out. And it surprised him. Maybe Faith wasn't the only one who had forgotten how to laugh over the past few months.

He had to admit Evie was a genius when it came to kids. Somehow she'd known exactly what his niece needed. Faith lived and breathed sports, but she'd quit the track team after Dan was injured. Not only had she walked away from something she loved, but she'd lost the physical outlet to deal with the additional stress on their family.

And he'd been totally oblivious to all that. Until now. For Faith's sake, he decided to trust Evie's unorthodox teaching methods.

"Ready, Evie?" Faith's eyes gleamed with the light of competition as she gave the basketball an impressive spin on the tip of her index finger.

"Ready, *Evie?*" Sam repeated in disbelief. "Haven't you ever heard the saying blood is thicker than water?"

"It depends on who's grading your papers," Evie retorted.

Feeling more lighthearted than he had in weeks, Sam knocked the ball out of Faith's hand and went in for a layup. Evie came out of nowhere and stole the ball, lobbing it toward the net. It hit the backboard and swished through the hoop.

Faith whooped in delight at the stunned look on Evie's face.

"Beginner's luck," Sam muttered as he jumped up and caught the rebound.

Family loyalty aside, Faith gave Evie encouragement and advice as they played. Somehow Evie had reversed their roles. She looked to Faith to teach her the rules of the game. Trusted her commands. Accepted correction.

Her strategy, Sam acknowledged, was brilliant. Evie didn't expect to win Faith's trust and respect, she wanted to earn it.

Faith would have played until dark if Sam hadn't noticed Evie's slight limp and called the game. And he didn't miss the grateful look Evie shot in his direction.

"Sam, I'm going to shower and work on my math for a while, okay?" Faith took one more shot from the makeshift free-throw line and did a little victory dance when it swept through the net. "You played a great game, Evie. Don't let anyone tell you you're just a science geek." She gave her a cheeky smile and dashed into the house.

"Did my niece just say she was going to work on her math? Without empty threats or shameless bribes?"

"She did." Evie took a folded tissue out of the pocket of her khakis and blotted her forehead. "She's a great kid, Sam. You'll get through this."

Sam had a feeling she wasn't referring only to adolescence and her next words confirmed it.

"I know about your brother. Dad asked me to pray for your family when it happened, but I didn't realize it was *you*. Not until yesterday."

"You've been *praying* for us?"

"Since March," Evie confirmed.

Three months ago, and Dan was still on a downward spiral. His lips twisted. "I wish I could tell you it's helped. Dan isn't walking yet."

"God is more interested in healing hearts than bodies," Evie said.

The simple words blindsided him.

"I'll be back tomorrow afternoon." Evie walked toward the car but Sam beat her to it and opened the driver's-side door.

"I'm going to toss some steaks on the grill. Why don't you stay for supper?" Sam had no idea which wire in his brain had short-circuited and disengaged his mouth from his brain.

Evie shook her head. "I can't."

No apologies. No excuses. Maybe he'd been impulsive to ask her to stay, but Sam still felt a stab of disappointment at her blunt refusal. He told himself it wasn't unusual to want to know a little more about the woman he'd hired to be Faith's tutor—but part of him chided himself for not being completely honest.

The truth was, Evie McBride intrigued him.

Sam reached the phone on the third ring. It was within Faith's reach but she was stretched out on the sofa with her eyes closed, headphones firmly in place.

After Evie had left, she'd retreated back into her shell. Lake Superior, for all its changing moods, had nothing on adolescent girls.

"Hello?"

A harsh crackle grated in his ear.

"Sam? This is...Patrick... Evie...needs help... Think we've...got a problem on your end." Static distorted the words and Sam frowned. "Take care...her."

"Patrick, I can barely hear you," Sam said. "What did you say about Evie?"

Patrick's voice broke up again and Sam felt a surge of frustration. "One more time, Patrick. The connection is terrible. Are you and Dad at the lodge yet?"

"Go...Evie. Might...danger." The line went dead.

"Patrick?" Sam hit Redial and got a busy signal.

Now what?

Sam tried to convince himself he'd imagined the word *danger*. But why had Patrick called him instead of Jacob?

Sam glanced at his watch. Seven o'clock. Evie had left half an hour ago. She'd think he was crazy if showed up out of the blue to check on her. And he'd have a lot of explaining to do if he told her Patrick had called *him*.

He still hadn't found the right time to tell her what their fathers were up to. The truth was, he'd been hoping he wouldn't have to.

Ten minutes crawled by as Sam paced the living room, waiting for Patrick to call back. Finally, he shook Faith's knee to get her attention.

"I'm going to drop you off at Sophie's for a few minutes, okay? I've got an errand to run."

Faith, eager to play with Rocky, didn't question him.

When he got to Evie's ten minutes later, he saw a van parked close to the house. His stomach knotted. Beach Glass was closed for the day, and he doubted Evie had made friends in the short time she'd been staying at the house.

He knocked on the door but didn't wait for someone to answer it. Giving in to an overwhelming sense of urgency, he turned the handle and went inside.

Chapter Seven

"Miss McBride?" Seth poked his head into the kitchen. "Wow. Something smells good."

"Garlic bread." Evie wiped her hands on the old-fashioned pinafore apron she'd found in a box of linens at the shop. When she'd gotten back from Sam's, she'd found Seth still hard at work in Patrick's office.

Feeling a little awkward with someone else in the house, she'd reheated some leftover pasta from the night before and lingered in the kitchen, hoping Seth would finish soon. She wanted the house to herself to sort through the strange jumble of emotions she felt whenever Sam Cutter cruised the perimeter of her personal space.

She drew a deep breath. Even when he wasn't around, the man had the most unsettling way of creeping into her thoughts. "Are you finished?"

"No. As a matter of fact, I've got a little problem. Your dad gave me his password but he must have changed it and forgotten to tell me. Think you can take a look? Most people use familiar words. Birthdays. Names of children. That sort of thing."

"I can try." Evie followed him into the office and sat down in the chair.

"Here's what I've got so far." He pushed a piece of paper in front of her. "Charlotte. Sara. Jo. Do you see a pattern there? Are they middle names? Old girlfriends?"

Evie didn't think the last comment particularly funny.

"There's more than one password?"

Seth smiled and shrugged. "You know Patrick."

That she did. Her dad probably thought he needed a password to protect his password.

"They aren't middle names." *Or old girlfriends.* She studied the names a few more seconds and started to laugh. "I can't believe Dad remembered. We had an aquarium when I was growing up. Every time we got a new fish, my sisters and I named it after the heroine of a book we were reading at the time. Charlotte is from *Charlotte's Web.* Sara is in *A Little Princess* and Jo is one of the March sisters in *Little Women.*"

Seth leaned closer, his eyes strangely intent. "What's the next one?"

"Let me think…." Evie bit her lip. Nancy Drew? No, Caitlin had vetoed that one. It had been a blue betta fish and according to Caitlin's logic, a fish named Nancy Drew had to be *red.* No wonder she'd started an image consulting business after graduating from college.

"Evie?"

The sound of Sam's voice startled her. She twisted

in the chair and saw him standing in the doorway behind her.

"I knocked but you must not have heard me."

"Sam. What are you doing here?" Once again her first thought was for her father. She rose to her feet but Seth's hand snaked out and caught her wrist.

"I've got two more calls to make this evening, Miss McBride." The faint bite in the words surprised her. Seth hadn't mentioned other appointments. And he certainly hadn't seemed to be in a hurry to finish up before now.

Evie gently tugged her wrist free. "This will only take a minute."

"Sure." Seth's lips worked into a smile. "No problem."

Sam leaned against the door frame and stuck his hands in his pockets. "I forgot to give you Faith's reading list for her book reports when you were over this afternoon. I saw the lights on and decided to drop it off."

Not exactly an emergency, Evie thought. Maybe he'd had another argument with Faith and wanted to talk about it. "I'll be right back, Seth."

As soon as they were in the hall, Sam took hold of her arm and guided her toward the door. When Evie opened her mouth to protest, Sam tapped his finger against her lips, shocking her into silence.

Once they were outside, she pulled away from him and planted her hands on her hips. "What do you think you're doing?"

"Who is that guy?" Sam asked tersely.

"Seth Lansky. Dad hired him to install some software."

"Your dad set up the appointment? He told you about it before he left?"

"No. He forgot. But that's nothing new—"

"Evie. Think about it." Sam's eyes held hers intently. "Patrick wouldn't hire someone to install software. Not when he's got a computer-savvy daughter coming to stay at his house for two weeks."

Evie's mouth went dry. "What are you getting at?"

"What did Seth ask you to do?"

Evie noticed Sam Cutter had an annoying habit of answering a question with a question. "Dad isn't very knowledgeable about computers. He set up multiple passwords when one would have been sufficient." There. That should prove her point.

"Maybe he set up multiple passwords on purpose." Sam edged her into the shadows between the house and the shop. Evie squeaked as he backed her against the wall, angling his body so she was hidden from view and bracing a hand on either side of her.

"That's crazy. The only thing Dad keeps on his computer is his personal budget and the financial records for Beach Glass."

"If this guy is *installing* software, why does he need to access your dad's files?"

Evie stared up at him. "I don't know."

Disbelief and fear skimmed across Evie's face.

Good, Sam thought. Now they were even. The vehicle parked in the driveway had made him uneasy, but finding Evie sitting at the desk, with an all-star wrestler wannabe leaning over her, had shaved ten years off his life.

"When did this guy show up? Did you ask him for any identification?"

"Right before I left this afternoon," Evie whispered.

Her failure to answer his second question was an answer in and of itself. He'd lecture her about that later. Right now he had to determine if Patrick's phone call and Lansky's showing up was a big fat coincidence.

"I'm going to take a look inside his van." He took a step forward and so did Evie.

"I'm not staying here."

"Now isn't the time to be nervous. You missed that opportunity. It would have been when a stranger came up to the door and you let him in your house." He knew he'd already made his point, but he couldn't help it. His heart was still doing jumping jacks in his chest, and he blamed it on the naive redhead standing in front of him. Apparently, there were times when her warm heart overrode her cautious nature.

He took another step forward. So did Evie.

"You can't spy on him alone. What if he sees you and you get hurt?"

Thanks for the vote of confidence, Sam thought wryly. "I'll be fine. Stay here and make yourself invisible. I'll be right back."

This time when he took a step forward, she stayed put.

Sam sidled around the house, pausing to take a quick look in the window. Seth had taken Evie's place at the desk and it looked like he was trying to figure out the password himself. Sam watched long enough to see him engage in the good old "hunt and peck" method of keyboarding. If this guy turned out to be a computer tech, Sam moonlighted as a gourmet chef. And everyone who knew him knew he lived on takeout.

He worked his way over to the van and tried the door. Locked. That was interesting. Apparently Seth wasn't as trusting as the woman who'd let him into her house. Keeping a wary eye on the front door, he circled the van.

And bumped into someone coming around the other side.

"I thought I told you to stay put." Sam said goodbye to another ten years. Only catching a whiff of a familiar floral scent in the air had prevented him from tackling the person first and asking questions later.

"Will this help?" The faint glow of a penlight illuminated Evie's face.

"As a matter of fact, it will." Sam plucked the key ring out of her hand, not prepared for the weight of it. "What do you have on here? A hammer? Never mind. Let me guess. *The essentials*."

He traced the interior of the van with the tiny beam of light. Crumpled potato-chip bags, soda cups and empty paper sacks littered the seat and floor.

"Where fast-food lunches go to die," Sam murmured. "Well, we know he's got high cholesterol. Let's take a look in the back and see what else we can find out about Mr. Lansky." He pressed the light against the back window and his blood chilled.

Okay, Dad, what have you and Patrick gotten yourselves into?

And more important, what had they gotten Evie into?

Evie stood on her tiptoes, her nose pressed against the glass as she peered inside. "What is all that?"

"Diving equipment."

Sam took a quick inventory and what he saw didn't make him feel any better. The gear wasn't amateur, weekend-warrior stuff. The front seat of the van might have resembled a college frat house, but the equipment in the back was practically arranged in alphabetical order. Expensive cameras. Oxygen tanks. Wet suits. And a very lethal-looking spear gun.

He lowered the light before Evie spotted it.

Sam's mind raced over possible scenarios and none of them included a computer tech. What he did have were two AWOL senior citizens with delusions of grandeur trying to track down clues to a sunken treasure. A frantic phone call from Patrick. A guy trying to access Patrick's computer files…and Evie somewhere in the middle.

The front door opened, tripping the motion light in the yard. Sam dropped to his knees, taking Evie with him.

She struggled against him and Sam saw the outrage and mistrust in her wide blue eyes. She didn't trust *him?* She let some guy into her house without asking for ID, and now *he* was the bad guy?

"Let me go." She struggled against him.

"Sorry." Sam eased away from her. "It looks like Mr. Lansky is done for the night and until we know if he's legit, I don't want him to catch us checking out his van. Time to work on your acting skills."

Sam did it again. He grabbed her hand, kept low to the ground and pulled her into the woods bordering the driveway.

"Play along," he whispered.

"Play along with what—" The words died as Sam rose to his feet, wrapped his arm around her waist and nuzzled her hair. Evie's feet melted to the ground, but somehow Sam managed to nudge her out of the shadows.

"He's watching." Sam breathed the words in her ear. "Let him think we were taking a romantic stroll."

Evie swallowed hard as she and Sam stepped into the light. Seth stood beside the van, scowling at them. When she'd met him that afternoon, Seth had reminded her of a teddy bear, but now his barrel-shaped frame and thick arms looked more menacing than cuddly.

Sam stiffened, as if he were bracing for a confrontation. Both men topped six feet, but even though Sam was muscular, he lacked Seth's solid bulk.

Evie had never been a flirt—she didn't even have a clue *how* to flirt—but she smiled playfully up at Sam and linked her arm through his. "Saturday sounds great…. Oh, hi, Seth. I'm sorry it took us so long but we had some things to…discuss."

She didn't have to pretend to be embarrassed that he'd caught them. She could *feel* her freckles getting hot.

For one heart-stopping moment, Seth stared at them, his fists clenched at his sides as he took a step closer.

"You two go ahead and finish on the computer, Evie." Sam tucked a strand of hair behind her ear and gave her a smile. "I'll make some popcorn and put in a movie."

Evie had never had a man look at her like that before—even if he *was* pretending. Her older sisters both had had their share of romances, but Evie had shied away from dating. In high school and college, she'd preferred reading to socializing and knew her serious nature turned off guys who wanted to have fun. Self-conscious of her pale skin, flaming red hair and gangly figure, Evie had discovered that even though she couldn't make herself physically disappear, she could get lost in the pages of a book. She could join adventurous people who didn't wear cardigans or carry dental floss in their purse.

"Honey?"

Honey?

Sam squeezed her hand and his eyes flashed a warning, reminding her to play her part.

Evie recovered and gave him an adoring look. "All right...dear."

Sam made a choking sound and Evie turned to Seth, giving him a bright smile. "Should we all go back inside? I'm sure I'll remember the password but I can always call my sisters. Maybe they'll know."

Seth looked as if he'd just swallowed broken glass. "I don't want to take up any more of your time. I'll finish the job when your dad gets back from his fishing trip."

He unlocked the van and climbed inside. As the van rattled down the driveway, Evie realized she was still clinging to Sam's arm. She let go and stepped away from him, crossing her arms over her chest.

"I think he bought it." Sam exhaled. "Or maybe he decided your house wasn't big enough for the both of us."

"What. Is. Going. On?"

Sam raked a hand through his hair. "I wish I knew," he muttered.

The man who'd given her the adoring, lopsided smile had disappeared. The man who replaced him looked as though he'd rather be treading water in Lake Superior than be with her. And it stung.

"You show up here out of the blue. Some guy is trying to access Dad's computer files. Why?" Evie's voice cracked on the last word. *Terrific.* She sounded like a hysterical female.

Sam pivoted and strode toward the house, leaving Evie no choice but to chase after him while he gave her a brief explanation. "I didn't show up out of the blue. Your dad called me."

"Dad? Why would he call *you?*"

"Believe me—I have as many questions as you do. The connection was bad but Patrick said you might be in danger. That's why I stopped by. And it's a good thing I did." He gave her a dark look.

"That's silly. You must have misunderstood him. Why would I be in danger?" A thought whisked through her, sending her heart speeding into overdrive. "Do you think Seth is planning to rob the antique shop? But why would he need Dad's password? Is *Dad* in trouble?" Fear spiraled through her. "I'm going to call the lodge and talk to him myself...."

Sam stopped so abruptly, Evie slammed into him. It was like running into a telephone pole.

"It might help if your dad was *at* the lodge."

"That must be where he called you from. According to my itinerary, they should have arrived there at six o'clock."

"Your *itinerary?*" he repeated.

"I plotted out their trip. Based on mileage. Number of stops. Packing the canoes and paddling to the island. My calculations could be off, but not by more than fifteen minutes."

Sam stared at her as if she'd spoken in a different language.

"That's it. We're going to Sophie's."

"What? Why?" She scrambled away from him when he reached for her hand. She was tired of being towed around like a piece of wheeled luggage.

"Because our fathers are having a delayed midlife crisis, that's why."

Evie managed to grab her purse as Sam took hold of her elbow and hustled her out the door.

Chapter Eight

"Oh, dear." Sophie took one look at Sam's face and put her hand to her throat. "Come in."

"Where's Faith?"

"She fell asleep on the couch. I think the puppies wore her out."

"We need to talk to you." Sam lowered his voice. "Is Tyson here?"

Sophie shook her head, casting an anxious glance at Evie. He didn't blame her for being concerned. If possible, Evie's skin looked more pale than usual. He'd expected to be bombarded with questions on the car ride over to Sophie's, but Evie had sat quietly, her hands twisting the straps of the gigantic purse in her lap.

"Come into the sitting room." Sophie bustled ahead of them. "We can talk there without disturbing Faith. Would you like something to drink? Tea? Coffee?"

"Sophie, I don't think—" Sophie speared him with a meaningful glance at Evie, who'd wilted into the worn velvet settee in the corner.

"Coffee." He had a feeling they were in for a long night.

He reined in his impatience until Sophie returned with a tray crowded with delicate china cups and a plate of paper-thin lemon cookies.

Sophie dropped two sugar cubes into Evie's cup before settling into a chair opposite them.

Sam had never been good at small talk, and he wasn't in the mood for it now. His stomach still clenched at the thought of finding Evie alone with the guy who'd managed to charm his way into Patrick's private office. Except Lansky hadn't gotten what he'd been looking for. Which meant he might come back.

"I got a call from Patrick tonight, Sophie. Before we got cut off, he said Evie might be in danger. When I went to the house to check on her, there was a man with her. A Seth Lansky. He told Evie that Patrick had hired him to work on his computer but it was clear he was really trying to get into the files." Sam watched the color ebb out of Sophie's face and felt a stab of guilt. Jacob would string him up for confronting her like this, but Sophie was the only person who might be able to explain Patrick's urgent phone call.

"You told me that Dad and Patrick were meeting with a friend about finding a ship that sank in Superior. Is there something you *didn't* tell me?"

Sophie's hands fluttered in her lap. "I'm afraid there's a lot I didn't tell you."

"We're listening." Sam softened his tone, reminding himself that Sophie had gone through a lot over the past year. But he had to make sure Evie was safe before he'd let her go back to the house alone.

"What are you two talking about?" Evie broke in. "Dad and Jacob are on a *fishing* trip. He never said a thing about meeting a friend…or searching for a…*ship*."

"He didn't want to worry you." Sophie sighed. "And the only reason I mentioned it to Sam the other day was because I thought Jacob had told him."

Evie leaned forward. "Told him what? Where *are* they?"

Sophie paused and closed her eyes. When she opened them, it was obvious she'd come to a decision.

"Shortly before I found out I had cancer, I'd started researching my family genealogy. I knew there'd been a scandal a long time ago. My grandmother always referred to it as the Graham family curse. It made me curious and I started contacting distant relatives, trying to find out what they remembered about it. Finally, I discovered a distant cousin who was thrilled to get rid of a box of old papers she'd had in her attic for years.

"My great-grandmother's journal was in it, along with letters she and her daughter-in-law, Dorothea, had exchanged. Dorothea and her husband had had a rocky marriage, and she blamed my great-grandfather, Matthew Graham. Apparently Matthew had been branded a thief and betrayed people who trusted him. Dorothea believed Matthew's actions had marked the family and no one would ever be free of them. I think that was why my grandmother referred to the scandal as a curse. But for me, it became a blessing. In the middle of reading through the journal and Dorothea's letters, I found out I had cancer. But I didn't feel hopeless because God had given me a purpose." Sophie paused and took a deep breath. "I decided to find out the truth. What really happened and if Matthew Graham was guilty or not."

"But what does this have to do with Dad? And Jacob?" Evie asked in confusion.

"They offered to help me."

Evie closed her eyes, relieved. "Dad is helping you research your family history? That makes sense. He'll spend hours sifting through books—"

"He's not looking through books," Sam interrupted. "He and my dad are looking for a ship. Or, to be more exact, something *on* the ship."

"That's impossible. Dad doesn't know the first thing about that kind of stuff." Evie looked to Sophie for reassurance, but the expression on the older woman's face caused a fresh crop of goose bumps to rise on her arms. Was she really supposed to believe that her quiet, scholarly father had gotten mixed up in a crazy hunt for a sunken treasure? If he had, she didn't blame Sophie. It had to be Jacob Cutter's fault.

"Sam is right," Sophie admitted. "They're looking for the *Noble*."

"What do you know about it?" Sam asked.

"Not a lot. According to Dorothea's letters, a ship came over from England in 1890. Over the past few months, Patrick and I searched through dozens of old newspaper clippings. We found several references to the *Noble,* a wooden steamer that sank in October the same year. It went down in heavy fog and only one person survived."

"Your great-grandfather."

Sophie nodded. "Matthew worked in a logging camp and his boss had hired him to go to England and escort Lady Dale Carrington back to the United States. Lady Dale's father had arranged for her to marry Randall Lawrence, the son of a lumber baron. She brought a wedding gift from her family with her. A dowry, if you will. I can't find a specific reference as to what it was. Maybe jewelry. A family heirloom of some kind. Whatever it was, it must have been extremely valuable. The loss of it stirred up more of a fuss in the Lawrence family than the loss of a prospective bride.

"Matthew claimed Lady Dale's dowry sank with the ship, but they found her betrothal ring in his possession. It was all the proof Randall needed. He accused Matthew of saving himself and the treasure. Matthew denied it, but his reputation was ruined. A few years later, he married my great-grandmother but something had happened to him. He drank heavily and couldn't keep a job. They barely scratched out a living."

"Not exactly the kind of life a man harboring a treasure would choose," Sam said. "If he'd managed to survive and keep the dowry, he would have moved far away and put it to good use."

Sophie gave him an approving smile. "My thought exactly."

"Who knows about the *Noble?*" Sam asked suddenly. "Is it common knowledge there was something valuable on board?"

"I don't think so. No one in my family ever said a word about a treasure—I didn't even know what Matthew had been accused of stealing until I read Dorothea's letters. She was the first one who had mentioned a dowry. The newspaper articles only reported that the entire crew had gone missing, their bodies never recovered. Some of my distant relatives know I've been researching the Graham family history, but only Patrick and Jacob know specific details about the *Noble* and Lady Dale's dowry."

Listening to their exchange, Evie remembered the diving gear in the back of Seth's van and a knot formed in her throat. "Are there people who look for sunken ships that might have a treasure on board?"

Sophie hesitated. "There are laws that protect wrecks from being salvaged in areas designated as underwater preserves."

"But what if the *Noble* sank outside a preserve?"

"Permits would need to be filed." Sam answered the question. "But some people might bypass that little detail."

"But Sophie said no one knows for sure where the *Noble* went down," Evie reminded him.

"Jacob's old friend, Bruce Mullins, is a diver. He's been credited with discovering several important wrecks in the Great Lakes over the past decade," Sophie said. "He's familiar with Superior and would know if there's a possibility the *Noble* can be found. I know Patrick and Jacob made it clear to Bruce that everything they told him was to be held in the strictest confidence."

Sam scrubbed the palms of his hands against his face. "I'm pretty sure someone knows about it now," he said grimly. "Do you have any idea why they'd be interested in Patrick's computer files, Sophie?"

Sophie bit her lip. "The day before they left, Patrick said he had a surprise for me. Something to celebrate my six-month checkup. He wouldn't tell me what it was, but maybe he figured out where the *Noble* sank."

"He's been documenting your research on his computer?"

"Dad hates computers." Evie felt the need to point it out. Again. Patrick may have helped Sophie pore over old newspaper clippings, but if she knew her dad, he'd taken notes using his trusty ballpoint pen and paper.

Sophie slid an apologetic look in her direction. "That's not quite true—he's actually quite knowledgeable about them. He also scanned Dorothea's letters and pages from the journal into his files. I have everything locked up, but Patrick thought we should have copies. I let him handle that part of it. Tyson has a computer but I never bothered with one."

Evie didn't think her dad bothered with them, either.

Sudden tears stung Evie's eyes and made her nose twitch. It was bad enough that Patrick hadn't confided in her about his real plans. And it was possible that someone else was interested in the *Noble*'s cargo. But everything Sophie had shared with them shrunk in comparison to one simple truth.

Her dad had broken his promise to her. A promise he'd kept since she was fourteen years old when he told her that he'd always be there for her. That he wouldn't do anything to put himself at risk...like her mother had.

* * *

"What do you mean you can't get in touch with them?" Sam paced the length of the telephone cord and reversed direction when he reached the end of it. He lowered his voice, aware of Evie and Sophie in the next room and Faith asleep on the couch several yards away. "What if there's an emergency?"

"Our pilot flies into the camps once a week with supplies," the proprietor of the lodge informed him. "Even in an emergency, the earliest we could get a message to your father would be next Monday or Tuesday."

Not good enough. Sam had to warn Patrick what had happened to Evie and find out who else was interested in the *Noble*. He already had a strong hunch *why* they were interested. Legends of sunken treasure lured hundreds of divers to the Great Lakes. Even though Sophie was right about laws existing to protect areas designated underwater preserves, there were unscrupulous people willing to break them.

Bruce Mullins, if he remembered correctly, had served in the Marines with his father. Maybe all he'd done was mention the *Noble* to a relative or friend he thought he could trust and it had sparked their interest.

But how had Seth Lansky zeroed in on Patrick's computer files instead of going to Sophie—the source of the information?

"Mr. Cutter? Are you still there? What is the message you'd like me to deliver?"

"Ah…could you tell the pilot to have him call home as soon as possible?"

Silence.

Sam rolled his eyes at the ceiling. Right. *Phone home.* That sounded like a legitimate reason to send a pilot on an unscheduled flight to an isolated fishing camp.

"I'll pass the message on, Mr. Cutter. Was there anything else?" Her tone made it clear she hoped not.

"No. Thank you." Sam hung up the phone.

The grandfather clock in the corner of the room came to life. Ten o'clock. The past few hours had disappeared, absorbed by Sophie's story about her family and Matthew Graham. Under any other circumstances, Sam would have been fascinated. But not now. Not with Jacob and Patrick out of reach and Evie alone at the house.

Another wave of helplessness rolled over him. He'd come to the Upper Peninsula to take a break from his problems, not add to them. But Patrick had called him. Warned him that Evie might be in danger and asked him to look out for her.

He couldn't leave her unprotected, especially if whoever was interested in the ship was convinced Patrick's computer files held the key to the *Noble* and her secrets.

Hopefully the incident with Lansky would prevent Evie from giving another stranger access to her home, but anyone could show up at Beach Glass during the day, pretending to be a customer.

As much as he wanted Evie to continue tutoring Faith, he didn't want to risk Evie's safety. When he'd pulled her to the ground so Seth wouldn't see them, her slender body had stiffened in his arms, tight as a bowstring. She was fragile. Vulnerable. There was only one thing to do. Convince her to pack her bags, close up shop and go home. And it probably wouldn't take much convincing. She was such a cautious little thing....

Decision made, Sam padded into the sitting room and saw the two women sitting shoulder to shoulder on the old settee. Hands clasped. Heads bowed.

Praying?

He paused in the doorway, feeling like an intruder, as Evie's soft voice filled the quiet.

"...and heavenly Father, we turn to you for strength. And for wisdom. Protect the people we love and bring them safely home. For now, we trust they are in Your care."

The words sailed through the empty places in his heart. What was it like to be so sure Someone was listening? Someone who really had the power to give strength? Over the past few months, his had drained away. Punctured by the bullet wounds in his brother's spine. Dan had always come to him for advice. But now, when Dan needed him the most, Sam found he had nothing. Nothing to give. Nothing to say. Nothing that could reverse the clock or give his brother hope for the future.

Dan hated him for it.

And Sam hated himself.

Chapter Nine

Evie lifted her head and saw Sam standing in the doorway. The raw pain in his eyes burned its way through her before the shutters slammed back into place.

"I can't get through to them until next week," he said flatly. "Bruce Mullins took them to one of the more isolated camps."

Evie felt a flash of hope. "So they did go fishing?"

"I doubt it." Sam stalked into the room. "Maybe you should stay with Sophie tonight."

He still thought she was in danger.

Evie wavered, remembering the way Seth Lansky's massive paw had circled her wrist. Had he given up or was there a chance he might come back?

You will keep in perfect peace him whose mind is steadfast, because he trusts in you.

The verse from Isaiah that Sophie had quoted while they'd prayed cycled back through Evie's mind. Peace followed trust. That's what she had to remember. "I need to go home. Dad might call again and he'll want to know I'm all right."

"If we can't contact them, they won't be able to contact us," Sam pointed out.

"I have plenty of room," Sophie added, concern for Evie evident in the slight furrow between her eyebrows. "Tyson reclaimed his old room upstairs, but the sofa in the living room pulls out into a bed."

Evie had forgotten about Tyson. Even though he was Sophie's son, something about the guy creeped her out. "I appreciate the invitation, Sophie, but I still have to open Beach Glass in the morning. I'll be fine. I think Sam spooked Seth Lansky enough that he won't be coming back."

The thought occurred to her that maybe that was why Seth had boldly talked his way into the house. With Patrick gone, he'd assumed she was alone. Vulnerable.

"Can you take me home, Sam?" Evie ignored the hollow pit in her stomach at the thought of going back to the isolated house again. "I know you and Faith are going out on the boat tomorrow morning. She needs a good night's sleep."

I'll keep my mind on You, Lord, and trust You to provide the peace.

"Let me know the second you hear from Patrick and Jacob." Sophie's eyes clouded over. "I wish now that I'd never gotten them involved in this."

"It's not your fault," Evie murmured, unable to resist a pointed look at Sam.

"Once Patrick found out what I was doing, he begged

me to let him help," Sophie continued. "That man does love a challenge."

"You mean Jacob," Evie corrected her gently.

"No. Patrick." A smile played at the corners of Sophie's lips. "I think he would have bought a wet suit and gone diving for the *Noble* himself if Jacob hadn't convinced him to contact Bruce Mullins first."

"Good old Dad. The voice of reason." Sam arched an eyebrow at Evie.

They *couldn't* be talking about Patrick McBride. The most challenging thing her dad tackled was the expert-level crossword puzzle book she bought him for his birthday every year!

The car's headlights barely made a dent in the darkness as Sam drove her home. Sophie had insisted he allow Faith to spend the night, and as Evie stared out the window at the thick stands of trees hemming the edge of the road, she wished she'd taken advantage of the offer now, too.

"Do you think Dad is in trouble?" Evie finally voiced the question churning in her mind since they'd left Sophie's.

"They're with an experienced guide," Sam said. "I'm sure they're fine."

Was it her imagination, or had he put the slightest emphasis on the word *they're*?

"I still can't believe Dad is involved in this," Evie murmured. "Helping Sophie is one thing but traipsing around, looking for a ship that may not even exist is totally out of character for him. And we have no idea who this Seth Lansky is. Or what he was trying to find."

"That's why you should go home."

Evie's mouth dropped open as the quiet force of the words vibrated in the silence. "Go home?"

"There's a real possibility you aren't safe here. Someone else is interested in the *Noble,* and they knew exactly who to go to for information. Patrick said you might be in danger. He would expect you to leave. Close up Beach Glass until I can make contact with them again and sort out this mess."

It was so tempting to grab hold of the suggestion. To put miles between her and whatever threat lurked around the corner. Would her dad want her to turn tail and run away?

You don't have to be here to talk to Dad, a logical voice in her head reminded her. *You can be at home just as easily.*

"The tourist season is just getting started," Sam continued in that calm, reasonable tone. "Even if you closed up the antique shop for a week, you wouldn't lose much business."

"I'm staying."

The announcement stunned Evie almost as much as Sam.

"There's no guarantee that you're safe," he said flatly.

Funny how those simple words shook her to the core. All her life, Evie had chosen *safe.* She'd built her life around it. Hadn't she learned that people who deliberately put themselves in dangerous situations eventually paid too high of a price? And so did the people they loved.

But what if her dad returned unexpectedly? Shouldn't she be waiting for him? And what about Faith? If God had brought them together, Evie had to trust she was under His protection and He'd give her the strength she needed.

"God brought me here for a reason," Evie said through dry lips. "I'm not leaving."

Sam didn't try to change her mind, but Evie had the feeling he wasn't happy she was staying. Or with the reason why.

"Hi, Evie."

At the unexpected greeting, Evie almost dropped the Depression-glass sugar bowl cradled in her hands.

"Faith." Evie looked at her in surprise before glancing at the row of whimsical cuckoo clocks mounted on the wall. Three o'clock. "Did you and Sam come in early today?"

Faith's face closed, reminding her of Sam's expression when he'd caught her and Sophie praying the night before. "Sam didn't want to take the boat out. It's supposed to storm later this afternoon."

The robin's-egg-blue sky, decorated with brushstrokes of wispy clouds, didn't look the least bit threatening at the moment, but Evie was glad Sam had chosen to believe the weather forecast over the clear sky.

"Is Sam with you?"

"Uh-uh." Suddenly, Faith became fascinated with

the canning jar next to the old-fashioned cash register on the counter.

Warning bells went off in Evie's head. "Faith, does he know you're here?"

"What's this?" Faith avoided the question, studying the contents of the jar on the counter as if she'd never seen anything like it before.

"It's beach glass." Evie gave the girl an exasperated smile. Science lesson or lecture? She decided there was time for both. "The waves and the sand work together like a rock tumbler until the glass is smooth and polished."

"Cool."

Evie smiled. One word that equaled high praise. "Go ahead and take one. Dad won't mind. Banks give out Tootsie Rolls, and Dad gives out pieces of beach glass. He says they last longer."

As soon as her thoughts returned to her dad, worry scurried back, chewing at Evie's peace of mind like a nest of field mice. She'd managed to keep her fear under control throughout the long night and most of the morning, but there were times it snuck up on her. Like right now.

"Look at this one. It looks like a piece of bubble gum." Faith held up a piece of glass in a shade of deep pink and for the first time, Evie noticed the girl's red-rimmed eyes and the faint pleats at the corners of her lips. "Pink is Mom's favorite color. Every Christmas, Dad buys her something pink even though he says it's a girlie color. He bought me a pink baseball mitt as a joke for my birthday once."

Faith bravely cracked open the door to her heart to see if Evie really cared about what was inside. She did. But now she had to convince her.

God, please give me the right words to say.

"Have you talked to your Dad lately?"

"When I called this morning, Mom said he was asleep."

The uncertainty in Faith's voice told Evie she didn't know if she should believe her.

"You must miss him a lot."

"I do." Faith dropped the piece of glass back into the jar. "But I heard Mom tell Sam that Dad isn't the same person anymore. Maybe…he doesn't miss me."

Evie drew in a careful breath, but it still felt like a knife sliding between her ribs. Obviously Faith had listened in on a conversation not meant for her ears. No one had been honest with Faith about her father's situation, and while Evie understood that her family thought they were protecting her, it had forced Faith to try to make sense of it on her own. And without wisdom and experience to temper her thoughts, Faith had come to the wrong conclusion.

"I'm sure your dad misses you very much," she contradicted softly. "But he has to accept some major changes in his life and that isn't easy. It isn't easy for anyone."

"I want things to be the way they were," Faith admitted in a small voice.

"They won't be the same." Evie knew she had to be honest. "But that doesn't mean they can't be better." She retrieved the piece of glass and held it on her open palm. "Look at this. It's still a piece of glass, right? But it's changed. At one point in time, it would have been sharp enough to cut you. But the waves and the sand gradually rounded the edges. Softened it. I'm praying for your dad, Faith. That he'll open his heart and trust that God is big enough to bring something good out of this situation."

She wrapped her arm around Faith's shoulders and felt them stiffen. And then Faith melted against her.

"I'll pray, too."

"Good girl," Evie murmured. "Now, how about I call your uncle, who's probably tearing apart the forest looking for you, and tell him we're going to have school earlier today?"

"Field trip?" Faith smiled hopefully.

"English first. Then maybe we can fit in a short field trip."

"Look at this." Faith squatted down and pulled a chunk of rock out of the ground.

"It's quartz." Evie stooped down to admire her find and smiled when she saw Faith's bulging pockets. The girl already had a good start on a rock collection. Evie's own pockets were full, a testimony to the fact she had a difficult time passing up interesting rocks, too.

"I'll give it to Sam for his desk. Then he'll see it every day."

"He spends a lot of time in an office?" The words rolled out before Evie could stop them, and she winced. Talk about blatant curiosity! Faith, thank goodness, didn't think there was anything unusual about the question.

"Dad always teases him about being a paper pusher or something." Faith rubbed the rock against the hem of her T-shirt and left a trail of grime on the fabric.

Evie wasn't surprised at Faith's affirmation that Sam worked in some kind of corporate setting. And she couldn't help feeling a little relieved, although she didn't want to examine *that* too closely.

When he'd left the night before, he hadn't been happy with her decision to stay in Cooper's Landing, and he'd made it clear he thought she was making a huge mistake.

It isn't as if you've shown a lot of backbone up to this point, Evie admitted to herself. She'd shaken like an aspen leaf when she'd seen that diving equipment in the back of Seth's van. No wonder Sam worried about her being alone. Some witness for God she was turning out to be. If Sam looked at her as an example of a believer, he'd think they were a bunch of wimps!

A raindrop splashed on the back of Evie's wrist. When she looked up, the blue sky had all but disappeared, filled with a slow-moving armada of dark cumulus clouds.

"Faith, let's get going. It looks like the storm that kept you off the lake is finally moving in."

A shard of lightning and a low growl of thunder in the distance underscored the point. Evie silently chided herself for being so focused on the ground that she hadn't paid attention to what was over their heads!

"We're going to get wet," Faith predicted.

Probably an understatement, Evie thought. *Soaked* was more like it. They had at least a two-mile hike back to the house. The beauty of the woods had enchanted them, luring them farther down the trail than Evie had originally planned.

She dug in her purse and pulled out her compact umbrella, popping it open and holding it over Faith's head. "Let's try this."

Faith grinned up at her. "You remind me of Mary Poppins. Remember, she had that great big carpetbag with a mirror in it? And a lamp?"

"I remember," Evie muttered as a gust of wind caught the umbrella and turned it inside out. "If I were Mary Poppins, my umbrella would behave."

They dashed down the trail as the light sprinkles, which must have been the opening preshow, became a pelting rain.

At one point, Faith slipped and fell. Rocks tumbled out of her pockets and she scrambled to gather them up again.

Evie quickly doubled back. "Don't worry, Faith. We can find more."

"I can't find the one I was going to give Sam." Faith had to raise her voice above the sudden screech of the wind.

Evie scooped a handful of soggy hair out of her eyes so she could aid in the search. "Look. Here it is." Rivulets of muddy water coasted down her arm when she picked it up. Soaked *and* dirty. With a new story to tell her students in the fall.

Faith cocked her head, reminding Evie of Sophie's puppies. "I hear a car. Maybe Sam is looking for us."

Evie heard it, too. For a brief moment, hope burst inside her. Until she remembered. "The gate was locked. It has to be a government vehicle of some kind."

"Maybe they can give us a ride!" Faith whooped and sprinted into the woods separating the service road from the trail.

Through the trees, Evie caught a glimpse of a white van creeping along the road.

It couldn't be.

"Faith! Wait." Evie was no track star but the rush of adrenaline rocketing through her blood pushed her into high gear. She caught up to Faith just before the girl stepped into the road.

"Hey!" Faith squawked in protest as Evie pulled her down behind a clump of foliage.

"It's not a government vehicle." Evie tucked Faith tightly against her as the van rolled past them, so close she could have reached out and touched the tire. A shiver ripped through her as she read the license plate, which bore the same number she'd seen on the one parked in her driveway.

Seth Lansky.

Was he looking for her?

Evie bit her lip, thinking quickly. If Seth really was following them, he probably thought they'd gone to the scenic overlook. That meant she and Faith had a chance to make it back to the parking area before Seth realized they weren't where he thought they'd be.

Thank you, God, for watching out for us.

And bless Faith and her adventurous spirit.

If they'd stuck to the service road, Seth would have spotted them immediately. Not that he'd pursue them on foot…

Out of the corner of her eye, Evie saw the red glow of the brake lights and watched as the driver nosed the vehicle into a narrow clearing.

He was turning around.

"Come on." Evie caught hold of Faith's hand and pulled her back toward the trail, their progress hampered by the brush dragging at their clothing and a grid of exposed tree roots that stretched out like a minefield beneath their feet.

"Evie, you're scaring me." Faith vaulted over a fallen log and clutched Evie's arm as she slipped on a slick bed of decaying leaves. "Who is that?"

"I'm not sure." It was the truth. Evie had no idea if the man driving the van was Seth Lansky…but it couldn't be a coincidence the three of them had wound up in the woods together at the same time.

The wind swallowed Faith's shriek as a shard of lightning hurtled out of the sky, incinerating a nearby tree. The ground trembled under their feet. Evie trembled, too, but didn't want Faith to know she was afraid.

"Not too much farther, Faith. You can do it."

Through the sheet of water cascading over the brim of her hat, Evie saw the gate up ahead. As they veered around it, she tripped over something. The heavy padlock that secured the gate to the post lay on the ground. Clipped off by something a little sturdier than a pair of pliers.

"I see the restrooms," Faith gasped.

Evie gave the girl's arm a reassuring squeeze. Tourists would be in the parking lot, waiting for the rain to subside. And Seth Lansky wouldn't dare approach them in front of witnesses.

Just as the terrain changed from dirt to concrete beneath their feet, Evie heard the faint, muffled purr of an engine. Fear seared her lungs and she scanned the parking lot.

Empty.

Chapter Ten

Evie stopped, bending over to massage the stitch in her side. Should they stay on the trail and try to make it home or take refuge in the restroom? Maybe Seth had checked them already and wouldn't bother a second time.

She had about thirty seconds to decide before Seth spotted them in the parking lot. Evie's gaze darted to the trail and gauged the distance. A straight shot fifty yards in before it took a slight turn that would conceal them from sight.

They didn't have time.

"Restroom," Evie decided, lurching toward the tiny building. Faith remained close at her heels and they skidded inside just as the van rattled around the gate.

Evie collapsed against the wall and Faith slumped to the floor beside her. Outside, the van's engine idled in harmony with their ragged breathing.

Keep going, Evie silently urged the driver. *It's pouring. You don't want to go out in this storm.*

The snick of a car door closing sounded more ominous than the crack of lightning that had demolished the top of a tree.

"You don't happen to have a phone booth in your purse, do you?" Faith hopped to her feet.

The complete look of trust in the girl's eyes stunned Evie. And goaded her into action.

"We don't need a phone booth. We need a distraction."

Think, Evie.

The restroom had been equipped with the bare essentials. Paper towel holder. A soap dispenser on the wall. And a locked cabinet under the sink.

Bingo.

"Faith, there's a package of gum in my purse. Unwrap all the sticks and give me the foil." Faith looked at her as if she'd lost her mind and Evie managed a quick smile. "Trust me. I'm a science teacher."

While Faith tackled her assignment, Evie peeled off the cabinet hinges with the miniature screwdriver on her Swiss Army Knife. Fear made her clumsy and she forced herself to take a deep, calming breath, praying the contents of the cabinet would yield what she needed.

"Here you go," Faith whispered.

Evie closed her eyes in relief when she saw the old bottle of drain cleaner stashed in the back of the cabinet with the rest of the cleaning supplies.

"Now I need you to look in the garbage for a large plastic soda bottle. Find one with a lid."

Faith wrinkled her nose but obeyed.

Evie licked her lips. Now came the hard part. She had to spot Seth before he spotted them.

"Faith, we're going to get out of here but we can't go home yet. There are some rustic cabins the Forest Service rents out on Porcupine Trail. Did you see them on the map?" At Faith's tentative nod, Evie patted her knee. "Good girl. We're going to head there and wait out the storm in one of them."

Hopefully by now, Sam would be looking for them, too.

Evie crept to the door and peered out. No one sat in the driver's seat of the van. Where was he? Evie edged out a little more and caught a glimpse of Seth's bulky frame near the trail. He had his back to them.

"When I give you the signal, head down the trail to the left."

"You're leaving me?" Panic flared in Faith's eyes.

"I'll be right behind you. I promise."

Faith's head bobbed. "What's the signal?"

"You'll know it when you hear it."

Evie filled the bottle with drain cleaner, shoved the foil into her pocket and sprinted toward the van. Seth had melted farther into the woods, and Evie knew she had only precious seconds before he realized they hadn't gone that way. Now she had no doubt he'd check the restrooms again.

Just as she skidded around the side of the vehicle, Seth appeared, lumbering back up the trail and heading straight for the restroom where Faith waited.

She shoved the foil wrappers into the bottle, screwed

the lid back on, eased the door to the van open and lobbed it inside like a grenade.

Thank you Brian and Tyler for your science fair experiment. Let's hope it works on a smaller scale.

Evie made it to the woods just as an explosion burst over the sound of the rain.

Seth's startled bellow told her it had.

The chill settling in Sam's bones had nothing to do with the sudden drop in temperature as two weather systems collided in the heavens above him.

Evie and Faith were nowhere to be found. The front door of the shop had been locked up tight. So had the house. Which could only mean one thing—Evie and Faith had taken another unscheduled field trip.

Sam's back teeth ground together. "I can't look out for you when you disappear on me, Evie."

The rain sheeted the car windows and lightning still backlit the clouds, accompanied by the low rumble of thunder. Hopefully, they'd taken shelter somewhere until the storm passed. Sam didn't want to consider the alternative.

"This is crazy." Sam twisted around, searching the backseat of the car for a discarded hat or jacket. Anything to prevent an immediate soaking when he got out of the car. The only thing his search yielded was the crumpled copy of *Captains Courageous* from Faith's summer reading list, a candy wrapper and a lime-green baseball cap. Way too small and not his color.

Evie's car was still parked by the garage, which meant they'd taken off on foot. If they'd stayed close to home, the storm would have pushed them back to the house by now.

Sam exhaled in frustration, wishing he knew the area better. He rifled through the glove compartment, remembering he'd shoved a bunch of tourist brochures into it on the drive up. A minuscule map showed a series of hiking trails less than three miles from Beach Glass.

Three miles. Judging from the map, he could drive in only as far as the rest area and then he'd have to hoof it from there. But he had to start somewhere. He wasn't a person who got rattled easily, but he'd feel a lot better knowing Evie and Faith were safe and sound. So he could chew them out for worrying him.

"What *was* that?" Faith's eyes were wide as Evie caught up to her on the trail.

"Just a little something I learned from the boys in my class."

"It sounded like a bomb."

"No, making homemade bombs is irresponsible. Reckless. I made a *distraction,* remember?"

"It was a good one."

"Thank you." The muscles in Evie's stomach cramped again, and she decided two miles a day on the treadmill didn't prepare a girl for running for cover over uneven terrain. "If my calculations are right, one of the cabins should be to the west of us about half a mile."

Rustic campsite didn't quite describe what they found at the end of the path, but at least it was a roof over their heads. Sort of. A one-room cabin fashioned from weathered cedar, equipped with screens instead of windows. A single bed frame complete with a questionable foam mattress. A fireplace layered with a thick coat of ash and a plank floor covered with droppings.

"Myotis lucifugus," Evie murmured.

"What's that?" Faith asked nervously.

"A bat." Evie scanned the ceiling to see if the culprit was still in residence. "Don't worry. All clear."

"I'm kind of c-c-cold." Faith wrapped her arms around her middle and perched gingerly on the edge of the bed.

Now that they'd managed to shake Seth loose, Evie had to concentrate on getting them dry. She rummaged in her bag and handed Faith a chocolate-dipped granola bar. "Here. Eat this. I'll try to start a fire." If she could find some dry kindling.

Faith read her mind. "We don't have any wood."

Evie poked at the ashes in the fireplace and turned up several chunks of charred embers. She wove her fingers together and closed her eyes.

"What are you doing? Did you get something in your eye?" Faith leaned forward.

Evie shook her head. "I was asking God for help."

"Starting a fire?"

"Of course. Have you ever heard the story of the loaves and fishes?"

Faith shook her head. "No."

"It's in the Bible. A huge crowd gathered all day to listen to Jesus talk. His friends told him to send the people away because everyone was hungry. Jesus asked what they had and all they could come up with was a few loaves of bread and some fish. Jesus blessed it and when his friends passed it out, those little loaves and fishes fed over five thousand people."

"Is that true?" Faith asked doubtfully.

"Yes, it is. And I'll tell you something else that's true. God cares about the small details of our lives as much as He cares about the big ones. I have the matches and few sticks and we'll let God handle the fire." She struck a match and held it against a splinter of charred wood, then blew carefully until a lick of flame chased up the length of it.

Another rumble of thunder rolled above them like a freight car, rattling the screens on the cabin.

"Look, Evie!" Faith stared in awe at the smoke curling into the air, born from the tiny flame that had begun to devour one of the chunks of wood.

"I'm going outside to make sure that smoke is going up the chimney like it's supposed to." Evie stood up and felt water squish in her shoes with every step.

Wisps of smoke emerged from the chimney, and Evie's gaze carefully moved from tree to tree. Maybe the heavy rain was a blessing in disguise. Seth didn't seem like the type of guy who carried an umbrella.

She eased back into the cabin and found Faith on her knees in front of the fireplace, hands splayed over the flames.

"Are we going to stay here for a while?"

Good question. And one Evie didn't have an answer to yet. She'd tucked some snacks into her bag before they'd set out but didn't normally carry a change of clothing! And both of them were soaked to the skin.

"Just until the rain subsides. Not that we can get any wetter."

Faith's eyes clouded. "Sam is going to be mad."

"He might be worried, but he won't be mad."

"It looks the same," Faith responded glumly.

"You might be right about that." Evie hid a smile. In spite of his annoying tendency to boss people around, Evie didn't doubt Sam's love for his niece. Not many men would take time off from work to care for a troubled adolescent, family or not.

"No one tells me anything." Faith stared into the fire, a frown puckering her brow. "I wanted to stay with Dad, but they didn't give me a choice. They made me come here."

They. It explained the tension between Faith and Sam. She blamed him for taking her away from her father. Evie didn't understand why Dan Cutter's family hadn't stayed to cheer him on during his recovery, either, but everyone had a different way of dealing with crises.

"Sometimes parents make decisions we don't understand," Evie said slowly. "But it's because they love us and want to protect us."

Faith's shoulders rolled in time with her heavy sigh. "So your mom did that, too? Did it drive you crazy?"

Laura McBride's face pieced together in Evie's memory like a tattered photograph. Her mother had loved her family but had chosen to protect everyone else. And where had that left Evie and her sisters?

"All moms do." Evie chose the safest response.

In a rapid change of moods, a mischievous sparkle

lit Faith's eyes. "We need more loaves and fishes." She poked at the fire with a stick and it flared back to life. "Dry ones."

Evie doubted she could find a dry stick in the forest at the moment, but the steady drum of the rain against the roof had quieted. "It doesn't seem to be raining as hard anymore. We should be able to leave soon."

"Do you think *he's* still there? The man you didn't want to see us?"

"I don't know." Fear pinched Evie again as she imagined the long trek back to the house. And the very real possibility that Seth was still out there somewhere, waiting for them. His deliberate search for her brought back a rush of doubts. Maybe retreat was the best option. She didn't want to put Faith in danger.

Maybe you should go home.

"Maybe you should pray," Faith said simply.

"Thanks for the reminder." Evie choked back a laugh. Out of the mouths of babes! "Don't get too close to the fire. I'm going outside to check the chimney again." A flimsy excuse, but she couldn't tell Faith she planned to sneak up the trail and make sure it was safe to leave.

The storm had exhausted its power, and Evie saw patches of blue sky through the trees as she picked her way cautiously down the trail. What she wouldn't give for a hot shower and a cup of tea…

The crack of a branch turned her knees to water. Not more than fifty yards off the trail, a man moved purposefully in the direction of the cabin.

Seth?

Evie ducked behind the thick trunk of a white pine.

Even above the sound of the rain, Evie was sure her ragged gasps of breath would give her away. Somehow, she had to get to the cabin before he did. Or, Evie thought with a flash of inspiration, draw him *away* from it.

Dropping to her knees, Evie scooted around the tree. "Okay, big guy. Let's see what you've got...." The words died as she found herself face-to-knees with the man towering over her.

He hauled Evie to her feet so quickly she barely had time to process the long legs encased in blue jeans, black sweatshirt stretched over a broad, muscular chest. And a soggy, lime-green baseball cap.

Eyes as gray as the storm clouds captured hers.

For one heart-stopping moment, Sam pulled her against him, his fingers combing through her tangled hair with gentle roughness. And then he let her go.

"I've got trouble, that's what I've got," Sam said softly. "It's about five foot five with red hair, blue eyes and a habit of taking unscheduled field trips."

Chapter Eleven

"A man was looking for us," Faith announced from the backseat of the car.

Sam's foot pumped the accelerator, spewing gravel off the back tires. Neither Evie nor Faith had said much on the trek back to the parking lot, and he'd assumed they'd taken refuge in the little cabin to wait out the storm. Until now. "What man?"

"A man in a white van. But Evie made a—"

"Distraction," Evie interrupted, shifting on the seat beside him.

"Uh-huh. A distraction." Faith nodded vigorously in agreement.

A white van. Seth Lansky again. Which could only mean one thing. He must have decided that since he couldn't get into Patrick's computer, he'd set his sights on the next logical source of information. Evie.

Sam had given in to her stubborn insistence to stay in Cooper's Landing once, but he wouldn't do it again. Not when Patrick had asked him to watch out for her. Evie had eluded Seth this time, but there was no guarantee she could do so again. Lansky might not be a physical threat, but Sam wasn't willing to take a chance.

"I'll drop Faith off to change clothes first and then I'll take you home." To make sure you pack your bags.

Evie didn't argue. Sam slanted a look at her, feeling an unfamiliar tug of *something* when he noticed the weary slump of her shoulders and the damp copper hair plastered against the nape of her neck. Hair he'd untangled with his fingers.

Sam's hands tightened on the steering wheel. He had no excuse for that. Maybe it was somehow connected to the relief that had slammed into his gut when he'd seen Evie scurry behind a tree near one of the Forest Service cabins. She'd looked as stunned by his unexpected embrace as he was. Immediately, he'd put some distance between them but that hadn't doused the confusing mix of emotions Evie always seemed to dredge up in him. And life was confusing enough at the moment, thanks, so now he planned to brush up on his grammar skills, take over as Faith's tutor and send Evie packing. For her own good. And maybe, Sam admitted, for *his*.

By the time they pulled up to the cabin, the sun was shining bravely again, gifting them with a spectacular double rainbow.

Faith propped her arms on the back of Evie's seat and gave them an engaging grin. "A rainbow is formed by the refraction and reflection of the sun's rays in the raindrops, right?"

Evie smiled. "That's true, but the Bible says it's also

God's promise never to destroy the world with water again."

"Really?" Faith blinked. "That's in the Bible? Like the story of the loaves and fishes?"

Sam felt Evie's questioning glance and hot color crept into his face. The Cutters tended to live by the old Pull Yourselves Up By The Bootstraps motto. All his life, Jacob had impressed upon his sons that they had everything in them necessary for life. Courage. Strength. Discipline. All they had to do was mine it out and use it. If they didn't, they had no one to blame but themselves. Asking for help from an unseen God was never offered as an option. The closest Sam got to Him was at Thanksgiving, when they bowed their heads and offered a weak prayer of thanks under Grandma Cutter's watchful eye.

When Sam had walked in on Evie and Sophie praying the night before, he'd felt something stir the emptiness inside and wondered if it was too late to approach God. And if it was a sign of weakness.

Jacob would think so. When a friend of Rachel's had asked the pastor of her church to visit Dan, Jacob had intercepted the man and politely told him to tend to his own "flock" and he would see to his.

The image of Dan, confined to a hospital bed, sawed through Sam again like the serrated edge of a knife. His brother's career and favorite hobbies required the use of his legs. He could still see the hopeless look in Dan's eyes. Even his wife and daughter failed to move him toward recovery. And instead of being encouraging, Jacob's admonitions to Dan—that if he set his mind on recovery, he'd be walking in no time—had only made Dan pull further into himself.

"Do you have a Bible, Sam?" Faith asked.

"No." The word came out more harshly than he intended.

"I'm sure Dad has an extra one. I'd be happy to let you borrow it, Faith," Evie said carefully.

Faith looked at him expectantly, and Sam decided that even though it might not help, it probably couldn't hurt, either. "I'm okay with it." He hoped the rest of his family would be, too.

"As long as you don't test me on it." Faith giggled.

"I make no promises." Evie turned back to Sam. "I'll wait here in the car while you get Faith settled."

"We've got towels inside. You should at least come in and dry your hair." Sam saw the blush that rose in Evie's cheeks as she glanced away. Strange. Evie wasn't exactly shy. The night he'd urged her to pretend they'd been on a romantic stroll, her fluttering lashes and adoring look had convinced Seth they were a couple. Just when his cynical self decided he was seeing an unexpected side of Evie McBride, she'd struggled to come up with an appropriate endearment. *Dear.* His lips twisted at the memory. Straight from a rerun of *Happy Days*.

As Sam followed Evie up the path to the cabin, he found himself wondering if there was someone special in her life. Jacob had mentioned all of Patrick's daughters were single, but that didn't mean Evie didn't have a significant other. Someone who could overlook her exasperating tendency to preplan every step and carry a bag guaranteed to make a tinker jealous...and who would appreciate the sapphire-blue eyes that could take a man down like one of the hapless ships at the bottom of the lake.

Where had that come from?

Sam's heart locked up. No, thanks. Been there, done that, had the scars to prove it.

He'd been engaged at the ripe old age of twenty-five to a woman who'd confronted him a week before the wedding, asking him to choose between her and his career. He must have hesitated a fraction of a second too long because Kelly had walked out the door, taking the choice away from him.

Some deep soul-searching and a game of one-on-one with Dan at midnight had left him with a broken finger, a bloody nose and the conclusion he wasn't the marrying kind. Lucky for him that Dan was. Sam could focus on his career with the added bonus of hanging out with his brother's family unit several times a month, enjoying home-cooked meals from Rachel's kitchen and the chance to be Faith's doting uncle without having to change diapers or do that burping thing.

After a week in Faith's company, he'd begun to think diapers and walking around with a towel tossed over his shoulder to catch whatever didn't stay down had been easier than the stage she was in now. Earlier in the day he'd caught her on the phone, trying to sweet-talk the receptionist into letting her talk to Dan. The woman had refused to put the call through, but for some reason Faith had blamed *him*. And then she'd taken off. He'd been about to go to Sophie's when Evie had called him to let him know Faith was with her.

Sam felt a pang of regret. Faith wasn't going to be happy when she found out Evie was leaving. Hopefully, he could make her understand.

Right. Like she understood when you took her away from her dad and brought her here.

Sam pushed the thought aside, more comfortable with action than feelings. "Faith, get some dry towels for Evie, too, okay?"

"Okay." Faith disappeared up the stairs to the loft, leaving them alone.

"I'll stay here. I don't want to drip on the hardwood f-floors."

The faint chatter of Evie's teeth reminded Sam that she'd been soaked to the skin for several hours. "I'll be right back." He disappeared into the bedroom and came back with a pair of clean sweatpants and a long-sleeved T-shirt. "Here. The bathroom is down the hall on the left."

Evie balked. "You're t-taking me home, right? I'll be fine for a few more minutes."

"Just wear them and put me out of your misery," Sam told her curtly.

A smile danced in Evie's eyes. "Now I *know* I look as horrible as I feel."

Horrible? Not the word Sam would have chosen. With her wide blue eyes and tousled hair, she reminded him of a stray kitten who'd been left out in the rain. "At least you don't look like a raccoon."

"Th-thanks."

She looked confused, so Sam figured he should clarify. "You don't have those dark runny circles under your eyes."

Her laughter reminded him of the wind chimes on the deck. "Those are from mascara. And I gave up on makeup when I realized *nothing* hides f-freckles."

Sam frowned as another shiver rippled through her. "I'll change while you put these on, and then I'll give you a ride home."

"He's bossy, isn't he, Evie?" Faith called from the loft as she leaned over the railing and dropped two colorful beach towels.

"You're insulting me?" Sam couldn't believe it. "The guy who rescued you this afternoon?"

Faith gave him an impish grin. "I think Evie's *bomb* rescued us."

"Bomb?" Sam narrowed his gaze on Evie, who shrugged.

"Actually…it was a *distraction*." Plucking the clothes out of Sam's hands, Evie scooted down the hall to the bathroom. She knew what was coming next. He was going to try to talk her into leaving. Again.

She turned the lock and sagged against the door, unsure whether her bones were rattling because the storm had turned her into a walking sponge or in a delayed reaction to their close call with Seth.

Hands shaking, she managed to strip off her wet clothes. As she tugged the well-laundered T-shirt over her head, the familiar blend of soap, fresh air and forest teased her nose. She buried her face in the crook of her elbow and inhaled, comforted by the scent. Sam's scent. It was strange how they barely knew each other, yet she recognized it so quickly.

The black sweatpants puddled around her feet, but at least they were dry. Evie rolled up the bottoms three times and decided it was the best she could do. But when she saw her reflection in the mirror, she stifled a groan. Maybe she didn't look like a raccoon, but Sam had neglected to mention she looked like a drowned rat! Her hair sprang every which way and there were faint scratches on her forehead from being attacked by a low-hanging branch.

When she emerged from the bathroom a few minutes later, she found a drowsy Faith curled up on the couch, headphones in place and a cup of hot chocolate cradled in her palms. She yawned and pointed to the kitchen.

Sam stood at the breakfast counter, slathering peanut butter on a piece of bread. "Coffee or hot chocolate? No tea in this house. Dad doesn't think it's manly."

Evie hooked her thumbs in the waistband of the sweatpants and hiked them up as she sidled into the kitchen. "Coffee. Please."

Sam turned and his gaze swept over her. A smile twisted his lips. "I should have given you something of Faith's to wear."

"This is fine. Thank you." Evie pushed the words out, self-conscious under the weight of his quiet appraisal.

"Foil and drain cleaner," Sam murmured, padding over to her and handing her the peanut butter sandwich she'd assumed was for Faith.

Faith had taken advantage of her absence and spilled the beans. "Seth was about to search the restrooms and Faith was trapped inside. I had to do something to distract him so she could get away."

"Very ingenious." Sam's eyes warmed to liquid silver. "The woman has brains...and beauty."

Beauty? Evie instantly rejected the notion. Caitlin and Meghan reigned as the unchallenged beauties of the McBride family. Caitlin's classic features, sable dark hair and pale blue eyes may have contrasted with Meghan's exotic green eyes and untamed strawberry-blond curls, but both women drew their share of appreciative glances.

Her sisters, only two years apart in age, had been the darlings of Abraham Lincoln High School. The phone had rung off the hook on the weekends. Boys called to take her sisters to a movie or out for a burger. They called Evie when they needed a lab partner.

Sam was probably used to dropping compliments. The night they'd fooled Seth into believing they were a couple, he'd turned on the charm without missing a beat. And his rakish good looks and easy confidence guaranteed a watercooler fan club out there somewhere. He was a man comfortable in his own skin, something Evie had never quite mastered. Old insecurities seemed to hang on like a piece of tape stuck to the bottom of her shoe.

It was a depressing thought.

"I want to go home." Evie closed her eyes as a wave of fatigue swamped her. She didn't deserve any praise. Not when all she'd done was help Faith escape from the dangerous situation she'd put her into to begin with.

"Sit down and eat the sandwich." Sam didn't wait for her to comply, just took her by the elbows and steered her toward the kitchen table. "You look like you're ready to fall over."

Evie decided she was too tired to argue and nibbled at the corner of the bread as he stalked away. He came back with two cups of coffee and straddled the chair opposite hers. "So you're going home. I think you're making the right decision—"

A chunk of crust took an unexpected detour down the wrong pipe. "Not my home," she managed to choke. "Dad's *home*."

Sam stared at her. "You're still planning to stay after what happened today? Knowing Seth is still interested in whatever he thinks you have? Knowing you might be in trouble?"

When he put it that way…

"Yes." She cloaked the word in bravery, leaning on the passage of scripture she'd tucked in her heart.

You will keep in perfect peace him whose mind is steadfast, because he trusts in you....

Sam's chair scraped against the floor as he pushed it away and rose to his feet. "Brainy, beautiful…and bullheaded."

Chapter Twelve

Evie decided two out of three wasn't so bad.

Still, Sam barely said two words to her on the way home. But he insisted on checking to make sure Beach Glass was still locked up tight and no one had broken into the house.

If his intent was to make her nervous, he was doing a stellar job.

He circled the kitchen and paused next to the telephone. "Looks like you have a message."

"Maybe it's Dad." Evie punched the button and listened impatiently while the prerecorded message went through the standard pleasantries.

"Ah...Miss McBride?" She gulped when she heard Seth Lansky's familiar voice. And it didn't sound half as friendly as it had when he'd asked her to help him with the passwords! "I want to talk and I think you know why. I'll be in touch. Soon."

The worst part was, Evie *didn't* know why.

"Change your mind?" Sam growled.

Evie shook her head. Because she couldn't form a coherent sentence even if she tried.

"I'll be right back." He gave her a look that clearly questioned her sanity and finished his rounds. After he rattled the sliding glass doors, Evie stepped in his path.

"If you wait a few minutes, I'll give you your clothes back. Or I can give them to you tomorrow when I meet with Faith."

"Tomorrow's Saturday. Faith and I are going out on the boat for the weekend."

"Overnight?" Evie's voice raised a notch.

"I believe the weekend would include an overnight, yes."

Evie's back teeth clamped together. She knew he was being difficult because she refused to take his advice and leave.

"I'm sure Faith will enjoy it," she said sweetly. "She has fifty math problems to finish by Monday and I'd like her to read the next short story in her literature book."

"I'll see she gets it done." Sam pivoted away from her and headed toward the door.

"Sam! Wait a second. I forgot something." Evie disappeared into her father's office and returned with a small, leather-bound book. "Here."

Sam stared down at the book. "What's that?"

"A Bible. I told Faith I'd lend her one. Remember?" When he made no move to take it, Evie pressed it gently into his hands.

Sam's thumb grazed the words embossed in gold on the cover. "I suppose it can't hurt."

Evie's heart softened when she saw the shadows skim through his eyes. "Faith was fascinated by the story of the loaves and fishes. Tell her to look up Matthew, the first book of the New Testament, and go to the fifteenth chapter." *God, what should I say to him? He doesn't re-alize he's holding the power to change his life.* "I read one of the Psalms every morning."

"Why?"

Was he baiting her? Evie decided it didn't matter. She wouldn't pass up an opportunity to share the truth. "The Psalmist, a man named David, didn't always understand God's ways but he wanted to know Him. And he wasn't afraid to ask Him tough questions along the way."

"Did God answer his questions?" Sam's voice carried an undercurrent of cynicism now.

"Not always," Evie said honestly. "But we don't find peace by having all our questions answered. We find it in God. He loves us and we can trust Him to bring something good out of everything that happens in our lives."

Pain darkened Sam's eyes. "Tell that to my brother."

"Faith? Are you ready to go yet?" Sam rapped his knuckles lightly against the fluorescent yellow Enter At Your Own Risk poster taped to the door.

He'd let Faith sleep away half the morning and then she'd holed up in her cabin again after breakfast. He hadn't minded being on deck alone to greet the sunrise. For the second restless night in a row, he'd watched the stars fade away one by one. Ordinarily he slept like the dead when they anchored the boat in one of the shallow bays for the night, lulled by the fresh air and the rocking motion of the waves. But not this time.

"You can come in if you want."

Sam gripped his chest with one hand and pretended to stagger. "Really? To the inner sanctum?"

There was a noisy exhale on the other side of the door. "That's what I said."

He chuckled and accepted the invitation before Faith changed her mind. "I'm surprised you aren't topside barking orders."

Reluctant as Faith had been to come to Cooper's Landing, she'd turned into a first-class first mate. She loved being on the water as much as he did. Not that Lake Superior provided an instant cure for the roller coaster of adolescence, but Faith seemed to be smiling a little more. And she'd even forgiven him for interrupting her unauthorized phone call to the care facility the day before.

Maybe it's Evie you should thank.

Sam shook the thought away even though he knew another one would replace it soon enough. That was the trouble. He couldn't *stop* thinking about Evie. The way she'd held it together and taken care of Faith when Seth had followed them into the woods. Her stubborn insistence on staying even though worry clouded her eyes.

He was starting to realize he'd underestimated her. Maybe she didn't laugh in the face of danger but she wasn't afraid to stare it down, either. And her faith was a wild card he had no clue how to deal with…

There you go again.

Sam yanked his wayward thoughts back in line and focused his attention on his niece, who lay on her back on the bunk bed, Evie's Bible propped against her knees.

"I wanted to finish reading something."

"Shouldn't you be doing homework?" As far as hints went, not so subtle, but the sight of Faith reading her Bible unsettled him. He still wasn't sure how Dan and Rachel would feel about it. He didn't know how *he* felt about it.

"I finished my math." Faith looked up at him. "Did you know Jesus healed people?"

"Uh-huh." Vague, but the best he could do on short notice.

"It says in here He healed all kinds of people. People who were blind and deaf." She paused for a second and sucked in her lower lip. "Even people who couldn't... walk."

It didn't take a biblical scholar to know where Faith was going with that. And Sam felt totally, completely out of his element.

He'd been there when Faith had let go of Dan's fingers and took her first wobbly steps. He'd taught her how to ice skate, slam dunk and do a mean imitation of a Tarzan yell. Although Rachel had never quite forgiven him for the last one.

Faith waited expectantly and Sam's throat closed. It was like seeing Dan all over again. Looking to him for answers. For comfort. For whatever.

You're wrong, Dad, Sam thought. *You said all I had*

*to do was look inside myself and I'd find everything I
need to tackle whatever life throws at me. Well, I'm coming up empty here. I've got nothing. Nothing for Dan.
Nothing for Faith. Nothing for me.*

"Evie told me the Bible is true." Faith tested the silence when he didn't respond right away.

"A lot of people believe that." People who, according to Jacob, didn't have the strength and know-how to
solve their own problems.

"Do you?"

Sam gave up and sat down at the foot of the bed.
"I've never thought about it much." At least not until
Dan was hurt. Ever since then he'd been bombarded by
the same relentless questions. What happened when a
man's life changed in an instant and he reached the end
of his own strength? What took over?

"Evie told me I should pray for Dad. If I do…"

Sam winced, bracing himself.

"Do you think he'll laugh again?"

The question sucker punched him. He'd expected
Faith to say she wanted her dad to walk again. But she
hadn't. She missed hearing him laugh. Easygoing and
fun-loving, Dan loved practical jokes. No one was ex-
empt as a target, whether it was the guys who worked
his shift at the police department or his immediate family. Sam had lost track of how many times his brother
had set him up over the years.

Regret burned through Sam, leaving a bitter taste in
his mouth. The last time he'd heard Dan laugh was the
day his brother was injured, when he'd called to invite

Sam over for the weekend to celebrate Faith's birthday. The phone call he'd received three hours later had been from a near-hysterical Rachel, telling him Dan had been shot while responding to a call for a domestic disturbance. He and his partner were walking toward the house when a guy, strung out on drugs, aimed a shotgun out the second-story window and opened fire. Diving for cover, Dan had been hit an inch below his Kevlar vest.

Sam tried to think of a way to encourage his niece without getting her hopes up too high. "Your dad is trying to find his way, Faith. And if you want to pray for him, go ahead."

Maybe God wouldn't listen to the prayers of a man like him, who'd always relied on himself, but Sam hoped He wouldn't turn a deaf ear to those of a young girl who wanted to hear her dad laugh again.

Faith turned her head away and Sam knew she didn't want him to see the tear sliding down her face. Too late. Now he'd do anything to see *her* smile.

Since they'd arrived in Cooper's Landing, he'd handled Faith's moods by retreating and giving her space because that's how *he* coped with pain. But Evie had shot that theory all to bits the day she'd brought over that rusty basketball hoop.

Surround Faith with the things she loves and everything else will fall into place.

He'd try it Evie's way.

"Why don't we stop by Sophie's when we get to shore and borrow Rocky for the rest of the day?"

"Really? Can we go now?" Faith sat up and hugged her knees.

"Sure." And maybe they'd stop by Evie's afterward. To drop off Faith's homework.

Sciurus carolinensis.

Evie groaned and yanked a pillow over her head to muffle the chatter of her alarm clock. Which happened to be the gray squirrel perched in the tree outside her window. At six o'clock on Sunday morning.

Fifteen minutes later, she gave up and tossed the covers aside. She peered at the squirrel through the screen. Now he sat on the empty feeder, his tail twitching with indignation. "Fine. You win. I'll replenish your corn supply."

Evie staggered to the kitchen in her pajamas, made a pot of coffee and poured herself a cup. Sunlight pooled on the hardwood floor, and in the distance the glittering surface of the lake looked as if it had been sprinkled with gold dust.

The heavens declare the glory of God; the skies proclaim the work of His hands.

The opening verse of Psalm 19 scrolled through her mind as she closed her eyes and said good morning to the Lord.

It's beautiful, God. You do all things well.

For a brief moment, she wished she could be out on the water. To feel the breeze brush against her skin. Have a front-row view of the towering sandstone bluffs. Watch the seagulls circling overhead in a graceful syn-

chronized choreography. Experience…a severe case
of nausea.

Evie decided she didn't have to be standing on the
deck of a boat to enjoy God's creation. She could just be
on a…deck. To prove her point, she took her Bible outside. Bypassing her dad's hammock, which, she noted
critically, probably wasn't good for his back, she chose
a cushioned cedar chair and flopped into it.

Curious black-capped chickadees landed on the railing to take a look at her, and Evie shared her bran muffin with them before closing her eyes and spending time
in prayer. Armed with scripture she'd memorized over
the years, she aimed a verse at every worry that crowded
into her thoughts. She prayed for Patrick and Jacob. Sophie. Faith. Faith's parents. And for Sam.

*Father, I think that Sam wants to talk to You but he
doesn't know how. Reveal Yourself to him. Show him
that he can find hope in You.*

*Thank You for watching out for me and Faith yester-
day. I know You want Your people to be courageous and
I fall so short of that. I'm tempted to go home but if You
want me to be here for Faith, I'll stay and I'll trust You.*

Evie kept her eyes closed for a few minutes, softly
humming the tune to one of her favorite praise cho-
ruses. Within moments, a verse drifted soft as a breeze
into her thoughts.

*Trust in the Lord with all your heart and lean not on
your own understanding. In all your ways acknowledge
Him, and He will make your paths straight.*

Thank you for the reminder, Lord.

That's what she wanted Sam to understand. If he

turned to God even when life didn't make sense, God wouldn't let him down.

She glanced at her watch, calculated how much time she'd need to get ready for church and decided she had time to take a short detour.

Chapter Thirteen

"I'm so glad you called." Sophie smiled as Evie opened the passenger side of the door and waited for her to slide in. "I was just thinking how lonely church would be this morning without your father to keep me company."

Tyson could go with you.

Evie bit the inside of her lip to prevent her from saying it out loud. When she'd stopped by to pick up Sophie, Tyson had been sound asleep on the couch.

"I didn't want to go alone, either," she said instead.

"I made chicken salad and a loaf of banana bread last night," Sophie said. "Can you stay for lunch?"

"I'd love to." The older woman's offer of friendship wrapped around her like a warm blanket. Caitlin and Meghan would love Sophie if they had a chance to meet her. And Evie had a feeling they would.

She looked forward to spending a few more hours with Sophie but hoped Tyson wouldn't be at the house when they returned. Evie made a habit not to judge people by the way they looked, but the unease she felt around Sophie's son wasn't due to his hygienically challenged outward appearance. Something in Tyson's cool, flat stare made her question what was going on on the *inside*.

Evie started her car and maneuvered it out of the church parking lot. "I came here for worship services last summer when I stayed a few weeks with Dad, but I don't remember seeing you."

"That's because I didn't know the Lord last summer," Sophie said matter-of-factly.

Evie blinked. "I… The way you talked about God and the way you prayed… I assumed you'd been a believer for years."

Sophie chuckled. "I'm afraid it's been just the opposite! You can give your father the credit for introducing us. When everyone else brought bestselling novels to read to the patients at the hospital, Patrick brought his Bible." Her eyes twinkled. "I have to admit there were a few times I wanted to throw it at him, but I didn't have the strength! He had a captive audience and he knew it. I couldn't get rid of him, so I started to listen to what he was saying.

"One afternoon he read a story about a woman who'd been sick for years. She risked everything to get close enough to Jesus to touch his robe. She wanted a new life. I could relate to her. The one thing I'd always wished for was the chance to live my life over again. Growing up, my family wasn't the kind you read about in storybooks. I met Tyson's father and hoped things would be different, but he walked out on us when Tyson was ten years old. I'd been wallowing in the past, wishing things had been different. The day Patrick read that passage I realized I wanted God to heal me, too. Not physically, but from the pain I'd lived with on the *inside*." Sophie's face took on a radiant glow. "Your father prayed with me when I gave my life to Jesus."

Tears stung Evie's eyes. Patrick had always had a gift for pointing people to the truth. She wasn't surprised he'd known exactly what story would touch Sophie's heart. "I'm glad Dad was there for you."

"So am I. Me and the Lord, we have a lot of catching up to do. I wasted so many years trying to muddle through life on my own." A shadow momentarily dimmed the light in Sophie's eyes. "Like Jacob."

"Jacob *Cutter?*" Evie asked cautiously.

"I've been on my knees for that man so often, I'm going to have to sew patches over the worn spots on my slacks," Sophie said. "Just about the time Patrick and I sensed him softening, his son was badly injured and he closed up again. When he came back from Chicago last month, he was so bitter. He made both of us promise we wouldn't talk about God." Sophie's smile returned. "But we never promised we wouldn't talk to God about *him*."

Evie laughed with her even as her heart ached for the Cutters. When Laura died, Patrick's unwavering faith had been a light that guided Evie through the dark valleys of grief. From the pain in Sam's eyes, it was clear he was stumbling through the shadows, looking for something to hold on to.

"Look at that." Sophie clucked her tongue as Evie

turned the car into the driveway. "Tyson is almost thirty years old and he still forgets to shut the door when he leaves. It's a good thing I locked Sadie and the puppies up in the laundry room or they'd be in the next county by now."

Evie followed Sophie inside and heard Sadie whining behind a door off the kitchen. The puppies joined her in a chorus of frantic yips.

"Tyson?" Sophie called above the commotion. "Are you here? We have company for lunch."

The hair on the back of Evie's neck tingled suddenly. Something wasn't right. Other than the sound of Sadie's obvious distress, an eerie silence filled the house. And that open door…

"Sophie, wait."

"I'll be right back." Sophie disappeared into the den and suddenly a sharp cry pierced the air.

"What is it? What's wrong?" Evie bolted into the room and her vision blurred as she took in the scene in front of her.

The room had been ripped apart. Furniture overturned. Shards of what had once been the porcelain figures in Sophie's curio cabinet littered the floor like confetti. The rolltop desk had been hacked to pieces.

Evie couldn't swallow. Had to consciously remind herself to breathe. "Sophie—"

Sophie knelt in the middle of the destruction, sifting through the papers scattered on the floor. "They're gone, Evie. The letters. The newspaper articles. Everything."

* * *

"Look! Evie's here." Faith squealed in delight at the sight of the familiar vehicle parked in Sophie's driveway.

Sam barely had the car in Park when she unbuckled her seat belt and launched herself out the door.

Sam followed at a more leisurely pace, the relief of knowing Evie was safe and sound soaking into his subconscious. He hadn't wanted to admit his concern for her had been part of the reason he'd given up a beautiful day on the open water and come back to shore early.

After her near miss with Seth on Friday and the cryptic phone message he'd left, Sam thought for sure she would agree to leave. Not knowing what Seth wanted or how much of a threat he posed had to make Evie feel vulnerable. She'd said herself that she didn't like surprises and the structured way she lived her life proved it.

So why couldn't he convince her to leave?

God brought me to Cooper's Landing.

Sam remembered the reason Evie had given and he rolled his eyes toward the sky. Billions of people inhabited the world. Sam had serious doubts that God had noticed one twelve-year-old girl who was failing her classes and that He had sent someone to help her. Even if he couldn't dismiss the fact that Evie, with her unwavering faith and loving concern, had somehow unlocked the key to Faith's heart.

Like she was trying to do to his.

When Faith wasn't paying attention, he'd snuck a look at the Psalms, the book Evie said she read from every day. The brutal honesty of the writer surprised him but what shocked him even more was that God hadn't taken the guy out for hammering Him with questions.

It eased the knot in his chest. He had a lot of questions, too, but he still wasn't sure how to ask them.

Sam reached out to grab the handle on the front door just as Faith blasted through it, almost toppling him back down the steps.

"Faith, for crying out loud—" The panic in her eyes squeezed the air out of his lungs.

"Sophie," Faith gasped.

Sam didn't wait for a longer explanation. He pushed open the door and met Evie on the other side.

"What happened? Is Sophie all right?"

"She's fine. But someone broke into the house." Evie's voice wobbled and Sam took her hand. Ice-cold. Automatically, he rubbed his thumb against her palm to stimulate the circulation.

"Where is she?"

"In here." Evie led him into the den and Sam exhaled slowly as he took a quick inventory of the damage. Whoever had broken in had had something specific in mind. And, judging from the amount of senseless vandalism, an ax to grind.

Sophie occupied the same chair she'd sat in the night she'd told them about Patrick and Jacob's search for the *Noble*. A search that had gotten out of control. Maybe it had started out innocently enough, like a trickle of water during a spring thaw, but now it had picked up both strength and speed. And was running roughshod over everything in its path.

"Have you called the police yet?" Sam recognized the shell-shocked look in Sophie's eyes and directed the question at Evie instead. She stood just inside the room, one arm looped around Faith, who'd wilted against her with Rocky cradled tightly in her arms.

"Not yet. We just got here."

"Evie and I went to church," Sophie added. "I don't know where Tyson is. When we walked in, we found this. Whoever broke in took everything Patrick and I collected about the *Noble*. It was all locked in a desk drawer. I don't know yet if anything else is missing."

"I'll be right back," Evie murmured. "I'm going to get Sophie a glass of water."

With a wide-eyed, fearful look at Sophie, Faith followed Evie out the door. After they'd gone, Sam dropped into the chair opposite Sophie and leaned toward her. "Was there any sign of forced entry?"

"No. But we never lock the door. There's been no need."

"And you said Tyson was here when you left?"

Sophie nodded. "He came home quite late. He must have been too tired to go upstairs because he was asleep on the couch when I came down this morning. I didn't want to disturb him."

Too tired or too drunk? Sam decided not to ask. The break-in was enough for Sophie to handle at the moment.

"I'll call the police and ask them to send over a deputy. They'll take photographs, so we can't clean up the mess yet. Have you checked the rest of the house?"

"No." Sophie closed her eyes. "I can replace the

newspaper articles but not Dorothea's letters and my great-grandmother's journal. I can't believe someone would do this."

Sam could.

"The *Noble* would be quite a feather in a treasure hunter's cap," he said quietly. "Not only because it's a new find but because there might be something valuable on board." And Sam was more convinced than ever that whoever wanted to find the *Noble* wasn't going to bother obeying the salvage laws.

"I know Patrick and Jacob didn't say a word to anyone about the treasure. And according to Jacob, he and Bruce Mullins were like brothers when they served together in the Marines. You know your father doesn't confide in people easily—he wouldn't be meeting with Bruce about the ship if he wasn't sure he could trust him."

Evie returned and Sophie accepted the glass of water she gently pressed into her hand. "Do you think that man, Seth Lansky, did this?"

Before Sam had a chance to comment, a strangled sound came from the doorway.

"Mom?" Tyson hurried into the room, fear etched in his face as he dropped to his knees in front of his mother and took her hands. "Are you all right?"

"I've had better mornings, honey," Sophie said, a faint glimmer of humor returning to her eyes.

"What happened?" Tyson's gaze swept the den and his lips went slack as he saw the extent of the damage.

Sam speared Tyson with a look. Sophie might want to downplay the seriousness of the situation for her son but that didn't mean Sam had to make it all touchy-feely for him. "How long were you gone?"

He hadn't meant for it to sound like an accusation, but Tyson scowled, immediately on the defensive.

"Not more than half an hour. I went into Cooper's Landing to get a newspaper to check the classifieds for jobs."

Which meant someone had been hanging around, watching and waiting for an opportunity to get inside the house. Sam's fists clenched at his sides. Lansky must have decided breaking and entering was a quicker way to get what he wanted than lying his way in, like he'd tried to do with Evie.

"Tyson, after I call the police, why don't we check out the upstairs to make sure nothing else is missing," Sam suggested. "Your mom will need a list when she makes a claim to the insurance company."

Resentment simmered in Tyson's eyes but he pushed to his feet. "What did they take, Mom? The computer? The DVD player?"

Yeah, because life just wouldn't be the same without that stuff, Sam thought in disgust. The molecule of respect that had formed when he'd witnessed Tyson's initial concern for his mother evaporated like a drop of water on a hot skillet.

"I'm not sure yet," Sophie said vaguely. "But Sam's right. You go with him and see if anything is missing upstairs."

Tyson's gaze lingered on the demolished rolltop desk. "Did you have anything valuable in there?"

Sophie smiled sadly. "Valuable, no. Irreplaceable, yes."

Sam saw the confusion that skimmed across Tyson's face. Apparently the guy didn't realize there was a difference.

By the time the deputies from the sheriff's department left, Evie felt as if she'd been put through the spin cycle of a washing machine. One deputy snapped photographs of the den while another took statements from her and Sophie.

Sophie listed the missing items but didn't offer any reason as to why she thought they'd been taken. Some old coins locked in the desk were stolen, too, and Sophie didn't correct the deputy's assumption they must have been what the perpetrator had wanted.

Something about Sophie's reticence caused Evie to resist the temptation to tell the deputy about Seth Lansky. When it came right down to it, what did she know about him? He hadn't broken in and stolen her dad's computer. He hadn't even threatened her that day in the woods or on the message he'd left on the answering machine. Suspicions were the only evidence they had.

Sam and Tyson escorted the deputies to the squad car, and Evie shooed Faith and the puppies outside so she could tackle the mess in the den. She found a broom and began to sweep up shattered glass while Sophie collected the pieces of desk that littered the floor.

They worked in silence until Evie happened to glance at Sophie and saw tears tracking her cheeks.

"Sophie?" Evie scrambled over to her and put her

arm around the woman's shoulders, mentally chiding herself for not banning Sophie to the living room with a cup of hot tea.

"Let me make you a cup of tea and something to eat." Evie guided her into the kitchen and into one of the wooden chairs at the table. She rummaged through the refrigerator until she found a block of aged cheddar cheese and some crisp apples and set to work cutting them up.

"As soon as we get in touch with your father, I'm going to insist he and Jacob come back." Sophie's voice barely broke above a whisper. "And I'm going to tell them to give up the search. Family is more valuable than any silly treasure that might be on board the *Noble*. What if Tyson had been home during the break-in? He could have been hurt. It's not worth the risk."

Ordinarily, Evie would have agreed. Maybe she *should* have agreed. But anger welled up inside her at the thought of people who didn't think twice about terrorizing a woman and destroying her property.

"I don't think Dad would want to give up," she heard herself saying. "And I don't think we should, either."

Chapter Fourteen

Had Sam really thought that Evie McBride, with her love of schedules and I-don't-like-surprises personality, was *predictable?*

Because she wasn't. In fact, she was turning out to be predictably *unpredictable*.

"What are you planning?" He could practically *see* the wheels turning behind those big blue eyes.

"I'm going to call Caitlin and ask her if she remembers the name of the last goldfish Meghan forgot to feed, and then I'm going to access Dad's computer files and make new copies of the documents for Sophie so Dad will have them when he gets back."

It was worse than he'd thought.

"Are you out of your mind?" Sam whispered in her ear, matching his steps to Evie's as they walked to her car.

Evie adjusted the gigantic purse—probably to balance the amount of strain on her shoulder—and looked him right in the eye. "No."

"I'm sorry. Did you think that was a question? I meant it as a statement."

"Dad wouldn't give up."

"He might not give up, but that doesn't mean he wouldn't want *you* to," Sam pointed out, feeling it necessary to do so. "He and my dad have no idea Sophie's place was broken into. Tyson is so freaked out he actually insisted Sophie stay with her minister and his wife for a few days."

"That's good. It shows he cares about her, although I don't think he's exactly bodyguard material."

Did she think he was? Because Sam was taking on the job whether he wanted to or not. He'd lost enough sleep over the weekend worrying about her safety. If he couldn't convince her to leave, there had to be some way he could keep a closer eye on her.

"I'll be over tomorrow afternoon to meet with Faith."

Faith heard her name and darted over, Rocky at her heels. "Can I keep your Bible a few more days, Evie?"

"Keep it as long as you like. It's an extra." Evie reeled Faith in for a hug, and Faith didn't squirm, kick or try to set Evie on fire with a glare.

Sam sighed.

Go figure.

Evie paced the floor for fifteen minutes, trying to decide which sister to call first. Caitlin had a memory like a steel trap and would no doubt be able to rattle off the names of all the goldfish the McBride sisters had nurtured throughout their childhood. But she'd also insist on knowing *why* Evie wanted her to remember them.

Meghan, on the other hand, wouldn't think to ask why, but she did have a tendency to be forgetful. Sticky notes wallpapered her apartment. And if Meghan didn't remember a cache of miniature chocolate bars hidden in her pillowcase—until after she put the pillowcase in the washing machine—Evie wasn't too sure she'd remember the name of the fourth goldfish that had taken up residence in the McBride household.

Evie took a deep breath and dialed Caitlin's cell. And got her voice mail.

"Hi, this is Caitlin McBride. I can't take your call right now but if this is Meghan, don't forget to mail out your car insurance. It's due this month. And if this is Evie, check your e-mail once in a while, would you? If you're a client, I'll get back to you as soon as possible. And have a nice day."

Check your e-mail.

Evie groaned. She hadn't booted up her laptop since she'd arrived. Patrick didn't have Internet service, although he'd mentioned the café in Cooper's Landing now boasted a wireless connection.

With only the songbirds at the feeder for company, Evie suddenly felt isolated and alone. And despite her confident words to Sam, she still felt a bit shaken from the break-in at Sophie's.

She'd called the lodge to find out if there'd been any word from Patrick and Jacob, but the proprietor had politely suggested she call back in a few days. Out of touch with her dad, Evie had a sudden longing to reconnect with her sisters. She decided it wouldn't hurt to drive into Cooper's Landing and get a cup of coffee while she caught up on her messages. At least that way, when she talked to Caitlin she could honestly tell her that she'd read them!

Evie didn't expect to see Sam and Faith until the next day, but when she got out of the car and paused to admire the sparkling sapphire water, there was no mistaking the tall, lean frame walking the shoreline. Or the puppy bouncing like a furry pogo stick at his feet.

Evie scanned the beach and relaxed when she spotted Faith, who'd staked a claim just out of reach of the waves to build a sand castle.

To Evie's astonishment, Sam flopped down next to Faith and began to scoop handfuls of wet sand to assist her in the project. Even from the distance separating them, she could see him laughing at something Faith said. And then he picked up a plastic shovel and used it to catapult water at her. Faith retaliated by soaking him with the contents of the moat she'd dug around the castle.

He'll be a great dad.

Even as the errant thought took root and bloomed, Evie felt her cheeks glow underneath the thin layer of tinted sunscreen she'd applied before she left the house.

And the practical side of her nature immediately voiced its disapproval.

Sure. He'll be one of those dads who take the training wheels off too soon. Or let the kids play tackle football in the backyard without the proper padding.

And if his wife dared to express her concerns, she'd

be labeled the family stick-in-the-mud. No fun. No sense of adventure.

No, thank you.

Still, she had to resist the sudden, overwhelming urge to forget about her e-mail and run down to the beach to join them.

She walked into the café and realized the rest of the world had decided to spend a beautiful Sunday afternoon *outside*. Every table was empty.

A teenage waitress wandered out of the kitchen. "You can sit anywhere you want to."

Mmm. A table with an unobstructed view of Cooper's Landing's quaint Main Street or a table with an unobstructed view of Sam?

She chose the table overlooking Main Street. Not as distracting. She put in an order for pie and coffee and opened her laptop.

The first three e-mails were from Caitlin. All of them began with a complaint about the lack of cell-phone towers in the "wilderness" and demanded to know why Evie was ignoring her. Evie suppressed a smile. Caitlin wasn't used to being ignored.

Meghan had written, too, accidentally sending her the same message twice, inquiring about their dad and expressing envy over Evie's "relaxing" summer vacation.

Evie rolled her eyes. She hadn't gotten past the dedication page on the first novel she'd intended to read, and the tomato plants she'd brought along were still waiting to be transplanted into their new containers on the deck.

Oh, it's relaxing all right, Meggie.

She erased some spam, skimmed through some general e-mails from the school administrator and came to one that said "Matthew 6:20" in the subject line. The sender's address wasn't familiar, and the last thing Evie wanted to do was set a virus loose in her hard drive.

Her finger hovered over the delete button. Some of her students had asked for her e-mail address so they could keep in contact over the summer, and she didn't want to inadvertently ignore one of them.

"Here goes." Evie clicked on the message and instantly a lithograph-type photo of an old map downloaded onto the screen. Along with a message from her father.

"But store up for yourselves treasures in heaven, where moth and rust do not destroy, and where thieves do not break in and steal. For where your treasure is, there your heart also will be." Matthew 6:20-21

Evie, please share this verse with Sophie. It's one of my favorites. See you soon.
Love, Dad

"Well, Patty McBride, aren't you just full of surprises?" Evie muttered, eyeing the verse superimposed over a sepia-toned map. "I didn't think you knew how to send an e-mail message let alone a background...."

Her heart slipped into the toes of her sensible shoes as she realized what she was looking at.

Seth Lansky had made a critical mistake. Patrick

hadn't stored the latest information about the *Noble* on his computer.

He'd sent it to hers.

"Sam?"

It had to be a hallucination. One minute Sam was staring at the water, thinking it was an exact match to Evie's eyes, and the next thing he knew, he heard her voice.

"Hi, Evie!" Faith jumped to her feet, kicking a spray of golden, sun-warmed sand against his leg. "What are you doing here?"

For a split second, Sam thought Evie had changed her mind and accepted Faith's invitation to spend the afternoon with them on the beach. Until he saw her expression. A warning bell clanged in his head.

"Look at the castle we made."

"It's great." Evie's smile seemed forced as she bent down to examine it.

Sam frowned. More warning bells. Tension coiled in his gut. Now what? Something to do with Sophie? Or their fathers?

"I put the flowers on it and Sam put the rocks along the top. To protect it from invaders." Faith rolled her eyes.

"Hey, you thought it was a good idea at the time." Sam gave Faith's ponytail a playful tug.

She dodged away from him. "I'll be right back. I'm going to find some sticks and leaves to make flags. Can you stay for a little while, Evie?"

"A few minutes."

"Good." Faith grinned. "I can give you a tour of the *Natalie*."

If anything, Evie's skin paled even more and she managed a jerky nod.

Sam waited until Faith was out of earshot. "Okay, what's up? I know you didn't come down here to build sand castles with Faith." He wished she would have. She'd stepped out of her comfort zone to play basketball, but the nervous little glances she directed toward the water, as if she were imagining a rogue wave rising out of nowhere and pulling her under, shot that hope all to pieces.

"Dad sent me an e-mail dated the day before I got here. The day he called Sophie and told her he had good news." She paused.

Okay, he'd bite. "What did it say?"

"I'd rather show you. I have my laptop in my purse. Can you take a few minutes and go to the café with me? I'll treat Faith to an ice-cream cone."

Was he imagining the faint glimmer of excitement in her eyes? "I doubt the owner of the café would believe Rocky is a service dog."

She gnawed on her lower lip. "Oh. I didn't think about him—"

"Do you want to see the boat now?" Faith returned, the puppy at her heels.

"Evie suggested ice cream." Sam stepped in, figuring Evie had already reached her quota of traumatic experiences for the day. "Why don't you keep working on the castle and we'll bring some back from the café?"

"That's all right." Evie smiled bravely. "I can see the boat first."

She continued to surprise him. He'd tried to let her off the hook, but once again she'd stepped out of her comfort zone for Faith. His respect for Evie went up another notch. Who was he kidding? Another ten notches. And suddenly Sam realized the needle gauging his emotions had somehow snuck past "like" and was hovering perilously close to…something else.

Sam's jaw locked. Attraction, maybe. That wasn't as scary. He wasn't blind. No one could blame a guy for getting caught in the depths of a pair of wide, sapphire-blue eyes. Or for knowing exactly how many cinnamon freckles dotted her nose. *Twelve.* But he didn't want to care about Evie McBride. Not that way.

Dan's injury had cut him loose from his moorings, setting him adrift in a sea of questions and doubt. The Cutter pride was the only thing keeping him from going under and who knew how long *that* was going to keep him afloat? Every time he remembered Dan saying that he wished he'd died on the way to the E.R., Sam felt his grip slipping a little more. The last thing he wanted to do was to pull someone else down with him.

Like Evie.

No, *not* just Evie. Not anybody.

"Okay, Faith, go ahead and lead the way." Evie marched stoically toward the dock as if she were going to have to walk the plank when she boarded the *Natalie.* Her purse bumped against her hip like unsecured cargo. Knowing how much stuff she had in that thing, she'd probably end up with bruises that wouldn't fade for a month.

"You don't have to do this, you know." Sam eased the bag off her shoulder and looped it over his arm, ignoring her look of surprise. He shrugged. "At least it's khaki and not pink with polka dots."

Her smile made a serious dent in the armor around his heart. "According to Caitlin, pink clashes with *this*." She sifted strands of silky, red-gold hair through her fingers. "My wardrobe consists of greens and browns and golds. And I accent with pumpkin."

"You lost me." Because the way the sunlight played on her hair had his full attention at the moment. He scrambled to catch up. "Who is Caitlin?"

"My older sister. The *oldest* sister. And proof that everything you hear about firstborn overachievers is true." Evie's eyes sparkled with obvious affection. "She works as an image consultant in Minneapolis and she has a lot of important clients. I surrendered my closet a long time ago, but so far Meghan, that's my other sister, refuses to be conquered."

"What does Meghan do?"

"She's a freelance photographer. She's in New England right now, working on a series of calendar photos for a private company. She and Cait are both pretty busy."

He detected a thread of wistfulness in her voice. "Which leaves Evie. A teacher with summers off. That must be nice."

"It is." She didn't sound very convincing. "I miss my

students, but it gives me a chance to spend time with Dad. He gets lonely."

He *gets lonely,* Sam thought with a sudden flash of insight, *or* you *get lonely?*

He'd assumed from comments Jacob had made that Evie acted like a mother hen when it came to her father, but now he wondered if there wasn't another reason for it.

"Do you travel much when you aren't teaching?" *Way to keep your distance, Cutter. Ask her about her life.*

"No." Evie slowed her pace as they neared the dock. "I read. Garden. That sort of thing. I put in so many hours at school that I'd rather stay home when I have the chance." She paused and dug a half circle in the sand with the toe of her shoe. "What do you do in your free time? Besides boating?"

She was stalling. Sam suppressed a smile. "I do some rock climbing. Sailing. Fly fishing." And he'd done every one of those things with Dan. Regret rocketed through him again. He'd lost sleep wondering how Dan would cope if he couldn't enjoy his favorite activities, but until this moment, Sam hadn't looked at it from his own perspective. Would *he* still enjoy them?

"Sam? Are you all right?"

When he glanced down at Evie, he wondered why she thought she'd needed to mix up a homemade bomb that day in the woods. The incredible blue eyes focused on him created enough of a distraction. She was five yards away from a dock that looked as if it had been built out of toothpicks, but the concern in her eyes was for *him.*

"I'm great." He lied through his teeth as he sealed up his emotions in a space marked by a sign similar to the one on Faith's door. Do Not Disturb.

Faith waved to them from the deck of the *Natalie*. "Come on, you slowpokes."

Sam hopped up on the dock and took three steps before he realized Evie wasn't following him. She stared at the boat, her complexion a bit green. She already looked seasick.

"She's tied up, Evie."

"*She's* still…bobbing."

Sam chuckled. "Boats tend to do that. Especially on the water." He retraced his steps, caught her hand and gave a gentle tug. She responded by digging her sensible shoes into the weathered wood and tugging back.

"I'm a coward," she murmured. "Ask my sisters. I don't like being on the water."

"In that case, you're good to go. You'll be on the boat, not the water." Still holding her hand, Sam urged her closer to the *Natalie*. He had to do something drastic to wipe the panicked look off her face. He remembered Evie's tendency to get defensive about her purse, so he let it go and it hit the deck with a dull thud. "We already have an anchor, but thanks."

"Very funny." Evie snatched it up but he noticed with relief that some of her color had returned.

Sam leaped across the narrow space separating the boat from the dock and stretched out his hand. "Ready?"

"Come on, Evie. You'll love it." Faith joined in the cheering section.

Evie cast another longing look at the beach.

"Come on, Evie. Trust me. I'm an expert at catch and release." Sam winked at her and Evie's burst of laughter went straight to his heart.

"That I can believe."

Chapter Fifteen

Evie focused on Sam's smoke-gray eyes instead of the enormous expanse of blue in the background. And jumped. True to his word, he steadied her and then promptly let her go. For a split second, disappointment outweighed her fear of the water.

"Faith, why don't you bring up a pitcher of lemonade. All that castle building works up a thirst."

"Sure." Faith disappeared down the short flight of steps that led belowdeck, and Sam motioned to Evie. "Step into my office and tell me about the message."

Evie perched in one of the captain's chairs, not sure where to begin. "Dad asked me to share a verse from Matthew with Sophie. That was strange enough, because he could have done that himself. But the background the verse is printed on is a…map."

"A map," Sam repeated.

Evie didn't take offense at Sam's skeptical look. It *did* sound a little far-fetched. She had her own doubts until she'd studied it more closely. "On the map, there's a ship just off the north end of a small island. It would make sense that the *Noble* would sail for the shelter of a bay if it got into trouble."

"You don't know if the ship depicted on the map is the *Noble*. Patrick could have pasted in that image from an old book or a pamphlet from a tourist center. It might not mean anything."

"That's why I *know* it means something. The map isn't a copy—he drew it himself." And the lines he'd drawn overlapped at the same point. On the tiny sketch of a ship.

"Even if Patrick has a general idea where the ship went down, don't you think if it sank that close to one of the islands, someone would have discovered it by now? Professional and recreational divers have combed this area for years." Sam scraped a hand through his hair in frustration. "And if by chance it is there and no one's found it, it means we won't, either. It's too deep or a reef smashed it to pieces and there's nothing left to find."

"Maybe. But that must be why our dads wanted to meet with Bruce Mullins. To find out if it was worth taking a look. When Sophie and I were on our way to church this morning, she mentioned Dad had found some old diary entries from a sawyer who had worked at one of the logging camps. He didn't have a chance to show them to her, but maybe Dad based the map on something he'd discovered written in them."

"You told Sophie about the map?"

Evie frowned at the sudden undercurrent of tension she heard in his voice. "I called her from the café. I thought she'd want to know that whoever stole the records didn't find the most important piece of the puzzle. She wasn't there so I left a message on the answering machine. Why? What's wrong?"

"I think—"

"I brought brownies, too," Faith interrupted them cheerfully, carrying a tray with a pitcher of lemonade and three glasses.

Evie smiled at the girl, glad to see that in spite of the scare they'd had at Sophie's house earlier that morning, she seemed to be fine. Or maybe Rocky had something to do with it. Faith and the puppy had become inseparable.

"Can I show her the rest of the boat now, Sam?" Faith asked hopefully.

"That's up to Evie. She might not have time."

A warm feeling trickled through Evie. Once again Sam was giving her an "out."

He had to be aware of her reaction to the water. And a man whose list of hobbies revolved around it probably wouldn't understand why she was afraid. She didn't quite understand it herself. When Faith suggested a tour of the *Natalie,* Evie had braced herself for a teasing comment or look of amusement from Sam. She'd been shocked when she didn't receive either one. In fact, the expression in his eyes when she'd agreed had stolen the breath from her lungs. It had almost looked like…respect? Affection?

Impossible.

Evie surged to her feet. At that moment, she would

have jumped overboard and dog-paddled to Canada if it took her away from Sam's unnerving presence. "I've got time. Let's go."

"This is where I sleep." Faith clattered down the steps and moved to the side so Evie could peek into the tiny room, roughly the same dimensions as Caitlin's walk-in closet! The decor was strictly functional. A narrow bunk covered with a navy spread. A pair of vintage maps in mismatched frames that hung crookedly above a corner desk.

Maps. Fleetingly, she wondered if she'd convinced Sam that they might have the *Noble*'s location. She still didn't know why his gaze had narrowed when she'd told him that she'd shared the information with Sophie. Maybe he thought she should have waited until they were sure so it wouldn't raise Sophie's hopes.

"What do you think?"

Faith's question coaxed Evie back to the moment. "It's cozy." And cramped. But if Evie kept her gaze from drifting out the window, she could almost imagine she was in a studio apartment. Almost.

"That's the desk Sam chains me to so I get my home-work done," Faith confided.

"I heard that!" Sam called down from the upper deck.

Faith grinned. "He has ears like a fox."

"I heard that, too."

Evie's heart listed, and this time she couldn't blame the waves. She found herself wishing she could take Faith up on her invitation to spend the rest of the day with them. But the thought of being out on Lake Superior in a boat like the *Natalie* turned her knees to jelly. She'd gotten seasick just watching the boat bump against the dock. Imagine how she'd feel if she actually…

The engine roared to life and Evie clutched the door frame. "What's he doing?"

"Sam always checks everything before we go out," Faith said blithely.

"Oh." Evie felt foolish. Of course he did.

"Come on. I'll show you the kitchen." Faith raised her voice above the gargle and sputter of the engine. She led the way while Evie trailed behind, trying to concentrate on her young guide's knowledgeable monologue about the boat.

The tiny kitchen charmed Evie. Even though there was barely enough room to turn around, it was outfitted with a sink, stove, refrigerator and a row of open-faced cabinets crowded with a mismatched set of dishes. Someone had added a whimsical touch by stenciling cherries and cherry blossoms along the ceiling, and the colorful rag rug on the floor repeated the bright yellows, greens and reds.

"Look." Faith opened one of the cabinets and proudly pointed to an enormous jar of peanut butter. "Sam lets me do most of the cooking while we're on board, but you can help me if you want to."

"I'm not going to be here for…" The boat pitched to one side and Evie caught her breath. "Wow. For a minute there it felt like the boat was moving."

Faith's eyes widened. "It is."

* * *

Sam heard Evie's shriek above the sound of the engine.

Five, four, three, two...

Her feet thumped up the stairs and she appeared in front of him, hands planted on her hips. "What do you think you're doing?"

"Taking you somewhere we can talk." Sam turned the wheel slightly to the left as the *Natalie* chugged cheerfully away from the dock.

The color ebbed from Evie's face, highlighting the constellation of freckles sprinkled across her nose. *All twelve of them.* "We can talk on land."

"This is more private."

"You *planned* this."

"No." Sam liked to think of it as taking advantage of the moment. The minute she'd told him she'd left Sophie a message telling her about the map, he knew he couldn't let her go back to the house alone. And it conveniently solved his dilemma on how to keep tabs on her.

"You attract trouble like a magnet." There. Something a science teacher would understand. "I promised your dad I'd look out for you. This is the only place I can do it."

"Whoever wants the information on the *Noble* got what they were looking for. They'll leave me alone now," Evie argued, keeping her voice low so Faith wouldn't hear them.

"Except for the map. Which you now have."

Evie's mouth opened and closed several times like a

beached whitefish. "The only people who know about it are you and Sophie...." Her eyes darkened. "You can't possibly think Sophie had something to do with this. You should have seen her expression when she saw the damage and realized all the records were gone."

She was right. He hadn't seen Sophie's expression. But he'd seen Tyson's.

Guilt had been written all over the guy's face. Forget about innocent until proven guilty. When it came to Evie's safety, Tyson was guilty until proven innocent. Sophie's son or not, Sam didn't trust him.

"Faith will be happy to have someone to bunk with." Sam kept his eyes trained on the water so he wouldn't cave in and take Evie back to shore. "Think of this as a field trip."

"Bunk?" Evie gulped. "I'm not staying overnight on this...*leaky bucket*. You have to take me back. *Now.*"

"We should be able to put a call through to our dads sometime tomorrow. Until then, I'm afraid you're stuck with me. And, just for the record, the *Natalie* doesn't leak."

"This is...*kidnapping.*" Her voice stretched thinly. "Sophie isn't going to tell anyone about the map."

He had to be honest with her. "Tyson might."

"Tyson?" The flicker of doubt in her eyes told him that she didn't trust the guy, either. "But he was upset when he saw the den and thought Sophie might have gotten hurt. He even arranged for her to stay with Pastor Wallis and his wife."

"He looked like a kid caught with his hand in the cookie jar." Sam's lips flattened. "I had a little talk with one of the deputies this morning. He recognized Tyson right away. He's been making the rounds at the local taverns lately and isn't choosy about the company he keeps. If he's out of a job and trying to support a drug habit, you can bet he's snooped around his mother's house. Maybe listened in on her conversations with your dad. He could have tipped off his so-called friends that Patrick had some interesting information about a sunken ship."

"You think Tyson knows Seth Lansky?" Evie slumped back down into the captain's chair and her purse slid to the deck. "Poor Sophie. When I saw the way Tyson reacted this morning, I hoped it meant he cared about her."

"I think he does." As cynical as Sam could be, the protective way Tyson had hovered around Sophie after the deputies left had seemed genuine. "Part two of my conspiracy theory? The break-in woke Tyson up to the fact that he's in deep with the wrong crowd and that's why he shuttled Sophie to her minister's house for a few days. He wants to keep her out of the way." *Just like I'm keeping you out of the way.*

As if she'd read his mind, panic flared in Evie's eyes. "If you take me back, I promise I'll check into a hotel."

Sam thought about it. For two seconds. The only way he'd get a good night's sleep was if he knew exactly where Evie was and who she was with. "Sorry."

"I don't have a change of clothes."

"Faith always keeps extra on board. And I have a spare pair of sweats." On cue, an image of Evie, looking adorably rumpled in his rolled-up sweatpants and T-shirt, downloaded into his brain. He shook it away.

"Beach Glass is open tomorrow—I can't just walk away from my responsibility."

"Neither can I."

"I'm not your responsibility." Evie folded her arms across her chest.

"Take that up with Patrick, okay? By this time tomorrow, we'll know if you're right about the map." And he'd find out if he was right about Tyson and Seth Lansky. And ask the deputy to run a check on Lansky, something he kicked himself for not doing sooner.

"You can't keep me—"

"You changed your mind about coming with us!" With what Sam considered to be an example of perfect timing, Faith rounded the corner and made a beeline to Evie.

And hugged her.

Evie's eyes met Sam's over Faith's shoulder. The smug glint in those smoky depths made her want to push him overboard. Except then no one would be driving the boat. And she'd actually been gullible enough to believe that Sam respected her fear of the water when all along he'd planned to lure her out into the middle of Lake Superior!

Her mouth felt as dry and gritty as the sand on the beach and Evie had to loosen her death grip on the straps of her purse in order to return Faith's impulsive hug.

For Faith's sake, she had to pretend to be a willing captive.

Her gaze shifted from Sam to the passing scenery as

the *Natalie* cut a choppy path through the waves, like a pair of dull scissors through satin. The waning afternoon sun coaxed out the deep golds and crimsons etched in the sandstone bluffs, and in the far distance, Evie saw the boxy silhouette of a barge against the horizon.

Hadn't she wished she could be out on the water with Sam and Faith? Watching seagulls coast on the air currents over her head? Feeling the spray of the water against her face?

So not funny, Lord.

"Evie." Sam's husky voice sent shivers down her arms. "Come over here for a minute."

Evie's eyes narrowed suspiciously. "Why?"

"We're going to make you an honorary sailor."

Faith giggled and flopped down on the vinyl-covered bench that curved in a semicircle around the cabin. Evie shot her a look. "Are you an honorary sailor, too?"

"Yup." Faith nodded vigorously.

Sam held out his hand, and Evie automatically grabbed it. He pulled her gently in front of him and curved her fingers over the steering wheel.

"Oh, no." Evie took a step back and bumped into the solid wall of his chest. "Absolutely not."

"You can do it. It's not much different than driving a car."

"Sure. Except for the treacherous underwater reefs."

"Come on, Evie." Faith's eyes sparkled. "Sam's right."

"That's one for the books," he whispered.

Faith wrinkled her nose at her uncle. "I'm going to check on Rocky. I'll be right back."

"She's going to put on a life jacket, isn't she?"

Evie felt Sam's low rumble of laughter down to her toes. "This should be a piece of cake for a woman who can put together a bomb in a wayside restroom."

"It was a *distraction*."

The movement of the boat had nothing to do with the nervous flutter in Evie's stomach. If she moved a fraction of an inch in any direction, she and Sam would be touching. She swallowed hard, aware of the corded muscles in the forearms braced on either side of her. And the warm strength of his fingers as they moved to cover hers.

She relaxed her grip and watched the blood rush back into her knuckles. She lifted her chin and felt the breeze cup her face and playfully ruffle her hair.

Okay, Lord, maybe this isn't so bad. After all, You created the land and the water and declared both of them good, right?

"It's different, isn't it?" Sam murmured. "To feel the movement of the waves instead of watching them from land. It gives you a whole new perspective."

Evie closed her eyes briefly. He'd not only read her mind, he'd just come close to describing her entire life. And lately she'd started to realize there was a difference between planning every moment of the day and actually living them.

"Hey." The tug of Sam's voice opened her eyes. Evie twisted slightly and looked up him, catching a glimpse of the half smile that tilted the corner of his lips. "Don't hit the island, okay? Rule number one—drive the boat with your eyes *open*."

"I'll remember that. *Captain.*" Evie raised two fingers to her forehead in a mischievous salute.

Sam's eyebrow arched. "Does this mean I'm absolved of all kidnapping charges?"

She tilted her head. "Maybe. But you have to promise me smooth sailing. And a blindfold wouldn't be a bad idea, either."

The breeze caught a few strands of her hair and blew it into her eyes. Before she could move, Sam reached out and tucked them behind her ear. He was so close she could see where the pewter-gray centers of his eyes deepened to charcoal.

Sunspots danced in front of Evie's eyes, and she felt curiously lightheaded. Probably the heat. Where was her straw hat when she needed it?

Sam shifted his gaze to a point somewhere in the distance. "I talked to Rachel before Faith and I left this afternoon."

Chapter Sixteen

"How is Dan?" The fragile thread connecting them gave Evie the courage to ask the question.

"It's not Dan." Sam's exhale stirred her hair. "There's been no change with him. It's Rachel…"

Evie held her breath and waited.

"You have to know Rachel. She's very emotional. Dan is easygoing but in their relationship, he's the strong one. I was afraid Rachel would fall apart when Dan got hurt, but she tried to keep it together for Faith. By the time the hospital moved him to the rehab facility, the stress was getting to her.

"I felt like Dad and I not only bailed on Dan, we bailed on her, too," Sam admitted. "Dan's doctor and the social worker…they didn't come right out and say it, but we were hurting Dan's recovery. He's bitter and angry and doesn't want to see me…*us.*"

The edge of pain in Sam's voice sawed through Evie's defenses. She couldn't imagine how she'd react if one of her sisters turned her back on the rest of the family and refused to let them help her.

"I check in with Rachel at least once a day. The first few times I talked to her, she couldn't make it through the conversation without crying."

"She's depressed?"

"I was beginning to think so. I even told her the last time we talked that I'd bring Faith back as soon as Dad got home, but today when I talked to her, she sounded... different. Better. She even made a joke about losing weight on the 'cafeteria diet.' I figured her good mood meant Dan was coming around, but when I asked if there was a change, she said no. I can't figure it out."

"Maybe she's decided she has to face whatever happens head-on."

Sam shook his head. "You don't know Rachel. She's not that strong. She has to hold on to someone. I think that's one of the reasons Dan is depressed. He knows how much Rachel depends on him. Now that we're not there, a friend of hers from work has been spending time at the hospital with her. Rachel mentioned she went to church with her this morning."

Evie thought about all the prayers being said on behalf of the Cutter family, and something stirred inside her.

Sam struggled with guilt for leaving Rachel and Dan alone but maybe he *hadn't*. Maybe God had intervened and cleared a work space at the rehab facility. And he'd started with Rachel.

God, You are so incredible.

"Maybe the change isn't in Dan," she offered tentatively, not sure how Sam would respond to her theory. "Maybe it's in *her*."

"What do you mean?" Sam frowned and adjusted the steering wheel.

"Maybe Rachel let God take over," Evie said simply.

"God?" Sam repeated.

"When you give God control of your life—and your heart—you don't have to muster up strength to make it through the day. He *is* your strength."

Sam stared at her, speechless.

It had to be a coincidence. Sam had taken Evie's advice and thumbed through the book of Psalms when he'd found it lying on Faith's bunk that morning. He had no idea where to start, so he'd randomly picked one out and started reading.

I love you, O Lord, my strength. The Lord is my rock, my fortress and my deliverer; my God is my rock, in whom I take refuge...

Sam hadn't expected the verses to lodge in his brain. Or brand his soul. He'd read the entire passage and remembered thinking that if God was everything a man named David believed Him to be, no wonder he'd loved Him. No wonder he'd turned to Him for help.

No wonder he'd trusted Him.

"So I should just let God take over? Not *do* anything?"

"Yes, you should let God take over. And no, I never said you don't have to *do* anything. The things we're responsible for—trusting, loving, believing—they're all acts of will. And they don't just happen once. We have to keep choosing them. Sometimes day by day. Sometimes second by second. Sometimes breath by breath."

Did he believe her? Evie wished Sam could see her in the classroom, confident and secure with her students, instead of worrying about Patrick and shaking like a leaf after her run-in with Seth Lansky. If she had half of Caitlin's fearlessness and Meghan's moxie, she knew she'd be a better example of someone who wholeheartedly trusted God.

"Hey, Evie!" Faith's muffled voice floated to the top deck. "Can you read through an essay I finished?"

"I'll be right down."

The corner of Sam's lips tipped. "Thanks, Evie."

Evie nodded mutely as she ducked under his arm and went belowdeck.

Had he thanked her for helping Faith? Or for something else?

"Do you want to help me make supper?" Faith closed her folder and with a twist of her wrist sent it hurtling toward the desk in the corner.

"I'd love to." Evie followed Faith into the kitchen to survey the well-stocked pantry. "Macaroni and cheese? Or ham sandwiches?"

One of the times she'd gone camping as a child stirred in Evie's memory. "Have you ever made shipwreck dinner?" she asked, trying not to wince as she said the name. Maybe they could come up with a new one. Like "safe-on-land dinner."

Faith made a face. "It's not raw fish, is it?"

Evie laughed. "I'll have you know that some people pay a lot of money for raw fish. But no, this has nothing to do with fish. We'll need hamburger, onions, carrots and potatoes. And foil."

"Okay. I think we've got all that." Faith gathered the ingredients while Evie kept one ear tuned to the sound of Sam's footsteps on the deck above them. As if by unspoken agreement, they'd given each other some space.

"Are you two ready to go ashore?" Sam called down.

Evie's heart bottomed out. "He's kidding, isn't he?"

"Sometimes we anchor and take the little boat into shore for a few hours."

"The *little* boat?"

"It's fun."

"If you say so."

Faith grinned. "I'll get you a life jacket."

"I look like a cross between the Michelin Man and Santa Claus," Evie said, striking a pose in the bulky vest.

Faith giggled. "I think that one is Grandpa's."

"It is." Sam came up behind them. "Let me see what I can do to make it fit better." He yanked on the belt and cinched it tighter around her middle. "Can you breathe?"

No. Not with you so close. "Yes."

"Good." Sam tugged on Faith's jacket and adjusted one of the shoulder straps. "The boat's ready."

Evie peered over the side of the *Natalie* and gulped. The dinghy secured to a line off the *Natalie*'s bow was the size of a bathtub. And the peaceful cove looked *very* far away.

"Faith, you get in first and I'll hand Rocky to you," Sam directed. "Make sure you hold on to him."

"I will." Faith practically skipped down the ladder and reached out to take the puppy.

Evie, not wanting to deal with the raft until absolutely necessary, focused on their destination instead. The cove was a smooth notch carved from the rugged shoreline, its backdrop a canvas of sandstone stained by the iron-rich water that trickled down its surface.

Her gaze traced the curve of the shoreline to the narrow finger of land that pointed to one of the smaller islands. Farther down, Cooper's Landing sprawled at the edge of a stretch of golden sand.

"Evie? Ready?" Sam's husky voice momentarily distracted her.

"Not even close," Evie muttered.

Sam didn't try to take her hand as she turned her back toward the water, grabbed the rails and settled one foot on the top rung of the ladder.

He smiled down at her. "Don't worry. If you fall in, you'll float."

"That's so comforting." Evie's foot found the next rung. "You should be writing the inside copy of greeting cards."

Sam laughed outright, almost causing Evie to lose her balance. He didn't laugh very often, and this one swept away the shadows that lingered in his eyes, arrowing straight to her heart. "I'll keep that in mind if I ever lose my job."

Evie inched the rest of the way down the ladder, and Faith shifted to make room for her.

The word *sardines* came to Evie's mind as she wriggled into place and watched as Sam practically swung from the deck of the *Natalie* into the boat.

Show-off.

He unhooked the line and Evie linked her arm through Faith's.

"Everyone okay?" Sam asked over the gurgle of the motor.

"Yup," Faith sang out.

Evie was relieved Faith answered the question.

Within minutes, they left the *Natalie* behind and were skipping over the waves toward shore.

"Look! There's another boat." Faith pointed out a boat close in size to the *Natalie,* but the similarity ended there. Its chrome accents gleamed like the edge of a new razor while the sleek lines and onyx finish put it into a completely different league.

Sam's eyes narrowed. "I see it."

He turned the boat to the left and nudged the throttle up another notch. The dinghy agreeably picked up speed.

Evie kept her eyes trained on the speedboat. Was it her imagination or had it changed direction, too? And instead of taking a wide berth around them, it set a course that would put them directly in its path.

"Don't they see us?" Faith asked worriedly.

"I'm sure they do." The grim look on Sam's face belied his reassuring words.

Evie cast a panicked look toward the cove and then at the boat rapidly closing the distance between them. Three-foot waves sloughed off her sides, gliding smoothly toward them like the dorsal fins of a school of sharks.

Sam shot a look at Evie. "Hang on tight. It's going to get bumpy."

Evie sucked in a breath and nodded. She could see people on the deck, but instead of witnessing a frantic effort to give them some space, the crew had lined up at the rail to watch.

To watch what? Their boat capsize?

Faith made a frightened sound and burrowed against Evie's shoulder as a wave slapped the side of the boat and tipped it. Before the boat had a chance to recover, a larger wave slammed against it. Cold water poured over the side and filled the bottom of the boat.

Evie closed her eyes and began to pray.

She prayed as she ground her feet against the floor of the dinghy and held tightly to Faith. She felt Sam's fingers grip her knee in an effort to keep her from pitching over the side.

Evie didn't open her eyes until the motor quit, and then she wished she hadn't. The sight off the bow squeezed the air out of her lungs. Instead of cruising past them, the black speedboat had cut its engine, too, positioning itself like a guard dog between their tiny boat and the shore.

It was close enough for Evie to read the name *Fury* scrawled across the bow, the red letters painted to resemble flames.

Sam half rose to his feet. "Are you insane?" he shouted at the man who came up to the railing and raised one hand in a casual salute.

"I like to think of it as *committed*." Seth Lansky grinned at Evie. "I thought it would be rude not to stop and say hello."

Sam wanted to keelhaul Lansky. Not for almost capsizing them but for the leering smile he aimed at Evie.

He moved to shield her from Lansky's view.

Seth looked offended. "What's the matter, Cutter? We're just being neighborly."

"By trying to drown us?" Sam called back irritably.

Seth shrugged. "Sorry. I guess I got a little close."

He was *still* a little too close, but Sam didn't bother to mention that. The waves had settled down into a gentle rocking motion, but they were still in a precarious position. Sam had no idea what Lansky was going to do next. His jovial greeting hadn't fooled Sam for a second. The guy was certifiable and, at the moment, they were sitting ducks.

"It's late in the day to be going out for a pleasure cruise," Seth mused.

"There's plenty of daylight left."

"We're doing some fishing this afternoon," Seth went on pleasantly.

"Good luck with that." Sam decided to dispense with the small talk and kept a wary eye on the *Fury* as he reached down and started the motor. It sounded like a Chihuahua growling at a Doberman, but Seth nodded to the man at the wheel.

The *Fury*'s engine roared to life, and Lansky strolled down the length of the rail, which gave him a bead on Evie again. "Miss McBride? Tell Patrick hello from me. And be sure to mention I'll see him around."

The *Fury* surged away, kicking up another row of waves large enough to swamp them. The little boat valiantly battled its way through them, but even when the water calmed, Sam's heart still hammered against his chest.

He didn't have to wonder anymore if he'd overreacted by keeping Evie close. If Seth had stolen Sophie's collection of records about the *Noble,* it meant he was getting desperate to find the location of the ship. And if Sam had to take a wild guess as to what that desperation stemmed from, he'd bet it had something to do with Seth's fear he wouldn't get to it first.

"Why did they do that?" Faith scrambled toward him and Sam caught her against his chest. "And why was Tyson with them?"

"You saw Tyson?" Sam looked at her intently. "Are you sure?"

"I saw him looking out the porthole at us." Faith twisted around. "Didn't you see him, Evie?"

Evie shook her head, but the weary resignation in her eyes told Sam that she believed Faith had.

Sam's stomach knotted. Seth and Tyson. Teamed up and getting antsy. And how was he supposed to tell Sophie that her son had been involved in the break-in at her home?

"Shouldn't we go back to the *Natalie?*" Evie asked quietly. "All our supplies are soaked."

Over her shoulder, Sam watched the *Fury* drop anchor a mere hundred yards from the *Natalie.*

"Let's just stick to our original plan for now."

* * *

Evie could have cried with relief when the bottom of the boat finally scraped against a shelf of sand in the shallow water. Their clothing was almost dry, compliments of the wind, and Faith no longer clung to Sam like a barnacle.

Not that Evie blamed her. The stomach-churning boat ride reminded her why she avoided amusement park rides.

Sam rolled up the bottom of his jeans and hopped out of the boat. He reached for Faith, but she gave him an armful of wiggling puppy first. He deposited Rocky on the sand and reached for his niece. As soon as Faith's feet touched dry land, she and Rocky scurried away to explore.

Evie peeled off her shoes and socks and wrung the water from them.

"Sandals are a good choice for the beach." Sam returned, eyeing the dripping socks with that familiar glint of amusement in his eyes.

She was glad he found something humorous about their near-death experience.

Evie stuffed the socks into the toes of her shoes. "You're forgetting one small detail. I wasn't planning to *go* to the beach today. And another thing...your methods of convincing me to *like* the water need some fine-tuning."

Sam's lips twitched. "Really? Because I thought you turned a much lighter shade of green this time." Before she could protest, he reached down and plucked her out of the boat and waded toward shore.

Evie smiled up at him. Which didn't make any sense. After what they'd just been through, and with the *Fury* looming like a specter right off *Natalie*'s stern, the last thing she should feel like doing was laughing. But she did. "That's all right, then. According to Caitlin, green is a good color on me."

"Evangeline McBride, you are…" Sam searched for a word.

Even without a thesaurus handy, Evie could have filled in the blank. *A worrywart*—Caitlin's personal favorite. *Organized*—Meghan's more tactful description. *Capable*—Patrick's loving moniker.

"Amazing."

That simple word would have been enough to render Evie speechless.

But then he kissed her.

Chapter Seventeen

He'd kissed her. Kissed her! And then apologized.

I'm sorry, Evie. I don't know why I did that.

At least afterward, Evie thought wryly, he hadn't asked her for her notes from her first class. The first kiss she'd ever received was from a boy who'd charmed his way through her defenses to bump up his ACT scores.

An hour had passed and she could still feel the warm press of his lips against hers.

Evie groaned silently.

She *couldn't* be falling for Sam.

She had a pretty good idea of the kind of man God would choose for her to spend the rest of her life with. Maybe a fellow teacher. Definitely someone who loved to spend quiet evenings at home and enjoyed home projects...

An image of Sam walking the roofline of the cabin, his T-shirt casually draped over his shoulder, came to mind. Evie shook it away. Replacing a roof wasn't the kind of home project she had in mind. Gardening. Painting a front door. They had to have some sort of common ground…some of the same interests and hobbies.

But more important, Evie knew her future husband's life had to be centered on Jesus' greatest commandment: *Love the Lord your God with all your heart and with all your soul and with all your mind…and love your neighbor as yourself.*

She sensed Sam's heart softening toward God, but it was obvious an internal battle waged inside him. She could tell he'd really been listening to her after he'd opened up about the change in Rachel, but Evie still didn't know if he'd put his trust in God.

Evie found herself frequently praying for Sam over the course of a day. And not only praying for him. Thinking about him. A lot.

When had she started to care so much?

Sam stalked the perimeter of Evie's personal space for over an hour after they came ashore, trying to figure out the best way to apologize. Because the way she kept avoiding his eyes told him that she hadn't forgiven him. She and Faith stuck together, making a private conversation with her impossible.

It wasn't until Rocky scampered down the beach and Faith chased after him that Sam had an opportunity to approach Evie. He followed the imprint of her shoes in the damp sand to a tangle of driftwood.

"Evie?"

Her shoulders tensed at the sound of his voice, but she didn't turn around. "Faith is doing really well in math. In fact, I think she might even be ahead of her classmates by fall. This week, we'll concentrate on grammar. She's still struggling a little with diagramming sentences, but she's smart. She'll get it."

Sam hadn't followed her to get an update on Faith's progress but the message was clear. *You hired me to be Faith's tutor.*

She put him firmly back in his place and the regret that weighted Sam down took him by surprise. That afternoon, when she'd told him about her sisters, he'd felt the first tenuous threads of *something* between them. And the threads had multiplied again when he'd confided in her about the change in Rachel.

He decided to try again anyway. "I'm—"

"Sorry. I know. You don't have to say it again." Evie sat down on a large piece of driftwood and stared at the horizon.

He didn't? Then why wouldn't she look at him?

Sam pushed his fingers through his hair. Maybe the fact she had to spend the night on the *Natalie* in the shadow of the *Fury* had her upset. "I know you don't like the water and I'm sorry I made it hard for you to go back to Cooper's Landing until tomorrow—" *Now* she looked at him. And it almost burned off the top layer of his skin. *Ouch.* "Okay…I made it *impossible* for you to go back to Cooper's Landing. But after what happened at Sophie's, I have to know you're all right."

"Why?"

The simple question ripped apart his prepared speech. Because she'd gotten under his skin? Because waiting to see what she was going to do next reminded him of trying to keep up with the changing wind currents when he sailed?

"I have no idea. You were just—"

"There. I know."

"No, you *don't* know. You make it sound like I would have kissed anyone," Sam said irritably.

Evie didn't answer.

Was *that* what she thought? That he made a habit of randomly kissing women standing within a five-foot radius?

Sam studied the faint blush of color on her cheeks in disbelief and realized that was *exactly* what she thought.

Maybe some guys' overinflated egos liked the idea of being labeled a "player," but it didn't sit well with Sam. "I don't play games like that," he said flatly. "Ever."

The confusion on Evie's face confused *him.* And then, almost as if someone turned on the proverbial lightbulb in his head, Sam knew. The day he'd told her she had brains and beauty, she'd totally shut down on him. He'd assumed she'd been reacting out of her fatigue, but now he wasn't so sure. Maybe her sudden retreat had been due to her rejection of his compliment.

The logical part of him, the part that was scared to death of giving Evie a weapon she could use against him in the future, urged him to go ahead and let her think he was some kind of Casanova.

But he couldn't do it.

"*You* were the reason I kissed you," Sam told her with quiet force. "You weren't conveniently in range. Or practice. Or a challenge. Or a chalk mark on the board. I kissed you because I'm attracted to you. And to tell you the truth, the only thing I really regret is upsetting you."

He rose to his feet and stared down at her. "Are we clear?"

She nodded mutely.

"Good. I'm going to find some wood to make a fire and try to concentrate on what to do about Lansky instead of kissing you again." Did he say that out loud?

Evie blushed.

Apparently so.

While Sam gathered driftwood for a campfire, Evie coached Faith through the dinner preparations. Which involved wrapping their food in tin foil and burying it in a hole they'd dug in the sand. It helped keep her mind focused on a task instead of Sam's stunning disclosure.

You *were the reason I kissed you.*

He'd stalked away, leaving her alone to sort out her tangled emotions. And to send up several fervent prayers asking for wisdom. She had a feeling she and Sam had just turned a corner. Instead of being nervous, she found herself actually looking forward to what would come next. Which made her more nervous. She didn't even *like* surprises.

"Earth to Evie." Faith waggled a stick in front of her nose. "When can we eat? I'm starving."

"In about an hour." Evie sat back on her heels and retrieved a handful of tiny packets of disposable washcloths from her purse. She peeled one open and wiped the sand off her fingers as Faith peered doubtfully into the makeshift oven.

"Does it really cook in there?"

"It'll be delicious. I promise." Evie handed her one of the packets.

"Who taught you how to make them?"

"My mom. We camped a lot when I was growing up." Funny how she'd forgotten how much time her family had spent camping and hiking through state parks over summer vacation. Laura saved all her vacation days for the months of June, July and August so she was free to travel with them.

Under their parents' watchful eyes, Evie and her sisters had learned how to bait a hook and clean whatever fish they caught. And cook it in the cast-iron skillet over an open fire. They'd also become expert outdoor chefs with gooey homemade "pies" cooked in a special iron and had copied Laura's famous recipe for "ship-wreck" dinner.

Evie caught herself smiling. She and Meghan loved to fish but Caitlin hated it. The only way they could get her to join in was to make it a competition to see who could catch the biggest one.

She could still see her mother flipping pancakes on the griddle or rigging up an outdoor shower. During the day Laura brought their attention to wildlife camouflaged by the trees and after the sun set she'd spread out blankets on the ground and point out the constellations as they lay on their backs under the night sky.

Somewhere along the way, Evie had forgotten those summer camping trips that had fostered her love for science. Her mother's passion and enthusiasm had been contagious—and out of the three girls, Evie had been the one who'd wholeheartedly embraced it.

As she let herself think about the past, Evie realized her memories had divided into two categories. "Life Before Mom Died" and "Life After Mom Died." And it occurred to her that she dwelled more on the ones in the second category. In many ways Laura's death had become the defining moment of Evie's life.

That day had drawn an invisible curtain between the past and the future and cast a shadow over the good memories the family had shared. And irrevocably changed how they created new memories.

After the funeral, Evie had made her father promise he'd always be there for her—that he'd take care of himself so nothing would happen to him.

Evie didn't even miss the camping trips the following summer. It would have been too difficult to enjoy them without Laura's presence. Patrick's hobbies changed from rock collecting to collecting antiques at auctions and estate sales. Evie spent her summers reading while Patrick remained close by, restoring vintage furniture to its original charm and then selling it to a local antique store.

Her dad hadn't seemed to mind staying close to home. And he'd kept his promise. Until now. Why had he broken it? Because of Sophie? His friendship with Jacob? Didn't he care that she was worried about him?

"Evie, can I ask you a question?" Faith dragged a path through the sand with the tip of a stick.

Evie took a ragged breath, still shaken by the bittersweet memories. Somehow she'd lost sight of the fact

that Laura had been a devoted mother and not just a respected police officer. "Of course you can, sweetheart."

"How old were you when your mom died?"

"Fourteen."

"How did… What happened?"

Pain shot through Evie. It wasn't the question she'd
been expecting, but it was the one she'd been dreading
since she'd found out Faith's father was a police officer.
"She died…at work."

Confusion clouded Faith's eyes. "Was she a teacher
like you and your dad?"

Evie knew there was no way around such a direct
question. "No. She was a police officer."

"Really? Like my Dad? And Sam?"

"Sam?" Evie's world suddenly tilted. "I thought you
said Sam works at a desk all day."

"He does. He's a chief of police."

Sam didn't mean to eavesdrop. He'd gone to get more
kindling and when he returned, Faith and Evie didn't
hear him come up behind them.

Faith's first tentative question welded his feet to the
ground. The second one nearly wrecked him.

Evie's mother had been a police officer? How could
Jacob have failed to mention that? He and Patrick had
been friends for months—he had to have known.

She died at work.

In the line of duty.

Sam's lungs burned at the pain he saw etched on
Evie's face. *Fourteen.* She hadn't been much older than
Faith when her mother died.

Because of Dan's injury, he had an idea what Evie's family had gone through. Sam had wrestled with the reality of losing his brother during the long surgery after the shooting. But even though Dan had survived, Sam discovered there were other ways you could lose someone you loved.

Just as he was processing how hard it must have been on Evie, Faith dropped her next question. And Evie's response ripped through him like shrapnel.

She thought he had a *desk* job?

Sam replayed conversations he and Evie had had since they first met and realized she'd never asked him what he did for a living. He'd assumed she knew. Apparently, their dads weren't the doting type that talked about their kids' accomplishments!

His law enforcement career had started at eighteen when he and Dan had applied to the tech school. But their careers had taken different paths. Dan loved being a patrol officer. He thrived in the middle of chaos and enjoyed dealing with the public. He had a reputation for being fair and even-tempered in the community while his zany sense of humor provided comic relief for his fellow officers during the course of a stressful day.

Sam had discovered his strengths rose to the surface while dealing with his peers and taking on roles of leadership within the department. While Dan had passed up promotion after promotion in order to stay on the road, Sam had taken every one they offered him. Eventually, he'd applied and been hired as chief of police in Summer Harbor, a small town in Door County.

The rare opportunity to make it to the top of command at the age of thirty had forced him to make some difficult decisions, but he hadn't regretted it. Even when his dedication to his career had meant sacrificing his relationship with his fiancée.

But now Sam realized he must not have loved Kelly at all. Because he hadn't experienced a tenth of the pain when she'd walked out on him as he did now when he saw the look of horror in Evie's eyes.

She'd looked doubtful enough when he'd described his favorite hobbies. There was no way she would willingly accept his choice of career.

Especially a career responsible for taking her mother's life.

Everything suddenly made sense to Evie.

Sam's suspicious attitude when Seth Lansky had wormed his way into her dad's house. His take-charge attitude. His innate confidence. The way he'd reacted at Sophie's.

Evie closed her eyes.

Sam had practically processed the crime scene. The only thing he hadn't done was file a report. He'd asked Sophie the right questions. He'd warned them not to touch anything until the deputies had an opportunity to photograph the damage.

All the signs had pointed to his profession, and she'd been totally blind.

A police chief.

Up until that moment, Evie hadn't known how deeply

her feelings for Sam had taken root. Until Faith's innocent disclosure about what he did for a living had ripped them out.

Chapter Eighteen

Evie wasn't sure what was more frightening: spending the night on the *Natalie* or spending another minute in Sam's company now that she knew what he did for a living.

No, not for a living, she amended. Dentists worked for a living. Lawyers worked for a living. Some people defined their lives by their careers, and some people's careers defined their lives.

Police officers, firefighters, soldiers…all of them fell into the second category. And Evie didn't miss the irony that every one of them put their personal safety at risk.

I guess that's it, God. You closed the door on a relationship with Sam.

At least Evie could be grateful she'd be going home in a week and life would return to normal. No more crazy stories about sunken ships. No more bad guys lurking around the corner. No more water. *No more Sam.*

So why didn't the thought of going back to her routine lift her spirits?

"Evie? Faith is ready for bed. She asked me to send you down to say good-night." Sam materialized beside her, wearing a navy-blue hooded sweatshirt. The department logo printed on the front slapped her with a reminder of what he was.

"Sure." Evie turned from the railing and averted her gaze. She'd managed to make it through supper and the trip back to the *Natalie* without talking directly to him. She could make it one more night. All she had to do was keep her distance....

"Evie? After you say good-night to Faith, can we talk?"

No, no, no.

She didn't want to talk to him. She didn't want to think about him. She didn't want to remember the look in his eyes when he'd told her she was amazing. Right before he'd kissed her.

"Please?"

She gave in. But only because she'd been raised to show good manners. And because there was nowhere on the *Natalie* she could hide. "All right."

Faith scooted over when Evie poked her head in the cabin, an invitation for her to join her on the bunk.

"Is the boat still gone?"

The worry in Faith's eyes told Evie she hadn't gotten over the scare of being caught in the *Fury*'s wake.

"Long gone." *Please, Lord, let them be long gone.*

Just when Evie had started to think they were going to be sleeping on the beach instead of the *Natalie,* Seth must have decided he'd toyed with them long enough.

The *Fury* circled the *Natalie* several times and then roared away, disappearing around the rock peninsula.

Without a word, they'd taken advantage of the window of opportunity and immediately packed up the supplies so they could return to the boat. As quickly as possible. Sam had kept one eye on the peninsula and Evie knew he was wondering, too, if the *Fury* had temporarily anchored there, waiting for them to venture back out onto the lake.

"Why was Tyson with them?"

The question tugged at a loose corner of Evie's frayed emotions. She had no idea what to tell Sophie about her son and his involvement with Seth.

"They must be friends of his."

"I guess so." Faith didn't look convinced. "He's always nice to me when I visit Sophie. Sometimes we watch basketball and he makes hot-fudge sundaes."

That would have surprised Evie if she hadn't witnessed Tyson's reaction to the break-in that morning. And the panic in his eyes when he'd asked Sophie if she'd been hurt. His concern for his mother had seemed genuine but it would still break Sophie's heart to find out Tyson had been the one who had told Seth about the *Noble*.

"Will you pray, Evie?"

Evie answered the unexpected question by taking Faith's hand. For the second time, Faith had unknowingly reminded her how to deal with her turbulent thoughts!

"Dear Lord, thank You for watching over us today. Thank You for calming my fear of the water so I could spend the day with Sam and Faith on the boat. Take care of Patrick and Jacob while they're...away. And Faith's mom and dad. It's hard to be apart from the people we love, Lord, but we trust they're in Your hands. And so are we."

She was about to close the prayer with an "Amen," but Faith took a deep breath and attached her own request.

"And I want to go home, God. Can you do something about that? Thanks."

Evie reached out and pulled the blanket up, tucking it around Faith's shoulders as she asked God to answer Faith's heartfelt, innocent prayer.

"Are you coming back soon?" Faith murmured drowsily.

They'd fashioned a mattress for Evie on the floor next to Faith's bunk from the extra blankets on board. Sam had folded one of his sweatshirts to make a pillow.

Practical. And thoughtful. Sam had proven himself to be both on so many levels since she'd gotten to know him.

"In a few minutes." She wouldn't spend any more time in Sam's company than absolutely necessary. "Sweet dreams."

"You, too."

The fragrant night breeze flowed over Evie as she made her way to the upper deck. Sam stood at the railing, his face tipped toward the sky. Pensive and...vulnerable.

The powerful rush of emotions that rolled through her reminded her of their hair-raising afternoon boat ride. She found it easier to guard her heart when Sam bossed her around, but it wasn't as easy when she caught glimpses of the sensitive man beneath the surface.

"It makes you feel pretty insignificant, doesn't it?" Sam asked without looking at her.

Even as a voice in her head warned her to keep her distance, Evie's feet moved on their own to join him at the railing. "No. Just the opposite. It makes me feel valued. And very…grateful."

"Grateful?" Sam slanted a look at her.

She didn't want to be near Sam, but she couldn't walk away from him when he was obviously searching. And just like Patrick's treasure map, she knew exactly where Sam could find the truth. She couldn't keep that to herself. If Sam was willing to listen, she had to be brave enough to talk.

"Because He not only created me, He loves me. When I look at those stars, I don't think about how small I am, I think about how *big* God is. And how much I mean to Him."

Sam didn't respond, and Evie was torn between wanting to say more and letting God fill the silence.

"Good night, Sam." She decided to let God take over.

Or maybe, Evie thought as she turned away, she was simply too much of a coward to stay any longer.

Sam watched Evie walk away, and it took every ounce of strength not to ask her to come back.

It was a good thing his officers weren't around to witness their chief totally losing his nerve.

He'd wanted to tell Evie he'd overheard her conversation with Faith. He wanted to talk to her about her mother and tell her he understood she fussed over Patrick because she didn't want to lose another parent.

He wanted to tell her he worked in a sleepy town not much bigger than Cooper's Landing. He'd leave out the part about living in a turn-of-the-century lighthouse only a stone's throw from Lake Michigan, but he could honestly tell her the most notorious crime his officers had solved was who'd put Jed Carson's VW Bug on the sidewalk on New Year's Eve.

But deep down, Sam knew none of that would matter to Evie. Whether he lived in a small town or a large city, police work always courted danger. The child of a cop, especially someone with firsthand experience of what the cost could be, knew it was the nature of the job.

Even if he told Evie what his life was like, there was no way he could convince her to embrace it. Or even to accept it.

And he had to face to truth. He *wanted* her to accept it.

Evie was a remarkable woman. Funny. Giving. Insightful. Patient. Beautiful. The kind of woman a man could imagine spending his life with. He'd started out thinking he had to protect her but somehow she'd become his *partner*. Watching out for Faith. Encouraging him to look outside of himself for strength. Facing her fears instead of running away from them. Finding humor in stressful situations.

Sam shook a blanket out and laid it on the deck. He wasn't going to sleep in his cabin and give Lansky another shot at them during the night. He stretched out on his back and folded his arms behind his head, staring up at the stars. The ones that made him feel insignificant and Evie, valued.

He didn't want to accept that the feelings stirring between him and Evie weren't as strong as their differences.

The engine wouldn't start.

Sam had planned to leave for shore right after breakfast, but the *Natalie* had a different agenda.

"Why did you decide right now to go temperamental on me?" Sam muttered, digging in the toolbox for a wrench.

Evie appeared in the doorway, looking annoyingly fresh in the wrinkle-proof khakis she'd worn the day before and Faith's favorite basketball jersey. "What's going on?"

"Something's wrong with the engine."

Evie moved closer to the engine compartment and watched him check the fluids. For the third time. Not that he was a slouch when it came to engines, but the *Natalie* had been around a lot longer than he had.

"It looks like the tube near the bottom is cracked," Evie said.

Sam couldn't believe he'd missed it. "That does pose a problem."

"You must have a backup motor on a boat like this."

"The key words are *on a boat like this*."

"No backup motor?" Evie frowned.

Sam searched for the roll of duct tape every man stashed in his toolbox. Apparently every man *except* his dad. "Do I smell sausage?"

"Faith is making breakfast. Are you trying to get rid of me?"

"Not if you have something to fix this."

"I'll be right back."

Sam sat back on his heels and waited for her to return. When she did, it was with a roll of duct tape.

"You carry that around in your purse?" Sam saw her expression and rephrased the question. "Thank you for carrying that around in your purse."

Evie gifted him with a small smile and some of the tension between them dissolved. "Why don't you let me try. My fingers are smaller."

"Be my guest." He regretted the decision as soon as she knelt beside him and the pleasing scent of maple syrup combined with Evie's favorite brand of perfume played havoc with his senses.

"There. That should hold. I'll stay here while you give it a try."

He took advantage of the escape route she'd offered and went on deck. A few seconds later, the engine came to life and Evie clamored up the steps. "It's working!"

"We make a good team," he said without thinking.

Shadows skimmed through Evie's eyes and she backed away. "I'm going to help Faith with breakfast. It's almost ready."

Regret pierced him.

Or not.

* * *

Within an hour, Evie's feet touched dry land again. And she wished she was back on the *Natalie* with Sam.

You are out of your mind, Evangeline Elizabeth. You don't like the water. And you can't like Sam.

But she did. That was the problem. In fact, she had nothing to compare her feelings to, but she wondered uneasily if they'd moved past "like."

"Evie?" Sam caught up to her as she hiked through the sand toward her car. "I'm going to stop by and talk to Sophie. Will you come with me?"

Was he asking because he needed her help or because he wanted to keep an eye on her?

"Yes." No matter how anxious Evie was to put some distance between her and Sam, she wanted to be there for Sophie.

"Do you know where her pastor lives?" Sam's expression closed, reminding her of the man who'd come to her door the night she'd met him and told her Faith needed a tutor. A man whose career forced him to ignore his emotions while he helped people deal with theirs during difficult circumstances.

"In a house right behind the church."

"Good." Sam nodded curtly. "Let's go."

Pastor Wallis met them at the front door of the parsonage, dressed casually in twill shorts and a white polo. Only in his mid-thirties, his approachable manner and compassionate eyes seemed to have a way of immediately putting people at ease. Evie had liked him from the moment her father had introduced them when she'd attended Sunday-morning worship services the summer before.

"Hello, Evie." Pastor Wallis's lively brown eyes lit with a smile that encompassed both of them. "It's good to see you again. I'm sorry I didn't get a chance to chat with you yesterday after the service."

"That's all right." Evie had noticed he was in deep conversation with several teenagers and hadn't wanted to interrupt. "Pastor Wallis, this is Sam Cutter."

"It's nice to meet you." Pastor Wallis extended his hand and gave Sam's a vigorous shake. "Would you like to come in? Barbara took an angel food cake out of the oven a few minutes ago."

"Actually, we're here to see Sophie."

Pastor Wallis frowned. "She's not here. Her son and his friend picked her up early this morning."

"But I thought she planned to stay for a few days." Evie's heart picked up speed.

"She did." The minister frowned. "But after she talked to Tyson, she packed up her things and told us she had to leave. To tell you the truth, Barbara and I both thought Sophie seemed upset. I was planning to call her this evening."

"Did you recognize Tyson's friend?" Sam asked tersely.

Pastor Wallis shook his head. "He didn't get out of the car. I only saw him from the window, and he was looking the other way. Sophie told us about her house getting broken into. Do you think something else happened?"

Evie and Sam exchanged a glance. "We'll stop by her house and make sure she's all right."

"I'd appreciate that."

Sam was already turning away but Evie hesitated. "Pastor, could we ask a favor? Sam's niece, Faith, is in the car. Is it all right if she stays here for an hour or so?"

The man's eyes lit with understanding. "Of course. My daughter, Samantha, would love the company. She's been complaining since school let out that there's nothing to do around here."

"She must be a teenager." Sam's guess brought a smile to the minister's face.

"She's thirteen."

"I'll get Faith," Evie said quickly. "And Rocky."

"That's right. We have one of Sophie's puppies with us." Sam winced.

"Not a problem. Samantha loves dogs. Bring them both in. I'll tell my two favorite girls we have company."

Faith was hesitant to stay with the Wallis family until Samantha Wallis ran outside, a soccer ball tucked under her arm.

Within minutes Faith waved a cheerful goodbye and the two girls disappeared around the corner of the house.

"That was a good idea until we know everything is okay with Sophie," Sam said. "I didn't even think about what we might be getting Faith into."

Evie tried to ignore the warm glow his words stoked in her heart. "I remembered they have a daughter close to Faith's age. Do you think Seth Lansky was the one with Tyson?" Evie murmured as they hurried back to the car. "Sophie will recognize his name if Tyson introduces them."

"I hope it wasn't him." Sam paused to open the car door for her before moving around to the driver's side. "I changed my mind about needing you to come with me. Do you mind if I drop you off at your house before I go to Sophie's?"

"Yes."

"Good. I'll—"

"Yes, I mind, not yes, you can drop me off. I'm going along."

Sam's lips flat-lined but he didn't argue. Until they got to Sophie's house. He stopped the car before the turn in the driveway and cut the engine.

"Do you mind waiting here for a minute?"

"Yes."

He flashed an impatient look at her. "Is that yes, you'll wait here or yes, you *mind* waiting here?"

"Yes, I mind waiting."

Sam's eyes narrowed. "Evie, I know what I'm doing and I won't be able to concentrate if you're with me. Please stay here while I evaluate the situation."

And let me do my job.

The words he didn't say hung in the air between them. Of course. Sam wasn't planning to walk up to the door and ring the bell.

Evie hesitated, not wanting him to go alone but not wanting to distract him, either. "I'll stay here." And pray.

Now he smiled at her grudging tone. "I'll be right back."

She watched as he melted into the trees instead of walking up the driveway.

As the minutes ticked by, Evie grew more concerned. Why wasn't he back yet?

Sam, where are you?

Lord, please let him be all right.

The two thoughts collided as Evie slipped out of the car and followed the path he'd taken into the woods until the house came into view.

No sign of Sam. Or Sophie.

Evie's heart picked up speed as she stepped out into the open and crossed the bright green patch of yard. Should she knock? Or just go in?

As she hesitated on the porch, a hand grasped her arm. "Sam? Thank goodness. I was starting to get—"

Her voice died in her throat as she saw the bruised and bloody face of the man holding on to her.

Chapter Nineteen

"*Dad!*" Evie's knees turned to water.

"Hi, sweetheart." Patrick smiled wanly and then swayed on his feet.

Evie instinctively caught her dad before he fell over, and her frantic gaze skittered over him. Blood congealed over one eye and angry red scratches crisscrossed his cheek. His muddy clothing hung loosely on his frame and she noticed his glasses were missing. "What happened? Where's Sam? Who did—"

The door flew open.

"Evie." Tyson stepped to the side and motioned for them to come inside. "Come and join the party."

She found her voice and turned on Tyson, anger over Patrick's condition overriding her fear of Sophie's son. "What did you do to him?"

Tyson ignored the question. "Let's go into the kitchen."

Where he kept the knives? Not a chance.

Evie balked and Tyson made an impatient sound.

Without ceremony, he nudged her away from her father and wrapped his arm around Patrick's waist.

"Let go of him." She glared at Tyson.

"It's okay, Evie," Patrick murmured.

Evie would have chosen a better word to describe the situation but because she couldn't exactly play tug-of-war with Tyson—with her dad in the middle—she gave in and followed him into the kitchen.

She took a silent inventory of the contents of her purse. If she could get to the travel-size can of hair spray in her bag, she could aim it in Tyson's face and get Patrick safely to the car. And then she could double back to find Sam…

"Oh, good, you found her, Patrick. Hello, Evie."

Evie blinked. Like watching a movie playing in slow motion, she tried to process the scene in front of her. Sophie stood near the kitchen table, calmly dabbing a washcloth against a jagged cut on Jacob Cutter's forehead while Sam knelt on the floor, holding a bag of frozen peas against his father's swollen ankle.

Sam glanced up and gave her a wry look. "I knew you wouldn't stay put."

Evie's face whitened alarmingly and Sam rose to his feet. His dad's sprained ankle could wait.

"Hey. It's okay." Sam drew Evie into his arms and she buried her face in his neck.

"I think we can take him," she whispered in his ear.

Sam choked back a laugh and felt Evie stiffen. "We don't have to take him," he murmured. "He's on our side."

"He's right, Evangeline," Patrick chimed in, wincing as Sophie turned her gentle ministrations to the scratches marking his face.

"But Tyson and Seth Lansky—"

Tyson hooked his foot around a chair, yanked it away from the table and dropped into it. "I can see I'm going to have to go over this one more time."

Sophie gave her son an affectionate smile. "I don't mind hearing it again."

Sam would have steered Evie toward a chair, too, but she took a protective stance near her father.

He didn't blame her. When he'd walked into the house and heard his dad and Sophie arguing over whether or not he needed stitches, he'd been ready to take Tyson apart, too.

And Tyson must have known it because he'd put the table between them while Sophie had intervened and explained the situation.

"It seems Tyson has a gambling problem," Jacob said, a little too jovially in Sam's opinion. "And he made some stupid mistakes. Go ahead and tell her, Ty."

Tyson didn't refute the accusation as he looked at Evie. "He's right. I needed money to pay off a loan from my friend, Gil. I heard Mom and Patrick talking about a sunken ship and I didn't pay much attention at first because I figured it was part of the boring genealogy stuff she's been researching. But when Mom said something about a ring, I got to thinking maybe there was something valuable on board.

"I was at the tavern one night and Gil started hassling me. Anyway, I'd had too much to drink and told him to be patient—that I was going to score some big money. But when I told him about the ship, he laughed and called me a stupid drunk. But the next day a guy called. Said he was a diver and maybe we could help each other out if I could tell him where the *Noble* went down. I did some snooping around here but couldn't find anything. I listened in on Mom's phone conversation and that's when I knew Mom had given Patrick the stuff about the ship." He drummed his fingers against the table and slanted a look at Evie. "I didn't think *she'd* be hard to get past. Seth was supposed to get the information off Patrick's computer without her knowing about it."

"But Sam came to her rescue." Jacob winked at Evie and her eyes widened. "That's part of his job, you know. Rescuing damsels in distress."

Sam groaned inwardly.

Dad, you are so not helping me here.

"Oh, I think Seth found out that Evie's pretty resourceful," Sam mused. "She's good at creating distractions."

There was a moment of silence as everyone in the room looked at Evie. But none of them looked the least bit surprised at his announcement. That seemed to fluster Evie more than anything else, and Sam smiled in satisfaction.

It was obvious from the expression on Tyson's face that he knew about it, too. With an encouraging nod from Patrick, Tyson continued, "When Seth didn't have any luck getting the stuff from Evie, he kept pushing me to find out if Mom had it. But I stalled, thinking

Jacob and Patrick would get back and he'd leave her alone and focus on them."

"Tyson is sure Seth is the one who broke in." Sophie picked up the thread of the story calmly, as if she'd already forgotten the trauma of finding her den torn apart and months of precious research missing.

Sam couldn't quite understand that level of forgiveness but he was pretty certain it had something to do with a mother's unconditional love. And maybe her unshakeable faith.

"But I didn't have anything to do with that. I didn't know you'd locked the records in your desk. Seth took a chance and ended up finding them." Tyson looked quickly at Sophie, who smiled reassuringly at him. "I confronted him about it and he threatened me. Said he paid Gil off and now I owed *him*. He'd been watching Evie and was pretty sure she knew about the ship. When she got on the boat with Cutter yesterday, he thought they were going to the wreck site. So we followed you," he added, looking at Evie.

"And almost capsized the boat," Evie reminded him.

Tyson squirmed in the chair but didn't look away. "Yeah. But I didn't know he was going to do that. The guy's crazy, man."

"When Tyson got here, he found Jacob and I camped out in the driveway," Patrick said. "I wanted Sophie to patch me up before I came home, but Tyson told us you were on the boat. Jacob and Tyson picked up Sophie at the Wallis's and brought her home."

"Then we all sat down and had a little talk." Jacob leveled a mock scowl at Tyson.

"I don't care what Lansky does to me," Tyson said in a low voice. "I don't want anyone to get hurt."

"It looks like two people got hurt." Evie's fingers closed over her father's shoulder.

"Oh, Seth Lansky didn't do this, sweetheart." Patrick patted her hand. "It was Bruce Mullins."

Sam pulled out a chair and Evie slid bonelessly into it. Without a word, he poured her a cup of coffee and pushed it in front of her. He'd heard the hasty summary of Tyson's involvement with Seth, but he hadn't heard this part of the story yet.

"This is where things get interesting." Jacob looked smug. "Mullins double-crossed us. We figured it out after we got to the lodge—that's why Patty called Sam and told him to look out for Evie. We asked Bruce questions about how to go about filing for permits and organizing the dive, but he started pumping us for information about where she'd gone down. Got kind of cranky when we wouldn't tell him, too, right, Patrick?"

"Yup. Cranky." Patrick's split lip curved into a smile.

"He wanted to find the *Noble* and file for salvage permits before we had a chance to?" Sophie asked.

"Permits?" Patrick sighed. "We can't prove it, but we doubt they were going to bother waiting around for permits. I think the plan was to salvage the ship before *we* filed for them. We would have followed the rules and come up with a big empty nothing because they'd have gotten to it first."

"But I thought you and Bruce were friends," Evie said in confusion.

Jacob snorted. "So did I. But when you say the word *treasure,* men can get greedy."

"Seth mentioned Bruce Mullins's name once when he was talking about a dive he'd gone on near White-fish Bay," Tyson said. "It didn't mean anything to me at the time, though."

"When Tyson told us about Lansky, we figured Bruce had sent him to nose around here," Patrick added. "Seth got lucky when Tyson's friend started making fun of him and his so-called treasure. We think Bruce's plan was to stall us until Seth had a chance to find out where the *Noble* went down, but he probably started to get impatient, thinking Sam and Evie would team up and go ahead with the search. We think he told Lansky to apply a little pressure."

"On Friday night, we waited until Bruce fell asleep and then we left. We spent the weekend trying to dodge him while we hiked back to the lodge. No tents. No food. Just the clothes on our backs, hey, Patrick?" Jacob reached out and cuffed Patrick's shoulder. "We were starting to worry about what was happening on the home front. Thought maybe you'd need our help."

The two men grinned at each other.

Sam saw Evie's expression. *Uh-oh.*

"Do you mean to tell me..." Evie said in a decep-tively pleasant voice "...that you were lost in the woods for two days?"

"Not lost, Evangeline. We had the miniature com-pass you pinned to the pocket of my shirt," Patrick said.

It didn't look like Evie cared about the compass.

"No food. No tent. Just the clothes on your backs," Evie repeated.

"And we had a great time." Jacob lifted his coffee cup and bumped it against Patrick's.

"A great time," Patrick echoed. "I'd say all in all, the fishing trip was successful."

"What are you talking about?" Evie asked, exasperated. "We all know you didn't go fishing."

"Oh, your dad went fishing, all right," Jacob said wryly. "Fishing for men as the Good Book says. If it hadn't been for Mullins's double cross, I would have thought Patty planned the whole thing."

Sam tensed. *The Good Book?*

"Never underestimate what God will use to get a man's attention." A glint of humor brightened Patrick's eyes. "All He had to do was get us alone in the wilderness with no food or water...and a sprained ankle... and Mullins hot on our trail...to get this stubborn guy to listen."

"Well, I listened, didn't I?" Jacob said irritably. "Some of us take more convincing than others."

"It has a lot to do with the thickness of the skull." Patrick tapped his index finger against his temple.

"Dad, what are you saying?" Because it couldn't possibly mean what Sam thought it meant.

"I accepted Jesus as my savior. Got my life right with God out there in the woods." He looked at Patrick. "Is that how you say it, Patty?"

Patrick's eyes misted. "That'll do."

Jacob looked at Sam and laughed. "You look a little befuddled, son. I'll tell you all about it. And then,

I'd like you and Faith to go back to Chicago with me. 'Cause your brother needs to hear it, too."

"I'm sorry I got you involved in this, Evie."

Evie stiffened when she heard her father's voice behind her. Under protest, he'd agreed to rest for a few hours at home before they met everyone again at Sophie's later. But when they got back to the house, Patrick hadn't rested. Instead, he'd printed out copies of Sophie's documents—something Evie had planned to do before Sam kidnapped her.

"I don't understand why *you* got involved." Evie still winced every time she saw the scratches on his face. Sophie had bandaged the cut over his eye but he still looked like a prizefighter who'd made it to the last round. "You promised—"

She caught herself. She hadn't meant to bring it up now that Patrick was home safe and sound. But she intended to make sure he stayed that way!

Patrick sighed. "The promise I made. I'm sorry—"

"It's okay, Dad. I forgive you."

Patrick gave her a gentle smile. "I'm not sorry I broke it, sweetheart. I'm sorry I made it in the first place."

"What?" Evie choked.

"I shouldn't have made a promise I couldn't keep, but you were young and we'd just lost your mother. I would have done anything to give you the security you needed. I said I'd never do anything that might take me away from you—even though I know our times are in God's hands—and that was wrong. Not only for you, but for me. I gave up things I loved because I didn't want to upset you…but I got restless after I retired. Your mother's been gone a long time but I found myself missing her more than ever. I needed some excitement. Something to make me feel alive again.

"When I met Sophie and she told me about her family genealogy and the scandal with Matthew Graham after the *Noble* sank, it gave me an opportunity to do something that mattered. Instead of selling people bits of the past, I could actually help Sophie connect with hers. She might have told you the search for her family history gave her a reason to live, but it gave me one, too."

Evie was speechless. She hadn't meant the promise to prevent her dad from enjoying life…or to make him give up things he loved, even if they were a little risky. She'd given them up, too. But she hadn't felt the void until she'd spent the day on the *Natalie* and relived the sweet memories of taking camping trips with her family.

She'd never known her father hadn't been as successful as her at forgetting those times. Or that he'd felt as though something were missing.

"Dad, I—"

Patrick held up his hand. "Just hear me out for a minute. Your mother was an amazing woman and I was blessed to have the years together that we did. Laura had a way of turning the most ordinary moments into adventures. She lived fearlessly and generously and she loved us the same way. I wouldn't have changed anything about her. Not even her choice of a career." Patrick gave Evie a tender smile. "You may think you and I are alike, Evangeline, but out of you three girls, *you* remind me the most of your mother. You're smart and curious and you care about people. Laura was that way, too."

All along, Evie realized with sudden, painful clarity, she'd been shaped by her mother's death instead of her life. And her father was right. Laura McBride had been an amazing woman. A dedicated police officer. And a loving mother.

"Some things are worth the risk." Patrick looked at her intently. "Friendship. Love."

Evie managed a smile as her heart struggled to recognize the truth she'd just discovered. "You love Sophie."

"Jacob loves Sophie," Patrick astounded her by saying. "And she loves him." He chuckled. "And he just might end up being worthy of her after all."

"Jacob and Sophie? Are you all right with that?" Unexpected tears welled up in Evie's eyes. She'd come to love Sophie, and she'd been ready and willing to welcome her into the McBride family.

"Oh, I'm more than all right with it. I've been asking God for months to give two people I care about a second chance at happiness."

Evie's lips parted. And no sound came out. She couldn't see Sophie and Jacob together. Sophie was deep and insightful. Jacob Cutter was, well, *Jacob Cutter*.

"They remind me a little of your mother and I," Patrick went on. "Different, but we brought out the best in each other."

Evie forced her mind to take a detour around thoughts of Sam. She couldn't let herself think about him right now. "Is all this talk about adventure your way of letting me know you're not giving up on the *Noble?*"

"Absolutely. And from what Sam told me, it seems I sent the map to the right McBride daughter."

"I was right?" Evie was momentarily distracted. "That *was* the map showing where the *Noble* sank?"

Patrick smiled in satisfaction. "I knew you'd figure it out and that you'd keep it safe. But now that I'm back, the rest of us can take over from here."

"You're really going to look for the ship?"

"We can't give up now. We have to get everything in order so we can hire a dive team to go down and see if Lady Carrington's dowry is still there. Prove that Matthew wasn't a thief."

"But what about Seth?" Evie asked helplessly. "You know he can't be trusted. And he's still lurking around somewhere, watching you."

"We've got some ideas. That's why we're meeting at Sophie's later. To have a planning session. But you don't have to come along, Evie. You're probably exhausted." Patrick's eyes twinkled as he hobbled away, rubbing the hip that had collided with a tree stump.

"I'll come along," Evie said grimly. "Planning sessions happen to be my specialty."

And, she thought with an aching heart, it might be her last opportunity to say goodbye to Sam.

Chapter Twenty

"God answered my prayer, Evie. I'm going back to Chicago with Grandpa and Sam tomorrow."

Tomorrow?

Faith's exuberant greeting pierced Evie's heart but she reached out and hugged her. "That's great news."

"Grandpa called Dad and I got to talk to him. I told him about Rocky and sleeping on the boat," Faith went on. "And I told him about you, too. He said to tell you thank-you for helping me with my homework. And for playing basketball with me."

Evie tried to swallow around the knot in her throat as Faith towed her toward the people sitting around the crackling bonfire in Sophie's backyard. Jacob and Sophie sat shoulder to shoulder, toasting marshmallows over the glowing embers, while Tyson stood several feet away from them, sharpening the end of a stick with his pocketknife.

For some reason, the homey scene brought tears to

her eyes. Maybe her dad was right about Sophie and Jacob being good for each other. And for Tyson.

Evie's gaze swept the yard but there was no sign of Sam anywhere.

"Sam didn't come," Faith told her, as if she knew who Evie was looking for. "He said he had too much packing to do if we're leaving tomorrow. He had to cover the boat and stuff like that."

Sam wasn't going to say goodbye?

Evie bit down on her lip to keep it from trembling. He'd barely spoken to her after he and Jacob had returned from their "talk" but she'd assumed it was because he was still in shock over his father's unexpected announcement. *She* could hardly comprehend that Jacob Cutter had surrendered his life to the Lord. She didn't know what it would mean for Sam and his brother, but she had a feeling that God had separated the entire Cutter family so He could work on them one at a time!

"Evie." Sophie rose to her feet and greeted her with a warm hug. "I was hoping you'd come over this evening with your father. Even though it might be kind of boring talking permits—"

"And strategy." Jacob chortled. "Tyson may have to pretend to be on Lansky's side for another few weeks so we can keep an eye on him and see what he's up to."

That sounded a little dangerous to Evie, but she saw the first real smile she'd ever seen on Tyson's face. "Boring? Are you kidding? Count me in."

Evie took a deep breath. "Me, too."

"Are you sure, sweetheart?" Patrick came up and

linked his arm through hers. "I don't want to take up any more of your summer—you said you had plans."

Plans. Yes, she did have plans. To paint her front door and read through a stack of books. And do some gardening. And she fully intended to check off every one of those things on her list...

After they found the *Noble*.

"Special delivery for Evangeline McBride."

Evie heard the mischievous tone in her father's voice and set aside the box of china she'd been unpacking.

"I hope it's iced tea because I'm—" Her voice trailed off when she saw the huge bouquet of summer flowers in Patrick's arm. Daisies. Roses. Snapdragons. Lavender. All nestled together in a cloud of airy white tulle. "Where did those come from?"

"A florist, I suppose." Patrick smiled at her. "A deliveryman just brought them to the house." He transferred them into her waiting arms and Evie buried her face in the scented blooms.

"There's a card."

"I know." But she didn't want to read it. Already tears clawed at the backs of her eyes. It had been almost a month since the Cutters had left. She knew Patrick and Jacob kept in contact, but it was as if Sam Cutter had disappeared off the face of the earth.

Or maybe just from your life.

And hadn't she wanted it that way? There couldn't be a future for her and Sam. It was one thing to venture beyond the perimeters she'd put around her life, another to deliberately risk her heart by starting a relationship with a police officer. That was something she didn't think she'd ever be ready for.

"Why don't you put those in some water and I'll finish unpacking the boxes?"

Maybe the flowers weren't from Sam. Maybe Caitlin had sent them as a guilt offering for not being able to visit over the Fourth of July. Or Meghan. Sometimes she did things like send flowers or chocolates for no particular reason other than to "celebrate the day" as she called it.

Evie walked up to the house and let herself inside through the patio door. Vase first. Card later. She carefully unwrapped the filmy netting and the layer of tissue paper underneath it. The tiny linen envelope fell out, drifting gracefully to the table. Reminding her it was there.

"I'll get to you in a minute."

She put the flowers in water and took her time arranging them in an ironstone vase. And then she wiped up the table and rinsed out the dishcloth.

With fingers that shook, she finally tore open the envelope and pulled out the small square of paper inside.

Therefore, if anyone is in Christ, he is a new creation; the old has gone, the new has come!
—2 Corinthians 5:17

Evie sagged against the counter as she stared at the signatures.

Jacob Rachel
Dan Faith

And Sam.

In the same tidy script he'd used to sign his name were two more words. *Thank you.*

Overwhelmed, Evie sagged against the counter.

All of them, Lord?

And then she burst into tears.

"He's a good man, Evie." Patrick draped her cardigan around her shoulders and settled down on the dock beside her.

"I know." Evie's gaze didn't shift away from the deep blue seam where the water met the sky in the distance.

Shortly after reading the card, she'd driven to Cooper's Landing and walked to the end of the dock. The *Natalie,* preening in a bright yellow canvas cover, bobbed a greeting. For a minute, she'd let herself remember the strength in Sam's hands as they'd covered hers while she steered the boat out of the harbor.

"Did I imagine it, or was there something happening between you and Sam?"

Something she'd walked away from. Evie drew a careful breath. "We're too different, Dad."

"Are you sure that's the real reason?"

She should have known her father would see through to the truth. "I was too young to realize how dangerous Mom's job was until she didn't come home that day, but now I do *know.* And I can't do it." Evie twisted her fingers together in her lap. "God brought me to Cooper's Landing to help Faith. I'm happy Sam is a Christian now but that doesn't mean we're meant to be together."

"I love you to pieces, Evie, but ever since your

mother died you've tried to cocoon yourself from anything that might be painful. And I know I'm partially to blame for going along with it. You won't even go barefoot on the beach."

"That's because there might be broken glass in the sand," Evie muttered in her own defense.

Patrick smiled gently. "The last few weeks, I've seen changes in you. Good ones. And I'd like you to consider something. Maybe God didn't bring you here for Faith and Sam. Maybe He brought Faith and Sam here for *you*."

Tears spilled down her cheeks. "It might be too late, Dad. He didn't even say goodbye."

Patrick patted her knee. "Maybe because he hoped it wouldn't be."

"Hey, Chief. Mrs. Mattson called and wants us to check out a suspicious truck parked outside her house again."

Sam's chair creaked in protest as he leaned back. "Does this one happen to have the words FedEx printed on the side, too?"

Officer Tony Faller laughed. "I don't know. But I'll take care of it."

"Let me." Sam rose to his feet, once again battling a familiar restlessness that had dogged him the past few weeks. "I could use a change of scenery from the city budget right about now."

"Yeah." Tony made a face. "Sorry about that. It was one thing watching over the town, another one taking on the city council and all those numbers. All I can say is I'm glad you're back."

"You did a great job. At least now I know I can take a leave of absence if necessary." Sam suppressed a smile when he saw the panic in Tony's eyes, but he couldn't help giving the officer a hard time.

Tony had been employed at the Summer Harbor P.D. for only three years, and the mayor had questioned Sam's choice of men to take his place during the month he was in Cooper's Landing. But Sam had pushed and eventually got his way. In personality and dedication, Tony reminded Sam of Dan.

Thanks, Lord.

Every time his brother came to mind, it was the only thing Sam could say. Two simple words, but they came from the depths of his soul.

He still couldn't believe the changes in his family. In a lot of ways, he felt like Dan. Like he was starting from scratch. What had Evie said? Moment by moment? Breath by breath? He hadn't understood what she meant at the time. But now he did.

A hundred times over the past few weeks, he'd wanted to call Evie and fill her in on Dan's progress. But she hadn't made any attempt to contact him since he'd left Cooper's Landing, and that told him, more than anything, exactly where they stood.

Apart.

Even after he'd sent her a bouquet of flowers, she hadn't called or sent a note.

After that, he carefully avoided asking questions

about Evie when Jacob called. He knew that, thanks to Tyson, Seth Lansky was being formally charged for possession of stolen property, while Bruce Mullins claimed Seth had acted entirely on his own. Sam even heard subtle references to Jacob's budding romance with Sophie. But Jacob didn't mention Evie, and Sam assumed she'd gone home, as planned.

It was clear that even though they now shared the same faith, Evie didn't see them sharing anything else.

"Not even a pizza," Sam muttered.

"You want to order a pizza?"

"No." He and Tony were friends but he wasn't ready to talk about Evie yet. "I was talking to myself."

"Michelle says you've been doing that a lot lately," Tony said, a glint in his eyes.

"Really?" Sam stalked toward the door, careful not to open it so quickly that Michelle, who probably had her ear pressed against it, would fall over. "What else does Michelle say?"

Tony followed him out. "That you sent flowers to someone name Evangeline McBride."

Sam stared at him in disbelief. "How does she know that?"

Tony shrugged. "She and the florist are second cousins."

"I should have stayed in Chicago."

Michelle, his loyal secretary and the department's efficient dispatcher, pretended to file papers when he rounded the corner.

"Cousins, huh?" He arched an eyebrow as he strode past.

"You weren't supposed to tell him!" She pouted at Tony, who winked at her.

"I'll be back. I'm going to check out the suspicious truck on Mrs. Mattson's street and then I'm going to stop home for a few minutes." Sam took his sunglasses out of his pocket and shook them open before reaching the door.

"Oh, that's right," Michelle called after him. "My mother's aunt Thelma reupholsters furniture and she said you can drop the recliner off anytime this weekend."

"Thanks." He planned to make his brother pay for the damages Rocky had inflicted on his favorite chair. In a moment of what Sam could only claim as temporary insanity, he'd offered to take care of Rocky until Dan came home. Rachel had changed her mind about having a dog in the house but the hours she and Faith spent with Dan at the rehab center weren't conducive to training an active puppy.

Neither were his, but he'd offered anyway.

Rocky missed his littermates and didn't like being cooped up all day, so he'd taken out his frustration on Sam's recliner. And a pair of boots. And the leg of a coffee table.

"I'll be back later. Don't call me unless it's an absolute emergency."

"Absolute emergency. Got it."

Sam glanced over his shoulder and saw Michelle curtsey and Tony salute.

Comedians. Both of them.

Sam rolled his eyes but tamped down the laughter

welling up inside him. The price he paid for being the chief of police in a small town. And he loved it.

If only he could convince Evie that she would love it, too.

Chapter Twenty-One

"You knew about this, Lord," Evie said out loud as she read the bright blue, wave-shaped sign that greeted visitors at the city limits.

Summer Harbor.

Of *course* it was on the water. The little town Sam had promised to protect and serve curled around a sparkling, diamond-shaped bay like a contented tabby cat.

Evie tapped the brake as the speed limit sign suddenly took a radical drop from 55 mph to 25 mph. She didn't want to get picked up for exceeding the speed limit!

She refused to let herself be charmed by the tidy, old-fashioned main street with its brass light poles and wrought-iron benches. Or by the planters, overflowing with pink and white petunias, strategically placed at every corner. She could see the top of an old stone lighthouse jutting from the top of a hill that overlooked Lake Michigan.

There was no sense admiring a town she might only

be visiting for fifteen minutes. Depending on how Sam reacted to her unexpected—and unannounced—arrival.

In a town of five thousand people, it didn't take Evie long to locate the police department. One squad car was parked in front of the brick building with the engine running.

Evie's heart jumped.

Okay, God. I'm taking a risk here. Don't leave me.

She pushed open the door and the dispatcher, a young woman with spiky blond hair and jewel-studded glasses perched on her nose, smiled at her from behind the Plexiglas window. When she stood up and waddled over, Evie was surprised to see she was *very* pregnant. "Can I help you?"

"I'm looking for Sam Cutter."

"He's not here right now," the dispatcher said. "Would you like to speak with Officer Faller?"

"No, thank you." Evie gnawed on her lower lip as she tried to determine what to do next. Wait? Go back home?

The second choice was tempting, but she'd driven almost half the day to see Sam.

As she waffled, the door opened behind her and Evie's knees turned to jelly.

"Evangeline McBride?"

Evie turned toward the unfamiliar voice and saw a man in uniform standing there, looking just as surprised as she was.

"Yes?"

Behind the glass, the dispatcher gasped. "You're Evangeline McBride?"

Evie's gaze cautiously slid from one to the other. How did they know who she was? Was it possible Sam had *talked* about her? To the people he worked with? A flutter of wild hope took wing in her heart.

"I ran your license plate before I came in," the officer said cheerfully. "I'm Officer Faller, by the way."

"And I'm Michelle Loomis." The dispatcher grinned.

"It's nice to meet you both," Evie stammered.

"I told her Chief's not here." Michelle gave Tony a meaningful look.

"I can come back—" If she didn't lose her nerve.

"No!" Their combined voices drowned out her weak suggestion.

"He won't be gone long. Why don't you wait in his office." Officer Faller stepped in front of the door, effectively blocking her path.

Evie eased around him. "No. Thank you. Really. I'll come back…later."

Michelle and Tony exchanged skeptical looks.

"He said we should call him if it's an absolute emergency," Tony mused.

Michelle ignored Evie's strangled protest and nodded thoughtfully. "If she is Evangeline McBride, I think she definitely falls into the category of an absolute emergency."

Evie tried not to overthink Michelle's remark as the dispatcher scrawled something on a piece of paper and pushed it toward her through the narrow slot in the divider. "Here you go, honey. But don't tell him where you got it. I happen to like my job."

* * *

Rocky greeted Sam at the door, a tattered baseball cap clamped in his jaws.

"Found a new hat, huh, boy?" Sam held the door open and Rocky charged past him, on a mission to find the perfect spot to bury the hat. Just like he had the coffee table leg.

The July sunshine beat down on him and Sam loosened his tie as he followed Rocky's crooked trail down the beach.

The remnants of an elaborate sand castle caught his attention, and he immediately thought about Evie.

When *didn't* he think about Evie?

Given the short time they'd known each other, Sam was amazed at how many things reminded him of her. When he looked out his living room window at the water, he remembered the afternoon on the *Natalie*. And her blue eyes. If he saw a woman on the street with a hair color similar to Evie's, his heart rate spiked in response.

Rocky let out a sharp bark and Sam lifted one hand to shade his eyes against the sun. The woman walking toward him on the beach wore a large straw hat. Just like Evie's.

There you go again.

Sam whistled but Rocky ignored him and made a mad dash for the woman, his stubby legs churning up sand like the wheels of a dune buggy.

"He's friendly," Sam shouted across the distance, hoping she wouldn't think his crazy dog was about to attack her.

"I know."

The laughter in the voice—even the voice itself—sounded like Evie. The heat was getting to him. No doubt about it.

As the woman reached down to pet Rocky, he saw the gigantic purse slung over her shoulder.

Somehow, Sam's feet kept moving. Even though everything inside had frozen solid.

"I can't believe he's gotten so big." The straw hat listed to one side and Sam caught a glimpse of sunset-red hair. And a straight little nose dotted with freckles. *Twelve of them.*

He couldn't believe Evie was standing three feet away. Almost within reach. Sam blinked, just to make sure she wasn't a hallucination.

"What are you doing here?" He hadn't expected to see her, not unless circumstances forced them together. Sam had discovered his newfound faith meant trusting God when it came to his relationship with Evie. And that had become his greatest challenge.

As the days slipped by with no contact between them, Sam had started to lose hope that she could accept his career. And not only accept it, but support it.

Sam knew God was the only one who could wipe away the last barrier standing between him and Evie. But she had to *let* Him. Accepting that had been tough for Sam, especially when he wanted to crash through those barriers himself and *make* Evie see they were meant to have a future together. Sam had come to the realization that trusting God took guts, a lot more than trying to do things on his own!

"They got the permits." Evie smiled uncertainly. "Yesterday."

She'd driven all the way to Summer Harbor to tell him about the *Noble?*

"That's great. Sophie will be happy." He'd talked to Jacob the night before, but somehow his father had failed to mention the latest news. Maybe because they'd sent Evie to deliver it in person?

Why?

Sam was afraid to hope.

"The local news interviewed Sophie and our dads last night. They're celebrities now. Even a national network called to find out what was going on."

"Great." Sam tried to muster some enthusiasm. He was glad the months of research had yielded some results, but he found himself wishing Evie would have come to Summer Harbor for another reason other than playing messenger. "Have you been in Cooper's Landing the whole time?"

"I went home last week."

"How's the garden?" Sam winced. Okay, there'd been a grain of sarcasm in the question, but seeing Evie again had knocked him off center.

He stuffed his hands in his pockets, not sure how much longer he could hold out before taking her into his arms.

He wasn't making this easy for her. But then, this was a Sam that Evie didn't recognize. He'd had his hair cut since the last time she'd seen him and the five-o'clock stubble that shadowed his lean jawline was gone.

He'd traded in his blue jeans and faded T-shirt for charcoal-gray Dockers and a crisp white shirt, paired with a conservative tie. The pockets displayed an assortment of pins. And his badge.

Sam didn't look like a windblown sailor anymore. He looked like a cop.

And she fell in love with him all over again.

From the minute she'd followed the path down to the beach and saw Sam walking by the water, she wondered why she'd let so much time go by. And why she'd let her fears control her future.

She'd put that control right where it had always been—in God's faithful hands. And she planned to leave it there.

Now she just had to convince Sam. If she hadn't waited too long already.

"It's a pretty town." Small talk. So maybe she wasn't as brave as she hoped to be!

"It's on the water," Sam pointed out.

Evie ignored the slight challenge in his tone. "I think it's prettier than Cooper's Landing, with the marina and the lighthouse."

"You like the lighthouse?"

Evie nodded.

"Come on. I'll show it to you."

Evie blinked. Had she imagined Sam's hint of a smile? "Really? I'd like that." She'd like anything that kept him with her.

Sam whistled for Rocky and this time the puppy bounded over and followed them up the beach. The stone lighthouse was smaller than others Evie had seen, but still quaint and well preserved. Probably due to being the target project of a local historical society.

Sam shocked her by following the uneven flagstone path right to the front door.

"You can go inside?" Evie frowned. "Is it open to tourists?"

Instead of answering, Sam turned the handle and stepped to one side.

"Are you sure?" She hesitated. "Don't we need permission?"

"After you." Now Sam did smile. And she would have followed him anywhere.

Evie decided the town must own the lighthouse and, as chief of police, Sam had permission to show it to visitors.

Rocky galloped over to them, his tail wagging proudly as he deposited a shoe at Evie's feet.

"Oh, no, you don't," Sam growled. "I happen to like that pair."

While he wrestled for control of the shoe, Evie turned in a slow circle and scanned the interior. Comfortable furnishings reflected a rustic, nautical theme and Evie realized the lighthouse had been converted into someone's…home. The truth suddenly dawned on her.

"You live in a lighthouse."

God, you knew about this, too! Are there any more surprises?

She hoped so. She was beginning to enjoy them.

"I bought it already fixed up. Over the years it's been a gift shop and an artist's studio, but the last owner put it up for sale within days after the police and fire commission hired me." Sam shrugged. "I couldn't resist."

Evie walked over to the circular staircase that wound up to the second floor.

"Do you want to take a look?"

"I don't like heights." A reluctant confession. Sam was going to think she was still afraid of her own shadow.

"Neither do I," Sam surprised her by saying. "But the view is worth it."

His cell phone rang and he flipped it open. "Excuse me, Evie. I have to take this."

So formal. So professional. When had Sam become the cautious one? And what was she going to have to do to prove to him that her perspective had changed?

"Of course." *I guess I've taken up enough of your time.*

While Sam stepped into the next room, Evie walked blindly outside into the sunshine.

Had she been wrong about Sam's feelings? Had she read too much into his unexpected kiss that day at the beach? Maybe he'd realized he didn't want to pursue a relationship with someone he thought couldn't accept his career.

Rocky followed her and made a beeline toward the lacey waves lapping against the shore. Without thinking, Evie peeled off her shoes and dropped them in the sand as she followed him into the shallow water.

He fished a wet stick of driftwood out of the surf and danced up to her. Evie laughed and tossed it into the water, unable to avoid getting splashed as he went after it.

They played the game for several minutes before Evie felt Sam's presence. She turned around and there he was, right behind her. Her shoes in his hand.

The warmth in his eyes took her breath away. And gave her the courage she needed.

"I'm sorry, Sam. I should've told you how I felt about you but I was scared and—" Evie decided words weren't enough this time. She stood on her tiptoes and reached up to frame his face with her hands. And kissed him.

Her shoes hit the sand with a thud as Sam drew her into his arms and looked down at her.

"Barefoot, Evangeline?" he murmured. "That's a little…adventurous, don't you think?"

She smiled up at him. "What can I say? I'm my mother's daughter. Do you think you can live with that?"

"I'm looking forward to it," Sam whispered in her ear. "For a very long time."

Epilogue

"Okay, Dad. Why did you call us all here? Did you find the treasure or not?"

Evie suppressed a smile. Leave it to Caitlin to cut to the heart of the matter. Several days before, everyone in the Cutter and McBride families had answered a mysterious summons to come to Cooper's Landing. E-mails flew back and forth but no one knew what was going on. When Evie called her dad to try to pry some information from him, all he told her was to pack her bag for the weekend.

So she had. And she'd picked up Sam along the way.

By midafternoon on Saturday, Sophie's backyard was crowded with people. Caitlin and Meghan had managed to get the weekend off, although Evie had a hunch their quick response had more to do with wanting to meet Sam than to find out what, if anything, had been discovered in Lake Superior!

Tyson was a quiet presence but Evie noticed Jacob was careful to include Sophie's son in the conversations.

According to Patrick, Tyson had joined a support group for people with addictions. He still shied away from attending church services with Sophie, but he'd met Pastor Wallis several times for breakfast.

And it was good to see Faith again, too. And to finally meet Dan and Rachel.

Evie felt an immediate connection with Sam's twin brother and his wife. To her embarrassment, both Dan and Rachel made a point of seeking her out and thanking her again for tutoring Faith. When Evie tried to downplay her role, Rachel met her gaze evenly and told her it wasn't only the tutoring sessions that had put their daughter on the right track. The piece of beach glass on the table next to her bed proved it. When Faith had returned to Chicago with Sam and Jacob, she'd told her father about Evie's prayer asking God to bring something good out of the accident. And, Rachel assured Evie, He had.

It wasn't the only good thing God had done, Evie thought as she felt the warmth of Sam's fingers laced through hers. When Sam had time off, they'd been spending it together. Sometimes he drove to Brookfield to see her, and other times she made the trip to Summer Harbor. Each time she visited, it got harder to say goodbye. Not only to Summer Harbor, but to Sam. Once upon a time, she could never have imagined herself with a police officer. Now she couldn't imagine life without him.

"I agree with Caitlin," Dan said with a grin. "Not that we don't appreciate all this wonderful food you've provided, but we want some answers now."

Sam's fingers tightened and Evie gave him a reassuring squeeze. She knew what he was thinking. Dan was walking now with the use of canes, but the doctor was optimistic he could retire them in time for Faith's basketball season.

Jacob's laugh drew Evie's attention back to the moment. "We can all go in the house and then Sophie can tell you. She's the one who started this whole thing."

Everyone squeezed into Sophie's tiny living room and Sophie set a plain brown folder down on the coffee table. "While the dive team was looking for the *Noble,* Patrick and I kept looking for more information about my great-grandfather Matthew. A few days ago, a retired pastor sent me something.

"The Church on the Hill was the first church in Cooper's Landing, started in the late 1800s by a circuit preacher at the request of the settlers here. It closed its doors about twenty-five years ago, but the original building is still there and so is the cemetery. The records of all the births and deaths were turned over to the local historical society. The pastor I contacted is a member of that society and he was very interested in Matthew's story. The name *Graham* caught his attention and he did some detective work for me."

Sophie hesitated and everyone in the room was silent, waiting for her to continue. Instead, Sophie removed a photograph from the folder on the table.

Evie looked closer and saw an image of an old headstone, pitted and scarred by the elements.

D. C. Graham
Beloved Wife

Born January 10, 1870
Died October 23, 1890

Sam frowned. "Another relative of yours, Sophie?"

"In a matter of speaking." Sophie's eyes misted over. "This headstone is in a section of the cemetery designated to remember people who died but weren't able to be buried. People who perished in blizzards and were never found. Or people who…drowned."

Judging from the confused expressions on the faces gathered around her, Evie knew she wasn't the only one having a hard time following Sophie.

"We think D.C. stands for Dale Carrington," Sophie explained softly. "While I researched our genealogy, I didn't find anyone in my family with those initials."

"But the last name is Graham. And it says beloved wife," Meghan said.

"Exactly." Patrick winked at his middle daughter.

Evie stared at Sophie and Patrick in amazement. "You think Matthew and Lady Dale were *married?*"

"We had a difficult time believing it, too," Sophie said. "But when we saw this photo, everything fell into place. It explains why Matthew had Lady Dale's family ring in his possession when he was rescued. He hadn't stolen it, she'd *given* it to him. According to relatives, Matthew was a changed man after the ship went down. Bitter. Burdened by guilt. But now I believe the guilt wasn't because he'd stolen Lady Dale's dowry—it was because he hadn't been able to save her."

"But wasn't she engaged to that lumber baron's son?" Rachel asked.

"Yes, but Matthew and Lady Dale would have spent a lot of time together, not only at her family estate in England but also on the journey over," Sophie said. "Stranger things have happened. The Lawrence family had a lot of money but lacked respectability. The Carrington family was just the opposite—that's probably why the marriage was arranged. It's possible Matthew befriended Lady Dale and offered her a way to avoid a marriage with a man described as selfish and hot tempered. Or they were simply two young people who fell in love. Whatever the reason, the ship's captain had the authority to perform a wedding ceremony on board the *Noble*."

"But if they got married, why didn't Matthew tell anyone? It would have saved his reputation," Caitlin asked, clearly skeptical.

"The proof went down with the ship," Patrick said. "The Lawrence family had a lot of influence in this area. Who'd believe a titled lady would give up everything for a lumberjack?"

Meghan gave the barest of smiles. "I would. God knows what He's doing when He brings two people together."

Sophie smiled up at Jacob and he turned red. "Yes. Well. I guess I can go along with that."

Evie felt the warmth of Sam's gaze. "So can I."

"So there's no treasure?" Tyson sounded disappointed. "All that work was for nothing?"

"The treasure is right here." Sophie tapped the photo with the tip of her finger. "For me, it was always about finding the truth."

"I suppose." Tyson sighed.

Patrick's lips twitched. "Maybe you should show him the other photo."

Sophie took something else out of the folder and slid it toward Tyson. "We turned these over to the underwater salvage and preserve committee yesterday. They were pretty excited, to say the least."

Tyson looked dazed. "Gold coins? There has to be at least—"

"Fifty of them," Patrick finished.

"Where—"

"Aw, that's up to the committee to decide." Jacob cleared his throat. "Doesn't matter to me what happens to them. Or even that we cleared Matthew's name. I think we found something a whole lot more valuable than a bunch of old coins."

Sam's eyes glistened as he brushed his lips against Evie's hair. "So do I."

"Did you see those two?" Jacob chuckled. "Who would have guessed?"

Patrick joined him at the window and saw Evie and Sam standing together in the moonlight, deep in conversation.

"We have a lot to be thankful for, my friend."

Jacob blew out a gusty sigh. "Isn't that the truth? But you know something, now that we found the *Noble,* I am going to miss the excitement."

"Mmm." Patrick smiled slowly. "Maybe we don't have to miss it yet."

"What do you mean?"

"After we made the six-o'clock news last week, I got a call from someone."

"About what?"

"Let's just say it may involve another…fishing trip."

Jacob grinned. "Count me in. Partner."

* * * * *

Dear Reader,

Many stories are born from the simple question "What if?" What if a young woman who doesn't like to take risks is suddenly pushed into an adventure? And what if the things she views as flaws, or weaknesses, in her personality turn out to be strengths when they're put to the test?

I love that God created each of us with unique personalities. And I love that He puts us in situations guaranteed to stretch us beyond our abilities—so we learn to trust Him more.

I hope you enjoyed teaming up with Sam and Evie in the romantic adventure, *A Treasure Worth Keeping*.

Blessings,

Kathryn Springer

QUESTIONS FOR DISCUSSION

1. What is your first impression of Evie? Does it change over the course of the book? Why?

2. How did Evie's and Sam's childhoods differ? How did Jacob Cutter, Sam's father, influence Sam's faith (or lack of it)? How did Sam's childhood differ from the way Patrick raised his daughters? Think about the legacy of faith in your own family as you were growing up. How would you describe it?

3. Dan's injury caused Sam to question what he believed. Has anything happened in a similar situation in your own life? Describe what happened and how it changed your perspective.

4. Evie was a believer, but there was an area in her life where she struggled with totally putting her trust in God. What was it? What did it stem from?

5. When did Sam's opinion of Evie begin to change? Why?

6. What is your favorite scene in the book? Why?

7. Evie compares herself to her sisters and thinks she doesn't measure up to them. What is the danger in comparing ourselves to other women? Why do you think we tend to do this?

8. Have you ever researched your family history? Do you think it's important? Why or why not?

9. In what way did losing her mother affect the way Evie lived her life? How did it impact her relationships? Why do you think that Evie had to be the one to reach out to Sam at the end of the book?

10. What would you say is your greatest "treasure"? Why?

HIDDEN TREASURES

In this way they will lay up treasure for themselves as a firm foundation for the coming age, so that they may take hold of the life that is truly life.
—*1 Timothy* 6:19

To Norah—
Always listen for the sound of wild geese,
stop to pick dandelions, study the clouds…
and reach for the stars. And remember,
you are fearfully and wonderfully made!

Prologue

"I knew I'd find you hiding in here."

"Technically, it's not hiding if the person is in plain sight." Meghan McBride shot a mischievous smile at her sister Caitlin who sauntered into the room with her usual catlike grace, still wearing the periwinkle-blue stilettos she'd stepped into at eight o'clock that morning.

Meghan had kicked off an identical pair hours ago. It was too much to hope Caitlin hadn't spotted her bare toes peeking out from under the netting of the tea-length gown she wore. She'd probably already noticed that Meghan's hair had managed to break free of the grid of bobby pins anchoring it in place. It wasn't fair that the breeze skipping off Lake Superior during their youngest sister's outdoor wedding ceremony had ignored Caitlin's neat French twist and set its sights on Meghan's mop of curls—the ones the stylist had spent an extra half hour trying to restrain.

"Evie and Sam are getting ready to leave. She was

wondering where you were..." Caitlin frowned. "Is that *frosting* on your elbow?"

Shoot. Meghan inspected her arm and made a half-hearted attempt to scrub off the pink smear with her thumbnail. "I think so. I warned Evie that she shouldn't have asked me to cut the cake."

Like a magician, Caitlin somehow produced a delicately embroidered handkerchief out of thin air and handed it to her with a sigh.

That was the trouble with sisters. They knew every chink in a person's armor. Caitlin's sharp eye for detail made her wildly popular as an image consultant and wildly annoying as an older sister. Evie had waved the white flag of surrender and turned her closet over to Caitlin years ago, but Meghan had refused to go down without a fight. She *liked* going barefoot and wearing blue jeans and T-shirts. Not only did she spend most of her spare time with children and paint, every time she bought something new, she ended up getting a stain— or two—on it. What was the point?

"I still can't believe our baby sister is married," Caitlin murmured.

Meghan couldn't believe it, either. The previous summer, she and Caitlin had sweet-talked Evie into managing Beach Glass, their father's antique store, while he went away on a two-week fishing trip. Evie's brief stay had turned into something straight from the pages of an action-adventure novel. She'd discovered that her father and his friend Jacob Cutter were searching for clues they hoped would lead them to a sunken ship. Their cautious sister, who ordinarily steered clear of anything risky, had dodged a corrupt group of treasure hunters and fallen in love with Jacob's son Sam.

"Right out of a fairy tale," Meghan murmured. "Who would have guessed?"

Caitlin made a noise that sounded suspiciously like a snort. Except that image consultants *didn't* snort. "Sam's a good guy."

The understatement of the year. "He's perfect for Evie. And she deserves to be happy." Meghan knew her sister couldn't argue with that.

"She does." Caitlin's expression softened. "We better get back to the reception before she hunts us down—"

"Too late!" The words, accompanied by Evie's lilting laugh and the rustle of satin, preceded her into the kitchen.

Meghan took one look at her sister and the lump that had lodged in her throat—the one that had formed while she'd watched Sam and Evie recite their vows—swelled to the size of an orange again. Evie looked spectacular in the ivory gown Caitlin had found in an exclusive shop in the Twin Cities, where Caitlin and Meghan lived.

Meghan ignored a pinch of envy. It's not that she wasn't ecstatic for Evie. She just couldn't help but wonder what it would be like to feel that way about someone. Caitlin was openly cynical when it came to love, but Meghan knew it happened to some people. Like their parents. And now Evie and Sam. But for reasons she kept to herself, she wasn't convinced she was ever going to be one of them.

"Sam and I are going to sneak away while the orchestra is playing the last song." Evie's gown swished around her feet as she crossed the room and drew them into an affectionate hug. "I wish I could take you to Paris."

"Oh, Sam would love that," Caitlin said drily.

"Have fun," Meghan commanded. "And don't worry about Dad. I'm planning to stay until next weekend and I promise I'll take good care of him."

Evie's smile faded slightly, proving she still had some progress to make when it came to letting their father manage on his own. Evie had an exasperating tendency to fuss over Patrick, although Meghan thought she understood why. Evie had been a freshman in high school and the only one of them still living at home when their mother, Laura, had passed away unexpectedly.

"I have a list of reminders—"

Meghan's howl drowned Evie out. "I don't do lists! I lose lists, Evie. You *know* that."

"That's why I made copies." Evie looked smug. "Several of them. And they're posted where you can't miss seeing them."

"On a package of Oreos?" Caitlin said under her breath.

Meghan bit back a protest long enough to glare at Caitlin. When she turned back to Evie, she pasted a smile on her face. No need to upset the bride on her wedding day. "Dad and I will be fine, Evie. Don't worry about a thing."

"Megs is right. It's not like Dad is a toddler who's going to get into trouble the minute your back is turned."

Evie didn't look convinced. "I wouldn't be too sure about that," she said darkly. "Remember what happened last summer."

"The entire Cutter family became believers. Sophie and Jacob got engaged. And you met Sam." Meghan believed in looking at the positives. If she didn't, she'd never have been able to gather the courage to launch her own photography business.

"That's true." Evie gnawed on her lower lip. "But he's up to something. I can always tell. He and Jacob were in a huddle earlier this afternoon and he's been spending a lot of time online lately."

Caitlin opened her mouth but Meghan shot her a warning look and looped an arm around Evie's slim shoulders. "I'll watch out for Dad. And I've got one word for you. *Honeymoon.* Now go. Sam's probably waiting in the car."

Evie's cheeks turned as pink as the miniature roses in her bouquet. "I'm going. And I'll call—"

"When you get back," Caitlin interrupted.

"When I get back," Evie promised.

Meghan didn't believe it for a second. Judging from the skeptical look on Caitlin's face, she didn't, either.

"Evie?" Sam poked his head in the doorway and his pewter gaze zeroed in on his wife. "Are you ready?"

"Just hugging my sisters before we leave."

"There's always time for that." Sam's warm smile encompassed all three women and once again Meghan found herself thanking God that He'd brought Sam and Evie together.

You wouldn't happen to have another Sam hidden somewhere, would you, Lord?

Caitlin cleared her throat. "Go on, you two. The

sooner you get out of here, the sooner I get my post-card of the Eiffel Tower."

"I taped a backup list to Caitlin's mirror in case you lose yours," Evie called over her shoulder.

Evie and Sam disappeared and Meghan felt the weight of the sudden silence, knowing that no matter how happy they were for Evie, things would be different now.

"I wish I could stay with you and Dad a few extra days, but I'm booked from now until September." Caitlin broke the silence.

"Dad and I will be fine," Meghan said. "You know Evie. She has a tendency to worry, that's all. Like you said, what kind of trouble can a retired English teacher get into?"

Chapter One

Dad, you are in so much trouble.

Meghan surveyed the papers fanned out on her father's desk. The ones she'd discovered when she'd shouldered her way into the study to deliver his afternoon cup of green tea and plate of Oreos. Evie's list had specified fig bars—in capital letters, no less—but over the course of the week Meghan had fed those to an adorable family of gray squirrels. That the discovery the squirrels liked fig bars had taken place *after* she'd dumped the cookies out the window was entirely coincidental.

She picked up a stack of photos, every one of them depicting a work by a well-known artist named Joseph Ferris. Either her dad had shifted his interest from antiques to art or else he was planning to become an art *thief.*

Which could also explain the blueprints of what looked to be a sizable estate fanned out on the desk blotter.

She'd gotten suspicious when she'd seen the light

glowing under the door of her father's study two nights in a row. At midnight. Patrick always went to bed promptly after the ten o'clock news. Both times she'd ignored it, not wanting to draw attention to her late-night forays into the kitchen for leftover wedding cake.

But the night before she'd heard the phone ring a few minutes after twelve and then her father's muffled voice on the other side of the door as she padded down the hallway. She'd assumed he was talking to Evie, but when she'd asked about it at breakfast, her father had almost choked on his whole-grain bagel and mumbled something vague about talking to a friend.

Right. Suspicious, she'd pushed a special code on the phone and listened to a nice little robotic voice recite the number of the last incoming call. From an area code somewhere in Upstate New York.

Meghan had to face the truth. Evie's list had turned her into…Evie. But there was no going back now. She had to find out what he was up to.

Ever since Patrick had discovered the whereabouts of the *Noble,* a ship Lake Superior had claimed in the late 1800s, and solved the mystery behind a century-old scandal that had plagued Sophie's family, random people had started to contact him. Some asked for help researching their genealogy while others wanted to hire him to locate missing family heirlooms.

In spite of his daughters' initial misgivings, Patrick had actually taken on some "clients" over the winter and, judging from the growing number of inquiries, his reputation must have spread.

Meghan blew out a sigh. She didn't want to be the

wet blanket that snuffed out the fire of enthusiasm in her dad's new hobby, but a person couldn't be too careful nowadays. Hadn't Patrick learned that lesson the summer before, when a man he'd thought he could trust had turned on him and Jacob Cutter while they'd searched for the *Noble?*

She put down a photo of Joseph Ferris's haunting watercolor *Momentum* and pivoted toward the door. And came nose to nose with her father.

"Meghan."

"Dad." Meghan crossed her arms and did her best imitation of Caitlin. It must have worked, because a deep red stain crept out from under the collar of her father's oxford shirt and worked its way to his cheekbones.

Patrick coughed. "Ah…I was wondering where you were."

I'll bet you were.

"It's three o'clock. Tea and cookie time."

"My watch must be slow," Patrick muttered.

Meghan sighed and decided to stop being Evie. And Caitlin. Especially Caitlin. Her suspicions were ridiculous. This was her father. Patrick McBride. The absentminded professor. Mr. Integrity himself.

"Why the sudden interest in Joseph Ferris, Dad? And please tell me that you aren't planning to supplement your retirement income by becoming an art thief." Meghan laughed.

Patrick didn't. Instead he gave her a thoughtful look. "Do you think it falls under the label of *stealing* if a person is taking something back that technically belonged to them in the first place?"

Meghan groped for the plate of Oreos she'd set on the desk. "Does the something that *technically* belongs to someone else happen to be a work by Ferris?"

"Yes."

Meghan shoved a cookie in her mouth. Never mind twisting the two sides apart and delicately scraping out the cream center. "You're going to...to *steal* a Joseph Ferris?"

Patrick smiled. "Of course not. I wouldn't begin to know what an authentic Ferris even looks like."

"Well, that's a relief—"

"That's why I was hoping you'd do it."

"Let me get this straight." An hour later Meghan had a new appreciation for Evie's suspicions about their dad's dedication to his side business. Her younger sister had tried to warn her, after all. "A woman named Nina Bonnefield contacted you by e-mail, claiming she knew Ferris personally. He supposedly left a gift for her on an estate he visited in northern Wisconsin almost *twenty years* ago. And she hired you to find it for her."

"That's it in a nutshell," Patrick said, way too cheerfully in Meghan's opinion.

Of their own volition, Meghan's fingers walked across the desk toward the plate of Oreos. Until she realized she'd eaten them all. "Why doesn't this Nina Bonnefield go back to the estate and retrieve it herself? If it really belongs to her."

There, she'd said it.

"That's…complicated."

Of course it was. "Dad, this whole thing sounds kind of fishy to me. You said she isn't even sure if the gift Ferris left for her was a painting. Maybe it was a coffee mug. Or a souvenir toothpick holder."

"For reasons Nina—*Ms. Bonnefield*—can't share, she can't go back. That's why she needs my help. There's a rumor the island is going up for sale and—"

"Wait a second. Did you say *island?*" Meghan interrupted.

"The Halloway estate is on a private island on Blue Key Lake, near the Chequamegon National Forest. It's been in the family for years but they closed it up in the late eighties."

Halloway. Halloway. The name stirred up something in Meghan's subconscious, but another thought darted in and pushed that one aside for the moment.

"So Nina is somehow related to the family that owns the island?"

Patrick's gaze bounced around the room and finally came to rest on Meghan. "No offense, but I promised Ms. Bonnefield I'd keep that part confidential. Jacob and I checked out her story, and both of us believe she's telling the truth. She sent me a copy of the letter from Ferris and it does sound as if he left something for her. A thank-you of some sort for her friendship and encouragement."

"That would be some thank-you," Meghan muttered. "His paintings are valuable?"

"Paintings, drawings, sculptures. He dabbled in everything. Ferris is one of those artists who gained fame postmortem. By the time the critics finally noticed him and acknowledged his genius, he was in the final stages of pancreatic cancer. The collection of his work isn't all that sizable because his career was short, so what's out there got snapped up right away. If there's still one floating around, I'm sure someone would have noticed. It may have already been sold."

"Or tucked away in a closet on an estate in northern Wisconsin."

And Meghan thought *she* was an optimist.

She tucked her teeth into her bottom lip and tried to figure out a way to discourage her father from getting himself into a potentially sticky situation. And helping oneself to a valuable piece of art definitely fell into that category, no matter who claimed ownership. "There has to be a way Nina Bonnefield can find out if the Ferris is there without involving *you*."

"There is a reason, but I can't tell you what it is. It's—"

"Confidential. I know." She hated to ask the obvious. "So what's your plan?"

Patrick's eyes lit up and Meghan tried not to groan. Somehow she knew she wasn't going to like the answer.

"The house is going to be opened up temporarily for a family wedding in a few weeks. According to my sources—"

Meghan blinked. *His sources?*

"—after the wedding, the Halloways plan to auction off the contents of the house before the actual sale of the island goes through. From what I've heard, the family used to be quite a patron of the arts. There's a sizable collection of paintings and sculptures there. I'm more familiar with antiques, so I wouldn't be much help."

Meghan's eyes narrowed. She had a background in art. She remembered what *her* dad had initially said about *her* finding the Ferris. She'd assumed he'd been kidding. Now she wasn't so sure.

"Dad, please tell me you aren't thinking I'm a shoo-in for the job."

"Of course not, sweetheart." Patrick looked surprised by the suggestion. "I told Ms. Bonnefield you're a photographer."

That much was true. Meghan relaxed a little, relieved she and her dad were on the same page. It didn't sound like either of them would be of much use to the mysterious Ms. Bonnefield. Thank goodness.

"So she decided to find someone else to play Nancy Drew?"

"Not quite." Patrick plucked off his glasses and rubbed them against his shirttail.

Warning bells suddenly went off in Meghan's head. That particular gesture meant her father was either nervous—or stalling. *"Daaaad?"*

"I had no idea she was going to pull a few strings."

"What *kind* of strings?"

"Parker Halloway has hired you as her wedding photographer."

"Wedding..." Meghan surged to her feet. "I don't photograph *people*. Didn't you tell Ms. Bonnefield that?"

"I did." Patrick smiled. "But she made you an offer I couldn't refuse."

* * *

Meghan's teeth rattled in her head as the small fishing boat bounced over the waves toward Blue Key Island. She kept her gaze trained on the slate-shingled roof peeking through a shield of poplar trees. Proof, at least, that one of Nina Bonnefield's claims was true. The Halloway house really did exist.

Meghan sincerely hoped the woman hadn't been making up the rest of the story.

She still couldn't believe she'd adjusted her work schedule to accommodate a visit to the Halloway estate in the first place. But like Joshua scoping out the Promised Land, a reconnaissance mission was all Meghan would agree to. Unlike her father, she didn't trust a woman who'd suddenly appeared out of cyberspace, claiming a friendship with a famous artist but not willing to disclose the nature of her sketchy relationship with the Halloways. Or why she couldn't simply knock on the door and ask for her property back.

It took several days of negotiations with Patrick, but in the end Ms. Bonnefield had reluctantly accepted Meghan's terms. If Meghan happened to spot an authentic Ferris hanging on the wall, it was up to its owner to figure out a way to claim it.

Meghan didn't trust Ms. Bonnefield but she trusted her dad. And it wasn't his fault that the thought of hunting for a work of art wasn't nearly as nerve-racking as playing wedding photographer. Even though she couldn't argue with Patrick's assertion that it made sense for her to be in a position where she could wander around the island—and the house—with a camera.

The boat tripped over a wave and Meghan grabbed the side to steady herself.

"It's a little choppy today," Verne Thatcher shouted above the roar of the outboard motor. "Storm's moving in quicker than they predicted."

Meghan glanced from the grizzled old fishing guide to the batting of dark clouds unfolding across the sky.

She and Patrick had spent the better part of the afternoon roaming through the sleepy little town of Willoughby, trying to find someone with a boat who was willing to take her across. With a major thunderstorm in the forecast, no one seemed eager to go out on the water. Or maybe it had something to do with the reason for Meghan's trip to the island.

Judging from the closed expressions on the faces of the locals whenever Meghan and Patrick mentioned the name *Halloway,* it was clear the family wasn't going to win any popularity contests. Meghan didn't want to speculate as to the reason why.

Close to giving up, they'd settled into a booth at the local diner to discuss their options when a shadow fell across Meghan's laminated menu.

The man standing beside their table was short and wiry, with features that looked as if they'd been carved from a piece of teak. Dressed from head to toe in field khaki, the only thing that prevented him from looking like a game warden was the Hawaiian-print handkerchief casually knotted at his throat.

He flicked the brim of his hat, which was studded with fishing lures. "Hear you're looking for a boat to the island. We better get there before the rain does."

Meghan barely had time to kiss her dad goodbye before Verne Thatcher tossed her suitcase into the back of his rusty pickup and hoisted her into the cab, where she found herself wedged between two damp, liver-spotted spaniels named Smith and Wesson.

Now, close enough to the island to see the dock jutting out from the gentle contours of the shoreline, a fresh crop of doubts stirred up the butterflies in Meghan's stomach. Just as a raindrop splashed against the back of her hand.

"Someone expecting you?" Verne barked the question as he eased back on the throttle and the boat agreeably slowed down.

"Yes."

It was the truth. They just weren't expecting her to arrive a full week before the wedding.

She'd talked to Parker Halloway's wedding planner, a young woman named Bliss Markham, on the phone the day before and told her that she wanted to come a few days early to find the best spots for a photo shoot. Bliss thought it was a marvelous idea. She'd even repeated the word *marvelous* several times. In the same sentence.

Listening to the woman's fake British accent fade in and out, Meghan thought it was a good thing her father had drafted her for the mission instead of Caitlin. Caitlin would have made mincemeat out of Bliss Markham.

According to Bliss, she wouldn't be the only one on the island. The caretaker, a man the wedding planner had simply referred to as "Bert" and who apparently lived on the estate year-round, was also expecting a landscape team hired to spruce up the grounds and a cleaning service to tackle the inside of the house.

Verne muttered something under his breath. "When I pull up to the dock, jump out and grab your stuff."

Meghan blinked. "Why?"

Verne pointed to the sky, where lightning flickered in the underbelly of a dark bank of clouds. "That's why."

Meghan quickly judged the distance between the dock and the house now visible through the trees. Her breath caught in her throat as she got a close look at it for the first time. She'd never believed in love at first sight. Until now.

For some reason she'd expected the Halloway estate to be a typical north-woods vacation home hewn from rustic logs. Instead it looked as if someone had plucked a château out of the French countryside and deposited it on an island in the middle of a chilly Wisconsin lake.

Meghan forgot about the rain as her eyes absorbed the two-story house painted a sleepy blue, with faded poppy-red shutters and a multicolored slate roof.

Smith and Wesson roused from their nap and lifted their noses, sniffing the air. Then looked accusingly at Meghan.

She figured out why a few seconds later when the heavens opened up.

"Mr. Thatcher, you should come with me up to the house until the rain stops," she shouted over the pelting rain.

Verne's eyebrows met over the bridge of his nose. "No, thanks. I'll take my chances on the water," he shouted back.

Before Meghan could respond to the cryptic remark, her suitcase sailed out of the boat and bounced onto the dock. She had no choice but to follow it. When she turned to thank Verne for his trouble, the boat was already spearing a path through the waves toward the opposite shore.

Meghan lifted the suitcase and held it over her head. The lopsided old boathouse built on stilts over the water wasn't nearly as charming as the château, but it was probably dry.

The light show dancing in the clouds above her head helped make up her mind. Meghan tucked the camera bag under the hem of her shirt and made a break for it.

Fumbling with the rusty latch, she shouldered the door of the boathouse open and tossed her suitcase in first to protect the bag of Oreos she'd stashed inside of it.

Her eyes adjusted to the gloom of the boathouse more quickly than her nose adjusted to the musty smell emanating from a mound of moldy life jackets stacked in the corner.

From the sound of the rain battering the window, Meghan guessed she'd be stuck here awhile. She wrung the water out of her hair, wrestled a sweatshirt out of the bottom of the suitcase and pulled it on over her wet T-shirt. Picking through a mishmash of garden furniture, she unearthed an old wicker rocking chair. Minus the cushion.

Meghan settled into it and tucked the headphones from her iPod into her ears, while she attacked the first row of cookies, vowing to stop after four. Or five.

Closing her eyes, Meghan let the praise music wash over her. If she couldn't work in her studio, music was the next best thing to guide her thoughts back to God. And at the moment, she knew she needed a long conversation with Him so she wouldn't unravel at the seams.

I don't have a clue what you have planned, Lord, but here I am. Or here am I, as Isaiah would say. I'd rather photograph animals than people, but I want to help out Dad. For some reason he thinks Ms. Bonnefield is a wounded soul—and you know Dad can never turn his back on a wounded soul.

Something she and her father had in common.

Meghan's "Amen" came out in a yawn, reminding her she'd been up since dawn. She pushed aside the package of Oreos and decided to rest her eyes for a minute. When the rain subsided, she'd find the caretaker and explain why she'd shown up a week early.

The lightning had moved *inside* the boathouse.

Meghan's eyelashes fluttered and she realized she must have dozed off for a few minutes. Confused, she blinked at the bright beam of light aimed directly at her face. It wasn't lightning. It was a flashlight.

Panic suddenly slammed her heart against her chest.

Because on the other end of the flashlight was a... man. The shadows obscured his features but she could see the broad outline of his shoulders as he loomed above her.

She struggled to sit up, shielding her eyes with one hand.

"Are you the caretaker?" She croaked. Rats. What was his name? She couldn't remember. "Mr. Um…"

The light suddenly shifted from her face, trailing a path down her soggy frame and lingering a moment on the package of Oreos balanced on her knee.

"Bert," he finally said.

Meghan wondered if all the men in the area had something against speaking in complete sentences. She plucked the headphones out of her ears—no wonder she hadn't heard him sneak up on her—and pushed her fingers self-consciously through her tangled curls.

Way to make a first impression, Megs. Soaking wet and sound asleep. And probably smelling a bit more like Smith and Wesson than a person in polite company should smell.

Not that the present company seemed very polite…

She took a deep breath. "It's nice to meet you. I'm Meghan McBride."

"You're the…wedding planner?"

Meghan's laugh rippled around the boathouse. He thought she was Bliss Markham? Caitlin would be on the floor when she heard that one.

"No. I'm the wedding *photographer*."

Chapter Two

And Cade had assumed the day couldn't possibly get any worse.

Since breakfast, he'd had three phone calls from his aunt Judith, all reminding him about wedding details he'd rather forget. The owner of a local landscaping business had been next, telling him they were backing out of the agreement "for reasons they'd rather not discuss." This meant Aunt Judith had been calling them with reminders, too. But they had the luxury of being able to simply walk away from her constant micromanaging. Unlike Cade, who was family. All he could do was exercise the self-control his father had spent years developing in him and attempt to bring some sanity into the nightmare everyone else insisted on referring to as a wedding.

In the afternoon he'd had a surreal twenty-minute conversation with a woman named Bliss Markham, whose voice fluctuated between a clipped British accent one minute and a Southern drawl the next.

And then he'd lost the dog.

And accidentally found the wedding photographer.

He hadn't even known his sister had hired one. The last he'd heard, Parker had decided against a professional photographer and wanted disposable cameras available for the guests. Cade had a hunch Aunt Judith had had something to do with the latest reversal in plans.

His lips twisted. Aunt Judith had something to do with most of the changes made in the past few weeks. When she hadn't been able to change Parker's mind about her choice of a groom, she'd retaliated by attempting to take over everything else instead.

Not that Cade blamed her. It was a Halloway family trait they all shared to some degree.

A polite cough yanked his attention back to the moment. And to the woman sprawled in the wicker chair.

Staring down at Meghan McBride, Cade pushed aside the unwelcome thought that she looked like a pre-Raphaelite model come to life. Oval face. Wide-spaced, gray-green eyes. Damp copper curls spilling over her shoulders. The only thing that didn't fit was the wide, engaging smile on her face.

Cade suddenly realized she'd extended her hand. Time to play nice. He reached out and closed his fingers around hers, but instead of immediately releasing his grip, he drew her to her feet.

It was getting late and he still had to find the dog.

Something hit the floor and Meghan McBride gave a startled yelp. Cade pointed the flashlight down and watched sandwich cookies roll away in every direction.

Meghan's sigh echoed around the room. "Did you ever have one of those days?"

Cade turned toward the door, surprised by a sudden urge to smile. "Never."

"Right." The undercurrent of laughter in her voice sent Cade off balance. And he wasn't sure he liked the feeling.

There'd been more than enough upheaval in his life over the past few weeks. The only reason he'd returned to the island was to tour the estate before meeting with the Realtor. He hadn't voluntarily signed up for his sister's unexpected waltz down memory lane, but when Parker had gotten wind of his plan to sell Blue Key Island, she'd insisted on getting married there.

At least one of them had fond memories of the place.

"I guess I must have dozed off for a few minutes." Meghan McBride's voice had the kind of lilting cadence that sounded as if she were reciting poetry. It should have been annoying. But it wasn't. It was…soothing.

Cade circled the flashlight on the wall until he spotted the switch, hidden beneath a stained baseball cap on a hook just above it. He'd avoided the boathouse since his arrival, but suddenly a hat brought back a whole lot of memories he didn't have the energy or desire to sort through at the moment. Maybe never.

He flipped the light on and turned his attention back to Meghan. Her lips moved as she silently counted the number of edible cookies left in the package.

"Care to explain why you're in the boathouse?" *And why I didn't have a clue you were arriving today?*

"It started to rain the minute we docked. This was closer than the house."

"Who brought you over?" Cade took a quick inventory of Meghan's belongings—a small suitcase, a duffel bag and a camera case—and wondered where she'd stowed the rest of her things.

"Mr. Thatcher," she murmured distractedly.

"Verne Thatcher?"

The incredulous note in the caretaker's voice made Meghan lose count. She glanced up at him and felt the same jolt of stunned surprise when she'd caught her first glimpse of the house.

The man scowling at her didn't *look* like a caretaker. Or a *Bert*.

When Bliss had mentioned the estate's caretaker, Meghan's imagination had immediately conjured up a middle-aged, scruffy-looking hermit in practical coveralls who puttered around the lonely estate, making sure the pipes didn't freeze in the winter.

So much for her imagination.

This caretaker wasn't middle-aged…or scruffy-looking. Unless a person considered the faint shadow that outlined his angular jaw *scruffy*. And Meghan decided, charitably, not to. Hair as dark and sleek as an otter's pelt lay flat against his head, a testimony to the fact she hadn't been the only one caught in the downpour earlier.

The pristine-white polo shirt and tan cargo pants he wore looked more suitable for an afternoon of sailing than for physical labor, but it was Friday. Maybe he had the weekends off.

"You said *Thatcher* brought you over?"

Meghan had been so distracted by the man's looks she'd forgotten he'd asked her a question. And then their eyes met and she found herself distracted all over again. Given his coloring, his eyes should have been chocolate-brown. Or hazel. Not a startling shade of dark blue that reminded her of a summer sky right after sunset.

He arched a brow and Meghan's face heated. "We met Mr. Thatcher at the café in Willoughby," she said quickly.

"We?"

"My dad and I." Meghan watched the cobalt eyes narrow and guessed the reason. He probably thought his peaceful island had come under siege. "We didn't know where to leave my car, so Dad dropped me off until after the wedding."

"Is the wedding ever going to be over?" he muttered, plowing his fingers through his hair as he stalked toward the door. Meghan assumed it was a hypothetical question. "You can go up to the house until I figure out where to put you. There's a fire in the library."

"What are you going to do?"

He threw an impatient look over his shoulder. "I lost…something. And I have to find it before it gets any later."

Meghan scrambled to collect her belongings and managed to squeeze through the door just before it closed. She hurried to catch up with him. "I'll help you."

There wasn't a hitch in his long-legged stride. "Not necessary, Miss McBride."

"Two are better than one, for they have a good return for their work." It was a verse from Ecclesiastes Meghan liked to use to encourage Caitlin when she went into control-freak mode. He shot Meghan a look that should have sent her scurrying for cover. If she was the scurrying kind. Which she wasn't.

"We're...*I'm*...looking for a dog. A spoiled-rotten, annoying, undisciplined dog."

Meghan would have laughed except it looked as if he meant every word. "Does this, um, spoiled, annoying, undisciplined dog have a name?"

"Of course it has a name," he replied irritably.

Someone had definitely skipped the Mister Rogers' episode about good manners. "Dogs *have* been known to respond when their owner calls their name."

"That might work. *If* I were the ungrateful rodent's owner."

The animal lover in Meghan rose up in immediate protest. Points for good looks, major demerits for the rodent comment.

"What kind of dog is it?" Meghan followed him onto a footpath that disappeared into the woods. Only the flashlight beam Bert swept back and forth kept her from tripping over the roots that had erupted through the hard-packed soil.

"I told you."

"You told me it was annoying and spoiled—"

"And undisciplined."

"Right." Meghan cleared her throat. "That may or may not describe its temperament. But what *breed* of dog is it?"

"Some kind of powder-puff thing." The words came out grudgingly.

"I don't think the American Kennel Club officially registers those." Meghan heard a snort from the shadow moving ahead of her.

She stumbled over another root and dropped the duffel bag she now wished she'd left at the boathouse. Pressing a hand to the stitch in her side, she made an executive decision. She put her fingers between her lips and let loose a piercing whistle.

The flashlight beam pooled on the path and then swung in her direction. "If you wanted to get my attention, all you had to do was tap me on the shoulder."

Meghan planted her hands on her hips. "Actually, I'm trying to get the *dog's* attention. But it would help if I knew his name."

Silence.

"This is crazy, Mr...." Was Bert his first or last name? She had no idea. "He could be two feet away—" *Hiding from you.* "But if the storm scared him, he won't come out unless he hears a familiar voice call his name."

"It's a she," he finally said. "Miss Molly. And please don't sing the words to the song," he added swiftly. "It's been done before. Frequently."

Meghan hummed a bar instead and heard Bert groan. She grinned, not sure why she took such delight in irritating him. She didn't even know the man. "Thank you. Now we're getting somewhere. *Miss Molly—*"

Her lips had barely gotten the words out when a small, furry object suddenly hurtled out of the brush and bumped against her leg, whimpering. Meghan lifted Miss Molly up and cuddled the animal against her chest.

From the shape of the dog and its soft coat, she guessed it was a bichon. "I think I found her."

He turned around and strode back down the path, eyeing the bedraggled animal in disgust when he reached Meghan's side. "It's about time."

You're welcome, Meghan thought. If he would have swallowed his manly pride and simply called the dog by her name, they probably wouldn't have had to trek through the woods to find her.

Miss Molly wiggled in Meghan's arms and gazed adoringly at Bert.

Hey, who was the one who rescued you? Meghan wanted to remind her. *This guy called you a rodent....*

Bert stripped off his lightweight nylon jacket and tucked it around the dog. Then he took Meghan's duffel bag and slung it over his shoulder. "Let's go."

Meghan smiled as she followed him back down the trail. So there *was* a heart beating underneath the little polo player embroidered on his shirt.

When they emerged from the woods, Bert ignored the flagstone path and cut across the yard toward the house. Meghan could see a collection of strange silhouettes in the shadows and silently kicked herself for falling asleep in the boathouse. Now she'd have to wait until morning to explore the island.

"Did you find her?" Light spilled onto the grass as a woman suddenly appeared in the doorway.

"We found her," Bert replied tersely.

"We?"

Meghan felt a sudden urge to jump behind a shrub as the woman's head turned in her direction. For the hundredth time that day she wondered what she'd gotten herself into. Or, more accurately, what had her dad and Nina Bonnefield gotten her into? And why had she agreed?

Because Ms. Bonnefield had somehow figured out that while Meghan wouldn't be swayed by a generous personal check, the offer of a sizable donation to a ministry close to her heart would tip the balance in her favor.

"Come inside, both of you. You must be soaked to the skin." The woman stepped back as they reached the semicircle of flagstones in front of the weathered red door. The elements had stripped most of the original paint away and left the lion's head door knocker tarnished.

What exactly was the caretaker taking care of? That's what Meghan wanted to know.

She unveiled Miss Molly and the little dog almost leaped out of her arms when she spotted the other woman standing in the hall.

Their reunion gave Meghan a chance to covertly study Miss Molly's owner. She looked to be in her late fifties, but the combination of a petite figure and ash-blond hair, shot with silver and cut in a short, low-maintenance style, gave her an almost pixielike appearance.

"I take it she belongs to you." Meghan gently eased the dog into the woman's arms but not before Miss Molly swiped Meghan's cheek in a polite doggy thank-you.

"She does, but over the past few days, I think she's

decided she'd rather belong to *him*." The woman's eyes sparkled behind delicate gold-framed glasses. "That's how she got lost. She snuck out of the house and went looking for her new friend."

Meghan hid a smile when Bert winced.

"Follow me. I have a fire going in the library. I know it's the middle of summer but on nights like this, there's nothing more comforting than a cup of tea in front of the fireplace."

Meghan liked the woman immediately.

"I'm Meghan McBride. The wedding photographer." Maybe if she said it often enough, it would eventually sink in.

"Elizabeth Ward. But call me Bert—everyone does."

"Bert?" Meghan frowned.

"I'm the caretaker here."

"But he told me that *he* was the caretaker." Confused, Meghan shot a glance at the man who'd dropped into the chair closest to the fire and stretched out his long legs.

The woman frowned and shook her head. "Cade, what on earth are you up to?"

Meghan glowered at him. *Yes, Cade, what are you up to?*

"I didn't tell you I was the caretaker," he said mildly. "You couldn't remember the name, so I simply told you what it was. Filled in the blank, so to speak."

Meghan silently replayed their conversation and re-alized he was right. Drat the man. But he must have known she'd assume he was Bert and he hadn't both-ered to correct her. "Then who are you?"

"Cade Halloway."

"Cade *Halloway,*" she repeated. "But that means—"

The sudden glint in his eyes did nothing to calm the sudden surge in her heart rate as he finished the sentence she couldn't.

"I'm your boss."

Meghan stared up at the ceiling, wrapped in a cocoon of butter-soft blankets, and wondered if she could swim to shore before anyone noticed she was missing.

Cade Halloway's unexpected presence on the island was a glitch she hadn't been prepared for.

A very attractive glitch.

Meghan ruthlessly pushed the thought aside. Maybe he was attractive but he seemed way too serious and uptight. And he had the same keen, watchful look in his eyes that Caitlin had. The kind that said nothing got past him.

It would make her reconnaissance mission that much harder.

Meghan knew there'd be family members arriving for the wedding, but she'd hoped to have enough time to wander freely around the house and grounds without raising anyone's suspicions. On the day of the wedding, she'd smile, snap some photos, convince her father there was no Ferris on the premises and go home.

Meghan shifted restlessly and lavender stirred the air. She inhaled deeply and burrowed into the feather mattress. The upstairs room she'd been assigned to, a cozy nook tucked under the slanted eaves, was perfect. Thanks to Bert. There'd been a few uncomfortable moments in the library when Cade Halloway had suggested

Meghan spend the night in one of the small cabins located on the other side of the island. Bert insisted on putting her up in the main house.

"The cleaning service hasn't shown up yet and those cabins are first on the list. They haven't been aired out in years. Meghan wouldn't sleep a wink."

"Oh, I don't think Miss McBride has trouble falling asleep," Cade had murmured.

The memory of Cade catching her napping in the boathouse instantly surfaced. But even though Meghan now knew who he was, she refused to be intimidated. So she'd smiled sweetly and agreed with him.

"I'm sure they're full of mice." Bert, bless her heart, had tried again.

Cade had shrugged. "Miss McBride seems to like rodents."

Meghan had choked back a protest while Bert folded her arms across her bright red Wisconsin Badgers sweatshirt. "Cade, there are plenty of empty rooms in the house. You can't possibly—"

"Please, I don't want to be a bother." Meghan saw the light of battle in Bert's eyes and jumped into the fray. Even though Bert seemed to be comfortable enough with Cade Halloway to call him by his first name, she didn't want to get the woman into trouble with her employer. "You weren't expecting me to show up this early. I can sleep right here on the sofa...."

"That's not necessary." Cade had abruptly risen to his feet, his expression remote. "Bert will get you settled and in the morning, you can tell me about yourself. And how Parker found you."

Meghan plopped a pillow over her head, stifling a groan. No wonder she couldn't sleep.

She couldn't tell Cade Halloway either of those things.

Chapter Three

Cade woke up to the haunting, liquid cry of a loon on the lake.

Forty-eight hours ago, his alarm clock had been the low keen of sirens and the rhythmic pulse of rush-hour traffic outside the window of his condo in St. Paul.

He glanced at his watch and closed his eyes. Ordinarily he'd be showered, dressed and pulling into the Starbucks' drive-thru by now. Not still horizontal in the twin bed he'd slept in as a child. Even the comforter was familiar—a lumpy bundle of goose down sandwiched between two soft pieces of flannel.

Cade's nose twitched. The blanket even *smelled* the same. A pleasing blend of sunshine and cedar that whisked him back in time. Whether he wanted to go there or not.

In fact, it seemed as if the entire estate had been frozen in some sort of time capsule. Nothing had been updated. Or repaired. Even though Cade knew no one in his family had set foot on Blue Key in years, he'd still been shocked at how neglected the house looked when he'd arrived. The paint on the shutters had bubbled and faded. Scabs of dark moss crusted the roof. The flower gardens his mother had lovingly tended during their summer visits had turned into a matted tangle of weeds.

Douglas Halloway, Cade's father, had refused to sink a penny into the place for twenty years. Except for the generous weekly paychecks mailed to Bert.

Bert.

Cade winced and closed his eyes. He hadn't seen her for years—had to admit he'd all but forgotten his mother's best friend—but from the moment he'd stepped onto the dock, she'd fussed over him as if he were ten years old again. It didn't seem to matter that his presence on Blue Key Island meant she was about to lose both her job and her home.

Cade reminded himself that Bert had to have known the estate would eventually be sold. And she'd been well-compensated over the years for simply *living* in the house. But knowing those things still didn't prevent him from feeling like a first-class jerk.

Especially when Bert treated him with the same indulgent affection and warmth she had when he was a boy, scratched and dirty from climbing the birch tree on the point or dripping water on the floor as he raided the refrigerator for an afternoon snack.

He hadn't given Bert more than a few hours' notice about his arrival…or Parker's upcoming wedding…and yet she'd hugged him fiercely when he'd arrived and told him that he had his mother's eyes.

Cade was glad his father hadn't been there to hear

Bert's observation. He'd spent years making sure his children didn't resemble Genevieve in any way. But not even Douglas Halloway, as powerful as he was, could change the color of a person's eyes.

The sun shifted a fraction of an inch, recreating a stencil of the lace curtain on the scuffed hardwood floor. For the first time Cade noticed a water stain in the corner of the ceiling above the window and mentally adjusted the price of the house. Again.

Whoever bought the island would probably raze the place and put up a structure more suited to its surroundings. He hadn't listed the island with a Realtor yet, but already he'd had inquiries from a developer interested in building a luxury lodge catering to executives-turned-weekend-anglers.

Guys like him.

Not that it mattered what happened to the place after it sold, Cade reminded himself. He had a job to do and the sooner he wrapped things up, the sooner he could get back to civilization. And his business. It had taken a long time for Douglas to turn over the reins to the family's architectural firm and Cade didn't want his father to regret the decision.

Murmured voices, followed by a ripple of delighted laughter, drifted under the door. And worked its way right under his skin.

Meghan McBride. Memories of the evening before came rushing back to Cade and guilt sawed briefly against his conscience. He hadn't exactly been a model host. Okay, he'd been downright rude. He wasn't sure why he hadn't told her who he was when they'd met in the boathouse. Maybe he could put it down to a day that had, thanks to Aunt Judith and a bichon frise that wouldn't let him out of her sight, spiraled out of control. And Cade didn't like it when things got out of control.

Or when something disrupted his concentration. And at the moment, his concentration centered on getting the estate ready to sell. He didn't have time to play the attentive host. Not even to the wedding photographer. Maybe *especially* to the wedding photographer, whose winsome smile just might make him forget he hadn't come to Blue Key to relax and enjoy the scenery.

After he interviewed Meghan and discovered why she'd shown up a full week before the wedding, he'd settle in behind the old oak secretary in the library and start making a list of the contents of the house. And try to hire a new landscaper.

The unmistakable smell of bacon and maple syrup teased his senses and Cade pushed himself out of bed, resigning himself to renewing his gym membership when he got back to the Cities. He'd forgotten how much Bert loved to cook. The day before she'd caught a stringer of bluegills off the dock and fried them up for supper in a cast-iron skillet the size of a hubcap.

He'd told Bert he didn't expect her to cook for him, but she wouldn't listen. In fact, she'd informed him in no uncertain terms that she got tired of cooking for one and he should just "simmer down" and let her spoil someone besides Miss Molly for a change.

And judging from the feminine laughter coming from the kitchen, it sounded as though Bert had added another person to her list of people to spoil.

Good. If Bert kept Meghan McBride company, he wouldn't have to.

Fifteen minutes later Cade padded into the kitchen. Meghan stood guard at the stove, tending Bert's favorite skillet. Barefoot and wearing loose-fitting jeans with a white shirt knotted at her waist, she didn't look old enough to be an established businesswoman.

But her unconventional clothing wasn't what made Cade's breath hitch in his throat. The night before she'd looked as wet and bedraggled as Miss Molly. But the hair he'd assumed was auburn had dried, lightening to an incredible shade of strawberry blond that fell in a tangle of curls to the middle of her back. He couldn't think of one woman in his circle of friends who would let her hair grow to that length. Especially Amanda, who scheduled her six-week appointments at a trendy salon a year in advance.

But then again, he couldn't think of anyone who'd wear what looked like a man's dress shirt and jeans to an interview, either.

Cade frowned. Maybe Meghan McBride didn't realize that although Parker had hired her, he had the final say as to whether or not she *stayed* hired.

Without turning around, Meghan knew the exact second Cade walked into the kitchen. And it wasn't because of the subtle, musky scent of his cologne or the husky "good morning" he growled at Bert.

It was because the skin on her arms prickled.

She had goose bumps.

And Meghan *never* got goose bumps.

Rattled, Meghan scanned the counter for the pancake turner but couldn't remember what she'd done with it.

"It's in your apron pocket," Cade said helpfully.

Meghan opened her mouth to argue that she wouldn't put a cooking utensil in her pocket, but glanced down first, just in case he was right. And he was. Why did she get the feeling that Cade Halloway was always right?

Bert cruised past with a platter of hash browns and scrambled eggs, pausing long enough to flip on the fan in the hood above the range. "All set, Meghan?"

Meghan nodded, even though she was pretty sure she wouldn't be able to eat a bite of Bert's fabulous breakfast.

Once they were seated, every time Cade's unnerving cobalt gaze settled on her across the table, she knew he was silently questioning her qualifications. She refilled her plate—frequently—because basic etiquette said it was impolite for a person to talk with their mouth full.

"I can help you clean up, Bert." It would buy her a few extra minutes before Cade's interrogation…Meghan swiftly amended that negative thought…*interview.* That's what it was. An interview.

"Don't be silly. What else do I have to do?" Bert made a shooing motion with her hands. "Cade wants to talk to you and he's not the kind of man who likes to be kept waiting."

Meghan had figured that much out for herself. She hated to make snap judgments about people, but it was Saturday morning and Cade had dressed as if he were on his way to the office. The only thing missing was a conservative silk tie.

So maybe he *had* been blessed with traffic-stopping good looks but he was so…serious. The only time she'd seen the hint of a smile soften his features was when Bert had reminded him that it was *his* turn to catch their supper.

At least if she had to meet with Cade, it would give her an opportunity to pay more attention to the paintings hanging on the library walls.

She took a deep breath and tried to work up a smile.

"Come in, Miss McBride."

She would have, if she hadn't frozen in the doorway. How in the world did Cade manage to lower the temperature in a room as welcoming as the library? Instead of taking one of the chairs by the fireplace like he'd done the night before, he'd positioned himself at an antique secretary to conduct his interrog—*interview*.

"You can call me Meghan." Because it would be harder to fire her if they were on a first-name basis. Wouldn't it?

Cade's eyes narrowed.

Okay, maybe not.

He motioned to a chair but Meghan decided *not* to sit down. It would give him too much of an advantage. Instead she took a casual lap around the perimeter of the room to check out the artwork, sucking in a breath at the some of the signatures she saw. Nina Bonnefield hadn't been exaggerating when she'd told Patrick that the Halloway family supported the arts.

She was used to seeing paintings of this caliber displayed behind a satin rope in a museum or in an upscale gallery, not in a casual arrangement on a backdrop of sun-faded wallpaper.

Her stomach knotted at the sudden realization that maybe there *was* a Ferris somewhere on the premises.

"…found you."

Cade's voice filtered into her thoughts and snagged her attention. Meghan mentally kicked herself for getting lost in the paintings. "I'm sorry. What did you say?"

He frowned slightly. "Maybe we should start with how my sister…found you."

Found her? As if she were a stray cat?

Meghan bit down on her lower lip to prevent a smile. She'd already rehearsed the answer to this question. Her parents had taught her that honesty was the best policy and she'd made a promise to herself—and Ms. Bonnefield—that she wouldn't tell a lie to explain her presence on Blue Key Island.

"The usual way. By referral. An acquaintance of mine heard your sister was looking for a photographer… someone who didn't mind coming this far off the beaten path for a wedding."

He couldn't argue with that, now could he? Not only was Blue Key Island way off the beaten path, a person had to take a boat to get there. And she wasn't even charging them for mileage.

Cade's fingers drummed against the top of the desk. "What studio are you employed with?"

The knot in Meghan's stomach tightened. "I'm a freelance photographer."

"Freelance." Cade repeated the word as if he'd never heard of it.

"That's right. I have my own business."

"Really."

It didn't escape Meghan's notice that Cade's sentences had gotten shorter as the interview progressed.

"I apprenticed with a master photographer for two years before opening my own studio five years ago." Which she ran out of her apartment, but Cade didn't need to know that. As her reputation had spread, she'd begun to travel more frequently but still tried to keep regular business hours.

"But you specialize in weddings."

It sounded more like a statement than a question, but since Cade seemed to be waiting for some sort of response, Meghan gave him a truthful one. "I take pictures of a variety of subjects." *And please don't ask what they are.*

"I'm sure my sister asked for references." Cade's fingers drummed against the top of the desk again.

Meghan simply smiled. She'd never met Parker Halloway in person and she had no idea if Parker had checked out her website. If she had, she would have discovered Meghan McBride *did* photograph a variety of subjects. Most of them just happened to have four legs. And occasionally, feathers.

Cade's eyes met hers and Meghan did her best not to flinch under the cool appraisal. "My sister can be a little… impulsive but she is a stickler for details. When you come back this weekend for the wedding—"

"Come back?" Meghan interrupted without thinking.

"It's only Saturday," Cade reminded her. "Parker and the rest of the wedding party won't arrive until

Friday morning. I assumed you came to check things out today...."

And then leave.

Meghan silently filled in the rest of the sentence Cade Halloway was too polite to finish.

Now what? She needed a legitimate reason to explain her extended stay on the island and not compromise her promise to stick to honesty.

The cry of a loon filtered through the open window and with a flash of inspiration, Meghan found her reason. "I know I'm here early, but I happen to be free this week." Also the truth. "I'd love to photograph some of the wildlife."

The lean fingers on *both* of the man's hands made a series of tapping noises. Meghan realized Cade Halloway didn't vent his emotions. He "drummed" them instead. "I have a lot of work to do. I thought I'd be alone on the island before the wedding chaos started."

What a coincidence. She'd thought the same thing!

"You won't even know I'm here," Meghan added. In spite of his words, she sensed him weakening.

"Somehow I doubt that," Cade said under his breath.

The telephone suddenly rang, saving Meghan from having to respond. Cade reached for it with a terse, "Excuse me," and Meghan took that as a cue their interview was officially concluded.

She slipped out of the library, quietly closed the door and collapsed against the wall.

The Ferris was somewhere in the house.

Cade Halloway was in the house.

Meghan decided it was going to be a very long week.

Chapter Four

Meghan grabbed her camera—just in case Cade saw her—and stepped outside. Into wonderland.

Why hadn't she seen this the day before?

Probably because the pelting rain had forced her to keep her head down. And because she'd been so taken with the house, she'd failed to notice the yard.

Meghan took a hesitant step forward and paused, not sure where to begin. The strange silhouettes she'd seen in the shadows while she'd tripped along after Cade Halloway came to life in the bright morning sun. *Sculptures.* But not the kind a person found in the gardening section of the local discount store.

Meghan's gaze settled on a blue heron created out of angle iron and followed the elegant arch of its neck to the unblinking marble eye and the fish trapped in its beak.

To the right of the heron, a trio of baby raccoons clung to the trunk of a birch tree—their mother perched on a sturdy branch above them. They'd been soldered together with bits and pieces of discarded metal, but each of their masked faces somehow conveyed a different expression.

Automatically, Meghan's feet moved toward a bald eagle, hewn right from the stump of the tree it sat on, poised for flight.

Incredible.

Some of the sculptures were larger than life, but others, like the whimsical turtle made from a clam shell that peeked out from under the broad leaves of a hosta, were so small a person could walk right by and not notice them.

They not only differed in size, they differed in design. Some were primitive, a simple sketch of an animal or bird created with minimal materials, while others were so detailed they looked as if they were about to come to life right in front of her eyes.

She'd studied the works of Joseph Ferris in the car on the way to Willoughby and wondered if she was within reach of one of his creations. Ferris had worked in several mediums but seemed to favor watercolor. And although he'd been a product of the pop art culture of the sixties, he'd been more influenced by the early Impressionists. Meghan guessed that was the reason why his work had gone unnoticed until after his death.

She wandered through the sculpture garden, looking for something that reflected the spare lines and luminous colors Ferris favored.

"Amazing, isn't it?"

Meghan, who'd dropped to her knees to peer at a

stained-glass replica of a dragonfly, started at the sound of a voice behind her.

"I didn't see any of this yesterday." Meghan's heart resumed its natural rhythm and she smiled up at Bert, who stood several feet away with Miss Molly nestled comfortably in the crook of her arm. "And I'm not sure *amazing* describes it." She reached out to pick up the dragonfly and then changed her mind. Maybe *someone* had instigated a No Touch rule.

"Go ahead."

"Are you sure?" Without thinking, Meghan glanced toward the house.

"I'm sure." Bert's low laugh told Meghan she'd guessed the reason behind her hesitation. "Besides, the dragonfly is one of mine."

Meghan picked it up and cradled it in the palm of her hand. "You're an artist?"

"I work with stained glass."

"It's beautiful."

Bert's eyes sparkled at the compliment. "I have a few minutes. I'll take you on a little tour of the island and show you the rest."

"There's more?"

A mysterious smile touched Bert's lips. "Oh, there's more."

Cade put down the phone and blew out a sigh, wondering if a photo of his aunt Judith was being faxed to every landscaping business in the county. He couldn't find anyone willing to come to the island and fix up the grounds before the wedding.

He walked over to the window but found his view almost completely obstructed by a hedge of fragrant arbor vitae desperately in need of a trim.

Without warning, a memory of his mother kneeling on a folded beach towel in the garden returned. While he and Parker had spent summer afternoons fishing for perch or catapulting themselves off the end of the dock, Genevieve had turned the island into an eclectic hodgepodge of gardens and objets d'art. A direct contrast to the formal decor of their house in Minneapolis.

He and Parker had grown up rattling around their father's childhood home in a neighborhood where the air still carried the faint whiff of "old money." Aunt Judith's influence had prevailed even there in the subdued neutrals and the furnishings arranged with museum-like perfection. Genevieve didn't so much as rearrange the jade statues on the mantel above the fireplace, but when Douglas purchased the island she'd practically designed the entire house, decorating it with airy fabrics and bright colors.

In Minneapolis, dinner guests were chosen from his father's business associates and potential clients; the conversation around the table as carefully planned as the menu. On the island, people dropped by with no advance notice and stayed as long as they wanted.

Judith had visited Blue Key only once that Cade could remember. She'd hated the water and the sand, declaring the place a tasteless "amusement park." And she'd never set foot on the island again.

Cade, who'd sensed the tension between his aunt and his mother even as a child, had a hunch Judith's refusal to visit Blue Key was fine with his mother. In fact, it suddenly occurred to him that Genevieve had smiled and laughed more when they were on the island than she had in her own home.

The carousel just beyond the concrete fountain in the center of the courtyard was a testimony to Genevieve's unusual taste. The painted horses had faded and patches of rust stained the metal canopy like a bad rash, but Cade remembered his mother's excitement when she'd discovered it during one of her frequent trips to the salvage yard.

The next time they'd visited the island, there it was.

He'd spent hours playing on it—the horse he "rode" reflecting the adventure he'd chosen to pursue at that particular moment in time. When he wanted to be a cowboy, he jumped on the brown bronco with wild eyes and a lasso painted over the saddle horn. If he was a knight, it was the black horse with its armored headpiece and sword.

Parker always claimed the white horse with a flowing mane and tail. The garland of roses around its neck hinted it was a derby winner, but from Cade's boyish perspective, flowers were flowers and he wasn't going to have anything to do with them.

All the horses were carved out of wood, the paint on the saddles and bridles original. As a piece of American history, the carousel must have been worth a fortune, but Genevieve had let him and Parker scramble on it as if it had been purchased from the back lot of a discount store.

Cade shook his head, not sure why they hadn't gotten rid of the thing years ago. Maybe he could donate it to one of the local museums. He'd been right to come back before listing with a Realtor. The rusted sculpture garden and the unusual objects his mother had collected might detract from the aesthetic value of the property.

He was turning away from the window when he caught a sudden movement out of the corner of his eye. Bert rounded the corner of the house with Meghan one step behind her.

Meghan's chirp of surprise must have had something to do with the carousel because she made a beeline directly over to it. With a delighted smile, she ran her hands up the white horse's face and over its mane as if it were real.

Cade knew he shouldn't be spying but stood there, riveted in place, as Meghan hoisted herself onto its back and wrapped her arms around its neck.

He winced as the camera, hanging by a cord around her neck, slammed against the horse's chest, but it didn't seem to faze her. He would have thought a photographer would be a little more careful with the most important tool of her trade.

When Bert slipped between the horses and fished around inside the mechanical box, Cade's shoulders tensed.

He doubted the thing worked after so many years. Even as a kid, he'd thought the simple tune the carousel played sounded muffled and rather tinny. Like the song a jack-in-the-box played right before a clown popped out of the top.

After a few minutes Bert gave up and Meghan slid

off the horse's back. And headed toward the mermaid fountain. Another one of his mother's salvage-yard finds that had found its way to the island.

Maybe that was why no one in Willoughby would talk to him, Cade thought sourly. No doubt the old-timers remembered having to transport his mother's purchases to the island by fishing boat.

"…it work?" Meghan's lilting voice drifted through the screen as she started to scoop handfuls of wet leaves out of the fountain and drop them on the ground.

The fountain. Cade shook his head. One more reason to talk Parker out of her crazy idea to hold the wedding ceremony and reception on the island. Without an army of landscapers to tackle years of neglect, the place would never be ready for guests by the following weekend.

And Parker would have a fit if she saw the state the house and grounds were in. No doubt she still carried the memories of the way it was when they were children—not realizing Douglas had forbidden Bert to do anything other than the simplest maintenance projects in the house.

Cade still didn't understand why Bert had stayed on. He knew Bert and his mother had been close friends. "Twins separated at birth" was the way Genevieve laughingly introduced Bert to visitors to the island. When he'd asked Douglas why Bert had stayed, his father had brushed aside the question in his typical gruff manner and muttered something about Bert not having anywhere else to go.

That didn't surprise Cade, since Bert belonged to the

group of artists that Genevieve had counted as friends. What surprised him was his father's benevolence. Especially since Douglas had completely wiped out any reminders of Genevieve.

After Cade's mother walked out on them, they'd simply continued on as if Genevieve had never been a part of their lives. Judith had moved into the suite of rooms in the east wing of their home and taken over the household.

And Cade had never seen his mother again.

The one time he'd gathered the courage to ask if she was coming back, the look of raw pain in his father's eyes had discouraged him from ever bringing up the subject again.

Aunt Judith however, hadn't been as silent with her opinions. There'd been anger, not pain, in her voice when she'd explained that Genevieve had found being a wife and mother too confining. That she'd gone back to the lifestyle she was more suited for.

Cade shook away the unwelcome memories that crowded in. The sooner he wrapped things up on the island, the sooner he could leave. All he had to do was convince Parker that without a landscape team working around the clock—for the next six months—Blue Key Island wouldn't be the romantic setting for the wedding of her dreams she imagined it would be.

Cade had never understood, given Douglas's keen business sense, why his father had held on to the island all these years. He'd seen the tax bills. Why keep shelling out money for a place they hadn't visited for years?

When they needed a getaway, they took advantage of their ownership in a luxury time-share.

He'd make sure Bert had a generous retirement package and close this particular chapter of Halloway history for good.

Selling the island was the logical solution.

Meghan couldn't believe Cade wanted to sell the island.

Everywhere she turned she saw evidence that the house and the surrounding grounds had been, at one time, someone's pride and joy.

A fountain, complete with a mermaid perched regally on a pearl inside an algae-stained oyster shell, created the centerpiece of the courtyard. Layers of decaying leaves filled the bowl instead of water and the rusty spout looked as if it hadn't been used in years, but the fountain hadn't lost its charm.

And even though grass had pushed its way through gaps in the stone footpaths and weeds vied with overgrown beds of perennials for sun and soil, when Meghan looked closely she could still see the outline of the garden's original design.

And an honest-to-goodness *carousel* stood in the shade of a sugar maple. She still couldn't get over that.

Meghan unearthed a green penny from the bottom of the fountain and scraped off a thin layer of slime with her thumbnail.

"Did you find something?" Bert asked.

Meghan held out the penny. "Someone forgot their wish."

Bert's smile was pensive as she took the coin from Meghan's hand. "I'm afraid there are a lot of those in there."

"It's such a shame—" Meghan bit back the rest of the sentence. She liked Bert and didn't want the woman to think she was being critical. It would have been impossible for one person to keep up with the maintenance required for a piece of property the size of Blue Key Island.

"Things are in such disrepair?" Bert finished the sentence for her.

"I didn't mean—"

"Don't worry. I know you didn't," Bert interrupted. "Repairs to the house are the only ones I'm able to authorize. To tell you the truth, I'm more like a well-paid, permanent houseguest than a caretaker." There was no undercurrent of bitterness in Bert's tone, only a quiet resignation that wrenched Meghan's heart.

"You must love it here." Meghan did, and she'd only been on the island twenty-four hours.

A spark of humor extinguished the shadows in Bert's eyes. "I love it enough to put up with mosquitoes the size of hummingbirds and the weather. Which, by the way, the locals refer to as nine months of winter and three months of poor skiing."

"You don't get lonely?"

"I have a few close friends in Willoughby who make sure I don't become too much of a hermit. And, of course, I have Miss Molly for company." Bert gave the dog an affectionate cuddle before setting her down on one of the multicolored path stones. Miss Molly immediately bounded toward the house with a joyful bark.

Meghan and Bert exchanged a grin. It wasn't difficult to guess where she was off to.

"We'll let her keep Cade company while I show you the stone cottage."

"Stone cottage?"

"The old studio. Years ago, it was quite the gathering place for the writers and artists who came here for inspiration."

Meghan's heart picked up speed. Artists like Joseph Ferris? Nina Bonnefield's story about a friendship with the man didn't sound so far-fetched anymore.

They hiked almost the entire width of the island until the woods opened up to reveal a flat, grassy area ringed by a stand of birch trees. In the distance, the lake shimmered in a changing pattern of blues and silvers.

Other than a few loose shingles on the roof and the crumbled corners of the foundation, the stone cottage seemed to be in better shape than the main house.

Someone had painted the front door of the cottage with a checkerboard pattern in blue and yellow. A collection of wind chimes harmonized in the trees. Once again, Meghan was charmed by the whimsical decor and wondered who was responsible for it.

They walked past a rocking chair fashioned from willow branches and Meghan couldn't help reaching out and setting it in motion.

Bert caught her. "Maeve Burke made that chair. You've probably never heard of her, but she's a well-known ceramics artist now. She visited Blue Key as a graduate student, when she was still trying to decide if she should pursue a career in art."

Meghan *had* heard of her. Maeve Burke was a native of Minnesota and some of the more exclusive shops carried her designs. In fact, Meghan had splurged and bought Evie and Sam a set of Maeve's signature jade and cream glazed coffee mugs as a wedding gift.

The breeze carried the scent of mint and Meghan spotted it next to the door, planted in an old galvanized washtub along with clusters of parsley and chives spiked with lavender flowers.

"I broke the rules and keep the herb garden weeded," Bert confided. "I love to use them when I cook."

"You rebel." Meghan couldn't resist teasing the older woman.

Bert laughed. "Come in. I have a feeling you'll feel right at home in here."

She was right.

Paintings in a variety of sizes crowded the walls, creating a mural all their own. Meghan gravitated toward a large watercolor in a rustic driftwood frame. She recognized the boathouse where she'd taken refuge from the storm. And met Cade for the first time.

Instant goose bumps again.

What was that about? Meghan impatiently rubbed them away with her fingertips and scanned the corners of the painting until she spotted the artist's name. "Who is G.H.?"

"Genevieve Halloway." Bert walked over and stood beside her.

"Halloway?"

"My best friend. And Cade and Parker's mother."

Chapter Five

"She's very good." Meghan studied the muted colors and delicate brushstrokes.

"Yes." Bert's guarded tone sent a shiver of unease up Meghan's spine.

Now she had no doubt it was Cade's mother's influence she saw everywhere she looked. And she could think of no other reason for the obvious neglect other than Genevieve's...absence.

Bert must have seen the questions in her eyes. "After Genevieve left, Douglas got the island in the divorce settlement. He closed up the place to...visitors...and the family stopped spending summers here. Until Cade showed up a few days ago, I hadn't seen him since he was ten years old."

It explained a lot but left many questions unanswered. And raised a whole host of others. Like why hadn't Douglas ever returned to the island? And why hadn't Bert been forced into exile with the rest of Genevieve's friends? But, Meghan reasoned, if Nina

Bonnefield had, it might explain why she didn't feel comfortable approaching the Halloway family about the gift Joseph Ferris had supposedly left behind for her.

"Genevieve loved Blue Key—I think she considered the island her real home. All the things you see—the gardens, the fountain, the carousel—they're here because of her. I still can't believe everything is going to be auctioned off."

Neither could Meghan. If Cade had spent his childhood summers on the island, why didn't he feel more of a connection to it?

She tried to make sense out of the bits and pieces Bert had shared. It sounded as though Genevieve had been the one who'd instigated the divorce. The house the Halloways loved had been closed up, no longer welcoming friends or providing a peaceful retreat for the family.

With a start, Meghan realized Bert had stopped talking. Probably because she'd noticed Meghan had stopped listening!

"I'm sorry," Meghan said simply. And she was. When Meghan was younger, she'd try to bluff her way through situations like this by smiling, nodding and making eye contact. Or by catching a few words that hadn't sifted through her thoughts and trying to *guess* what the person had just said.

Caitlin had put an end to that one day in her usual, no-nonsense way.

Megs, you zone out on people and they think they're boring you. And then they wonder if they're boring the rest of the world, too. If you lose track of the conversation, just say you're sorry and ask for a recap. Easy.

Not so easy, but Meghan had taken her advice. She didn't want anyone to think they were the reason she was distracted. That's why she preferred working with animals instead of people. Less pressure. They never seemed to mind if her thoughts jumped around or she lost her place in the middle of a conversation.

Growing up, Meghan had been described by her exasperated teachers as sweet, but also "dreamy" and "imaginative." They coaxed her to try harder. To pay attention. When she struggled to remember things she'd read and the lectures she heard, she'd wished she was smarter, like Caitlin and Evie. No matter how often she'd grit her teeth and force herself to concentrate, she had a difficult time staying focused on a task.

Although popular in school, Meghan began to withdraw from social situations where following multiple conversations became stressful and she was afraid people would notice something different about her and she'd be slapped with the "weird" label. Fortunately, her strengths were in the artistic, creative areas so being quirky was more acceptable, but she still couldn't count the number of times she'd heard the familiar greeting "earth to Meghan" uttered by her classmates. She'd laugh…and then stare up at the ceiling at night and cry, wondering why it was so easy to get lost in her own thoughts that she missed what was going on around her.

It wasn't until Meghan was in college that she'd found out she had Attention Deficit Disorder. And she had Evie to thank. Her sister, a high school freshman at the time, had stumbled on the signs of ADD while writing a research paper. For the first time, Meghan understood why she was the way she was. Accepting that ADD wasn't something that would go away, like a bad cold, wasn't as easy.

It had helped when Evie had started to refer to it as Attention Deficit *Design*. She'd carefully written out the verse from Psalm 139 and framed it for Meghan, reminding her that God had designed her and she was "fearfully and wonderfully made."

The day she'd hung it on the wall, Meghan had decided she was going to work with her strengths instead of wishing away what some would view as weaknesses.

Even now, seeing herself mirrored in Bert's friendly gaze, Meghan had to resist the urge to scold herself for letting her thoughts drift away.

"Woolgathering?" Bert smiled. "Don't apologize. I do that myself on occasion."

"Not just gathering," Meghan admitted. "Carding, spinning and turning into sweaters."

Bert laughed and linked her arm through Meghan's. "You remind me of an old friend."

Genevieve? Or maybe Nina Bonnefield?

Meghan was tempted to ask but her dad had made her promise, at Nina's request, that she wouldn't mention his client's name to anyone.

But that hadn't raised any red flags with Patrick. No, of course not.

At this point, Meghan had more questions than answers. Bert seemed to be familiar with the people who'd visited the island. It was possible the two women's paths had crossed. Maybe they'd even been friends. But if that was the case, why wouldn't Nina have contacted Bert directly about the Ferris?

The bottom line was that even though she liked Bert, she didn't know her—or the situation—well enough to disclose any more information. And Bert's first loyalty would be to her employer. Who also happened to have the power to fire Meghan if he took a notion.

"I'm going to start lunch soon, but we can take the long way back to the house, past the cabins," Bert said.

Meghan wanted more time to study the artwork in the studio, but didn't want Bert to get suspicious. She decided to come back later. Alone.

She started to follow Bert when a trio of charcoal sketches, each showcasing the same tree but in a different season, caught her eye. "These aren't signed."

Bert paused. "That's not unusual. The artists who came here weren't under any pressure to produce something salable. Some of them needed a quiet place to think. To share ideas. Creative people find different ways to express themselves. Genevieve understood that. She put as much thought and effort into her gardens as she did in her paintings."

Meghan understood, too. Photography was her first love, but when she wasn't traveling or in the studio, she volunteered with Sidewalk Chalk, a citywide children's art ministry sponsored by local churches. Meghan didn't consider herself a painter, but she loved turning a wall or sidewalk into a mural that brought beauty to a color-hungry neighborhood.

With a sinking heart, she also realized that dozens of unsigned works scattered around the island would make it that much harder to identify an unsigned work by Joseph Ferris.

"I can't count the number of people who came here weary and burned out, but left the island refreshed."

Meghan wondered if that was because of the peaceful surroundings or the woman who'd welcomed them.

"Genevieve…she'll be here for the wedding, won't she?" Meghan had a sudden urge to meet the woman who'd turned an entire island into her own unique art gallery.

"I don't—"

"My mother has missed every milestone in Parker's life for the past twenty years. I doubt she'll break tradition and show up for this one."

Meghan pivoted and saw Cade standing in the doorway.

He had to stop sneaking up on her like that. *She* was supposed to be the one doing the sneaking.

Cade regretted the words as soon they came out of his mouth.

He had enough to do without sorting through the skeletons in the family closet. Especially in front of witnesses.

His eyes locked with Meghan's across the room and he saw a flash of compassion in their velvety-green depths. He looked away. Quickly. In the space of twenty-four hours, Meghan McBride had managed to set foot everywhere on the island he'd been trying to avoid.

He'd decided to talk to Bert about hiring a new landscaping crew, but by the time he'd walked around the house to the courtyard, she and Meghan had disappeared.

Miss Molly, who managed to get herself lost on a regular basis but had a knack for finding *him* at any given moment, had taken over the search. He'd hoped the cabins were her target, but she'd veered off the main path and charged toward the clearing, her destination obvious.

Cade hadn't meant to eavesdrop on their conversation, but they'd left the door standing wide-open and he couldn't help overhearing part of it. Meghan and Bert were in Genevieve's studio, so it didn't surprise him to discover they'd been talking about his mother. What surprised him was the confidence in Meghan's tone when she brought up the wedding. As if there were no doubt that no matter what the circumstances, Genevieve, the mother of the bride, would be attending.

Because that's what a mother would do.

But not his mother.

As if it had taken place yesterday, he remembered the unsettling question Parker had asked him several days after Justin proposed. She'd stopped by the office to coax him into going out for lunch with her and Cade thought he knew what was on his sister's mind. Their aunt hadn't taken the news of Parker's engagement well and she needed him on her side. Judith had plans for her niece's future and none of them included her marrying a missionary with no assets or family connections.

It turned out, however, that Aunt Judith hadn't been the reason she'd wanted to talk to him. She'd waited until they were halfway through dessert before dropping the bomb on him.

Do you think I should let Mom know I'm engaged?

Cade's response had been an immediate *no*. Instead of getting angry or pouting, two tools Parker utilized on a regular basis for getting her way, she'd listened patiently until he'd run out of reasons. And even on such short notice, Cade had been able to come up with quite a few.

Parker hadn't argued with him—another unusual occurrence—and when he'd finally asked her why she'd even consider letting Genevieve know about the wedding, she told him it had been Justin's idea. Apparently her fiancé had strong feelings about lugging "personal baggage from the past" into their future.

Cade had dismissed the idea immediately. It was healthier for people to move forward than to constantly be looking back, trying to make sense of a past they couldn't change.

He'd never understood how their mother could simply walk away from her family and never contact them again, but *she'd* made the choice. And the hole Genevieve's absence had left had slowly closed over the years.

Cade didn't see the point of prying it open again.

Parker had changed the subject after he'd suggested she and Justin deal with any "baggage" during their premarital counseling sessions. But he'd still felt uneasy she'd brought it up at all.

The bottom line was, he didn't want his sister to get hurt. Or rejected. He and Parker were both adults now—if Genevieve wanted to get to know them, there was nothing to prevent her from contacting them. The fact she hadn't could only mean one thing. She didn't want to.

He couldn't remember Parker ever bringing up the subject of Genevieve. He had quite a few memories of her, but Parker, who'd only been six years old when Genevieve left, hadn't understood just what had fractured their family.

Cade envied her. Which was another reason why Parker needed to leave the past in the past...

"Did you need something, Cade?"

Bert's cautious question yanked him back to reality. Once again the past had derailed the present. He blamed Blue Key Island. "A landscaping crew."

"I thought Parker had lined one up."

"She did. But Aunt Judith must have gotten their phone number."

"Ah." Bert, who'd met Aunt Judith once and had probably never forgotten the experience, tried not to smile.

"I've been trying to get in touch with Parker to talk her into having the ceremony at the church instead."

"It's a little late to change the location now, isn't it?" Meghan blurted.

Cade gave her the Look. The one he used to put upstart summer interns in their place. It didn't seem to work on upstart wedding photographers. He gave in. "Until a few weeks ago, Parker and Justin had reserved the church for the wedding. It's probably still available."

"The church might work out, but what about the reception?" Bert frowned. "The country club is booked two years in advance. Especially for a July wedding. I doubt Parker is going to want to hold the reception in the fellowship hall of a church basement."

Cade doubted it, too. Parker had a reputation for wanting—and expecting—the best of the best. He still had a hard time believing his sister had willingly given up her "fairy-tale" wedding—Cade thought the description "high-budget production" more appropriate—to get married on the island. Aunt Judith was still fuming over that decision.

"If Parker saw this place, she'd agree the fellowship hall is more suitable." Cade heard a stifled gasp and arched an eyebrow in Meghan's direction. "Something to add, Miss McBride?"

"The island is *perfect* for the wedding and reception. My sister Evie just got married in an outdoor ceremony a few weeks ago at our father's home and it was beautiful."

"I'm sure it was. I'm also sure the lawn didn't look like the set from *Jurassic Park*."

Meghan's chin lifted. "There has to be a lawn mower around here somewhere. Right, Bert?"

Bert made a choking sound. "Yes, there is."

"What are you suggesting?" He had a feeling he knew. He just wanted her to say it out loud.

"I'm *suggesting* we don't need a landscaping crew. I can pull a few weeds and mow the grass. Between, um, taking pictures of the loons."

He glanced at Bert and she shrugged, not even trying to hide her amusement.

"Tell her she'd be fighting a losing battle, Bert."

But the challenging gleam in the caretaker's eyes told Cade she was throwing her line in with Meghan. Her next words confirmed it. "I've wanted to give the courtyard a makeover for years."

Cade's brain began to break down the situation, organizing it into his usual list of pros and cons.

He was too busy to add anything else to his to-do list. The auctioneer expected Cade's phone call by the end of the week to set up an appointment to inventory the contents of the main house. Cade had planned to have a detailed list of his own before then.

On the other hand, it probably *was* too late to find a suitable place for the reception....

"Great," Meghan said. "Can you show me where the gardening tools are, Bert?"

Cade frowned. Had he missed something? *Like saying yes?*

It occurred to him that working on the courtyard meant he'd be spending more time with Meghan.

Cade, whose logical brain always knew exactly where things fit, suddenly wasn't sure whether to file that on the "pro" side or the "con" side.

And why did he get the unsettling feeling that Meghan McBride was the kind of woman who demanded a column all of her own?

Chapter Six

What happened back there, Meghan? Did you or did you not just offer to perform manual, backbreaking labor free of charge? In between taking pictures of the loons?

Yes, she had.

And all because she'd stood up for a piece of property that didn't even belong to her.

Meghan pulled on the pair of leather gloves Bert had given her and surveyed the courtyard, not sure which section to wade into first.

It was all Cade Halloway's fault. If he hadn't said the island "wasn't suitable" for a wedding, she wouldn't have felt the need to express her opinion.

Not suitable.

Cade Halloway had *no* imagination.

Without closing her eyes, Meghan could picture luminaries hanging from the branches of the trees while the fountain provided the background music for the ceremony. If it still worked…and the carousel horses would wear garlands of real flowers around their necks.

Meghan couldn't think of a more beautiful spot for a couple in love to say their vows.

Too bad she knew as much about landscaping as she did about photographing weddings. And how was she supposed to find the Ferris when she'd be on her knees pulling weeds in the courtyard instead of doing her best Nancy Drew impression *inside* the house?

She had to make an emergency call to Caitlin. Caitlin not only had a gift for helping people make the most of what God had given them, she could apply that gift to just about anything. Cramped apartments. Messy closets—Meghan knew that firsthand—and cluttered desks—again, firsthand knowledge. Why not gardens?

She could take photos with her camera, send them off with an SOS and get some input from a professional.

Bert had offered to help, so it wasn't as if she were in this alone. She'd gone inside to make a salad for lunch but Meghan expected her back to provide moral—and trowel—support any minute now.

"Having second thoughts?"

Meghan's trowel clattered to the stones at the sound of Cade's voice and missed her foot by an inch. "Stop. Doing. That."

"Doing what?" He looked genuinely confused.

"Sneaking up on me."

Now he looked genuinely exasperated. "I didn't sneak up on you. You were lost in thought." A slow smile turned up the corners of his lips and worked its way to his eyes. "Or maybe regret."

The courtyard wasn't overwhelming. That smile was. It transformed his features, igniting a warm blue flame in his eyes and carving out a captivating indentation in his left cheek. One that would have been labeled a dimple on anyone else's face.

But whatever it was called, the sight of it sucked the air right out of Meghan's lungs.

She knelt down to retrieve the trowel. And give her voice a chance to recover. Her heart would have to catch up later.

"Are you sure you know what you're doing?" Cade asked.

"I'm going to start by pulling out everything that doesn't look like a flower." She pushed a confident note into her voice. The same one she'd used on the loan officer when she'd filled out the paperwork to open her studio five years ago.

"Fine by me. Let's go."

"Go where?" Panic shot through her. Another interrog…*interview?* To make sure she was qualified to pull weeds?

"I'll rephrase that," Cade said patiently. "Let's get started."

For the first time, Meghan spotted the garden tool in his hand.

"You're—" Meghan gulped. "Going to…*help?*"

The crease in his cheek made another brief but memorable appearance. "Two are better than one, for they have a good return for their work."

"You took my verse." Meghan couldn't believe he

remembered it. And quoted it. Verbatim. Was it possible Cade Halloway was a…believer?

Or did he just have a good memory?

"I surrender." Bert swept off her white straw hat and waved it above her head. "The weeds win this round. At least for today. I should spend some time in the studio while the natural light is still good."

Meghan sat back on her heels and blotted the moisture from her forehead with the back of her glove, surveying the small section of garden stones she'd been clearing. The three of them had been working for close to three hours, stopping only for a light lunch, and they'd barely made a difference.

She glanced at Cade under her lashes, waiting for him to say *I told you so.* And knowing she probably deserved it.

Lord, I think you should assign a crossing guard to me instead of a guardian angel. Someone who will yell STOP if I'm about to get myself into trouble.

Meghan smiled at the thought, knowing God understood its origins. Her sisters did claim she had a tendency to leap before she looked. Meghan preferred to think of it as exercising her faith.

But in this instance, maybe even she'd been overly optimistic. Not that she'd lost her vision of how the courtyard *could* look after some TLC. Okay, a *lot* of TLC. The challenge was getting it to that point in time for Parker Halloway's wedding.

Meghan's heart locked up when her eyes met Cade's

across the courtyard. One eyebrow arched in a silent question and Meghan realized she was still smiling.

She looked away, breaking the connection.

Even with that slightly arrogant eyebrow, Cade Halloway was downright dangerous to her peace of mind. Here she'd been ready to dismiss him as the poster boy for the serious, alpha executive, not knowing there was a smile lurking below the surface capable of short-circuiting every neuron in her body.

When they'd set to work, she'd quickly discovered Cade was a dedicated multitasker who could pull weeds *and* conduct part two of his interview. The one she'd thought she'd successfully survived that morning.

Apparently not.

Oh, he'd been subtle. This time his questions had come under the guise of making friendly conversation. A barrage of questions was difficult enough to process—Meghan had to sort through them all and hope none of them slipped through the cracks—but screening them first to make sure she didn't blow her cover was even more stressful.

When had her interest in photography started? Where was her studio located? How many weddings did she usually photograph during a summer?

The first question had been easy. Meghan had always been the designated family photographer but didn't realize she had a knack for it until the yearbook adviser encouraged her to come on board her sophomore year of high school. She didn't bother to mention the peace and quiet of the dark room relaxed her. She even loved the sour smell of the chemicals. But most of all, she loved seeing the photographs, amazing moments of *life* captured in time, developed in the trays right in front of her eyes.

Cade Halloway struck her as a just-the-facts, give-me-an-answer-in-ten-words-or-less kind of guy. Kind of like Evie's Sam, except her brother-in-law's frequent smiles were warm and easygoing. Cade's sense of humor, if he had one, was hidden as well as the Ferris she was searching for.

She'd seen the flash of disbelief in his eyes when she'd reluctantly relayed the address of her studio. And even though loyalty to her quaint but underappreciated neighborhood had immediately surfaced, she'd resisted the urge to defend it. Her aching knees reminded her of what had happened the last time she'd attempted to defend a piece of property.

Fortunately, Bert had appeared, saving Meghan from having to answer his last question. Which would have been *none*. Unless she counted the German shepherd, dressed in a tuxedo, which she'd photographed for a "faithful friends" calendar the month before.

Meghan had taken advantage of Bert's presence and offered to help her clear another section of stones. Far enough away from Cade that he couldn't talk to her without shouting.

Interview over. Meghan had breathed a sigh of relief when Cade had turned his attention to the fountain. And away from her.

They'd all worked in relative silence until Bert had made her weary announcement and "surrendered."

"I've got some phone calls to make, too." Cade stood

up, his lean frame unfolding with the fluid grace of a natural athlete.

Meghan guessed tennis. Or golf. Bert had mentioned the country club. Wasn't that where wealthy, successful businessmen kept in shape and networked?

He and Bert were both looking at her now and Meghan took the hint.

"I'll take a break, too," she said. It wasn't that she didn't want to. She just wasn't sure her cramped muscles would cooperate and she didn't want to fall flat on her face in front of Cade.

"Help yourselves to some lemonade. And there are sugar cookies in the jar by the coffeepot. I'll be back in time to make supper. That is, if Cade catches something for us to eat." Bert shaded her eyes against the sun, judged its strength and set off in the direction of the studio.

And just like that, they were alone again. Meghan didn't count Miss Molly, who'd spent the last few hours napping next to Cade.

"I forgot I was supposed to catch supper." Cade scrubbed a hand over his jaw. "What are the chances of Louie's Shrimp Shack delivering this far?"

Meghan laughed, surprised he knew about the humble little seafood restaurant slouched on the corner of a street not far from where she lived. "I doubt it. And Bert might be suspicious when you bring her the fish already breaded and in a little white box."

"Good point." Cade continued to stare at her until Meghan began to wonder if she had a smear of dirt on her cheek.

Please, Lord, I can't take round three of the interview!

"What are your plans for the rest of the afternoon?"

To stay as far away from you as I can. "I'm going to scout out some places on the island that might make good photo ops." Because that's what the wedding photographer would be expected to do.

At the mention of the wedding, a shadow skimmed across Cade's face. "If I were you, I'd pass up any place that involves sand, water and anything my sister might step in or trip over in high heels."

Meghan's lips parted, but she didn't have time to form a comment before Cade muttered a terse see-you-later, snapped his phone open and strode away. A man on a mission.

Well, she had a mission, too. And it was time she started focusing on that mission instead of wondering what it would take to coax out that fascinating dent in Cade Halloway's cheek again.

"I'm sorry. The connection is bad…I can't hear you very well." Cade managed to catch two words before static choked off the rest of them.

I quit.

Bliss Markham, wedding coordinator extraordinaire, had apparently become the next casualty in Aunt Judith's war on the wedding plans.

Who was next? The cleaning crew?

If that was the case, Meghan would expect him to wash windows and sweep out those old relics…*cabins*… when what they really needed was a match.

A smile tugged at the corner of Cade's lips and he shook his head.

He still couldn't believe she'd talked him into letting her and Bert clean up the courtyard. He wasn't sure what had tipped the balance in Meghan's favor. Had it been the sudden image of the way the courtyard had once looked or the stubborn tilt of Meghan's chin when she defended it?

Not that it mattered. He could predict what would happen. They'd spend hours working in the hot sun and Parker would burst into tears upon arrival.

He knew his sister. Even if a professional landscape design team took on the grounds, they wouldn't meet her high standards.

Even though he was still a little taken aback by the changes he'd seen in his sister since she'd met Justin, Cade put them down to her wanting to make a good impression on the man she loved.

Parker had started planning her wedding long before she'd had a serious boyfriend. If Cade wasn't mistaken, she'd started dreaming about it in the sixth grade. By the time she graduated from high school, she had a folder bulging with pictures of satin gowns, wedding cakes and flower arrangements.

So what was she trying to prove, changing the location from the country club chapel to Blue Key Island? And would it make a difference if she knew her wedding planner, the woman she'd hired to take care of all the details, had jumped ship?

There was one way to find out.

Cade punched in the code for Parker's cell but the call went directly to her voice mail.

Parker only rerouted her calls for two reasons. If she was doing some serious shoe shopping or if she was hiding. And if Judith had called Parker half the amount of times she'd tried to call him in the past few hours, Cade guessed she was hiding.

He buried a sigh and looked down at Miss Molly, who'd sprawled across his foot during his conversation with Bliss Markham.

"I guess we don't have any more excuses. If we want something to eat for supper, we better go fishing."

As if she understood every word, Miss Molly bounced to her feet and bolted toward the house without a backward glance. Letting him know in no uncertain terms that fishing was strictly a pastime for humans.

"Fine. Be that—" Way. Cade groaned. He was talking to a *dog*. Now he knew the heat was getting to him. Or maybe it was the island.

When he was young, he'd thought Blue Key was the most magical place in the world. And his mother had encouraged the notion by scattering odd little collectibles around the island.

It hadn't been unusual for Cade to go exploring and discover hidden treasures. A metal chest filled with smooth stones. Animals, sculpted from wood and metal, peering at him from the brush. An old pocket watch or an arrowhead nestled in the notch of a tree, waiting to be found.

He'd hunt down Genevieve and pull her along, anxious to show her what he'd found. The delight on her

face always looked genuine—as if, Cade thought cynically, the things he'd discovered hadn't been strategically planted for him to find.

Someday you'll bring your family here and you can
tell your sons and daughters that this is a place where
dreams come true.

Cade's jaw tightened at the memory.

By fall, Genevieve was gone. And Cade didn't remember the island as a place where dreams came true.
He remembered it as the place they'd fallen apart.

Chapter Seven

Meghan eased the door open and slipped inside the library.

The thud of her heart threatened to drown out the quiet, methodical tick of the grandfather clock in the corner and she forced herself to take a deep breath.

Cade had taken the boat out and Bert was in the studio. It was a golden opportunity to have the house to herself to look for the Ferris.

Meghan paused in front of a group of paintings and checked the signatures. All of them were signed but none with the signature she hoped to see. She shifted her attention to a watercolor of a boat anchor half buried in the sand. Instantly she recognized it as one of Genevieve Halloway's.

Once again the attention to detail, right down to the single seagull feather ruffled by an unseen breeze, amazed her. And made her wonder about Cade's mother all over again.

She hadn't missed the touch of bitterness in Cade's

voice when he'd told her Genevieve had missed all the important milestones in Parker's life.

And in his.

Meghan closed her eyes briefly as memories pressed against an old wound, resurrecting a familiar ache.

Every time she and her sisters had huddled together to make wedding plans, Meghan felt the weight of their mother's absence and wished she could have been there with them.

Meghan had been a freshman in college when Laura McBride, a police sergeant, was killed while assisting a stranded motorist during a storm. She could still remember the exact moment she'd gotten the phone call from Caitlin. Five-seventeen. She'd curled up on the bed in her dorm room and stared at the clock. Everything inside of her had frozen solid but the clock kept ticking away the minutes. Pushing her forward into a life without Laura McBride's wisdom and loving guidance.

She'd learned that night that life is as short as it is precious and she couldn't understand how some families allowed things like misunderstandings, unforgiveness… or even indifference…to steal away the time they had.

No matter how bitter the Halloways' divorce had been or the circumstances behind it, Meghan couldn't imagine Genevieve walking out of her children's lives. Not being there for birthdays and graduations. Or her only daughter's wedding.

She reached out and traced the picture frame with the tip of her finger.

It didn't make sense. Everywhere Meghan looked, she saw evidence of a woman who had been nurturing. Someone who saw beauty in the unexpected and generously shared her home with people who needed a place to rest.

Genevieve Halloway still has time to reconnect with her family, Lord. They can start over. There isn't anything broken that you can't put back together. It's not too late. Can't you somehow show them that?

Whatever had happened, Meghan believed it wasn't beyond God's reach. Nothing was.

The grandfather clock began to chime the hour, a reminder she had more rooms to search before Bert— or Cade—returned.

Ten more minutes convinced her that none of the paintings in the library were by Joseph Ferris.

Meghan stepped back into the hall and hesitated, not sure where to go next. Upstairs or downstairs?

Her bedroom was on the second floor, so she'd have more opportunities to look around up there without making anyone suspicious.

Downstairs it was, Meghan decided.

She bypassed the kitchen and half bath and headed down to the end of the narrow hall. Door number one, two or three? Cade was staying in one of the rooms but she wasn't sure which one.

She nudged the first door open and breathed a sigh of relief. Once upon a time, this room must have been Parker's.

Airy dotted Swiss curtains trimmed with white pompoms welcomed the sunlight and the walls had been painted a delicate seashell-pink. Twin iron beds, covered by matching comforters, flanked the oak ward-robe like bookends.

Meghan took a quick lap around the room, pausing in front of each picture. All the artwork on the walls was dried flowers or leaves, carefully preserved under glass.

She ducked out again and closed the door, mentally crossing Parker's room off her list. Evie would be proud to know she actually had a list.

She probably had time to search one more room.

Meghan's heart bunched up when she peeked inside the next room and saw the expensive leather case at the foot of the bed.

Somehow she would have expected Cade to choose the master suite that overlooked the sculpture garden.

Meghan would have backed right out of the room if she hadn't spotted a small painting of a rowboat hang-ing above the headboard.

Her heart picked up speed as she padded into the room, her eyes fixed on the painting. Ferris had done several paintings of boats on the water using the same sparse style.

Her gaze traced the silhouette of the man sitting in the boat, his face lifted toward the sky. The soft play of light on the horizon hinted it was either dawn or just after sunset. Obviously the artist left that to the imagi-nation of the person looking at the painting.

She swallowed hard and looked at the corner. No signature.

With trembling fingers, she lifted the painting off the wall to see if there was a name on the back of the canvas.

"What do you think you're doing?"

Meghan almost dropped the painting as she whirled around and her eyes met Cade's. "I…"

A movement in between the pillows grabbed their attention and Miss Molly poked her head up, a sock dangling from her mouth. Her ears perked up at the sight of Cade standing in the doorway.

"Ah…Miss Molly," Meghan said, hoping, praying, those two words would explain her presence.

"I wondered where she disappeared." Cade's eyes rolled toward the ceiling before coming to rest meaningfully on the painting still clutched in Meghan's hands.

"I…was curious who did this."

"Why?" The word came out like a single shot and blew Meghan's confidence to bits.

Meghan looked at Miss Molly, who wasn't inclined to rescue her a second time. "The light…the way the man is looking up at the sky instead of the water. It almost looks as if he's…praying—"

"Don't bother looking. It isn't signed."

"Oh." Meghan moistened her lips. Would Cade know if Ferris was the artist? "Do you know who did it?"

Cade hesitated a fraction of a second. "I did."

"I…*you* painted this? I didn't know you were an artist." Meghan looked down at the canvas and then at Cade, still frozen in the doorway. "Where do you show your work?"

"I don't. I'm not an artist, I'm an architect." Cade stalked into the room. Which suddenly felt a lot smaller as he entered the perimeter of her personal space.

"But this is the way you express yourself." Meghan

smiled, warmth stirring inside her at this unexpected glimpse into Cade's personality.

"I express myself in my *work,*" Cade said sharply. "And just so we're clear, I painted that when I was ten years old and I haven't picked up a brush since then."

He plucked the painting from her nerveless fingers and tossed it casually onto the bed. It landed upside down. Meghan would have rescued it but something in the tempered blue flame of Cade's eyes warned her not to.

"Ten years…" Meghan's voice trailed off. Impossible. If he possessed this kind of talent, someone would have encouraged it. Helped him refine it. "But how could you…stop?"

Cade stilled. When he spoke, his voice was soft. "I didn't stop because I never *started.* I painted a picture on a rainy afternoon when I was bored. That's it."

Meghan refused to believe that was it. If a ten-year-old boy could capture such raw emotion with no formal training, where would he be now if he'd pursued it as a career? "But you have a gift."

"A gift." Cade repeated the words. "Do you know how many people I met on this island with that gift? But looking back, I doubt any of them could have come up with a month's rent, let alone support themselves. Or a family. It's a self-centered, reckless pursuit that I'd call a burden, not a gift."

"Sometimes a gift does feel like a burden," Meghan admitted, remembering the sleepless nights and countless hours she'd spent on her knees, asking God if she should start her own business. Even now, the path wasn't always smooth but Meghan couldn't imagine the alternative. Following her dream had deepened her relationship with God in ways she'd never expected. With every stumbling step forward, the faith in knowing she was pursuing the seed of a dream *God* had planted inside her had given her the strength and courage to take the next one. "But if it's there inside of you and you ignore it—or give it up—you take on another kind of burden."

An emotion Meghan couldn't quite define flickered in Cade's eyes. "Not many artists are successful enough to make a living."

"Maybe some of them think it's more important to make a life," Meghan said quietly. Reaching for the painting, she stretched up on her tiptoes and hung it back on the wall.

Stepping back, Meghan realized that in the few seconds it took her to align the frame against the faded square on the wall, Cade had left the room.

Cade's hands clenched at his sides as he retreated down the hall.

A dreamer. No wonder she seemed right at home on Blue Key. The island had been tailor-made for people like her.

His instincts about Meghan McBride were right. He should have known they were right when she'd reluctantly told him the address of her studio. His firm's monthly utility bill was probably higher than the rent in the run-down neighborhood where Meghan's business was located. She must be barely making ends meet if she couldn't afford office space that didn't come equipped with bars on the windows to keep the non-paying customers out!

If Meghan had attained any level of success in the five years she'd been on her own, the first thing she would have done was rent space in a better part of the city. The fact she didn't meant that she couldn't afford to. Which meant she was struggling. And the term "struggling artist" had been coined for a reason.

Cade cut into the library and tossed his cell phone on the desk, still rattled by the conversation.

But how could you stop?

It was the last question he'd expected Meghan to ask. And the last one he wanted to answer.

He might have some artistic ability but with his father's encouragement, he'd used it to pave the way to a lucrative career.

Why spend your life doodling in sketchbooks no one will see when you can design buildings? You'll have something to show for all your hard work at the end of the day and money in the bank.

During Cade's adolescent and teenage years, Douglas Halloway's favorite lecture had gradually drowned out Genevieve's gentle encouragement to follow his heart. As a child, he hadn't understood what that meant. But now he did. It was an excuse people used when they selfishly went after what they wanted without caring what—or who—they left behind.

His cell phone rang, jarring him out of the past.

"Cade?" His name was barely audible through the snap, crackle and pop in the background.

"Parker? I've been trying to get in touch with you

all morning." Cade's frustration leaked out in his voice. "Why haven't you been answering your phone? The landscape crew quit. And so did your wedding planner—"

"Her name is Bliss Markham…should be there tomorrow afternoon. I'm so glad you're on the island. Homeland security, you know." Parker giggled at her own joke.

Giggled.

"This is Parker, isn't it?" Suddenly Cade wasn't sure. "And did you hear what I said? The island won't be ready for a wedding this weekend." It wouldn't be ready for a wedding by *next* summer. "You're going to have to come up with another plan."

"What? I can barely hear you. Justin says hello, by the way." Another giggle.

Parker was twenty-six years old. Way past the giggling phase. Cade's back teeth ground together. "Tell him hello." He tried another tack. "Meghan McBride showed up yesterday."

"Meghan who?"

"McBride. Your wedding photographer." *The one I found asleep in the boathouse. Strawberry blond hair. Misty-green eyes.*

"That might be her name. A friend of a friend recommended her."

Cade frowned. "You didn't check her references yourself?"

"Listen…fading out. I'll call you tomorrow. Bliss has everything under control so I'm not worried…"

"Wait a second, Parker. Bliss—"

Call lost.

Quit.

Cade plowed his hand through his hair and then hit redial.

The call went right to voice mail.

"Parker…call me back. Now," Cade growled.

Ten minutes later, he gave up.

Parker wanted a wedding to remember. Cade had a feeling his sister was going to get her wish.

He'd have to call Judith and ask her to get the message about Bliss Markham to Parker. He hated to involve his aunt, but he didn't want his sister's wedding day completely ruined, either. If anyone could secure an alternate place for a wedding reception, it was Judith Halloway. She had more connections than the circuit board at the Mall of America.

He strode outside and then wished he'd stayed in the library. The courtyard was a mocking reminder of a well-planned schedule completely destroyed.

Cade paused, his gaze moving from the misshapen boxwood, once a family of topiary deer, to the flowering shrubs braided with wild grape vines.

Meghan had confidently declared it would a beautiful place for a wedding. Almost as if she had a clear picture of what the courtyard had looked like years ago. Or what it could be again with some attention.

That kind of vision was a one-way street to disappointment. Cade had decided a long time ago that if he was going to pour his time and energy into a project, he'd make sure he had something to show for it at the end.

* * *

Meghan heard the quiet slap of Cade's shoes against the dock and her pulse jumped in time with every step he took toward her.

She hadn't been able to stop thinking about their conversation. Or about him.

There were artists who spent a lifetime trying to achieve what Cade had accomplished at the age of ten. And he'd called it a burden because it didn't fit his qualifications of a "real job."

The look in his eyes when he'd mentioned his mother's friends had peeled back a corner of his soul and exposed an old wound. And made her wonder if ignoring his artistic ability was more a rejection of something Genevieve had held dear than choosing to channel his ability into a more stable career.

Cade stopped several feet away, but Meghan still felt as if she were being reeled in by an invisible tractor beam. Was she about to be fired for insubordination? Or for telling the truth? The glint in Cade's eye wasn't exactly encouraging...

"Are you admiring the fish I caught?"

Meghan exhaled in relief, knowing the proper response would be yes. Too bad she'd never been a fan of the proper response. Something she had a feeling Cade Halloway was used to receiving!

"Fish?" Meghan feigned confusion. "I thought that was the bait you'd been using."

Cade's eyebrow shot up and for some odd reason, it gave her an all's-right-with-the-world feeling. "I suppose you think you could do better."

"No." She bit back a smile. "I *know* I could do better."

"I accept the challenge."

Meghan gulped. "What?"

"I. Accept. The. Challenge. Grab the tackle box."

"Tackle box? Oh, I see. That was your first mistake."

"I know how to fish."

"Keep telling yourself that." In for a penny, in for a pound, as her grandmother used to say.

Cade made a strangled sound that sounded suspiciously like a laugh. But Meghan had never heard him laugh before, so she couldn't say for sure.

"You sound pretty sure of yourself."

Meghan could have argued that point—she'd only gotten good at pretending—but decided she'd stirred things up enough for the day. "Leave the tackle box on the dock and grab the night crawlers. We have about an hour before Bert comes back."

"Anything else?" Cade drawled.

"I get to drive the boat."

Chapter Eight

Fifteen minutes later Meghan decided the fishing competition was rapidly moving its way up the list of Very Bad Ideas. Right past letting the Evensons talk her into perching their cat—she *knew* the Santa hat would make him cranky—on the back of their Saint Bernard for their annual family Christmas card.

How was it she'd forgotten her original plan to put as much distance between her and Cade as possible?

A whopping three feet separated them in the tiny pram. If she moved her knee three inches to the left, it would be touching his.

"Meghan, your bobber."

Was nowhere in sight.

She stifled a squeak.

Concentrate, Meghan.

The line went taut and she grabbed the pole and set the hook.

"Beginner's luck," Cade muttered when she reeled in a nice perch.

"Beginner? I'll have you know that when my family went camping, I always caught the most fish." Meghan felt the sharp pinch of the memory and gave herself a moment to adjust to the pain. As much as it hurt to remember the vacations they'd taken, she'd never wanted to seal Laura's memory in a safe compartment of her heart just to make it easier to handle. "My sisters and I used to have fishing competitions, too. It was the only way Evie and I could get Caitlin in the boat."

"Which one just got married...*bobber*."

Meghan grabbed her pole again and reeled in another perch, smiling when she heard his soft huff of indignation.

"Evie." Meghan balanced the pole on the side of the boat and carefully took the fish off the hook before depositing it in the bucket. "She's the baby of the family."

"Where do you fit in?"

"Middle child." Meghan's attention drifted to the sun winking through the branches of the towering white pines on the other side of the lake.

It really was beautiful. No wonder the Halloways had fled Minneapolis to spend the summers here. She'd always thought of herself as a city girl, but Blue Key could change her mind. Who needed aromatherapy candles? Not when all she had to do was walk outside and breathe in the sweet scent of the woods that perfumed the air around her.

"Did you take the pictures at your sister's wedding?"

"No, they hired a professional for that." Meghan closed her eyes, feeling the gentle rocking motion of the boat, lulling her into...

"I thought *you* were a professional."

A false sense of security!

Meghan's eyes snapped open and she found herself pinned in place by Cade's steady gaze. Had he deliberately tried to trip her up or had she stumbled onto dangerous ground by letting her guard down?

"I am...but I was a bridesmaid, too." She held her breath, practically *seeing* the wheels turn in Cade's head as he processed that bit of information.

"I suppose it would have been hard to do both," he finally said.

"Very hard."

They stared at each other for another heartbeat as Meghan sent up a plea for divine intervention.

Cade's bobber disappeared below the surface.

"You have a bite."

Cade's attention immediately shifted, giving Meghan an opportunity to exhale.

Thank you, Lord!

He *still* doubted her credentials. And all it would take was the click of a mouse to locate her website and see the screen-size photo of her latest subjects—a herd of adorable miniature horses galloping through a sprinkler—to figure out she didn't exactly fulfill the requirements the Halloway family would have demanded for Parker's wedding.

Meghan's heart took a swan dive toward her toes as reality set in. She'd thought her assignment would be simple. Look for the Ferris. Photograph the wedding. Leave.

She hadn't figured in the amount of stress a wedding

created. Or becoming a volunteer gardener. Or being drawn into the mystery as to why the Halloway family had stopped coming to the island.

And she definitely hadn't figured in Cade.

Meghan slanted a look at the man sitting next to her in the boat, threading another night crawler on the hook to replace the one that had just been stolen. The weakening sunlight still had enough power to pick out threads of umber in his dark hair and the intense concentration he applied to the simple task created a slight furrow between his brows.

The sudden flutter of her pulse surprised her even as she rejected the notion. She *wasn't* attracted to Cade. And even if she was, he certainly wouldn't be attracted to her.

It was easy to see that he was the kind of man who'd constructed his life in a precise orderly way, from his career to the methodical way he *fished,* for crying out loud.

Cade was a color-inside-the-lines type of guy. Scribblers drove people like him crazy. She drove her sisters crazy but they loved and accepted her—quirks and all. It was in the fine print of their family code.

Anyone else?

Not worth the risk of rejection.

"Look, Cade! Do you see the eagle? It's sitting at the top of that tree on the point."

Cade hadn't noticed the eagle—but he had noticed Meghan's bobber had disappeared again.

"You have another one. I think your end of the boat is right over a weed bed. I can't believe your luck."

"Luck has nothing to do with it." Meghan summoned a haughty look. "It's skill."

"Skill?" Cade couldn't help but smile. Meghan might have called what she was doing "fishing," but she'd practically created her own sport. He'd never seen anyone so focused on everything except what she was supposed to be focusing on. That she still managed to be successful was nothing short of incredible. "Who did you say taught you to fish?"

"My parents. But I like to put my own spin on things."

"Uh-huh. Would that spin you like to put on things include trying to pierce my ear?" He'd had to duck at least a half dozen times while she recreated some strange contortion with her fishing pole that she insisted was "casting." The last time, the hook had zipped past his earlobe, missing it by an inch.

"That was an accident. And besides that, your ear was in the way."

Cade might have argued the point except that Meghan gathered her hair in her hands and tied it in a loose knot at the nape of her neck. And his brain and his ability to speak parted company.

Once again an image of Amanda materialized in Cade's mind. Amanda kept her hair under control in a short, sleek cut as professional as her navy blazer. If she took up fishing, he had no doubt she'd prefer the smooth, choreographed art of fly-fishing over angling for perch over the side of a rusty, flat-bottomed boat.

He'd met Amanda through mutual friends. They

were both independent and devoted to their careers. Shared similar taste in music and movies. They even attended the same church. If Cade had filled out an application for one of those online dating services, he wouldn't have found anyone more suited for him than Amanda Courtland. So why was he content to remain friends?

His head told him that falling in love with Amanda made perfect sense. His heart didn't agree. And right now, it was pounding against his chest wall in response to Meghan's smile.

Which only proved it couldn't be trusted.

"Megs, where are you?" Caitlin demanded.

Meghan held the phone several inches away from her ear, confident she'd still be able to hear her sister. Caitlin's voice echoed loudly in the predawn quiet of the woods.

"I stopped by a few times but you weren't there. At first I thought maybe you'd decided to stay with Dad another week but when I called him, he said you'd left."

Meghan nibbled on the tip of her ragged fingernail as she picked her way down the path to the narrow peninsula where she'd seen the eagle the evening before.

Maybe calling Caitlin *hadn't* been such a good idea. "I was only in Cooper's Landing for a few days. I'm on a shoot."

"Dad said you were on vacation."

A setup. She'd been right—her older sister and Cade were similar in temperament. "It's kind of…both."

"So tell me about it." It wasn't a request.

"You know, freelance work."

"Where?"

"Wisconsin."

"Could you narrow it down a little?"

"Northern?"

"I thought we stopped playing Twenty Questions when we were twelve."

If Caitlin didn't have such an aversion to sensible shoes, Meghan thought, she would have made a brilliant attorney.

"I'm photographing a wedding."

"You have *got* to be kidding me. I know there are people who think their pets are human, but come on. Who's performing the ceremony, Smokey the Bear?"

Meghan laughed, realizing how much she'd missed hearing her sister's voice. "It's a real wedding, Cait. With real people."

The sudden silence told Meghan she'd managed to achieve the impossible. Momentarily render Caitlin Rae McBride speechless.

"You don't photograph people. And you don't photograph weddings."

"Not usually."

"Not *ever*."

"Okay, not ever. But I did it as a favor."

"To whom?"

Maybe she hadn't missed Caitlin's voice as much as she thought. "Dad."

Caitlin made a noise that sounded similar to the one Meghan's bicycle tire made when she'd run over a nail. "I can't believe it. Evie was right. I should have known something was up when Dad hemmed and hawed on the phone and wouldn't tell me where you were."

"Evie *wasn't* right. I offered to do it. And it's a small wedding." Meghan assumed it was a small wedding. She'd never asked to see the guest list but how many people could crowd into the little courtyard? Twenty? Thirty?

"Mmm." Caitlin didn't sound convinced.

"You're beginning to sound like Evie. Don't worry so much. I could use some advice, though. Parker wants an outdoor wedding in the courtyard and it's a little—" Meghan searched for the right word. "Unkempt. If I sent you some pictures, could you give me a few ideas how to make it look good?"

"Parker." Caitlin repeated the name. "You don't mean Parker *Halloway*." A low chuckle trailed behind the last word, as if she knew Meghan couldn't possibly be referring to Parker Halloway.

"She's the bride."

"Parker Halloway."

"Um...yes."

"You're photographing *Parker Halloway's* wedding."

"It's a small ceremony—" Hadn't she said that already?

"Megs, have you met Parker Halloway?" Caitlin interrupted.

"Not exactly, but—"

"Well, I have. She's a princess. Her interior designer is a friend of mine and nothing is good enough for her. Her dad is one of the wealthiest men in the Cities and Judith Halloway, her aunt, is a pit bull in pearls."

"What about her brother?" Meghan ventured. Just because she couldn't help herself.

"Cade? He's brilliant. Great sense of style, though. He likes getting his way. Ruthless—"

Meghan remembered the way Cade had covered Miss Molly up with his coat. And the elusive indentation in his cheek that made an appearance when he loosened up...

"Ruthless seems a little harsh," she said without thinking.

Silence. The second time in less than five minutes she'd had that affect on Caitlin. Then, "How do you know?"

"I...met him."

"Where?"

This time Meghan opted for silence.

"Megs, tell me that Cade Halloway isn't *with* you."

"Well, he's not *with* me. But he's...here."

"Stay on the line," Caitlin commanded. "I'll be right back."

Meghan delayed her journey long enough to slump against the nearest tree for support. She should have known Caitlin would be familiar with the Halloway family. After all, her sister's business allowed her discreet access to the upper levels of the Twin Cities' social strata.

"I'm back. And I happen to have an excerpt from the Society column that ran in *Twin City Trends* a few weeks ago. Are you ready?"

No, Meghan wanted to say, but she didn't bother because Caitlin would tell her anyway.

"Society weddings of the summer…topping the list of brides to watch is Parker Halloway, daughter of architect and local entrepreneur Douglas Halloway. The themed outdoor reception will take place at the family's summer home and showcase the talents of Chef Michaela Cross of Cape Road Caterers."

Meghan was afraid to ask what "themed reception" meant.

"I'm just the photographer, Cait. Bliss Markham is handling all the wedding details. I'm sure everything is under control." Meghan thought about the courtyard and winced.

From what she was learning about Cade's sister, she couldn't imagine why Parker had chosen the island for her wedding. And suddenly her great idea to pull some weeds and hang luminaries from the trees would be better suited for an impromptu picnic than a reception "showcasing" the talents of a popular caterer.

"She hired Bliss Markham?" Caitlin's voice intruded on her thoughts. "You remember Bliss Markham, don't you?"

"No…" Oh, wait a second. Maybe she did. "She was your first success story, wasn't she?"

"You really do find the silver lining in the storm clouds. I still have nightmares about the woman. I almost closed up shop and took a job folding T-shirts at the Gap because of her."

"But you didn't."

"No, I didn't." Caitlin sounded as if she were pushing the words out between clenched teeth. "She still needs to work on that phony British accent, but she's

got a solid reputation as an event planner. I'm not surprised Parker hired her. She's the best."

Funny how two little words like "event planner"
could torpedo what remained of Meghan's confidence. A person only needed an event planner when
they planned an...event. The small, intimate wedding
she'd been imagining fractured into a billion pieces.

"You're wondering why she hired me, aren't you?"

"No." Caitlin responded so swiftly that Meghan believed her. "You're the best photographer I know, but
you prefer working with animals. And even though
Parker Halloway can be a bit of a cat—"

"Caitlin!"

"—I'm wondering why you took this particular job.
The stress around there has got to be off the charts.
And where does Dad fit into this?" Caitlin's questions
picked up speed. And volume. "And why is Cade Hal-
loway with you? The wedding isn't until next Saturday.
You aren't alone together, are you?"

Meghan could almost see Caitlin crossing her arms.
And *not* wrinkling her shirt in the process.

"I'd love to talk longer, Cait, but my battery is really
low." Meghan tapped the phone against the trunk of the
tree. "Oops. I think I'm losing the signal."

"Megs—"

"I'll have to get back to you. But I'll send those pictures of the courtyard soon." Maybe *after* the wedding.
"Bye."

The last thing she heard before she snapped the
phone shut was Caitlin's squawk of protest.

Lord, what have I gotten myself into?

Meghan closed her eyes; her stomach churning at the thought of the Halloways' A-list descending on Blue Key Island and finding the house and grounds a joke, lacking the country-club atmosphere they'd expected. Lacking *everything* they expected.

Even Cade didn't seem to appreciate that the estate had aged with the dignity and beauty of a vintage post-card. The changing seasons might have stripped some of the color from the paint and dulled the shine on the sculptures in the garden, but to Meghan, those things only added to the island's character.

She detached herself from the tree and stumbled down the trail until it narrowed into a path barely dis-cernable through the thick underbrush, more anxious to reach her destination than she had been when she'd started out.

Bert hadn't made an appearance when Meghan grabbed a banana muffin off a plate on the kitchen table and slipped out of the house to greet the sunrise. She'd only called Caitlin because her sister was awake by five every morning to organize her day.

Meghan had another plan.

Church.

Chapter Nine

Cade wasn't sure what woke him up.

He thought he heard the quiet snap of the screen door off the kitchen and wondered if Bert had gotten up early to work in the studio before breakfast.

He remembered his mother doing the same thing.

Sometimes he'd sneak out of bed and follow her. When he'd peek into the studio, Genevieve would smile as if she'd been expecting him. She'd stop painting long enough to pour milk into a mug and then add some coffee before handing it to him and continuing her work. He still drank his coffee that way....

Cade shook the memory away and silently scrolled through his day, not sure whether he should keep "landscaping" in his schedule or cross it off the list. Once he got in touch with Judith and told her about the state the house was in, he wouldn't be responsible for fixing the temperamental fountain.

The image of Meghan, a smudge of dirt on her cheek as she enthusiastically dispatched weeds from between the path stones, preempted his thoughts like a severe weather broadcast.

And right behind that one came several others, stored like digital photographs on an internal hard drive. Meghan shaking her head and making a "tsking" sound when he'd insisted on using a lure instead of a night crawler—which could explain why he hadn't caught anything. The warmth in her eyes when she'd talked about her sisters. The wry, almost resigned smile that tilted her lips whenever he pointed out that her bobber had disappeared and a fish was halfway across the lake with her worm....

Cade decisively shut down the program featuring "Meghan McBride" and got out of bed.

When he walked past the window, he didn't even have to look outside to know what he'd see. Brushstrokes of scarlet and tangerine painting the sky. Transparent gray patches of mist rising from the lake. The quicksilver flash of a bass surfacing for an early breakfast.

A handful of short summers on the island as a kid and the place had somehow gotten under his skin. He recalled waiting restlessly during the months bracketing his family's trips to Blue Key like a racehorse confined at the starting gate. To make the time go faster, he'd drawn maps during recess of the best fishing spots and filled pages of his science notebook with diagrams of tree forts and rafts.

By the age of ten, Cade had already decided he was going to live on the island when he was a grown-up. Not just for a few weeks out of the summer, either, but year-round. He'd eat fish three times a day and build a canoe so that he could paddle to shore for supplies when he needed them.

All those childish dreams. And in one summer—in one *day*—they'd come crashing down.

Pop psychology claimed that closure was necessary for a person to move on. Cade didn't buy it. He'd been fine until he'd made the decision to visit Blue Key one last time before it sold. He'd thought that coming back as an adult, with an adult perspective, would make the trip easy.

After all, he wasn't ten years old anymore. Over the years he'd accepted his parents' divorce as proof that love wasn't always enough and the whole "opposites attract" school of thought was a myth. Two people had to have similar backgrounds and temperaments to go the distance. He'd even accepted that his mother's unhappiness wasn't his fault.

So why did he stay awake half the night, battling memories from the past?

"Because you're an idiot." Cade answered his own question as he yanked a faded chambray shirt out of the hall closet on his way out the door.

Miss Molly, who'd materialized out of nowhere, barked a cheerful affirmation to his muttered comment.

"Why didn't you go to the studio with Bert?" He glared at the dog as he reached down to scratch the base of her silky ear. "You know I'm not taking you home with me, right? This friendship is only temporary."

She barked again and Cade put a finger to his lips. "Shh. Don't wake up Meghan."

He assumed she was still asleep. He hadn't seen her since supper, when she'd disappeared into the woods with her camera. Much later, at work on his computer in the library, he'd heard her low laughter mingling with Bert's outside the window.

The faint smell of smoke warned him that the two women had decided to make a campfire.

He'd resisted the urge to join them.

It was hard enough to keep Meghan from invading his thoughts without spending more time in her company than absolutely necessary.

"Which way?" He looked down at Miss Molly, who tilted her head, as if considering, before taking several tentative steps toward the lake. Suddenly her nose lifting and she changed course, taking an overgrown path into the woods.

Cade followed.

When the dog's destination became evident, Cade tried to call her back with a whistle. Which she ignored. "Next time I'm putting you on a leash."

Miss Molly glanced over her shoulder, laughed at him and kept going.

Cade's steps slowed as the path through the trees all but disappeared. As he neared the point, he thought about turning around and letting Miss Molly find her own way back to the house but determination—or stubbornness—kept his feet moving forward.

He'd been everywhere else on the island—why not the point? If he was looking for that elusive thing called "closure," he should probably just get it over with. Face the memory head-on instead of trying to avoid it.

A breeze stirred the aspen trees, setting the leaves in motion. Cade smiled humorlessly in response.

Drum roll, please...

He braced himself as he stepped into the open, ready to relive the moment his life had changed. The afternoon he'd searched for his mother and found her. In the arms of a man who wasn't his father.

The image never materialized.

Because another one took its place. And instead of letting his mind rewind to the past, this one held him firmly in the present.

And maybe, if he allowed it, gave him a glimpse into his future.

Meghan. Balanced on the trunk of the old birch tree growing off the end of the point. Eyes closed, face tilted toward the sky. Hands lifted above her head.

She was *praying*.

And if the sight of Meghan's openhearted display of worship hadn't jolted Cade enough, he was struck with something else.

The overwhelming desire to paint her.

And he hadn't painted—or *wanted* to paint—for years.

He took a step back, ready to retreat, but Miss Molly had other ideas. Before Cade could stop her, the dog spotted Meghan balanced precariously on the narrow trunk of the tree and zeroed in on her like a homing device.

Cade opened his mouth to call out a warning, but the words didn't have a chance to form.

Miss Molly bumped against Meghan's leg, the im-

pact enough to shift her balance. Meghan tried to re-
gain her footing, but both of them pitched off the side
of the tree into the lake.

And Cade couldn't help it. He laughed.

*I will praise you as long as I live, and in your name
I will lift up my hands...*

Hands still lifted, Meghan laughed softly as one of
the verses her "kids" had woven into a mural in the park
bubbled to the surface of her silent prayer like a spring.

Until a joyful bark interrupted it.

Meghan opened her eyes and saw a blur of white
hurtling toward her.

"Miss Mol—" Meghan pivoted, then gasped as her
foot slipped off bark slick with morning dew. As she
tried to right herself, the little dog barreled into her and
knocked her off balance.

Just before she hit the water, she thought she heard
someone laugh.

Meghan bobbed to the surface like a cork several
seconds later, but promptly went under again when Miss
Molly decided Meghan's head was closer and easier to
reach than the shore.

"Miss..." Meghan swallowed a mouthful of lake
water as she tried to touch the sandy bottom she knew
ought to be below her feet...but wasn't.

"Hold on. There's a drop-off somewhere around
here." She recognized the husky growl of Cade's voice
somewhere close by.

"I think I found it," Meghan sputtered. She heard a

splash as water streamed down her face and blurred her vision. "You were…did you *laugh?*"

"Laugh. Not me." Cade materialized beside her. "Hold still."

Miss Molly stuck her paw in Meghan's eye while Cade tried to untangle the dog from her hair.

"I'll take care of the dog."

"But—"

"Swim back to the tree."

Meghan peeked through her spiky lashes and saw the solid, muscular outline of Cade's shoulder. She reached out and latched on to his arm like a barnacle.

And accidentally dunked him.

He came up coughing and tried unsuccessfully to peel her away. "What are you trying to do?"

"I can't s-swim."

"Then tread water. Everyone can tread water." Cade tried to disengage her fingers, one at a time, from the death grip she had on his shoulder.

"Is that a proven fact?" Meghan gasped, using both hands to fist the soggy fabric of his shirt during his second attempt to shake her loose. "Because I'm pretty sure I s-sink."

"Just kick your feet and move your arms…"

She could do that.

"You have to let go first."

Meghan wasn't sure she could do *that*.

"Meghan." The warm puff of Cade's breath in her ear instantly multiplied the goose bumps on her arms. "I have a dog on my head and you clinging to my arm. I have to get rid of either you or the rodent. You dec—"

She let go of Cade's arm. From the sound of Miss Molly's ragged panting, the dog wasn't enjoying her impromptu swimming lesson any more than Meghan was.

"I'll be right back. Don't panic."

Easy for him to say, Meghan thought as she made a halfhearted lunge toward the trunk of the birch tree. Her water-logged jeans tugged her down, refusing to let her arms and legs cooperate. She hadn't realized until now that the place she'd chosen to stand, where the birch arched over the water, was at least five feet above the water. And over a drop-off.

"Rule number one. Always swim with a buddy." Cade had returned. He slipped an arm around her waist and pulled her against his side.

Meghan found herself looking right into his eyes. Close enough to see the fascinating merge of color where the cobalt irises deepened to rings of midnight blue.

"I wasn't planning to s-swim."

But hey, if she needed a buddy...

Meghan choked and saw Cade frown.

"Are you all right?"

She nodded mutely, not quite sure how to answer the question. Was she all right? Or did the increase in her heart rate have more to do with Cade than being over her head?

Or, Meghan wondered in panic, were they the same thing...

This was so not good.

She let him tow her toward the shallow water, but as soon as sand sifted between her bare toes, she pulled away. Stumbling up the bank, Meghan collapsed on the first sun-warmed rock she encountered.

Cade dropped down beside her. A little closer than Meghan would have liked, given the unsettling epiphany she'd just had.

"That wasn't exactly on my agenda, but it was an interesting start to the day." Cade scraped his hand through his hair and sent droplets of water raining down.

He had an agenda. Somehow, that didn't surprise her one bit.

"How did you know I was here?"

"You have to give the dog credit for that. She's convinced she's part—"

"Bloodhound." Meghan finished his sentence and smiled. And then it occurred to her that Cade might have seen her *before* she'd fallen in the lake. When she was balanced on the arch of the tree, soaking in the beauty around her, hands lifted in praise.

"How did you know about the drop-off?" Panicked he'd comment on it, Meghan grabbed hold of the first question she could think of.

"That birch tree has been growing off the point since I was a kid. Although it was smaller back then."

"Did you fish here?"

"Not really. My parents insisted on having me in visual range when I took the rowboat out, and you can't see this part of the island from the main dock. I claimed the point as my thinking spot. Parker was too little to make it this far and everyone else thought this side of the island was too wild." Cade's voice sounded detached, as if he were talking about someone else.

Meghan wasn't fooled. The island had to have been a small boy's paradise. For some reason, it became important to Meghan to find a way to reconnect Cade with a place he'd obviously once loved.

"This was the setting for your painting, wasn't it?"

"How did you know that?" Cade's voice tightened.

How had she known? Meghan wasn't sure. Small details had provided clues but it had been more of a feeling than anything. Until now. But the set of Cade's jaw told her that she better have a more logical explanation than intuition. "The curve of the shoreline over there. The aspen trees—"

"I didn't paint the aspens," he interrupted.

Meghan discovered she could raise one eyebrow, too. And it felt pretty good. "The silver-gray splotches in the foreground? Those aren't the aspens?" She dared him to deny it.

He didn't. But he looked away, shielding his eyes. And his emotions. "How did you manage to find your way here? It's not exactly on the main path."

She understood the invisible No Trespassing sign and backed off. What she didn't understand was why he got so touchy about painting.

"I saw the eagle land in the pines last night when we were fishing and I hoped I'd see it again."

"That would have been hard with your eyes closed."

Meghan stifled a groan. He *had* seen her.

"I was praying. But I suppose it might have looked a little…unconventional."

Cade frowned again and it cut straight through to her heart. And put her on the defensive.

"People stand up and cheer when a football player makes a touchdown and no one thinks it's strange," she pointed out. "I think jumping up and telling God wow for a beautiful sunrise is perfectly acceptable."

"Do you always live with such…" He hesitated and Meghan wondered if she should be offended it was taking him so long to find the right adjective. *"Abandon?"*

Abandon, Meghan decided, had a very nice ring to it.

"According to my family, yes," she admitted. "But I prefer to call it *expectation*."

From the expression on Cade's face, it didn't matter what she labeled it. It was still cause for suspicion. She exhaled noisily. "Don't you believe in God?"

Cade swung around to face her and the startled, almost offended, look in his eyes answered the question. "Of course I do."

"What do you believe about Him?" Meghan blurted, even as it dawned on her this probably wasn't the best time, considering they were both shivering and soaked to the skin, to be talking about what Evie liked to call "the meaning of life."

Cade was silent for so long, Meghan thought he was going to ignore her.

"That He's orderly. Everything He created has an intricate design. A reason for being. He has a plan and He sticks to it."

"The master architect?"

"I didn't say that." The color that crept into Cade's

cheeks had nothing to do with the warmth of the sun beating down on them.

"What about the rest of the design? The beauty? The color? Trees? Mountains? Rivers? Aren't those parts of the plan, too?"

"Sure." He shrugged the word. "But they're not necessary."

Meghan blinked. "Not necessary?"

"They're…additions. For instance, if I strip a house down to the frame, it still has a form. A structure. But the siding, the roof, even the furniture and the pictures on the walls…those things aren't necessary. On their own, they don't hold anything together."

Meghan floundered in the face of that kind of logic. He was totally missing the point. "If all God cared about was a frame, or a structure, He could have divided the land and sea—in His orderly way—and left it at that. But He added beauty…just for the sake of beauty. He declared all of it *good*. I think those things are important to Him, too. God didn't stick Adam in a cubicle. He put him in a *garden*."

The words stumbled out and Meghan didn't know if she was making sense or not. She didn't believe the man sitting next to her—the man who had, at the age of ten, managed to recreate ripples on the water with a few dabs of cerulean—thought that if something wasn't practical, it didn't count. That it wasn't necessary.

She tried again. "When you painted the picture of your dad in the boat—"

Cade's expression suddenly iced over, freezing the

rest of the words before they left her mouth. "That wasn't my dad. Ferris was a friend of…he was one of the artists who visited the island."

Chapter Ten

Ferris?

Meghan couldn't believe it. Her breath hitched in her chest but she tried to inject a casual tone in her voice. "You painted Joseph Ferris? *He* was the man in the boat?"

Cade looked surprised she recognized the artist's name and belatedly Meghan wondered if she shouldn't have pretended ignorance. But it was too late now.

"Why?" Cade's lips twisted. "Are you a fan of his work?"

"I know a little about art." A slight prevarication, but true. She exhaled slowly before releasing the question she had to ask. "Did he…paint…anything while he was here?"

Cade abruptly rose to his feet. "We should get back and change into dry clothes before Bert wakes up and wonders where we are."

I get it, Meghan thought ruefully. Conversation over.

She stood up and rivulets of water poured off her soggy jeans and ran down the rocks.

Miss Molly, who, Meghan noticed with envy, had dried with the speed of an airy white hankie clipped to a clothesline, trotted beside her as she scrambled up the bank to catch up with Cade.

She didn't know why the mention of Joseph Ferris had shut Cade down but the connection between them had been severed. Keeping her distance from Cade Halloway was the wisest thing to do, but disappointment still carved out a hollow in her chest.

And even though everything inside Meghan rose up, waving and shouting, to remind her that Cade wasn't the type of man who needed a friendly hug of encouragement, that's exactly what she wanted to do.

Because he was hurting.

She knew it. She just didn't know why.

Yet.

Your mission, remember? It's to find out what happened to the Ferris, not the Halloway family.

"Don't bother wasting your time in the courtyard today." Cade's voice cut tersely through her thoughts. "Parker is going to have to find another place for the wedding."

"But she won't have time," Meghan protested.

Hadn't they agreed on that the day before? Even though she'd had her own doubts after her conversation with Caitlin, Meghan resisted defeat. But why? Parker's wedding didn't have anything to do with her. In fact, if Cade convinced his sister to move it to another place, it would make life easier. Cade would leave. She would leave…

And you'd never see each other again.

Maybe the pesky little voice in her head had a direct link to her heart but Meghan tried to shoo it away.

"But the cleaning crew is coming tomorrow. And Bliss Markham…"

"Bliss Markham quit."

"What?" Meghan gasped. "Why doesn't anyone want to work for you?"

Cade glanced over his shoulder at her as they reached the main path. "It isn't me they don't want to work for. It's my aunt Judith."

"But Cait—" Caution won out. Meghan didn't want Cade to know she'd been talking to her sister. "I've heard Bliss Markham is the best."

"If Parker hired her, she is."

Meghan tried to keep up with his long-legged stride but she was barefoot and had to keep a wary eye on the roots jutting out of the ground, threatening to send her flat on her face. "If Parker hired Bliss, why would she quit because of your aunt?"

Cade didn't slow down. "You've never met my aunt."

A pit bull in pearls. Meghan had thought Caitlin's description a bit harsh but now she wasn't so sure.

"The cleaning crew isn't a problem. I need them here anyway," Cade continued, still forging ahead as if he couldn't get away from her fast enough. "To get the place in shape for the Realtor's inspection."

Meghan tossed her head toward the sky, appealing for patience.

She waited but it didn't come fast enough.

"I can't believe you're going to sell the island. Parker must have good memories. And she could bring her family here." *So could you.* The thought scraped against a sensitive spot on her heart. The one that spending time with Cade had already softened.

He gave an exasperated snort.

Right back at you, Meghan thought.

"You have so many memories here," she murmured more to herself than to him.

But Cade heard her. Because he stopped dead in his tracks and turned around to face her.

"Selling the estate is a business decision," he said flatly. "And no matter what you might think, not all childhood memories are good ones."

She might have believed him.

If he hadn't added the last part.

Cade's fingers drummed an uneven beat against the top of the desk as he tried to concentrate on some of the work he'd brought with him to Blue Key.

Unfortunately, the image of Meghan—hands lifted to the sky, palms open, offering praise to God even as it looked as if she were waiting to receive something back—kept intruding on his thoughts.

Once again, his fingers itched to hold a paintbrush.

He drummed them against the desk to distract them, but when they idly picked up a pen and started to sketch the curve of the birch tree on the back of an envelope, he surged to his feet.

Meghan hadn't even caught his veiled attempt at sarcasm when he'd asked her if she always lived life with abandon. The question had been based purely on self-preservation. He'd thought it would shut the conversation down. Instead her honest response had pushed it to another level.

Expectation.

That's what she'd called it.

And that's what he didn't understand.

As far as he was concerned, that way of thinking was an open invitation to disappointment. If you didn't expect anything—or more importantly, if you *made* things happen—you didn't end up with...nothing.

Their conversation cycled back through Cade's mind.

He'd never discussed his faith in such an unconventional setting before, but it wouldn't have surprised him to find out *she* had.

Of course he believed in God. He attended the church he'd been raised in faithfully and gave generously when the offering plate went by. He talked to God but tried not to bother Him with what he considered to be insignificant details as he went about his day-to-day routine. His faith fit neatly into his life. It didn't spill over the edges and disturb anything around him.

Why was that a bad thing?

Earlier in the spring, Parker had invited him to church for a special evening series designed to encourage people to "live what they believed" but Cade had declined, assuming he was already doing that. Parker had gone without him and that's when she'd met Justin, a missionary back in the States on something called "furlough" while he waited for his next assignment.

They'd dated for a month before announcing their engagement.

Way too fast, Cade had thought. Less than the expiration date on a gallon of milk.

If he ever decided to pursue a relationship, Cade knew he wouldn't let his heart rule his head. It would be based on mutual interests, not emotions. Conversations would be like a game of chess. Well thought out. Reasonable.

Unlike his last conversation with Meghan.

Talking to Meghan was like playing…verbal Twister.

A reluctant smile tilted the corners of Cade's lips when he remembered his parents having similar "discussions." Never arguments. Discussions. That's what they'd called them. How he and Parker, young as they were, had been able to discern the difference, he wasn't sure.

Maybe it had something to do with the undercurrent of respect in their voices. Or the sparkle of laughter that never left Douglas's eyes, no matter how heated the debate. Or the way Genevieve would catch Cade's wide-eyed stare and wink at him while he listened. An argument would have shut him out, but Genevieve's mischievous wink subtly included him.

"We don't agree on much," Genevieve would tell her children cheerfully when she tucked them into bed, "but we agree on what's important."

Cade had believed her. Until the evidence became too strong not to.

He took a restless lap around the library and a scraping noise outside in the courtyard snagged his attention.

Before he reached the window, he knew what he'd see.

And he was right. Meghan on her knees pulling weeds, her bright hair covered by a floppy hat that shaded her face from view.

Stubborn.

That's what she was.

Why was restoring the courtyard so important to her? She didn't have any connection to the island or to his family. She challenged him. Questioned him. Irritated him.

Inspired him.

Cade turned away from the window but the thought lingered, weighting the air around him.

"Inspires me to what, God?" Cade muttered, directing the question to the only one who could possibly understand. "To do something that wastes my time and energy? I'm maximizing what you gave me, just like the servants in the parable of the talents. Isn't that what we're called to do?"

While Cade waited for an answer, he realized this was the first time he'd talked to God directly from his heart instead of his list.

And somehow, in some way, he knew Meghan was responsible for that, too.

Sheer stubbornness drove Meghan to spend the majority of the afternoon pulling weeds. She discovered that yanking them out released some of her pent-up frustration with Cade. So it was kind of like a two-for-one special.

After dropping the bombshell on her that she didn't

need to bother with the courtyard—which she decided to ignore—he'd spent the day holed up in the library and hadn't bothered checking on her and Bert's progress.

They'd just finished pushing a patch of rebellious brown-eyed Susans back to their original borders when a pontoon boat crowded with a lively group of Bert's friends pulled in near the dock. They'd coaxed her on board and encouraged Meghan to come along, but she'd already decided to walk down to the cabins before the cleaning crew descended on them the next morning.

She hoped Genevieve Halloway's habit of displaying artwork in unexpected places meant she'd decorated the walls of the rustic cabins with her friends' paintings, too.

The walk across the width of the island should have given her time to regroup and collect her thoughts, but they remained stubbornly centered on Cade.

He drives me crazy, Lord.

Meghan wanted to say more, but that one complaint kept circling through her mind like the horses on the old carousel as she made her way through the woods.

The four cabins, constructed from peeled logs, hugged the shoreline a stone's throw from the water. At close range, they looked as flimsy as the card houses Meghan and her sisters used to construct on the living room floor.

A stone chimney sprouted from each blue-shingled roof and all of them had screened porches. Forget-me-nots bloomed around the foundations but the wind had reseeded them in random spots, creating a patchwork quilt of blue and pink everywhere Meghan looked.

Meghan eased the door to the first cabin open and took another step back in time. Hot, stale air that begged for a breeze filled the room. Meghan obliged, rattling the windows until the paint congealed in the crevices loosened so she could force them open.

She gave the interior a quick once-over. No flat-screen television. No television at all. No microwave oven. None of the comforts of the new millennium.

Meghan loved it.

And just as she suspected, a collection of water-colors, oils and charcoal sketches, preserved in mismatched frames, decorated the knotty-pine walls.

Judging from the way Cade had reacted when she'd asked about Joseph Ferris, Meghan had the uneasy feeling that he'd disliked the man. But if that were true, why would he have painted his picture?

She paused to study one of the oil paintings, a portrait of a woman in her late twenties or early thirties. Dressed casually in a red-and-white-checkered shirt with a matching scarf tied around her sable hair, Genevieve Halloway's warm smile was reflected in a pair of dreamy, dark blue eyes.

The artist could have interpreted his subject any way he liked, but Meghan had a feeling she was seeing the real Genevieve Halloway. This was the woman who had paid such loving detail to the gardens and carried it into the watercolors she painted. This was the woman who'd proudly framed the flowers her daughter had picked and displayed her son's artwork next to paintings by artists whose work commanded thousands of dollars.

This was the woman Cade no longer wanted in his life.

Remember why you're here, Meghan.

Reluctantly, Meghan moved to the next painting. And the next.

By the time she'd toured the last cabin, the sun was setting and her initial doubts about finding the Ferris had begun to creep in. Anything could have happened to it over the past twenty years and she was running out of places to look.

Bert spent a lot of time in the studio, so other than the time she'd walked Meghan through, there hadn't been an opportunity to check out all the nooks and crannies there.

She stepped out of the cabin and spotted a fishing boat just beyond the point.

And immediately recognized the broad shoulders of the man sitting in it. Cade.

He'd gone without her.

Relief bumped aside Meghan's initial disappointment as she reminded herself she wasn't ready to face him yet.

Farther away, she could see the pontoon boat chugging along the shoreline and hear the faint laughter of the people on board.

The soft tug of loneliness Meghan felt wasn't unfamiliar.

It wasn't that she didn't enjoy being with people. She did. She just chose the people she spent time with very carefully. Evie and Caitlin were her best friends, but she also had a small, close-knit group of people, men and women, she'd known for several years. They were as different as a box of assorted chocolates when it came to ages, hobbies and occupations, but they all had one thing in common—their faith. They valued the things that mattered and they gave Meghan space. Space to grow. To take chances. To make mistakes. To be herself.

And she tried to return the favor.

It suddenly occurred to Meghan that her friends were probably a lot like the people who'd gathered on Blue Key at Genevieve's invitation.

The people Cade had scoffed at.

What did his social calendar look like? Dinner at a trendy restaurant with a private table overlooking the Mississippi? A standing golf date once a week? A black-tie charity event with a woman on his arm who was comfortable in that type of setting?

Even with a little black dress and Caitlin's expert advice, Meghan knew she'd never fit into that crowd.

The low drone of hundreds of mosquitoes emerging from the woods to hunt for their evening supper reminded Meghan it was time to head back to the house.

With Cade and Bert out on the lake, she might have a few minutes to check the upstairs bedrooms. If nothing turned up there, she wasn't sure what to do.

Give up?

It was tempting. By the time Cade got back to the house, she'd be asked—politely—to pack her bags and head back to the city. Cade would have had plenty of time to talk to Parker over the course of the afternoon and his aunt Judith had probably already summoned her minions to find an alternate place for the wedding.

Animals were much less complicated.

Just as Meghan reached the house, she heard the

faint strains of music coming from the courtyard. Out of curiosity, she rounded the corner, stunned to see the carousel horses moving slowly, methodically, up and down. As if trying to remember what it was they were supposed to do.

"Hi." Meghan spoke the word softly, not wanting to startle the woman sitting on the back of the white thoroughbred.

The woman didn't bother to look up. "Bliss?" The name was accompanied by a sniffle.

Funny, Meghan had been wondering the same thing. When she'd spotted her, she'd felt a wild surge of hope that maybe the wedding planner had decided not to quit.

"No. Meghan McBride. The photographer." Meghan moved closer.

As the white horse came back into view, Meghan saw the woman more clearly. Close to her own age. Wearing a printed sundress paired with strappy sandals. Sunglasses perched on top of the artfully streaked hair. And even though only one of the colors matched the sable brown of Cade's, Meghan knew she was about to officially meet Parker Halloway.

Another sniffle. "Oh. I'm sorry you wasted your time coming here."

Meghan's first thought was that Parker was crying because she'd seen the shape the courtyard was in. Her reaction would certainly fit with Caitlin's description of Cade's sister.

She watched for an opportunity and grabbed the gold pole of the black charger as it went by, swinging onto the platform of the carousel. "Wasted my time?"

"There isn't going to be a...wedding."

"Because you can't find another place for the reception?" Meghan gripped the pole tighter as the carousel shuddered and then lurched to a complete stop.

Parker shook her head. "Because I gave Justin back his ring. I can't m-marry him."

Chapter Eleven

Cade came in off the lake shortly after the sun melted into the horizon and took a few minutes to pack away his fishing gear.

He had a nice stringer of fish. The weather had been perfect. The solitude of the lake appealing. But something had been missing.

Meghan.

He should have been happy not to have to dodge her wild casts or compete with her for perch. But instead he'd found himself missing the play of sunlight on her hair and the small frown of concentration that settled between her eyebrows when she baited the hook.

What was she doing to him?

He refused to let his thoughts formulate an answer to that, knowing he was afraid of the answer.

"Come on. Rise and shine." He glanced down at Miss Molly, who'd fallen asleep on a musty boat cushion while he cleaned the fish. "Let's find…" *Meghan?* He quickly ad-libbed. "Something to eat."

The dog's ears perked up at the word "eat" and for once she followed him obediently up the path to the house.

Cade had almost reached the front door when he heard music. Carousel music. He recognized the grating tune immediately.

Only one person could have coaxed the ancient contraption to life. And that one person had to know that some things were off-limits.

Shadows already filled the spaces between the flowering bushes and shrubs as Cade veered around the hedge of arbor vitae.

The music stopped abruptly and so did Cade.

Meghan sat on a willow bench near the carousel, one arm curved around the shoulders of the young woman hunched over beside her.

It took a few seconds to realize it was his sister.

"Parker?" Cade walked toward them but Parker met him halfway, launching herself into his arms.

He couldn't remember a time when his sister had been anything but calm, confident and in control. And the last time she'd turned to him for comfort was when she'd fallen off her tricycle and skinned her elbow.

"Hey." Awkwardly, he pushed the damp strands of hair off her face as she burrowed against him. "What's going on?"

He asked the question even though he could guess the answer. Parker had seen the courtyard and now she finally believed what he'd been trying to tell her.

He peeled his sister off his chest, about to give her

a gentle shake to remind her to pull it together, but Meghan's fingers closed over his. And squeezed. Hard.

"We should go inside," she murmured.

Cade hesitated and then nodded curtly, guiding Parker up the path to the house while she clung to him like a limpet.

"Who brought you over? Is Justin here?" Cade thought the questions were simple and straightforward enough but all they did was trigger another bout of tears.

Meghan had the door open, waiting for them, before they reached it. He would have led Parker into the library, but Meghan got in his way and somehow the three of them ended up in the kitchen.

Cade assumed Meghan would leave them alone to talk but she set a box of tissue down in front of Parker. "Tea? Coffee?"

Cade opened his mouth to tell her neither one was necessary but closed it again when Parker melted against the chair and let out a long, shuddering breath. "Tea. Please."

Cade didn't know if he should be relieved or frustrated that Meghan had stayed. It was family business, after all, and he'd never seen his sister so rattled. He pulled out the chair opposite Parker and straddled it, folding his arms across the back. Parker honked loudly into a tissue, seemingly unaware of the black streaks of mascara running down her cheeks.

"I tried to warn—" The rattle of teacups interrupted him. When he glanced at Meghan, the message in the misty-green eyes was clear. No *I-told-you-so's allowed*. Maybe she had a point. And he didn't want to be responsible for opening another set of floodgates, either. "Don't be upset, Parker. We can fix this. Have the ceremony at church and let Aunt Judith find another place for the reception. We've got time and everything else is good to go, right?"

In spite of his brotherly pep talk, tears pooled in her eyes again.

To Cade's astonishment, Meghan slipped a cup of tea in front of Parker and put a comforting hand on her shoulder. What was even more surprising was Parker's reaction. Instead of moving away from Meghan, his sister reached up and grasped her hand as if it were a lifeline.

"I'm not upset because of the courtyard. It's p-perfect." Just as Cade tried to wrap his mind around that, Parker dropped another bomb on him. "Justin and I… I c-called it off. The wedding is off."

"What happened?" Cade tried to mask his relief. He hadn't expected such a neat little solution to all their problems.

Parker shook her head mutely, staring into the teacup, and Cade glanced at Meghan. She looked away, but not before he saw mixture of disbelief and disappointment in her eyes. She'd accurately read his thoughts, another unsettling habit of hers.

Cade tried to tell himself that she, as an outsider, didn't understand the whole situation. How could she know that Parker, whose idea of "roughing it" was skipping her weekly spa appointment, wasn't being realistic about linking her future to a missionary used to going without the most basic necessities? Like clean drinking water. Or outlets to plug in the dizzying array of tools Parker used to style her hair.

Parker's stubborn insistence to plan a wedding in three months, before Justin returned to Mexico, had only added to the family's concern that she was letting her heart rule her head.

But no one had been able talk her out of it. Not even Judith. For some reason Parker was blind to the fact she and Justin were as ill-suited as…their parents.

"It's better this way," Cade said cautiously instead. "One of these days, you'll look back and be glad you called off the wedding. You wouldn't want to find out Justin wasn't the right one for you *after* you got married."

Meghan had heard enough.

She had to leave the room before she muzzled Cade with the nearest dish towel. And she was taking Parker with her.

Before Cade had interrupted them, Parker had started to open up to her about the reason she'd broken up with her fiancé and fled Minneapolis for Blue Key Island.

Her. A complete stranger. Finding things out about Parker that none of her family members seemed to know.

Which wasn't surprising, Meghan thought darkly, if the Halloways considered lectures and interrogations "the art of conversation."

"Cade, I'll bet Parker hasn't had anything to eat all day. Why don't you make her a veggie omelet while I help her unpack." Meghan phrased it as a statement, not a question.

Cade opened his mouth to say something but his jaw snapped shut when Parker offered him a watery smile. "That sounds great."

"Great," Meghan echoed cheerfully.

The suspicious glint in Cade's eyes told her that he knew she was up to something. Her answering smile told him she didn't care.

Parker followed her down the hall like a sleepwalker and Meghan moved to the side as Parker stepped past her, into the pink bedroom she'd slept in as a child.

"It looks exactly the same." Parker's voice came out barely above a murmur as she ran her hand over the sun-bleached taffeta spread.

Meghan didn't hear any bitterness in the other woman's tone, only quiet resignation.

"Those shoes have to be killing your feet," Meghan said, eyeing the railroad-spike heels. "I have some slippers you can borrow. I'll be back in a flash."

She slipped out of the room and her nose twitched at the pungent scent of garlic permeating the hall. Apparently, Cade had taken her advice.

When she returned, Parker was perched on the side of the bed, examining her face in a compact mirror.

"I look horrible." She snapped the mirror shut without bothering to repair the damages.

"You look a little…rumpled." If Meghan would have said anything else, Parker would have known she was lying. "But that's understandable."

She offered her the dog slippers—a gag gift from Caitlin when she'd opened her studio—complete with tails and the curling, pink felt tongues she was forever stepping on.

Parker studied them for a few seconds before pushing the slippers on her feet. She wrapped her arms around her knees like a little girl and looked around. "This room seems a lot smaller than it did when I was six. I love it here."

Love. Present tense, Meghan noticed, not past. And unlike Cade, no bitterness leaked into Parker's voice. How could it be that two people who shared the same memories had such different feelings about the island?

"When J-Justin and I started making plans, I couldn't imagine another place I'd rather say my wedding vows," Parker continued softly. "It just seemed to be the right place for a new...a new beginning."

Meghan silently agreed. She'd fallen in love at first sight, too. Even in the neglected state it was in, the house retained an inviting, comforting warmth. The grounds reflected Genevieve Halloway's attempts to work with the wild, untamed beauty of the island instead of trying to subdue it.

"Now I wonder if there really is such a thing as a new beginning. If a person can really change." Parker picked at a loose thread in the bedspread, her expression pensive.

Meghan's forehead furrowed. "Were you hoping Justin would change?" she ventured.

Parker looked up, startled. "Why would I want Justin to change? He's the most amazing man I've ever met. Strong. Sensitive. Funny. Caring. Unselfish." Her voice wobbled slightly on the last word. "His faith is...different. It took me a while to figure out it was what made *him* different. He knows God in a way I never thought a person could. In a way that *I* could."

"I understand."

Parker pinned her with a sharp look, then relaxed. "You do, don't you? I can see it in your eyes."

"What I don't understand is why you broke your engagement," Meghan said candidly. "It's obvious you love Justin."

"Love isn't always enough," Parker muttered.

"Do you really believe that? Or is that someone else talking?" *Say, someone a smidge over six feet tall, with cobalt-blue eyes?*

Parker stared at her for a long minute and then her gaze shifted to the rocking chair in the corner. "Why am I talking to you? Who are you? I don't even know why you're here."

Meghan wasn't intimidated by the unexpected glimpse of the Parker Halloway that Caitlin had described. The sudden retreat behind familiar walls had to be a defense mechanism. Something Meghan understood all too well.

"You do know why I'm here. Because God obviously thought you needed someone—" *other than your brother* "—to talk to you about why you're willing to walk away from the man you love."

Parker's response was to bury her face in one of the daisy-shaped pillows piled at the end of the bed and Meghan strained to make out the muffled words underneath them. "I think God is going to give up on me. I keep trying...but I keep messing up."

"What is it you're trying to do?"

Parker sat up, ticking off the list on each manicured finger. "Be friendly. Polite. Generous. Kind. Unselfish—"

"You're trying to be a Girl Scout?"

"I'm trying to be a missionary's wife," Parker blurted. "And I can't do it. Aunt Judith is right. If I really love Justin, I have to accept I'm not the kind of woman he needs by his side. He would end up hating me and I couldn't stand that."

Meghan had to send up a silent prayer, asking God to forgive her bad attitude toward Judith Halloway, before she spoke again. Obviously, Parker's aunt had failed to break up the engagement by telling her niece that Justin wasn't right for her. But she'd succeeded by playing on Parker's doubts that she was right for *him*.

"You accepted Christ into your heart recently, didn't you?"

The smile on Parker's face answered her question even before she affirmed it out loud. "In the spring. Two weeks before I met Justin. But it's harder than I thought it would be." She lowered her voice. "I still like to shop."

She looked so guilty, Meghan choked back a laugh. "I've been a Christian since I was twelve years old, and trust me, there are a lot of areas in my life still under construction. The difference is that now, instead of trying to manage those areas on my own, I let God in so He can deal with them.

"I don't know if anyone shared this verse from Romans with you, Parker, but it says God demonstrated

His love for us in that while we were still sinners, Christ died for us.

"He didn't wait until we had our act together before He decided we were good enough to love. He loved you before you knew Him and He loves you now. And He doesn't expect you to do your own heart makeover, either. That's His job. I've found it's spending time with Him that changes me. It's not something I have to force. If that's the case, it becomes all about me again, when really, it should be about Him."

For the first time, hope sparked in Parker's eyes. But then the doubts returned and she chewed off the last smidge of color remaining on her bottom lip. "I don't know, Meghan. I might drag Justin down. I don't have the books of the Bible memorized and I'm not sure if I'm praying the right way. I don't even know how to make a casserole if the church has a potluck dinner—"

"How old is Justin?" Meghan interrupted.

"Twenty-eight."

"I may be wrong, but Justin has probably met plenty of women who know how to make cheesy potatoes and Jell-O fluff. But he didn't fall in love with one of them and ask her to marry him. He asked you. He loves *you*. If you really believe God brought you and Justin together, don't let your fears get in the way. Or your aunt Judith."

"Aunt Judith." Parker shook her head. "She means well."

Meghan wasn't so sure about that, but was saved from having to comment by a light rap on the door.

"Ladies, dinner is served." Cade bowed low, a white dish towel draped over his arm.

Parker giggled and jumped off the bed.

Cade looked down at her feet as she padded toward him. "Interesting choice of footwear, sis."

"They're Meghan's."

"Really?" Cade smiled, and the tiny crease in his cheek made a guest appearance.

Meghan swallowed hard against the lump that suddenly formed in her throat. Fatigue? Discouragement that she hadn't found the Ferris during her search of the cabins? Or because she'd expected Cade to be all business but he'd somehow known that what Parker really needed was her big brother?

And that small, silly gesture scooped out another piece of her heart. If Cade Halloway kept it up, it wouldn't be long before he had the whole thing.

And that scared her more than anything.

"Aren't you coming, Meghan?" Parker paused, and glanced back.

"I should take Miss Molly for a walk since Bert won't be back until later."

Parker's eyes narrowed and Meghan had the sudden, uncomfortable feeling the other woman could see right through the flimsy excuse. And why she'd made it.

"What time do you get up in the morning?" Parker asked.

"About seven." Curiosity overrode caution. "Why?"

"Because I've only got five days to plan a wedding and I need your help."

Chapter Twelve

Cade watched his sister tuck away three-quarters of the omelet he'd made, plus two pieces of toast. All the time eyeing the slice of ham he'd cooked up for himself.

With a sigh, he slid it onto her plate and received a sunny smile in return. He still couldn't believe the transformation in his sister after ten minutes in Meghan's company. Apparently he wasn't the only Halloway susceptible to her wide-eyed optimism.

"Dad called." Cade reached for the teapot and topped off Parker's cup.

"You didn't tell him I was here, did you?" Panic flared in his sister's eyes.

"He was worried."

"He'll tell Aunt Judith," she predicted gloomily. "And she'll airdrop a team of deprogrammers on Blue Key by tomorrow morning."

"I can always set a trap for them. It worked pretty well the last time I tried it, as I recall."

Parker smiled. "You didn't expect it to, though, did you? I'm glad I still have all my toes."

Cade grinned. "We won't talk about that."

Silence settled between them and the laughter in Parker's eyes faded. "There's a lot we won't talk about, isn't there, Cade?"

He shrugged, knowing what she was referring to and yet reluctant to go down that road. "There's no point in digging up the past. Especially when it comes to Dad and Genevieve. She wanted something else out of life and she left. She left Dad. She left us. End of story."

At least that's all Parker needed to know.

"You never call her Mom," Parker murmured.

"I don't know anything about her. And it's hard to call someone Mom who you haven't talked to in twenty years…" Cade leaned forward, stunned to see tears form in his sister's eyes again. "What?"

She took a deep breath and met his gaze. "I talked to her."

"When?"

Parker flinched and Cade realized he'd put more force in the word than was necessary. He counted to ten. And then to fifteen. His voice softened. "When?"

"In April."

April. The same month she'd met her fiancé. A dozen questions surfaced and Cade swiftly ranked them in order of importance. "Does Dad know?"

"I wanted to tell him."

So, no. Some of the muscles in Cade's neck loosened. He could only imagine the fireworks that confession would have created in the family.

"Why after all these years of silence, did you think Genevieve would want to know—would *care* to know—about Justin?"

Silence stretched between them and Cade realized his little sister was trying to decide if she could trust him. And it stung. Maybe as far as sibling relationships went, they weren't extremely close but he'd always kept a watchful, brotherly eye on her from a distance.

"I didn't call Mom to tell her I met Justin. I called to tell her that I met…Jesus."

It was the last thing he expected her to say. "Parker—"

"I know what you're going to say but just listen to me for a minute, Cade. I have a relationship with God now. And it's different. When we went to church, it was a Sunday-morning appointment. Like getting my nails or hair done. If I paid attention to anything, it was what the other women were wearing. And it's scary how I thought that was normal. That it was *enough*. But something happened when I started going once a week to hear the missionaries talk. It was like listening to a different language that everyone could speak but me. They talked about God as if He wasn't just glaring down at everyone from heaven, but like He was right there with them. And that He loves them. Cares what happens to them. I…I wanted that. And I never knew I wanted it until then.

"I'd been meeting with the pastor's wife, studying the Bible with her. We talked about forgiveness one day and I realized it was crazy that our family split apart so completely, no matter what the reason. That because our parents divorced when I was six years old, I have to live the rest of my life without knowing my mother."

"It's what Genevieve wanted."

"It's not what I want." Parker's voice was soft but emphatic.

Cade dropped onto the willow bench and closed his eyes, even though darkness cloaked the courtyard and he couldn't see anything more than two feet in front of him.

Bert had returned from her boat ride, thrilled to see Parker again no matter what the circumstances, and he'd turned his sister over to her for a reminiscing marathon, grateful for the chance to escape.

Too bad he couldn't escape his thoughts as easily.

He was still having a hard time processing what Parker had told him. That she'd been in contact with their mother. That Genevieve had hinted she'd like to see Parker sometime if Parker was agreeable. And Parker seemed more than agreeable. She was actually excited about the possibility of, in her words, starting over.

That was another thing Cade didn't get. Starting over. No one could reclaim twenty years. Parker had been in first grade when Genevieve left and now she was an adult. They were more like strangers than family members.

And why was Genevieve suddenly interested in getting to know her daughter?

According to Judith, Genevieve had signed the papers granting total custody of her children to Douglas without protest. And his aunt had hinted the generous settlement their father had given Genevieve had played a significant part in the decision.

They didn't know anything about Genevieve or the kind of life she was living now. Judith had judged Genevieve selfish, but she could also be an opportunist, ready to take advantage of her only daughter's desire to reconcile.

The thought made Cade shifted restlessly and his hand bumped something on the bench beside him. He reached out and picked it up. Meghan's camera. She must have left it here when he'd found her and Parker sitting together earlier.

Cade shook his head. It wasn't the first time he'd seen it lying around, but he couldn't believe she'd left it outside—what if it rained during the night?

"Cade?" Meghan suddenly stepped out of the shadows, as if conjured up by his thoughts. "How is Parker doing?"

"Carrying on with her wedding plans." *Thanks to you.*

Cade didn't say the words out loud but he didn't have to. The unspoken accusation hung in the air between them.

"What do you have against Justin?" Meghan finally ventured.

"I don't have anything against Justin," Cade said, surprised. "I've met him and I think he's a great guy."

"Then why…" Meghan's voice trailed off in confusion.

"They're complete opposites," Cade explained patiently. "Justin is soft-spoken and thoughtful. He's used to making sacrifices. To putting other people first. Parker is used to getting her own way. Very loudly, on occasion. The qualities they're drawn to in each other will eventually drive them crazy." *And drive them apart.*

"Maybe. But they could complement each other, too."

"Like oil and water?" Cade asked cynically.

She tilted her head. "Like hot fudge and ice cream."

"Like my parents?"

The corners of Meghan's lips turned up. "Like mine."

"I think you're overestimating my sister."

"And I think you're underestimating two people who are committed first to Christ and second to each other," she said quietly. "Maybe what they bring to the relationship might be different, but they're building on the same foundation. Their faith."

Cade didn't know what to say. Maybe understanding that was what had sparked the peaceful glow he'd seen in Parker's eyes after she'd talked to Meghan.

His fingers closed around the camera and he held it out, grateful for the chance to take a detour from the path their conversation was going down.

"You left your camera on the bench," he said abruptly.

Meghan took a tentative step forward to take it and her fingers brushed against his. The slightest touch, but Cade felt the jolt down to his toes.

"Someone should invent one of those beeper things for cameras." Her soft laughter stirred the evening air. "Then I'd always know where it was."

"Or you could put it back in the same place every time you used it." Cade thought the suggestion was a reasonable one, but it snuffed out the sparkle in her eyes like a bucket of water on a campfire.

"I'll keep that in mind."

Cade watched her walk away and disappear into the shadows, feeling like an insensitive clod. The worst part was, he wasn't sure why.

"Did you get the pictures I sent? How do we start?" Meghan surveyed the courtyard, hoping her sister had formulated a plan.

"Mmm. For starters, I'd recommend a backhoe. Definitely a backhoe. And a bulldozer."

"Caitlin!"

"Is Parker Halloway's themed reception a recreation of Gilligan's Island?"

"I need advice, not a stand-up comedy routine."

"Who's joking?"

"Cait—"

"Fine. What time is the ceremony?"

"Three o'clock?"

"Reception?"

"Five." Meghan smiled as Parker sidled closer and she held the phone out a few inches to include her in the conversation.

"Too bad. Darkness would have definitely worked in your favor. But I suppose the times are etched in stone." Caitlin expelled a "look what I have to work with" sigh.

"What's etched in stone?" Parker whispered.

"The ceremony and reception time," Meghan whispered back.

"No, it isn't. What does she have in mind?"

"Parker said it isn't. What do you have in mind?"

Silence. And then, "Are you sure she's really Parker Halloway and not an impost—"

Meghan squeaked and jerked the phone back but it was too late. Parker had heard. "It's really me, Caitlin," she sang out cheerfully.

"I'm never going to work in this town again," Caitlin muttered.

"Yes, you will. Now focus. Wow, it feels good to say that to *you* for a change. Now, one more time. What do we need?"

"Bliss Markham," Caitlin admitted. "But I heard she took a flight to Paris for a long weekend. Something about needing to recuperate?"

Parker rolled her eyes and mouthed the words "Aunt Judith."

"Okay, this is a list of what I need to start with." Caitlin got serious and shifted into image-consultant mode. "Measurements of the courtyard. Number of guests. Menu. Weather forecast for the weekend. Floral arrangements… Megs? Are you still with me? Repeat what I just said."

Meghan winced. "Ah…menu?"

"Maybe you should write this…never mind. Let me talk to Parker."

"Be nice." Meghan whispered the warning before handing the phone to Cade's sister.

Bert came outside, carrying a tray with a pitcher of orange juice, a plate of cinnamon rolls and a carafe of coffee.

"Fuel," the caretaker said succinctly.

Meghan glanced at the door behind Bert, waiting for Cade to make an appearance. If he was still on the island. She'd sensed the change in his mood last night and wondered if he was upset that Parker was going ahead with the wedding plans.

If Caitlin met someone like Justin, Meghan knew she'd be thrilled to welcome him into the family. Evie had been blessed with that kind of man in Sam, and Meghan couldn't have been happier for her younger sister. Their wedding had been a celebration of God bringing two people together in His name.

Her brother-in-law was a new believer, like Parker, but his faith was already bearing fruit. Evie had shared that Sam had started the process to create a chaplain's ride-a-long program through the Summer Harbor Police Department, not only to encourage the officers but to reach out to families in the community.

"Penny for your thoughts." Bert deftly poured a cup of coffee and pressed it into her hands.

Meghan smiled. "I was thinking about my sister's wedding. It was perfect. Not everything-just-so perfect, but perfect in its…imperfections, I guess you could say. We decorated the tables with white linen and crystal but the centerpieces were wildflowers in antique glass vases. My dad's friend, Sophie, made the wedding cake. It was important to Evie that all of us contributed something to make the day special. It wasn't an event. We were celebrating how awesome it is when God brings two people together."

"That's what Justin and I want."

Meghan hadn't realized Parker was eavesdropping

on their conversation. "But *Twin City Trends* said your wedding was going to be the one to watch," Meghan reminded her.

"That wasn't my dream wedding, it was Aunt Judith's. And it also happened to be the one that got canceled yesterday." The mischievous gleam in Parker's eyes—eyes a shade lighter than Cade's—brightened. "Which means the wedding we're planning now can be anything we want it to be."

Parker put the phone back to her ear. "Caitlin? Are you still with me? Guest list, let's say twenty. Six o'clock ceremony. Eight o'clock reception." She nudged the phone down her chin and looked at Bert. "I no longer have a florist or a caterer, but can you whip up some hors d'oeuvres? And a wedding cake?"

"I'd love to." Bert grinned.

"Great. Caitlin? I'll call you back. Before we go any further, I need to make one more phone call and ask Justin to marry me."

Later that afternoon, sketchbook under her arm, Meghan broke away from the frenetic whirlwind of activity and headed for the point in a quest for peace and quiet...and the opportunity to fall apart without witnesses.

Somehow, Parker had assumed she was as qualified as Bliss Markham to oversee the wedding preparations.

"Maybe it's because she thinks you've photographed so many weddings you have a handle on the way these things are supposed to work," Meghan muttered as she stumbled along the uneven path.

Guilt pinched her for the first time since she'd come to Blue Key Island.

No one can serve two masters...

The scripture reference scrolled through her mind and Meghan shook it away.

Completely out of context, she told herself firmly. Technically, she did have two employers—Parker Halloway and Nina Bonnefield—but she'd thought she could keep the two jobs separate. She didn't realize she'd find herself at cross-purposes. But she didn't know she'd be drafted into service as a stand-in wedding planner, florist and gardener, either! Fortunately, Bert had taken on the role of supervisor for the cleaning crew that arrived just before lunch to shoo the mice out and transform the cabins into acceptable living quarters.

Parker's wedding had been ruthlessly scaled down from a "summer event" to a small, intimate gathering of close friends and family, but Meghan had still spent the afternoon trying to create what Caitlin liked to refer to as a "plan of attack."

But then, General Caitlin thrived on that sort of thing. Three hours later, Meghan was retreating into the brush, ready to surrender.

Except that Parker was counting on her. And explaining why she didn't have a hundred simple wedding solutions right off the top of her head would mean explaining the real reason she'd signed on to photograph the wedding.

Meghan felt another pinch of guilt.

To tell Parker the truth now would not only break the confidentiality agreement she'd made with her father's client but could jeopardize the fragile bonds of friendship between her and Cade's sister.

And it didn't take a degree in rocket science to figure out that Cade wouldn't be happy when he found out she'd been scoping out the island for a valuable painting. A painting its original owner might be planning to "reacquire."

Meghan groaned.

She was in a pickle, no doubt about it. And she had no one to blame but herself.

All afternoon, she'd smiled and nodded. Making and listening to suggestions, pretending everything was under control so Parker wouldn't worry. She'd taken notes but couldn't remember where she'd put them. As she tried to concentrate on one task at a time, old tapes began to play in the background of her thoughts.

You're going to fail. You're going to disappoint people. They're going to think you're strange.

Panic had set in, sending Meghan running for cover. For some time and breathing room to drown out the thoughts with truth.

Lord, the things I'm expected to accomplish over the next few days aren't just out of my comfort zone or things that aren't registered on my spiritual gift list, they're almost...impossible.

Discouraged and tired, Meghan stepped off the path and dropped down on the bank, resting her forehead on her bent knees.

You know the drill, Megs. Evie was an ocean away, but Meghan heard her sister's gentle encouragement as if she were sitting right beside her. Maybe because

Evie had told her the same thing a thousand times before. *When you're under attack, pick up the sword of the spirit and parry. Fight lies with the truth.*

Evie might have been the youngest of the McBride sisters but she'd surrendered her life to Christ at an earlier age and many times Meghan felt as if her little sister was the more mature one when it came to spiritual things. And she was also Meghan's biggest cheerleader. Somehow, she understood Meghan's struggles with ADD in a way that Caitlin, who didn't see why Meghan couldn't keep her thoughts focused by sheer determination, didn't always understand.

Meghan closed her eyes, letting her soul absorb the silence as she leaned on the familiar verses that had shored her up during difficult times in the past.

My grace is sufficient for you, for my power is made perfect in weakness.

There'd been a time in her life, like the Apostle Paul, when she'd pleaded with God to take away her weaknesses. To reconnect what she viewed as faulty wiring in her brain. He hadn't. And in the mysterious ways of grace, she'd realized that a one-time miracle of healing hadn't changed her as much as the day-to-day appeals for strength that had deepened her faith.

Quietly, she recited other verses she'd memorized for days like today.

I can do everything through Him who gives me strength.

I am fearfully and wonderfully made...

The last verse snuck in, uninvited, and Meghan sucked in a breath. There it was. The basis of her fears. That people would see the "real" Meghan Mc-Bride and find her lacking. People she was beginning to care about.

Meghan sighed. Another visit to a battleground the Lord had already fought—and won—in her life. As much as she tried to move ahead, there were times she returned. The landscape not comfortable but all too familiar.

She opened her eyes just in time to see a bald eagle skim over the surface of the water and then ride the wind current up again.

Meghan choked back a delighted laugh, awed by the unexpected gift. And the reminder.

But those who hope in the Lord will renew their strength. They will soar on wings like eagles; they will run and not grow weary; they will walk and not be faint.

Did planning a wedding, when you had no clue what you were doing, fall under that promise?

Meghan hoped so. Because at the moment she felt more like a fish out of water than an eagle soaring in the sky.

Chapter Thirteen

"So, what do you think?" Parker scratched the tip of her nose with the back of her gardening glove, looking way too pleased with herself.

Which was why Cade didn't have the heart to tell her the truth. "You've made some…progress."

With some strategic planning, he'd managed to avoid getting caught up in wedding preparations for most of the afternoon. Until his sister finally tracked him down and pried him away from the desk, insisting he look at the courtyard.

She wrinkled her nose at him. "We *could* use some more help. But not from the bulldozer that Caitlin Mc-Bride recommended."

Cade decided he liked Meghan's older sister. "Maybe the cleaning crew could take an extra day and help out with the landscaping."

"They might. If they didn't already have a month's worth of work condensed into five days. Bert's friends offered to help with the food, but I think we're going to have to bribe some people from Willoughby to come over." She gave him a hopeful look.

"I hate to fog up your rose-colored glasses, Parker, but the people in Willoughby aren't exactly rolling out the red carpet for the Halloway family at the moment."

Parker anchored her hands on her hips; a familiar gesture that made Cade wince. *Here it comes,* he thought. Level One of what would rapidly morph into the adult equivalent of a temper tantrum. Tools that Parker had used in the past to get her way.

"That's because you're selling the island. It may have been twenty years ago, but a lot of people remember being invited to the island for fish boils and corn roasts. To them, you aren't just selling a piece of property, you're selling a piece of local history."

"It's business. And maybe if the people in Willoughby understood that business requires change, they wouldn't be struggling to keep their little town alive."

He braced himself for Level Two, which could take one of two directions. Shouting or pouting. Personally, he preferred the latter. Much easier on the ears.

Cade blinked in surprise when Parker laughed. *Laughed.* "Can you hear yourself? You sound just like Dad." She walked over and shocked him even more when she reeled him in for an affectionate hug and tweaked his cheek. "Never mind about going into Willoughby to round up some reinforcements tomorrow morning. I'll ask Meghan. I have a feeling she can charm the birds out of the trees. But if she can't get some help and there are still a few weeds on Saturday, we'll have the bridal party stand on them and no one will notice."

She winked and sashayed away while Cade stood rooted to the spot like one of the statues in the sculpture garden.

Who are you and what have you done with my sister?

The question got bumped to the side as Parker's teasing comment replayed in Cade's mind.

You sound just like Dad.

Cade wasn't sure why that statement rubbed him the wrong way. He respected his father. Douglas Halloway had constructed his life in much the same way he'd built his business. In an organized, thoughtful way, controlling—and minimizing—the number of unknown variables. There were fewer surprises that way. Let this in. Shut this out. It worked for them.

He watched Parker kneel down on the cobblestone path and start plucking weeds again, humming a cheerful off-key tune. He couldn't remember ever seeing her so...content. In fact, he'd witnessed emotion meltdowns over things as insignificant as a friend canceling last-minute dinner plans. And although he'd been listening the night before when she'd earnestly described her change of heart, he'd still been skeptical. Until he saw actions to back up her words. Not only would the "old" Parker have demanded nothing less than perfection for her wedding day, she wouldn't have handled the obstacles with a wry sense of humor.

It occurred to him that the change he saw in Parker, the one he'd originally attributed to wanting to put on a good show for her fiancé, might have more to do with a changed relationship with God rather than her relationship with Justin.

Cade wasn't ready for the unexpected stirring in his soul. The uncomfortable realization that his relationship with God looked a lot like his relationship with his own father. Correct but distant. But the truth was, Cade wasn't sure he wanted it to be different. Case in point—Parker. She'd sought a deeper relationship with God and ended up engaged to a missionary. And he still wasn't convinced the match made sense. They didn't have to look any further than their parents for an example of the fallout that occurred when opposites attract.

"Fine," he heard himself say out loud. "I'll go into Willoughby tomorrow and see if I can sweet-talk someone into helping you. I'd hate to have you break a nail."

"Too late. I've sacrificed three already." Parker grinned. "You should take Meghan with you. She isn't such a scowler."

The gleam in Parker's eyes sent warning bells clanging in his head. She didn't think...no, she couldn't think he was interested in Meghan.

"I'm not a scowl—" Okay, he was scowling. But who wouldn't be under the circumstances? "I'll ask her. But only to be the official smiling-person."

Parker shrugged and gave him an innocent look. "Sure. Whatever."

"I think I liked you better before," Cade growled.

Parker's smile turned pensive. "No, you didn't."

"Are you ready?"

Meghan's heart took a swan dive at the sound of

Cade's voice behind her. She was going to have to attach a jingle bell to his Rolex, that's all there was to it.

She gave a jerky nod, not sure how to answer his question. Because she still wasn't sure exactly how she'd ended up with Cade as her buddy for a trip to town. It had started out innocently enough. Parker had asked her during dinner the night before if she'd go into Willoughby and inquire at the café about getting a grounds crew together, maybe a few teenagers who'd welcome the chance to earn some extra spending money. It wasn't until after she'd agreed that Parker had blithely informed her Cade was going along, too.

The man she kept trying to avoid. Which was really difficult, given the fact they were on an island.

Nothing seemed to be working in her favor lately.

And did he have to look so good?

Cade hadn't gone native yet—he still favored khaki pants and button-down shirts—but the wind had ruffled his hair out of its conservative style and he hadn't bothered to shave off the five-o'clock shadow that enhanced his jawline. The result was an intriguing combination of business casual and… professional swashbuckler.

Now there was a new style waiting to be discovered, Meghan mused.

"…sent lunch along." Cade hefted an enormous wicker picnic basket into the boat and vaulted in after it. "She must think it's going to take a while to find some help."

Meghan hoped not. She scrambled into the boat and sat down, plucking loose strings out of the frayed hems of her denim cutoffs.

It's for Parker and it's only a few hours, she reminded herself.

Cade must have been thinking the same thing. Because judging from the rate of speed in which he pushed the boat toward shore, he obviously didn't want to spend any more time alone with her than was necessary, either.

"Where to first? The chamber of commerce?" Cade parked his car along the curb in the middle of the main street and turned toward Meghan.

"How about the churches?"

"Churches? Why the churches?"

"Because believers aren't supposed to hold grudges. Which means that out of all the people in Willoughby, they shouldn't be upset you're selling and they should be willing to help someone in need," Meghan explained.

Cade shook his head at her logic. "How about I go to the chamber of commerce, you go to the churches, and we'll meet back at the park in an hour to see who hired the most people."

"Are you turning this into a contest? Like the night we went fishing?" Meghan asked suspiciously.

"Why not?"

Meghan clicked her tongue. "Men are so competitive."

"Winner gets to drive the boat back."

"You're on."

Cade was late.

So late that Meghan began to wonder if his "divide and conquer" suggestion had really been a plot to ditch her.

At least, Meghan thought in satisfaction, she had the picnic basket.

She pulled her sketchbook out of her bag and began to scribble. Absorbed in the drawing, she didn't see Cade until he dropped down beside her on the blanket she'd spread out under an oak tree.

"You first. How many?"

"Seven," Meghan answered.

"You're kidding me."

"The church youth group at Faith Fellowship needed a community service project." Meghan tried not to sound smug.

"Unbelievable."

"They'll be there tomorrow morning. All we have to do is provide snacks and bottled water and—" Meghan snapped her fingers "—the weeds are history. What did you come up with at the chamber of commerce?"

"You mean, other than a map for a self-guided walking tour of the Willoughby cemetery, which was established in 1864, compliments of Obadiah Willoughby, in case you were wondering—"

"I get to drive the boat, don't I?"

"You get to drive the boat." Cade stretched out his legs in the grass and glanced at the sketchbook in her lap. "What were you drawing? Main Street?"

Meghan closed the sketchbook. But not fast enough.

"Let me see that."

Absolutely not. "I was just...doodling."

"Uh-huh." Cade held out his hand.

"You really don't want to—" She gave in when his

eyebrow lifted. *Never,* she thought, *underestimate the power of the eyebrow.* "Fine. Here."

Cade flipped through the sketchbook, pausing to linger over some of the pages while Meghan chewed on her fingernail, wishing she could disappear in a puff of humiliation.

"This looks familiar." He frowned down at one of the pages.

Meghan smiled. "It should. You probably drive past it every day. It's the time mural the children's art ministry painted last summer."

"Time mural?"

"You know, there is a time for everything and a season for every activity under heaven? Ecclesiastes?"

"You're involved with Sidewalk Chalk?"

Meghan was surprised, and pleased, that Cade was familiar with the ministry. "More like totally submerged." She didn't bother to mention she was the one who'd spearheaded the entire project. "Have you ever volunteered?"

Meghan would have remembered if she'd seen him on-site, but with the ministry expanding the way it was throughout the various churches in the city, it would have been possible their paths hadn't crossed.

"The firm makes a contribution every year." Cade continued to study the sketch that topped the list of Meghan's favorite murals.

Now Meghan remembered why the Halloway name had sounded so familiar the first time Patrick had mentioned it. She hadn't simply heard the name Cade Halloway because of his family connections, she'd *seen* it. His bold signature had been scrawled in the bottom right-hand corner of several checks giving generous donations to the ministry. There'd even been rumors a black-tie fund-raiser was in the planning stages, compliments of some local corporations.

Meghan didn't pay much attention to the finer workings of that side of the ministry. She was all about the kids and the paint.

"You're the one who comes up with the initial ideas?" he asked.

"I wish I could take the credit. That happens to be one of mine, but there are a lot of gifted people who design the murals. What I do is scribbling compared to some of the artists who donate their time. But I have a flexible schedule, I love kids and I don't mind getting paint in my hair, so it's all good." Meghan scraped up some courage. "If you have time on a weekend, you should help out."

"I told you I don't paint."

Meghan tilted her head. "Do you want to talk about that?"

"No." Cade's lips twitched. Whether from annoyance or amusement, Meghan wasn't sure, but she didn't push the issue.

"Hand out water bottles and peanut butter sandwiches then. If you believe in the ministry enough to support it financially, you should at least see what it is you're supporting. And we need more male role models for the boys—most of the people involved in Sidewalk Chalk are women." The passion and enthusiasm Meghan had for the ministry crept into her voice and

Cade shook his head, as if answering another unspoken question. Like, "Where did this woman come from and why am I with her?"

"I'm involved as much as I can be."

Or as much as you let yourself be, Meghan thought.

As much as the ministry relied on donations, she knew four little boys in her group alone who desperately needed someone like Cade in their lives. But what Cade didn't know was that he needed them, too. A lot of the people who worked with Sidewalk Chalk openly shared that although they'd initially come on board with the intent to give something to the children, they'd been the ones on the receiving end of a blessing.

"If you change your mind, all you have to do is show up and we'll put you to work."

"Are you by chance the head of the PR committee?"

"Nope." Meghan reached out to retrieve the sketchbook from his hands but as if he anticipated the movement, he inched away from her and flipped through several more pages.

Meghan tried in vain to distract him. "Should we have lunch before we head back to the island—"

Too late.

"What is *this?*" Cade's eyes narrowed as he tapped a sketch.

Without looking at it, Meghan knew which one he was referring to. The one she'd drawn right before he'd shown up. The one of *him.*

She peeked down at the sketch and saw him pointing accusingly at something.

"A...dimple?" Meghan supposed she should be relieved he'd demanded an answer to a question she actually had an answer for. It was embarrassing enough he'd discovered his likeness in her sketchbook without having to come up with a reasonable explanation as to why it was there.

"A dimple." Cade repeated the word softly. "Why did you give me a...dimple?"

"Because you have one?"

"I do not."

He sounded so offended that Meghan smiled. "Yes, you do."

"I've been looking at this face in the mirror for thirty years. I think I'd know if I had a *dimple*." A slight shudder accompanied the last word.

"That explains it, then. You can only see the dimple when you smile, so I'm not surprised you never noticed it before."

Apparently humor was wasted on him. Cade stared at the page and then touched his cheek in roughly the same spot Meghan had sketched the questionable dimple. He smiled. A wide, celebrity red-carpet smile.

"Is my finger gone?" he demanded. "Did it disappear into the deep crevice you drew on my face?"

Meghan's shoulders twitched as she tried to hold in her laughter. And failed. "I draws it the way I sees it."

As Popeye the Sailor impersonations went, Meghan didn't think it was half bad but Cade didn't look impressed.

"Give me the pencil. It's my turn."

"What? No!" Meghan reached for the sketchbook but

he twisted his body away from her, effectively block-ing her puny attempt to wrestle it away.

"Payback time. You can unpack the lunch Bert sent. This will only take a few minutes." The glint in Cade's eyes warned her that all her imperfections were about to be magnified by a master.

What had she gotten herself into?

Grumbling, Meghan opened the wicker basket and the yeasty aroma of fresh bread wafted out. Wrapped in a flour towel, the loaf still felt warm to the touch. Bert had added a generous wedge of black pepper cheddar and thin slices of roast beef. White cake with raspberry filling—the prototype for Parker's wedding cake—nes-tled beside two bottles of iced tea.

Meghan's stomach growled in response to the won-derful sight, momentarily taking her mind off the portrait Cade was drawing. Until she glanced over, in-stantly mesmerized by the quick, efficient movements of his strong, well-shaped hand.

He wasn't even *looking* at her. But then, she hadn't had to look at him, either. Somehow, over the past few days, her brain had imprinted every one of his features in her mind. And she had the funny feeling they were going to linger there a long time…

Cade had stopped.

It had taken him less than five minutes to sharpen her chin to a point, snub her nose and enlarge her eyes. Meghan sighed. "Let's get this over with. Although in my defense of the caricature I drew of you, I have to say I wasn't being mean. I didn't know you'd never seen the dimp— Ah, the slight crease in your cheek."

"Hmm?" Cade glanced up.

"Never mind. Just hand it over so we can eat lunch. I'm starving."

"I don't know what I—" Cade's jaw snapped shut, severing the rest of the sentence. With one swift movement, he tore the page out of the sketchbook and would have crumpled it up if Meghan hadn't guessed his intent, launched herself across the space between them and yanked it out of his hand.

Chapter Fourteen

"Don't bother sparing my feelings. I deserve…" Her voice trailed off as she stared down at the caricature. "I don't look like this."

Cade frowned. "Yes, you do."

"But caricatures are supposed to exaggerate a person's features. My head should be shaped like a…like a snowcone. And you made my nose *cute*. Not snubby."

"Give it back. I'll do it over."

"No." Meghan smoothed the wrinkles out of the sketch and held on to it protectively. "I love it. Thank you for sparing my fragile self-esteem."

Cade frowned. "What do you mean by that?"

"I've looked at this face in the mirror for approximately twenty-six years," she said, repeating a variation of the comment he'd made earlier in the conversation. "I know my eyes are too big. My hair looks like I stuck my finger in a light socket. My mouth is too wide…."

Cade's gaze suddenly shifted to her lips and Meghan had to work hard to draw in her next breath. Every fiber in her body tingled as he leaned closer and his thumb and index finger captured one of the long, corkscrew curls that had fallen free of her baseball cap and traced it to her shoulder.

"I draws it like I sees it," he murmured.

Their faces were only inches apart and Meghan was sure Cade could hear her heart beating. She stared into his eyes and wondered if the blend of confusion and hope she saw there was a reflection of her own emotions.

"Meg—" Her name came out in a husky growl and Meghan closed her eyes, anticipating the touch of his lips against hers.

"Cade?"

The feminine voice, saturated with disapproval, separated them as efficiently as a bucket of cold water.

Cade recovered more quickly than Meghan, his expression inscrutable as he stood up to greet the couple. Unlike Meghan, who sat cross-legged on the picnic blanket as if she'd been fused to it, he didn't look at all surprised to see them.

"Hello, Dad. Aunt Judith."

Judith Halloway's winter-blue gaze settled on Meghan. Judging from the woman's frosty expression, it was clear she'd made her own assumption as to what she and Douglas had interrupted.

"Dad, what happened to your arm?" Cade zeroed in on the aristocratic-looking older man, whose arm was encased in a cast from wrist to elbow and supported by a sling.

"It's nothing," Douglas said gruffly. "Just a little mishap."

"A little mishap." Judith scoffed at the description. "A gross error in judgment if you ask me. He decided to go rock climbing over the weekend."

"Rock climbing?" Cade's neutral expression slipped a little, revealing his disbelief.

"I thought I'd give it a try."

"So, what did you think? Mishap aside?"

"I'll probably stick to golf."

The deep undercurrents flowing between the two men rivaled those of the mighty Mississippi and Meghan's eyes bounced from father to son.

Douglas was an attractive, older version of Cade. Silver tipped his coffee-brown hair and he'd passed along the strong, angled jaw and aristocratic nose, but somewhere along the way, life had chiseled Douglas Halloway's lips into a hard, uncompromising line.

That's why the humor in his eyes was so unexpected.

"Now, enough about me. Aren't you going to introduce us to your friend?"

Cade recognized his cue and tried to organize his thoughts long enough to perform the necessary introductions.

"Dad, Aunt Judith, this is Meghan McBride…" *The woman I would have kissed if you hadn't interrupted us.*

His thoughts disintegrated again, leaving an awkward silence as everyone waited for him to finish.

"The wedding photographer," Meghan supplied helpfully. "It's nice to finally meet you both. I've heard so much about you."

Cade glanced sharply at her and the sunny smile she directed his way only managed to bring his attention back to her lips…

He cleared his throat. "What are you doing here, Dad?"

The question might have been directed at his father, but it was Judith who answered.

"We've come to get Parker and take her home, of course." Over the years his aunt had perfected a haughty sniff for occasions just like this one. "I'm not sure why she chose to come here of all places, but she sounded very distraught about canceling the wedding. She'll get over it, but your father and I are worried about her."

Cade and Meghan exchanged looks.

This is your family, a pair of mist-in-the-pines eyes reminded him.

Like he needed to be reminded.

"I was going to call you today—" Cade paused, not sure how to tell them the wedding was back on. And, from the plans he'd heard over the dinner table the evening before, it bore no resemblance to its original form.

In fact, Cade wasn't even sure if Aunt Judith and Douglas's names were still on the guest list.

"Cade was going to ask you both to come to Blue Key," Meghan interjected. "Especially you, Judith. You're right. We really need your help."

Judith drew herself up and pressed a hand against her silk blouse, fingering the triple strand of pearls nestled between the sharp points of the collar. "Of course I'll help. Parker is my only niece."

"I'm glad to hear you say that. Because Parker and

Justin are getting married Saturday evening and we need all hands on deck, so to speak."

Cade would have chosen a more subtle approach but when his aunt appeared speechless, he changed his mind and silently applauded Meghan's strategy.

"She changed her mind?" Douglas asked mildly.

Cade nodded, keeping a wary eye trained on his aunt for signs of escalating blood pressure and the other on his father, who didn't look as upset as he should have given the circumstances.

"Parker is very excited." Meghan's engaging smile, like a thousand-watt bulb during a blackout, conveyed the message that they should be excited, too.

"Excuse me." Judith's voice was sharp enough to etch glass. "What did you say your name was?"

"Meghan McBride."

"McBride." Judith's eyes narrowed as she opened the social register stored in her memory file and searched the "M's."

It triggered a protective streak inside Cade that he hadn't known existed. Just as he was about to step in and deflect Judith's verbal missiles, Meghan's eyes flashed a brief warning.

Sit tight on your white horse and let me handle the dragon.

"We've never met. No pedigree, I'm afraid." Meghan managed to sound relieved rather than sorry and Douglas's bark of laughter—quickly suppressed—told Cade that another Halloway had just fallen captive to her winsome charm. "You'll need a ride out to the island and since Cade and I happen to have a boat, you're welcome to come with us."

"Well." Judith stared at her.

Meghan met her gaze, waiting her out.

"Douglas? Shall we? The sooner we get to the island, the sooner I can save Parker from making a huge mistake." Judith smiled as if the idea had been hers to begin with.

Meghan didn't answer. She turned away and began to collect the sketchbook, picnic basket and blanket.

Cade bent down to help her. That's when he noticed her hands were shaking.

"Oreos?" he whispered.

"Double stuff. And I still get to drive the boat."

Cade had to fight the sudden urge to pull Meghan against him—right in front of his father and his aunt—and finish what they'd started. The only thing that stopped him wasn't the uncertainty of where it would end, but the unsettling feeling he wouldn't want it to.

Smile. Nod. Smile. Nod.

Meghan tried to concentrate on Parker's enthusiastic plans for the bridesmaid's bouquet but her thoughts kept returning to the point. Where the lap of the waves against the sand soothed like a lullaby and the eagle made his three o'clock appearance every afternoon like clockwork. It was as if God had lovingly provided a visible reminder that when she put her trust in Him, she'd have the strength she needed to make it through the next few days.

And Meghan needed strength.

"I'm boring you, aren't I?" Parker laughed. "I know we talked about this last night, but I wasn't sure about adding the forget-me-nots."

"You aren't boring me. I was just thinking." Meghan reached out and squeezed Parker's hand.

Given their different temperaments and backgrounds, the comfortable friendship that had sprung up between them had come as a surprise.

Their shared faith alone provided a strong foundation for friendship, but Meghan knew it was more than that. She truly *liked* Parker. As they worked together, Meghan had discovered Parker was a woman of depth and keen insights. For all her concerns about being shallow and useless, Cade's sister had an empathetic nature and the ability to listen without casting judgment. Qualities Meghan knew would be more important on the mission field than the ability to put together a casserole.

"I don't know what I'd do without you." Parker gave a gusty sigh. "Or Bert…and Dad."

Meghan didn't miss the note of wonder in Parker's voice and knew the reason. They'd expected Douglas to side with Judith about the change in plans, but over the past two days he'd proven himself indispensable… and supportive of the upcoming wedding.

"He manages pretty well with one arm."

"Rock climbing. Can you believe it?" Parker rolled her eyes. "He and Bert are finally talking."

Meghan had noticed that, too. When Douglas had arrived on the island, the tension between him and Bert had been as thick as evening fog. It had taken some time, but the two were now able to carry on a polite conversation. And the evening before, Meghan had spotted Bert carrying a tray of coffee out to the courtyard where Douglas had been puttering with the fountain.

Definitely progress, Meghan silently agreed.

Parker's aunt was a different story. If Meghan had her way, Judith Halloway would be the first person voted off the island. She had to recite every scripture that she'd ever memorized dealing with patience, taming the tongue and loving your neighbor just to be civil to the woman.

After a rocky confrontation with Parker soon after she'd stepped off the dock, Judith seemed resigned to the fact that her niece was going to marry a missionary on Saturday. Too resigned, in Meghan's opinion. She had a hunch the woman was plotting a final showdown and hoped it wouldn't be on the day of the wedding.

"I'm going to check on Dad and see if he needs anything." Parker stood up and stretched, unfolding her runway figure with the grace of a ballerina. "Maybe I'll try to pry Cade away from his desk. He's made himself pretty scarce over the past few days."

Out of the corner of her eye, Meghan caught Parker's speculative glance. And blushed.

"I'm sure he's been busy getting everything ready for the appraisal," Meghan said casually.

Or else he was avoiding her the way she'd been avoiding him.

As forgetful as Meghan could be, the memory of her afternoon with Cade remained stubbornly embedded in her thoughts, surfacing at random times during the day and playing havoc with her already frayed emotions.

"The sale." The sparkle in Parker's eyes faded. "He's determined to go through with it. I think even Dad might be having second thoughts. It's just that Blue Key…"

"Has so many memories?" Meghan gently prompted when Parker's voice trailed off.

"Not only that. It has so much of Mom. This place is the only connection I have with her. It's silly, but when Cade told me he was planning to put it up for sale, I got the strangest feeling. Like if the island was gone…she'd be gone. It was the connecting point for our family. No matter how busy Dad was and how many hours he put in during the year, we were a family here."

Cade might have hardened his heart against their mother, but judging from the wistful note Meghan heard in Parker's voice, she didn't share her brother's feelings.

"Does Cade have the final say as to whether the island goes up for sale?"

"I guess so. Dad shocked us all a few months ago when he revealed his five-year plan. He wants to retire at sixty, about a hundred years earlier than what we all expected. Aunt Judith thinks he's having some kind of midlife crisis. Anyway, Dad gave Cade the green light to start making decisions, and selling Blue Key was one of them. When I found out, that's when I realized I wanted to get married here. Mom might not be here, but it would *feel* like she was." Parker shook her head. "Justin reminds me to keep praying about the situation but I get confused. How do we know if God wants us to *do* something or if we're supposed to wait?"

Meghan was glad Parker didn't seem to expect an

answer. Because at the moment she was wondering if Cade had a five-year-plan, too. And what it included. Running the family business? Writing checks to worthwhile charities? Looking for a woman who looked up to Judith as a role model?

For some reason, it was a depressing thought.

Because the more she spent time with Cade, the more she sensed that he kept parts of his heart under lockdown. Not dealing with things seemed to be his way of dealing with them.

She'd tried that and it hadn't worked.

Eventually Meghan had discovered that giving God room to move through her life meant letting Him clean out the clutter. Sometimes all her soul needed was a daily dusting, other times, a complete renovation...not always painless but much more freeing.

"Oops. Quarter to three." Parker tapped the face of her Tiffany watch. "Time for you to go."

"Go?" Meghan played dumb.

Parker gave her a knowing look. "You know. To the place you disappear to every day around this time."

"Checking out photo ops?" Meghan offered weakly.

"I might believe that. If you took Miss Molly along."

Meghan choked. "How long have you known?"

"Awhile." Parker shrugged. "I checked out your website after Bliss told me your name."

"And you didn't care?"

Parker's eyes sparkled with mischief. "To tell you the truth, the wedding was turning into such a circus, I figured you'd be perfect for the job."

"Does…anyone else…know?" Meghan sucked in a breath and held it.

Parker wasn't fooled by the carefully worded question. "Not from me. You're a photographer, right? And from what I could see, a good one. That's all that matters."

Meghan knew she didn't deserve such loyalty. Especially when she'd come to the island for another purpose. She'd already decided to take one more walk through the studio to see if the Ferris was there. If it wasn't, she planned to hand in her junior spy manual and give up the search.

"I'm sorry—"

Parker held up her hand in a gesture that reminded Meghan of a crossing guard. "Don't you dare apologize. For accepting the job or for taking a break in the afternoon. My family would make most people run for cover." She smiled wryly. "It must have something to do with our charming personalities."

Charming.

And there was the rub, Meghan thought.

It was easier to keep her distance from Cade when he was in alpha executive mode. Much more difficult when he teased her. Or made a detour to the grocery store to buy her favorite cookies. Or told her that she was beautiful…not with words but with a charcoal pencil.

"Off with you." Parker gave her a gentle push in the direction of the path that led into the woods. "Your secret is safe with me. Go let out a primal scream, throw rocks, pray or whatever it is you do. I'll hold down the fort. No one will even notice you're gone."

Chapter Fifteen

Meghan was gone. Again.

Over the past few days, Cade had noticed a pattern emerging.

Meghan spent her time alternating between supervising the teenagers that came across to the island in a ragtag armada of borrowed fishing boats and putting out the fires that inevitably started between his aunt Judith and...everyone.

He'd been stunned and proud of the way his sister had respectfully but confidently stood up to Judith. She'd told their aunt that she was going to marry Justin and if she didn't have her blessing, Parker would understand if Judith chose not to stay on the island to witness their vows.

Judith stayed. And Meghan, through some kind of unspoken vote, had been appointed as Judith's official handler. No amount of icy looks, pursed lips or cutting remarks managed to cast a shadow on Meghan's sunny disposition.

Throughout the day, Meghan taste tested Bert's hors d'oeuvres, answered dozens of questions and sat at the kitchen table, painstakingly creating luminaries made from old canning jars and pieces of stained glass threaded on copper wire.

She'd even put his father to work.

Douglas had been given the dubious honor of taking a pair of hedge clippers to the overgrown topiaries to decide if the family of whitetail deer trapped inside the branches was worth saving.

And then in the afternoons, Meghan disappeared.

Cade wondered about it, but didn't seek her out. Since their almost-kiss in the park on Monday, it was as if they'd made an unspoken pact to keep their distance.

For him, it was purely self-preservation. It was bad enough that the sound of her laughter through the open windows could totally short-circuit his concentration. Or that whenever he caught a glimpse of her, his soul reacted like an oxygen-deprived diver taking in a draught of fresh air.

"Wow. What's the occasion?" Parker's teasing voice intruded on his thoughts.

"Occasion?"

"You came out of your lair."

"Funny."

"I try." Parker grabbed his hand and skirted a mound of fresh dirt, towing him along behind her. When Cade saw her destination was the carousel, he balked.

"It'll break."

"Sit down." Parker perched on the edge of platform

and patted the space beside her. "It's proven it can with-
stand the test of time."

Cade sat.

"Were you looking for someone in particular?"
Parker slanted a look at him.

"I needed some fresh air."

"Justin will be here tomorrow." Parker closed her
eyes with a blissful smile.

"Stop. I'm getting a sugar headache."

She jabbed her elbow playfully into his ribs. "You
should be glad to see him. He's bringing your tuxedo.
Oh, and Suzanne, my bridesmaid."

Cade looked at her sharply. He hadn't been tuned in
to all the wedding preparations, but he was pretty sure
Parker had, at one point, mentioned four attendants *and*
a maid of honor. "What happened to Kirsten?" he asked,
referring to the woman who'd been Parker's best friend
and sorority sister in college.

"She got a better offer. Venice. Paris. She was kind
of vague. It's all right, considering the guest list has
shrunk a bit now that only close family and friends
will be here."

"Mmm. So the guest list would be…"

"Fourteen."

"From?"

"Four hundred and thirty-two."

Cade gave a low whistle.

"I know. More cake for each of us. And cleanup
should be a breeze."

"Parker—"

She cut him off with a quick shake of her head. "You

remember the old saying that you find out who your real friends are when things get rough? Well, I'm revising it. You find out *if* you have any friends when things get rough."

Cade exhaled slowly. "I'm sorry."

"Don't be." Parker shrugged. "I don't blame people for wondering if frequent credit card use finally melted my brain cells. I love Justin. And I like me better now. For the first time in my life, I feel excited about the future even though I have no idea what's going to happen."

"You've never been impulsive."

"I'm still not." Parker looked at him in astonishment. "Is that what you think? That surrendering my life to Christ and accepting Justin's proposal were decisions I made on a whim? They weren't. I thought—and prayed—long and hard about them. I knew there'd be fallout from my friends and…family. I know what I'll be giving up. For a little while, I admit I panicked and ran away. But Meghan reminded me that if I believe God brought me and Justin together—which I do—I can't let my fears get in the way of our future."

Cade wasn't surprised to learn that Meghan "Miss Expectation" McBride had played a role in Parker's decision to proceed with the wedding.

"I know you have doubts," Parker continued quietly. "You remember how different Mom and Dad were, and you think their differences eventually drove them apart. When we talked on the phone, Mom said she didn't want to get into the details, but I got the feeling there was more to their breakup than what the courts like to call irreconcilable differences."

"She didn't want to get into the details," Cade repeated. "So Genevieve conveniently forgot to mention the affair she had with Joseph Ferris?"

Cade instantly regretted the words when he saw the color ebb out of Parker's face. But it was too late to take them back. And maybe time his sister knew the truth. Maybe knowing would put an end to her desire to "start over" with the woman who'd walked out on them without a backward glance.

"I don't believe you." Parker squeezed her eyes shut, as if blocking him out would block out the words he'd just spoken. "Did Aunt Judith tell you that? You know she never approved of Mom."

He'd opened the door to the conversation, so now he had no choice but to follow through.

"The summer right before they separated, Dad couldn't come with us to Blue Key, remember? He'd been working overtime on a project, so Mom brought us. When we got here, Ferris was staying in one of the cabins. You know how people came and went all the time. He told Mom he'd leave, but she encouraged him to stay for a few weeks to finish the painting he'd started."

He could tell by the expression on Parker's face that she remembered Ferris. A shadow of a memory, because she'd only been six at the time, but it was there.

Cade wished his memories were as vague.

He hadn't let Ferris invade his thoughts in years. Not until he'd caught Meghan holding the watercolor he'd painted of the man.

Bitterness rose up inside him like bile. For a few

short weeks that summer he'd idolized the artist. They'd explored the island together. Fished together. Ferris was the one who'd encouraged him to start painting, told him that he had a "gift."

In Cade's mind, his mother wasn't the only one who'd betrayed Douglas. He had, too. Not only because he'd befriended Ferris, but because he'd actually thought about following in the man's footsteps.

"Mom wouldn't have done that." Parker's voice shook. "She *loved* Dad."

"Genevieve and Ferris had a lot in common," Cade went on carefully. "They both painted. They had the same friends. Enjoyed the same things—"

Parker's chin lifted. "That doesn't mean anything."

She was going to make him say it.

"I saw them together."

"You're making this up and I don't want to hear it." Parker surged to her feet and sprinted across the court-yard, startling the teenagers who'd gathered near the fountain for an ice-cream break.

Cade winced when the screen door slammed shut behind Parker as she fled into the house.

You handled that well.

Scrubbing a hand across his jaw, Cade debated whether he should follow her but decided to give his sister some time alone to sort through things first.

He hadn't meant to be so blunt, but the fact that Genevieve wasn't willing to take responsibility for their parents' failed marriage had stirred up his emotions and temporarily overrode his ability to think before he spoke.

For years he'd kept what he'd seen a secret, although it was obvious that Douglas had found out. He remembered hearing his parents arguing behind closed doors when they'd returned to Minneapolis and it had sounded much different from the teasing banter he was used to. A week of cold silence from his father—and the sound of his mother crying behind her bedroom door—followed. Until the day he came home from school and found Judith in the kitchen, lecturing a middle-aged woman in a crisp white apron about her "duties."

And Genevieve was gone. Just like that. By the end of the weekend, Judith had replaced his mother with a cook, a day maid and her own watchful, but cheerless, presence in the house.

Douglas retreated into his career. The firm became his sanctuary and he used its walls to close out the parts of life he wasn't comfortable with. He let Judith decide how to deal with the fallout at home from his failed marriage. Cade guessed his father had told Judith not to mention the affair, because although his aunt had been openly scathing of Genevieve's decision to leave in what she tactfully referred to as "a pursuit of other things," she never mentioned another man. And Cade had never told them what he'd seen that day—but age and experience had gradually filled in the pieces of the puzzle until he had a clear picture of what had really led to his mother's abrupt departure from their family.

It didn't matter to Cade that his father had chosen not to confide in him. In his mind, Genevieve's affair with Ferris had simply been a by-product of her unhappiness. They'd tried to make the marriage work, but in the end, Genevieve had turned to a man whose lifestyle meshed with her own. And she'd walked away from twelve years of marriage and two children as if they'd been nothing but a burden she'd grown tired of bearing.

Cade glanced at the house again and felt the gut-wrenching guilt of being the one who'd told Parker the truth.

Chalk it up to an entire week that had refused to go according to plan.

Restlessly, he scanned the courtyard. Aware of the teenagers' curious looks, Cade felt the sudden urge to escape. He chose the closest path that disappeared into the woods and followed it.

There was only one place he knew of that could offer any kind of peace. And he was halfway there when the truth crashed into him with the force of a wrecking ball. It wasn't the solitude of the point he needed.

It was Meghan.

Meghan heard Cade before she saw him. And when she saw him, she knew right away something was wrong. The rigid set of his jaw warned her that he wasn't going to talk about it.

Tension radiated from him like a force field as he dropped down on the bank beside her and his fingers immediately began to tap out a code against his knees.

She spent the next few minutes trying unsuccessfully to decipher it.

Had he known she was there? Or should she leave?

Cade had claimed the point as his thinking spot years ago, but she'd taken up squatter's rights, figuring the hours he spent in the library meant he'd replaced it as his refuge.

It had certainly become hers.

On the point, the voices and the hum of constant activity were lost in the lap of the waves against the shoreline and the rustle of the aspen leaves.

She stayed there until her heart stopped racing and her thoughts came together once again in a steady, manageable formation. She poured her heart out to God until she could smile at Judith Halloway and mean it.

Cade had been right. No one wanted to push through the dense undergrowth that separated the peninsula from the well-traveled paths.

Except one person, Meghan silently amended. The strangest part was discovering she didn't mind sharing it.

With him.

Ordinarily, her stomach would have coiled into one gigantic knot at having her solitude disrupted without warning. But there was something warm and solid about Cade's presence. Something unexpectedly comforting in the scent of his cologne in the air.

That alone would have sent her fleeing into the woods if it hadn't been for one thing.

The eagle appeared. Right on schedule. And she never turned down a gift. Or hesitated to share one.

"Cade. Look up."

He did. Just in time to watch the eagle take a leisurely lap above their heads before its wing tips curled and it angled lower, skimming the surface of the water.

Close enough for them to see the helmet of snow-white feathers and the intimidating curve of its beak.

As if it knew it was playing for an audience, the bird collided with the water and surfaced almost immediately. The fish gripped in its talons flashed silver, like a mirror in the sun, as the eagle returned to the nest.

For a few minutes neither of them spoke. Cade's gaze remained fixed on the top branches of the white pine that cradled its nest.

His expression was remote and his fingers had started their measured tapping again. He obviously wanted to be alone.

Reluctantly, Meghan rose to her feet and took three steps before Cade's voice stopped her in her tracks.

"I told Parker something she didn't want to hear."

Meghan backtracked and sat down beside him again. She might have been tempted to push him into the lake, but heard the self-recrimination in his voice and sighed instead.

Poor Parker. Meghan had been trying to draw Judith's fire away from the bride-to-be for the past few days and now apparently she'd been submarined by her own brother. "Cade, you have to accept there is going to be a wedding here the day after tomorrow—"

"It wasn't about the wedding," Cade interrupted. "It was about Genevieve."

Meghan sucked in a breath and waited. Cade always referred to his mother by her first name and she guessed it was his way of detaching himself from the bond they shared as parent and child.

"Parker just couldn't leave well enough alone. And

she has no idea what Dad will do if he finds out she contacted Genevieve," Cade muttered. "My sister doesn't usually do things like this, but lately it's been one crazy decision after another. She's listening to her heart, not her head."

"Or maybe they're working together."

The impatient look Cade shot in her direction disagreed. "After all this time, Parker is willing to let Genevieve waltz back into her life. As if the woman went to the mall and happened to be gone for, oh, twenty years. Can you believe it?"

"Yes," Meghan said simply, astounding them both. "Parker is at a new place in her life. She's ready to forgive and move on. She's getting married…she and Justin might have a family of their own. It's all right if she wants to make some extra room for people she cares about."

She had never been in a situation like the Halloways', but she did know that holding on to bitterness and anger took up a lot of room inside a person and crowded out the fruit that God tried to cultivate in His children.

"Parker doesn't know anything about her," Cade said flatly. "She thought Genevieve left because she didn't want to be tied down by a family. I told her the truth to save her from getting hurt again."

Meghan swallowed hard and sent up a silent prayer for strength. Not only for herself, but enough to share with Cade. It was clear from the expression on his face that he was hurting, too. "What did you tell her?"

"That Genevieve had an affair with Joseph Ferris."

Meghan thought she'd braced herself for whatever

his response would be, but the impact still sent shock waves through her.

"But—"

"I saw them together." Cade designed his words to shut down any opposing arguments. "Right here as a matter of fact. Dad had shown up a few days early to surprise us and he sent me to find her. I looked everywhere—the point was the last place I tried. They didn't hear me but I saw them. Saw their arms around each other. I didn't understand what was going on at the time, but something didn't seem right."

Meghan couldn't imagine the confusion a ten-year-old boy would feel in that situation but denial struggled alongside compassion for Cade. Call her misguided, but something inside her refused to believe that Genevieve Halloway would willingly sacrifice her family for a summer fling.

"You didn't talk to your father about what you saw?"

"I talked to Aunt Judith. When we got home, she could tell something was bothering me and took me out for ice cream."

Meghan's mouth went dry as dust. "You told her you saw your mother with another man?"

"Dad had already told her."

Or else, Meghan thought, Judith had only pretended to know in order to extract information. She'd witnessed firsthand the woman's finely honed manipulation skills. It wouldn't have been hard to convince a little boy that he wasn't telling her anything she didn't already know.

The barbed comments about the house and grounds

that Judith frequently made bubbled from a hostility that still simmered below the surface. Twenty years later.

Judith refused to call her former sister-in-law by name and her lips pursed to the size of a keyhole whenever her gaze settled on anything connected to Genevieve. And because almost everything on Blue Key Island in some way reflected the woman's creative, winsome personality, Cade's aunt walked around wearing an expression that looked as if she'd been sucking on lemons.

But how could she tell Cade her suspicions about Judith when he'd witnessed his mother's indiscretion with his own eyes?

His ten-year-old eyes...

"Are you sure you didn't misinterpret what you saw?" Meghan asked carefully. "Some people are more demonstrative than others. The embrace you saw could have been between...friends."

Cade stared at her. "I can't believe you're defending her actions."

"I'm only saying that it's possible what you saw might have been inappropriate...but innocent."

"If that was the case, I doubt my parents' marriage would have ended," he said stiffly.

It might have, Meghan thought grimly, with a little additional help.

She caught her bottom lip in her teeth, knowing she had nothing to base her beliefs on other than instinct. And instinct told her that Judith had poured her own special brand of acid into a weak spot in the Halloways' marriage and waited for it to dissolve.

"I don't know why Parker can't let go of the past and move on," Cade murmured. "I have."

"No, you haven't."

The eyebrow tried to put her in her place. Meghan ignored it. "Stuffing your emotions isn't the same as moving on."

"I don't…*stuff*…my emotions."

"Really? Then why do you drum?"

"Drum?"

Meghan glanced down meaningfully at his hands just as he caught himself, and his fingers stilled. "You drum because you won't express yourself in the way God designed you to express yourself. You need emotional Drano."

"And that would be?"

Meghan deposited her sketchbook in his lap and tucked the pencil between his fingers. "You're a smart guy. You figure it out."

Chapter Sixteen

A soft light glowed inside the studio but Meghan wasn't put off because she knew Bert left one burning all night. And everyone was at the house. All accounted for.

This was it. The last time she was going to look for the Ferris. Her assignment would be officially over. Mission…unaccomplished. But Meghan had decided she was fine with that. Large donation to Sidewalk Chalk or not, now that she'd gotten to know the Halloways, she was no longer comfortable working as Nina Bonnefield's undercover operative.

Meghan flipped the latch on the door and stepped inside.

"Oh—" *No.* Meghan backed up when she saw the man standing in the shadows. "I'm sorry. I didn't mean to intrude."

"You aren't intruding, Miss McBride," Douglas Halloway said. "Please. Come in."

Meghan hesitated but Cade's father waved her inside. "Sometimes an old man needs more than his own thoughts for company."

If Meghan hadn't heard the melancholy echo in Douglas's voice, she would have been halfway back to the house by now. "You aren't old."

"The cast on my arm says differently."

"That could have happened to anyone. Young or old."

"Which means I'm clumsy." He sounded more disgruntled about that than being old.

"It means you're a beginner," Meghan corrected, bravely moving closer. "And you won't make the same mistake next time."

Douglas smiled and Meghan was amazed to see a tiny dent appear in his cheek. Why had she assumed it was Genevieve Halloway who'd passed on that appealing feature to her son?

"You're assuming there will be a next time. You know what they say. You can't teach an old dog new tricks."

"You don't believe that and neither do I." Amazed at her own temerity, Meghan braced herself for the fallout.

Instead, Douglas sighed. "Sometimes the evidence is too great to ignore. A man has to accept his successes. And his...failures."

Meghan got the distinct impression they were no longer talking about rock climbing. "But isn't it hard to discern sometimes which one is which? They can look the same, depending on your attitude."

"Has anyone ever told you that you're...astonishingly optimistic?"

"All the time," Meghan admitted. "But with a slight

twist. *Annoyingly* optimistic seems to be the most popular choice of adjectives."

Douglas gave her a shrewd look and then shook his head, a slight smile playing at the corner of his lips. "Well, no wonder."

"No wonder what?" Meghan blinked, thoroughly confused by the cryptic remark.

But Douglas didn't reply. His gaze had already shifted to the paintings on the wall and Meghan realized it was riveted on the familiar watercolor of a man in a boat.

Cade must have moved the painting from his bedroom to the studio so he wouldn't have to look at it. Relief that he hadn't tossed it into the burn barrel mingled with frustration at another example of Cade's stubbornness.

"Cade is very gifted," she said softly.

Douglas made an indistinguishable sound that neither confirmed nor denied her comment. "He's the best in the firm. His designs have won several awards."

"I meant as an artist. He painted the one you're looking at, you know."

Douglas hadn't known. It was obvious in the way his eyes widened in surprise and then darkened. With what, though, Meghan couldn't discern. Denial? Anger? Regret?

Or maybe a combination of all three.

"I can't take the credit." Douglas flicked a look at the painting, his previous good humor evaporating like a drop of water in Bert's cast-iron skillet. "This was Nina's influence."

At the mention of the familiar name, Meghan sucked in a breath.

Was it possible Douglas was referring to Nina *Bonnefield?* Had she been one of the artists who'd encouraged Cade to paint?

Meghan sent up a quick prayer, appealing for wisdom. If she admitted she'd heard of Nina, a woman who claimed to live several thousand miles away on the East Coast, Douglas might wonder how that was possible. In this case, anything she said had the potential to jumpstart a game of Twenty Questions that Meghan didn't want to play. But if she didn't follow up on the comment, she'd lose the opportunity to find out more about her father's mysterious client.

"Who is Nina?" Meghan hoped that since Douglas had been the one to bring up the woman's name, he wouldn't read more into the question than simple curiosity.

Douglas remained silent for a moment and Meghan held her breath. His eyes never left the painting. "Nina is Cade's mother."

The two words liquefied Meghan's knees and she sagged against the wall. "His *mother?*"

Was it possible that Douglas had been married twice?

"I…I thought Genevieve was his mother's name."

A dark red stain crept up Douglas's cheeks and he looked away. "Nina is…*was*…a nickname."

A husband's affectionate, intimate nickname for his wife. That explained why Meghan hadn't heard anyone else use it until now.

Just as the ramifications of Douglas's stunning disclosure began to pile up, he forced a smile and shuffled past her, looking ten years older than he had a few minutes ago. "If you'll excuse me, I'm going back to the house. It's getting rather late."

Meghan could only nod. Because she had no idea what to say to him.

But she had plenty to say to her father.

Stumbling into the courtyard, Meghan punched a number on her cell phone and then hit the send button.

"Hello?" In spite of the lateness of the hour, Patrick McBride didn't sound sleepy or disoriented. That alone should have made her suspicious.

"Nina Bonnefield is Genevieve Halloway, Dad."

Silence.

"Did you hear me? Genevieve and Douglas divorced years ago and she must have lost the estate in the settlement—" Meghan suddenly realized she hadn't heard a surprised exclamation. Or a horrified gasp. Nothing. Which could only lead to one conclusion. One hive-inducing, nauseating, instant insomnia-causing conclusion. "You...*knew*. Didn't you?"

"I knew."

Meghan dropped her head between her knees and groaned. *"Dad."*

"I promised Nina I'd keep that part confidential," Patrick explained. "She assured me it would be simpler that way."

Simpler for who? Meghan was tempted to shout. She groaned instead.

How could she begin to explain to her father that

her assignment had been difficult enough when she believed Nina Bonnefield had simply been one of Genevieve Halloway's acquaintances? But knowing Nina was Cade's mother—the woman he didn't bother to hide his bitterness for—added complications she didn't have the time, energy or desire to count at the moment.

Meghan stared blindly at the mosaic of colorful pottery pieces cemented in the path stones beneath her feet.

"Meghan?" Patrick's worried voice broke through her thoughts. "What's wrong? What's happened?"

What's happened?

Meghan had the strangest urge to laugh. And cry. What should she tell him? That she'd befriended the runaway bride? That she'd gotten way too attached to a place—and people—she'd probably never see again? People who, if they found out she'd come to the island under false pretenses, might stop speaking to her?

Or that she'd fallen for the best man?

"I'm fine, Dad." Which at the moment was an acronym for *freaked out, insecure, neurotic and emotional.* "But you better tell me everything."

So he did. But by the time Patrick had finished, Meghan didn't feel any better. If it were possible, she felt worse.

According to Patrick, Parker had contacted her mother shortly after her engagement to Justin. Not only was Nina ecstatic to hear from her adult daughter, she was floored by Parker's shy declaration of her newfound faith. In Nina's own life, that phone call had been a life-changing affirmation that God really did listen. That He really did love her.

Because apparently, while Parker had been attending special evening services at her own church and feeling as though God was trying to get her attention, hundreds of miles away, He'd been nudging Genevieve, too. The gallery and café she managed had become the gathering place for a trio of women who stopped in for dessert and coffee after their weekly Bible study. Over the course of a few months, she'd overheard enough snippets of their lively discussions to get a new perspective on people who lived out their beliefs.

When she'd finally pulled out a chair at their table and asked them to explain it to her, it had been like finding a treasure.

Nina had begun her own faith journey, never dreaming it would ultimately connect with her daughter's.

When Patrick finished telling Meghan what he knew about Genevieve Halloway, Meghan still had no idea what to do. Or who to believe.

"Dad, Cade Halloway is convinced that Genevieve—*Nina*—had an affair with Joseph Ferris. And he told Parker about it today."

"What!" Patrick's dismay sounded genuine.

"I didn't want to believe it, either, but now I'm beginning to wonder if it isn't true. I mean, it would explain why Joseph left a gift for her on the island."

"Nina told me that Ferris had been having some health problems and needed a quiet place to retreat. That's why he left something for her as a thank-you. She never mentioned anything about an affair."

"Maybe she thought you wouldn't help her if she told you everything."

They were silent, each of them absorbing the information they'd shared while trying to make sense of it.

The back of Meghan's head began to throb. She'd gone from defending Genevieve to doubting the woman's sincerity now that she knew who she really was.

"Did Nina tell you why she left?"

"No. Only that now she realizes she gave up much too easily."

Which could mean just about anything, Meghan thought grimly.

"I don't understand something. If Parker was open to meeting with Genevieve, then why did she send me here to look for the Ferris? Especially if the two of them were involved. If the family finds out, Genevieve has to know it's going to look as if the Ferris might be the real reason she's anxious to connect with Parker after so many years. Cade already believes she can't be trusted."

"Nina thought if you actually found the Ferris, she could show the family's lawyer the letter as proof and convince Douglas that it belonged to her. Then she planned to sell it for a down payment on the island. Parker had mentioned the island was going up for sale at the end of the summer. Nina said the house held so many memories, she didn't want to lose that connection to her family."

Tears burned the backs of Meghan's eyes when she realized what Genevieve had told Patrick closely paralleled what Parker had said about why she'd chosen the island for the wedding.

A grand gesture on Genevieve's part, Meghan

thought, but it would still be suspect. And the timing couldn't have been worse.

Meghan exhaled. "You have to let Genevieve know that Cade told Parker about the affair before they talk again. As soon as possible."

"Ah—that might be a little difficult." Patrick paused and Meghan had a sudden image of him plucking off his glasses and wiping the lenses on his shirttail.

Dread curled in her belly. "Why will that be difficult?"

"Because she's on her way there—"

"What! She's coming here? Why?"

"Because someone sent Genevieve an invitation to the wedding."

"Dad? What are you doing up so late?" Cade paused in the kitchen doorway, surprised to see his father sitting alone at the table, a bowl piled high with Bert's leftover strawberry shortcake in front of him.

"I could ask you the same question."

Douglas could, Cade thought, but that didn't mean he had to answer it. Which in turn raised another interesting point. Why couldn't he and his father talk about anything that wasn't work-related?

"Have you talked to Parker?" Cade asked. He'd tried to approach his sister several times earlier in the afternoon but she'd stuck like glue to Bert or the teenage help, not giving him the chance to talk to her privately. Later on when he'd tried to seek her out, she was nowhere to be found.

"I haven't seen her since supper. But I did have a chat

with your photographer friend. Meghan. She showed up at the studio."

Panic gripped Cade and he didn't even pause to wonder why his father had gone to the studio. "You talked to Meghan? About what?"

Instead of answering, Douglas aimed his spoon at an empty chair. "Sit down, son. You look a little tense."

Cade strode over and yanked the chair away from the table. "About what?" he repeated, hoping his father's abrasive personality hadn't roughed away a spot on Meghan's sensitive soul.

"About your artistic ability."

Cade winced. Wonderful. "I hope you weren't too hard on her, Dad. Meghan puts a high value on that—"

"It wasn't bad," Douglas interrupted. "The painting she said you did. Not as good as Nina's, of course, but not half bad."

Cade, who hadn't heard his father utter Genevieve's name in years, was momentarily stunned into silence.

"You quit, didn't you?"

Cade wondered if it was a trick question. A week ago the answer would have been a decisive yes. But today, the charcoal sketch of the eagle he'd drawn after Meghan left him at the point could be entered as evidence against him.

"Work keeps me busy. I don't have time for anything else." Douglas couldn't fault him for that. Not when he'd modeled Douglas's own intense brand of dedication to the firm all these years.

Instead of getting an approving nod, Douglas frowned at him. "There's more to life than work, Cade."

The berries in Bert's shortcake had obviously fermented. "Excuse me?"

"I was thinking this evening that maybe we shouldn't rush into selling this place," Douglas mused. "It might be a good place to retire."

"You want to retire. Here." Cade pinched the bridge of his nose between his fingers as the opening music to a popular old sci-fi series played in his head.

"I don't know. I'm just weighing my options."

"You can find something closer. Up by the boundary waters. This place is beyond repair—"

"Is it, do you think? Beyond repair?" The look of deep regret on his father's face cut off Cade's opening argument.

The two men stared at each other across the table.

The chair creaked in protest as Cade shifted his weight. "We haven't been here in twenty years, Dad. Why are we holding on to it? The yard is a scrap heap. The house is falling apart. Selling the island is a sound business decision. You agreed with me. I don't know why everyone gets so sentimental about it. Blue Key is just the place…" Cade bit back the words that had forged ahead of his thoughts.

"Go ahead and say it," Douglas prompted softly.

"All right. The place where Mom had an affair with Joseph Ferris that ended your marriage." Finally being able to say the words out loud didn't feel as good as Cade thought it would. "Or am I the only one who remembers that? She made a mockery of everything about this place."

"You can't put all the blame on Genevieve." Douglas sighed. "I made my share of mistakes."

"What mistake? Marrying a flighty artist who got tired of her life and changed it as easily as she painted over a canvas? 'I didn't get it right, so I guess I'll start over with someone else…'"

"Cade?"

Meghan's voice barely broke a whisper but he heard her. And when he saw her chalk-white face, he rose to his feet so quickly the chair almost overturned. "What's wrong?"

"I'm sorry to interrupt, but I need to…talk to you."

Cade glanced at his father. "Dad?"

"Of course." Douglas smiled reassuringly at Meghan but when he would have risen to his feet, she shook her head.

"Both of you."

"All right." Cade reached for her hand but she skirted away from him and went to stand by the sink. A cold trickle of unease skittered down his spine. "What's going on?"

"It's about…Genevieve. You need to know that she's on her way here…someone sent her an invitation to the wedding."

"Parker." Cade closed his eyes, wondering how, in spite of his best efforts, life had gotten so out of control. He looked at Douglas, ready for the fireworks. "I'm sorry, Dad. I should have told you that she contacted Mom, but I had no idea she would invite her to the wedding—"

"Parker didn't invite her," Douglas interrupted. "I did."

For the second time Cade felt as if he'd been sucker punched. "Why would you do that?"

"This is her daughter's wedding. Nina would want to be here. She *should* be here."

Anger warred with disbelief. "Don't you think after twenty years, she gave up her right to be included? She's the one who left *us*." As soon as Cade voiced his thoughts out loud, Meghan's soft admonition about people deserving second chances tweaked his conscience.

Right behind that tweak came the humbling realization that she was right. Where would he be if God hadn't forgiven him? If he wanted to live out his beliefs, forgiveness was a good place to start.

"I think this is a good time for us to join this family meeting." Parker's shaky voice interrupted her father and she nudged the woman standing rigidly beside her. "After you."

Before Cade had a chance to react, Meghan slipped past them and left the room. He would have followed her but his sister's stricken expression held him in place.

"Dad? Aunt Judith has something to tell you."

Chapter Seventeen

Cade stepped out into the courtyard and the breeze touched his face, carrying a hint of perfume from the flower gardens. He stared with unseeing eyes into the darkness until he felt someone beside him.

Parker linked her arm through his.

"No offense, but I'd like to be alone." He kept his voice even, careful not to let any emotion leach into it.

"That's why you shouldn't be." Parker leaned against him but Cade had the strangest feeling that his sister was offering *her* strength, not seeking his. "What do you think they're talking about?"

"Dad and Judith? After what happened tonight, I wouldn't begin to take a guess."

"I want to be angry with her but I feel…I don't know. Numb." Parker sighed. "I didn't believe Mom had had an affair with Joseph Ferris, but until I confronted Aunt Judith and asked her what she knew about Mom leaving, I never would have guessed she was capable of such coldhearted…*deception*. She still thinks she did the right thing. She threatened Mom because she was convinced we were all better off without her."

Cade swallowed hard against the knot in his throat. The one that had formed during his aunt's self-righteous tirade and showed no signs of easing. "An institution. Mom." He could hardly put the two words in the same sentence. "And she wasn't even mentally ill."

"I think in her heart Mom believed she wasn't a good wife and mother. And she was so sensitive, it made her even more susceptible to Judith's threats," Parker said softly. "Don't you remember how hard Judith was on Mom? How she made it seem as if Mom had some flaw in her personality because she marched to a different drummer? I'd guess that Mom was afraid Judith was right in believing something was wrong with her. She forgot to pick us up from school sometimes. She must have thought she was a disappointment to Dad because she wasn't a typical country-club wife. And then her relationship with Ferris became suspect."

That's when Judith had seen an opportunity and struck.

Cade closed his eyes but could still see his aunt standing in the kitchen just minutes ago, logically and coolly stating "her side" of the situation. Supremely confident that neither her brother nor the children she'd practically raised as her own could fault her for what she'd done.

The fact that Judith firmly believed Genevieve wasn't a fit parent and had taken steps to cut her sister-in-law off from the family only made the circumstances surrounding Genevieve's abrupt departure more terrible.

All three of the Halloways had listened to Judith's confession with a growing sense of horror. And for the first time, Cade had a glimpse of what his sensitive, vulnerable mother had gone through. Not only day-to-day but following that last visit to the island.

According to Judith, after they'd returned to Minneapolis, Judith sensed the tension in the household and had gotten Cade to confide in her about what had happened. To a woman who prided herself on her family's spotless reputation, it had been the last straw. She'd told Genevieve to leave. And she'd warned her that if she refused, she knew the family doctor would confirm it was his opinion Genevieve was suffering from borderline personality disorder.

Genevieve had left to save the family from embarrassment. And the fact that she'd given up without a fight proved that she believed there was something innately wrong with her.

Cade had a hunch that Parker was right. Judith's threat must have triggered Genevieve's own insecurities and she was afraid the stigma of being institutionalized—even for a short time—would hurt Douglas's reputation and have a profound affect on her children.

In the end, Genevieve had walked away. Not from them. But *for* them.

As the weight of that realization sank in, Cade wondered bleakly if their family could ever recover.

"Cade? Will you pray with me?" Parker's uncertain voice cut through his pain.

"I'm not sure what to say," he admitted in a husky voice.

"Just say what's on your mind. And in your heart."

Cade closed his eyes again as his sister took his hand. For a moment he struggled to find the right words. Freedom came when he realized that God didn't wait until he found them... He met him right where he was at.

"I think I hear a boat. Do you think it's Justin?" Parker lurched toward the window but Meghan grabbed her shoulders and held her in place.

"Hold still or you're going to pop a button on your gown. Remember, this kind of thing is Bliss Markham's forte, not mine." Meghan turned Parker toward the mirror again and their eyes met. Parker's were still red rimmed and puffy; Meghan's shadowed from a sleepless night. They shared a wan smile, silently acknowledging a promise to make the day ahead a celebration in spite of what had happened the night before.

"Bliss," Parker scoffed, stretching up on her tiptoes to try to see out the window. "If you switched careers, you'd give her a run for her money."

Meghan shuddered at the thought of being a full-time event planner. "I'll stick to critters, thank you very much. Now, go ahead and breathe."

Parker obeyed, although she didn't seem nearly as interested in what she looked like in her wedding gown as she did about the boat chugging up to the dock. "It's Bert's fault my dress feels a little tight. I can't say no to her buttermilk pancakes."

Meghan smiled. Parker looked beautiful. Her dress had arrived via special courier—namely Verne Thatcher—and she'd discarded the elaborate veil for a tiny cluster of wild roses tucked in her chignon. Justin's arrival had been delayed for a day due to an emergency meeting with his sponsoring church but Meghan hoped he'd be on the island soon. Although Parker had confided that she'd called him during the middle of the night, Meghan knew she needed the reassurance of his presence.

Bert had the reception well in hand, which left Meghan to continue her role as wedding planner. She'd ruthlessly put her own emotions aside in order to concentrate on Parker and Justin's wedding day.

"I have to see if it's Justin. He promised he'd be here right after lunch. Or maybe it's some of the kids from Willoughby."

In a generous display of hospitality, Parker had invited all the teenagers who'd helped clear and decorate the courtyard to the wedding.

"If you promise to stay put, I'll look."

"I promise." Parker fidgeted but only her eyes moved as she watched Meghan walk to the window.

Of course Cade had to be the first person that Meghan saw. Her heart constricted as she watched him stride down the narrow cobblestone path to the lake.

He wore a black tuxedo and a satin cummerbund over a crisp white shirt. Not rented, of course, but custom fit for his tall, lean frame. The breeze ruffled his dark hair and his set profile gave her no hints as to what was going on inside his head. Or his heart.

He hadn't made an appearance at breakfast, a subdued affair since Judith had opted to leave the island early that morning. Parker had confided in Meghan that she had no idea what her father had said to her aunt, but she'd intercepted her on her way out the door and encouraged her to stay for the wedding. Parker's willingness to forgive was a testimony to her deepening faith and—although Meghan didn't comment on it out loud—another affirmation that she and Justin would accomplish amazing things together for God.

After Meghan had left the family alone in the kitchen the night before, she'd grabbed a flashlight and made her way to the point to pray. She'd prayed for healing for the entire family. And she'd prayed for Judith.

By the time she'd returned to the house, there was only one light burning. In Cade's room. More than anything, Meghan had wanted to find out how he was doing. What he was feeling. And she might have summoned the courage to tap on his door if she hadn't remembered what he'd said about Genevieve.

She couldn't deny the attraction between them. And the kiss they almost shared in Willoughby told her that Cade felt it, too. But if Meghan had dared to hope the fragile threads of friendship could turn into something stronger—something lasting—it was crushed when she'd heard Cade disdainfully dismiss his mother as a flighty artist.

If she kept their relationship from progressing, he wouldn't get close enough to see the "real" Meghan. If she kept her distance, she could hide the things that he would see as flaws. And she wouldn't die a little inside every time he rolled his eyes in frustration. Or flash an impatient look at her when she misplaced her camera. Or her purse. Or her car keys. Or all three.

"Can you see who it is?" Parker's voice yanked her back to the present.

"Just a—" Meghan's voice died in her throat as she saw Cade pause as he reached the end of the dock. Her gaze shifted to the small motorboat and then settled on the person climbing out of it.

Not Justin. A woman. Tall. Slender. With a straw hat perched on her dark hair; the jaunty yellow flower fastened to the brim a perfect match to the formfitting satin sheath she wore. It wasn't until she swept off the hat and used it as a fan that Meghan saw the marked resemblance to Parker.

Genevieve.

Meghan sucked in a breath, recognizing the split second when mother and son recognized one another. Cade remained frozen while Genevieve stood poised on the dock, like a bird ready to take flight.

Please, God.

They were the only words her thoughts could form as she watched.

Cade took a few hesitant steps forward and held out his hand to help her from the boat. Genevieve took it and pressed it against her cheek. Meghan felt a tear slip down her cheek as Cade wrapped his arms around Genevieve and rocked her in his arms, as if she were the child and he were the parent.

"Meghan? Who is it? Is it Justin?"

"It's your mother," she whispered.

"I now pronounce you husband and wife. You may kiss the bride."

Cade averted his eyes—Parker was still his baby sister, after all—and his gaze moved to Meghan, who was snapping a picture of the couple's embrace.

She had stayed in the background for most of the day, catching candid shots of last-minute preparations and capturing moments of what the Society pages would no longer title "The Wedding of the Summer."

But the small gathering of people didn't seem to care that there was no orchestra, just the music provided by a temperamental fountain that had gurgled to life shortly before the ceremony started. Or that the elaborate six-course dinner had been replaced with simple hors d'oeuvres. Or that a frisky bichon was one of the guests.

The only thing that had shaken things up a bit was when Douglas walked into the courtyard with Genevieve on his arm. And they stood side by side as Parker and Justin recited their vows.

When Cade had seen Genevieve, the years had melted away. And so had his anger. Maybe he'd never totally understand everything that had happened, but he'd suddenly realized it didn't matter anymore. When he saw the uncertainty, and the hope, in his mother's eyes—eyes the exact shade of blue as his—he'd realized Meghan was right. There was a time to forgive and start over. A time to make room for people in your life.

He'd spent a lot of time talking to God and knew he'd no longer be satisfied with a faith confined to an hour on Sunday morning.

Once again, Cade's eyes drifted to Meghan, who was laughing as she knelt down to snap a picture of Miss Molly.

She was beautiful.

When the excitement surrounding the wedding ebbed, he planned to tell Meghan how he felt. About his desire to pursue a closer relationship with God—and with her.

Chapter Eighteen

For ten minutes Cade tried unsuccessfully to get past Caitlin McBride's receptionist. The young woman's curly blond hair and wide brown eyes made her look as good-natured and easygoing as a golden retriever puppy, but Cade had quickly discovered looks were deceiving. She was part guard dog. And she wasn't about to let him into the inner sanctum without an appointment.

It appeared that Caitlin's receptionist was either deathly afraid of the consequences of breaking company policy or else she… Cade noticed the panic in her eyes. No. She was deathly afraid of the consequences.

She seemed more afraid of angering her employer than keeping a potential client happy. Which made him rethink his decision to approach Meghan's older sister. But only for a split second. At this point, he was getting desperate.

"Listen, Miss—"

"Buckley."

"Miss Buckley. If you'll just let Caitlin know I'm

here, I'm sure she'll see me. I'm a…friend of the family."

"What did you say your name was?"

He hadn't said. "I'd like to surprise her."

Miss Buckley's eyes narrowed. "If you're a friend of the family, you'd know Miss McBride doesn't like surprises."

Cade tamped down his frustration. "Fine. I'll make an appointment. When is she available?"

He hoped it would be before lunch.

"Let me check." Miss Buckley turned to the computer and her fingers danced lightly across the keyboard. "The first week of November. What time works best for you?"

"November. You've got to be kidding me. Does everyone in this city have such low self-esteem that they have to—"

"Thank you, Sabrina." A terse but feminine voice interrupted him. "I have a few minutes to speak with Mr. Halloway before my nine-thirty."

Cade turned and saw a woman standing just inside the foyer, holding a disposable cup of coffee in each hand.

A woman who'd immediately known who he was even though he was sure they'd never been introduced.

Cade searched vainly for a genetic link that would identify her as Meghan's sister and couldn't come up with a match. Meghan, with her wild mass of curls, winsome smile and penchant for jeans and T-shirts had nothing in common with the serious, cool-eyed woman impeccably dressed in a pencil-thin black skirt, silk blouse and stiletto heels.

Maybe she was Caitlin's personal assistant....

"Of course, Miss McBride."

Or not.

Sabrina Buckley bobbed her head diffidently, as if addressing royalty. Cade half expected the secretary to curtsy.

"Follow me." Caitlin barely spared him a glance as she swept past, pausing long enough to deposit one of the cups on the reception desk.

Cade followed her to the office suite at the end of the hall but once she ushered him inside and closed the door, he was suddenly at a loss. A feeling he wasn't used to experiencing.

Caitlin didn't offer him a seat. Instead she remained standing and folded her arms across her chest. Waiting for him to make the next move.

But Cade was through playing games.

"Meghan won't return my calls," he said with blunt honesty. "I've stopped by the studio but she doesn't keep regular hours. When I called the minister who coordinates Sidewalk Chalk, he told me that Meghan had asked for a month off."

"Really." Caitlin didn't sound surprised.

"I have to talk to her."

"It doesn't sound like she wants to talk to you."

"She just thinks she doesn't," he muttered.

A fleeting smile skimmed across her face. So fleeting that Cade knew he must have imagined it. "I can't help you."

"Why not?"

"Because my sister is miserable. And I'm still trying to decide if it's because she let you into her life or because you're not part of it anymore."

For some strange reason, finding out Meghan was miserable made Cade feel a whole lot better. "I messed up. Big-time."

Caitlin's perfectly shaped eyebrow lifted in a tell-me-something-I-don't-know gesture.

"It would help if I…" For a split second Cade's pride tried to muzzle him. He hated to admit the truth. Especially to a woman who was already eyeing him as if he were a smear on a microscope slide.

But really, Cade asked himself, what did he have to lose?

Meghan.

Which translated to *everything*.

So he told the truth. "It would help if I knew *why* she won't talk to me."

Caitlin stared at him in disbelief. "You really don't know why?"

"Totally clueless."

"Talk to my sister."

"I would love to talk to your sister," Cade pointed out with exaggerated patience. "But I can't. That's why I was hoping *you'd* talk to me. Explain what's going on."

"You want closure."

"I want Meghan," Cade snapped.

Caitlin's shoulders stiffened, encouraging Cade to clarify the statement. Quickly. "I…care about her. I have to apologize and tell her how I feel."

Caitlin's gaze shifted, as if talking about emotions was uncomfortable for her.

Silence weighted the air between them and Cade waited, half expecting her to show him the door. She didn't. Instead, in a gesture that struck Cade as oddly vulnerable, she pushed her lower lip out and blew a sigh, stirring the wisp of bangs on her forehead.

"You can *tell* her, Cade," she finally said. "But getting her to *believe* you—that's going to be the tough part."

"Why wouldn't she believe me?"

"I don't know." Caitlin splayed her fingers and studied her French manicure. "Maybe because you disapproved of your sister marrying Justin. Or because you said your mother couldn't be trusted because she's a flighty artist. Or because—correct me if I'm wrong here—you label your tools and, if asked, you could find the receipt for the first Rolex you bought. In less than five minutes."

Meghan had obviously confided in her sister. Cade wasn't sure where to file that one on his pros and cons list.

"I think Parker and Justin make a great couple. I was being stupid when I described my mother as flighty. She's actually incredibly amazing. And I'm not sure what the rest of what you said has to do with anything." Frustration leached into Cade's voice. "Doesn't everyone keep receipts?"

Caitlin's expression softened for the first time. "Not Megs. She manages to lose them in her purse on the way home from the store. She can be a little…unorganized."

Cade thought the assessment unfair. "She orches-trated my sister's entire wedding reception. Kept my aunt Judith in line. Supervised a group of rowdy teen-agers." *And bullied me into painting again.*

"I know she did." Caitlin regarded him levelly. "That doesn't mean she wasn't out of her comfort zone. Or her galaxy, from the way she described it."

"Meghan seemed to thrive on all the commotion."

"'Seemed to' being the key words."

Cade didn't follow. "What are you getting at?"

"I'm not sure I should bother, considering you claim to care about Meghan and yet you don't know any-thing about her. I'll give you the benefit of the doubt, though, because Megs is a pro at masking her feelings. She helped with the wedding because it meant a lot to Parker, not because she, to borrow your word, thrives on activity. Her faith held her together, but I'll bet she found a place to hide and recharge."

"She—" Did. The argument Cade was ready to pres-ent disintegrated. His fists clenched at his sides. From the look in Caitlin's eyes, there was more. He also knew she wasn't sure she could trust him.

But he was running out of options. The only bridge between him and Meghan was Evie or Caitlin McBride. He would have preferred Evie, the nurturing junior high teacher. Instead he was at the mercy of another nail-chewing, firstborn overachiever. Someone a lot like himself.

Parker was right. God did have a sense of humor.

"Tell me the rest." He added the magic word. "Please."

"I better not regret this." Caitlin gave him a hard look. "If I had to guess, I'd say my sister thinks you wouldn't be able to deal with her ADD."

"Her what?"

"Attention deficit disorder."

Cade frowned. "Isn't that a kid thing?"

"That's what people hear about the most, but adults have it, too. Sometimes children outgrow it and sometimes they don't. Megs didn't. We didn't even realize she had ADD until she was in college. Evie had picked the topic for a term paper and during her research she realized Meghan had all the classic signs."

"That's the reason why she won't return my calls?" It didn't make sense to him.

"It hasn't been easy for her, but Meghan works *with* it. She designed her life—her interests and her career— to play to her strengths." Caitlin paused and met his gaze directly. "And she's just as careful when it comes to her relationships."

Cade sank into the leather chair opposite Caitlin's desk without permission as the enormity of her meaning began to sink in. For the first time he had a clear picture of the damage he'd unknowingly inflicted on Meghan over and over again with his careless words. Now he understood why she'd left so abruptly after the wedding. And why she'd rebuffed his attempts to contact her.

"Wow." Cade closed his eyes, bracketing his face with his hands. When he drew a careful breath, it felt as if someone had slid a knife between his ribs.

"Exactly." The sympathetic note in Caitlin's voice scared him more than her anger.

He opened his eyes and his gaze locked with hers. "So what do I do now?"

"Give up?"

"Not an option." And there was no way he was going to apologize for that.

"I'm not sure you understand. She's always going to struggle with attention issues, Cade. This isn't something that she can make go away if she tries hard enough. And for the record, I haven't seen her struggle with her self-esteem like this since she was first diagnosed. I'm sure you get the credit for that."

Cade absorbed the hit, knowing it originated from Caitlin's loyalty and love for her sister. He wouldn't expect anything less.

"There's something between us." Cade waited to see if Meghan's sister would deny it.

She didn't. Which fanned a tiny flame of hope inside of him.

"Megs is afraid she'd drive you crazy in less than a month."

"Does she drive *you* crazy?" Cade had a strong hunch Meghan's sister not only alphabetized her spices, but also her cleaning supplies and the paperback novels on her bookshelf.

"Of course she does." Caitlin grinned, and for the first time Cade saw the marked resemblance between the two sisters. Unguarded, Caitlin's smile was every bit as charming as Meghan's. "But she knows I love her exactly the way she is. She's Megs. I wouldn't want her to change."

"So, you're going to convince her to talk to me?"

"I already tried," Caitlin admitted, stunning Cade into silence. "But she doesn't see the point. She isn't being stubborn—she's protecting her heart."

From him.

Maybe it was too late to patch things up. She'd taken a month's hiatus from the ministry she poured her heart and soul into. Thanks to him, she was struggling once again with accepting the way God had designed her. He wouldn't let that one go without a fight. Not when she'd been the one who'd challenged him to seek out a deeper relationship with God.

"How do I get in touch with her?"

"You must be a glutton for punishment."

"She can kick me out after I apologize for being an…" He searched for the right words.

"Arrogant jerk," Caitlin supplied.

"Thanks," Cade said drily. "That about sums it up."

Caitlin seemed to make a decision. "Megs is out of town on a shoot for the rest of the week, taking photos of birds at a wildlife rehabilitation center for their brochure. But she *might* have mentioned something about visiting a friend on an island before she comes back to the Cities."

"She's going to Blue Key?" Cade couldn't believe it.

"I doubt she meant Hawaii."

He wasn't intimidated by the cool response. In fact, Cade was so "not intimidated" that he crossed the distance between them, framed her face in his hands and planted a light kiss on her smooth forehead. "I owe you, Caitlin."

"Just don't mess up. If I have to intervene again, I'm going to charge you a hundred and twenty dollars an hour."

Chapter Nineteen

Meghan shaded her eyes against the sun as Verne's fishing boat skipped over the waves toward the island. The maple trees already flashed bits of scarlet and gold high in the green of their branches, reminding Meghan of a Scottish plaid.

A little over a month ago, she'd caught her first glimpse of the main house and fallen instantly in love.

The house wasn't the only thing you fell in love with.

She shook the thought away before it left a mark on her heart.

Maybe she was crazy to come back to Blue Key so soon, but Bert had insisted she spend the weekend when Meghan had mentioned she'd be in the area on a shoot.

"Someone expecting you?" Verne called over the growl of the motor.

The question was almost identical to the one he'd asked her the first time she'd arrived; tears sprang into Meghan's eyes. She hoped Verne would attribute them to the wind.

"Bert knows I'm coming over."

Verne cut the motor and guided the boat along the dock. Smith and Wesson stirred at her feet and raised their noses, sensing the change in direction.

The fishing guide picked up Meghan's duffel bag but this time he deposited it on the dock as carefully as a bellhop handling a Gucci bag at the Ritz.

"I'll be back when you give me a jingle."

"I'm leaving Sunday afternoon. One o'clock. Remember?"

"You may decide to stay longer." He gave Meghan a cheerful wink as he grasped her elbow and helped her out of the boat.

"One o'clock—"

The motor drowned out the rest of the words as Verne revved it up for the return trip.

Two days on Blue Key Island would be more than enough. Meghan hadn't stepped on dry land yet and already memories of Cade were crowding in. It occurred to her that she'd run away from him and ended up in the very place they'd met.

Way to think things through, Meghan, she chided herself.

For several weeks she'd dodged his repeated attempts to get in touch with her.

Deleting the messages he'd left on her answering machine, both at the studio and on her cell phone, had taken more strength than stepping into Bliss Markham's shoes. But when she'd happened to see his name added to the list of volunteers for the next Sidewalk Chalk mural, she'd promptly requested some time off. The

shoot she'd just finished had been an answer to her
frantic prayers for a reprieve.

She hadn't realized that cutting Cade out of her life
would feel like undergoing open heart surgery—without an anesthetic.

It's for the best, she reminded herself. Maybe there'd
been a slight attraction between them, but nothing that
her many quirks couldn't snuff out in record time.

Meghan swung the strap of her duffel bag over her
shoulder, scanning the beach to see if Miss Molly had
heard the boat pull up to the dock.

There was no sign of the dog or her owner.

Walking up the path, she heard music coming from
the courtyard and cut through the sculpture garden to
follow it to its source.

The wedding decorations had been taken down but
Meghan could still picture the way everything had
looked that day. Parker and Justin standing under the
rose arbor, holding hands as they recited the vows they'd
written. Genevieve and Douglas standing side by side
in honor of their daughter, each little glance that passed
between them uncertain yet cautiously optimistic.

Parker had left a message on Meghan's answering
machine right before she and Justin had left for their
honeymoon, letting her know that her parents had met
for dinner—alone—several days after the wedding.

Judith had moved out of the family mansion and
bought a condo of her own in an upscale neighborhood
near the river. She'd also made a sizable contribution to
Justin and Parker's ministry fund. It was Parker's the-

ory that that was as close to an apology as Judith would ever make for what she'd done.

Meghan had no idea what was going to happen between Douglas and Genevieve. But whatever it was, she did know that God could help them reclaim those lost years when they'd let their insecurities drive their actions.

God, she knew, was very good at putting broken things back together. Piece by piece, He was doing the same thing in her life, too.

Maybe by the time she was eighty years old, her heart would look the way it had before she'd met Cade.

She followed the neatly groomed path around the side of the house and stopped as abruptly as if she'd hit an invisible wall.

Water bubbled from the mermaid fountain, catching the sunlight and creating a muted rainbow that fanned across the stones.

The summer flowers had faded a bit, replaced by pale peach mums that bloomed along the foundation. Asters had escaped the ornate Victorian fence and popped up in the courtyard, spilling across the ground to the…carousel.

Meghan blinked.

Someone had begun the painstaking process of restoring it. The knight's steed already sported a fresh coat of ebony paint.

The carousel was obviously going up for sale along with the rest of Genevieve's collection. It was the only reason Meghan could think of to explain the makeover.

Discouragement weighted her steps as she moved

closer to get a better look. She felt a little bit better when she realized that whoever had been hired to do the restoration was definitely qualified. In the interest of time, some artists would have simply chosen one color for the detailing. This one had accented the intricate medallions on the saddle and bridle with gold. Every decorative swirl and whorl on the crest of the chest plate had been meticulously highlighted with the sweep of a number four brush.

Meghan reached out and traced the arch of the horse's head with her fingers, wishing she could scrape up the money to buy the carousel and relocate it to a green space for the kids to enjoy.

A sharp bark came from the woods and she looked up just in time to see Miss Molly break out of the undergrowth.

"Hey, you." Laughing, Meghan scooped the dog up in her arms and cuddled her. "Where's Bert?"

Miss Molly barked a reply that Meghan couldn't decipher and squirmed frantically in her arms. That Meghan understood. She wanted down.

She set the dog back down. "Go find her. Go find Bert."

Amazingly enough, Miss Molly disappeared the way she'd come. When she returned moments later, the person who stepped out of the woods behind her wasn't Bert.

It was Cade.

Meghan's traitorous senses absorbed his familiar features like a dry sea sponge. He looked different somehow and she realized it was the first time she'd ever seen him wearing a pair of blue jeans that had seen better days and a worn-out cotton sweater, the sleeves pushed up to his elbows.

She wanted to run away but her feet wouldn't cooperate. By the time she got her bearings, he was standing in front of her, his eyes searching her face. Looking for something.

Meghan turned away, afraid he'd be able to read what was in her heart.

"So, what do you think about the carousel?" Cade asked, pushing his hands casually into his back pockets. As if they hadn't been apart for almost two months. As if she shouldn't find it strange that he was on the island, too.

"It looks good." Meghan tried to match his tone.

"Thanks." Cade grinned. "I think."

Realization slammed into her. "*You're* the one restoring it?"

"Yup. Someone suggested that I stop...ah, plugging up my creative outlet. I discovered that restoration satisfies my somewhat scary need for precision and order, and also keeps me from drumming my fingers."

Meghan tried to suppress a smile as the memory of that afternoon on the point slipped into her thoughts.

"Don't," Cade said quietly.

"Don't what?"

"Try to forget. I haven't been able to."

Meghan swallowed hard. "I suppose you're here to get things ready for the sale."

"We decided to hang on to the place. Parker and Justin need a place to stay when they come back on furlough…and Bert let Mom talk her into opening up the studio to the locals for beginning art classes. Dad is determined he's going to take up fishing when he retires. And this project will keep me busy for quite a while. Unless I can convince someone to help me. Do you know anyone who might be interested?"

"Cade—" Meghan took a step back. This was too hard. She had to make up an excuse and leave before he caused irreparable damage to her heart.

"Come on. I have something to show you." Cade took her hand before she could escape and led her toward the house.

"Where's Bert?" Panicked, Meghan looked around for an ally. All she saw was Miss Molly, who'd been won over to Cade's side long ago.

"She's working, but she said she'll see you at dinner."

"Dinner…" That was hours from now.

"It'll only take a minute. Please."

Meghan couldn't resist the please. She gave in and let him tow her into the house and up the stairs to the bedroom she'd stayed in.

He nudged her over to the window and pushed aside the curtain.

Meghan shifted her weight to the other foot but she could still feel the warmth of Cade's skin through the thin cotton shirt he wore. One slight turn and she'd be in his arms…

"Genevieve told me the real reason you came here."

It was the last thing she expected him to say but she shouldn't have been surprised. Is that why he'd been trying to get in touch with her? To chew her out for her trying to help his mother find the Ferris?

Meghan moistened her lips. "I stopped looking for it. I didn't feel right considering how I felt about—" *You.* "Your family. Dad gets involved in these crazy schemes sometimes and—"

"Meghan?" Cade interrupted softly. "Look down."

Confused, Meghan obeyed. "What—"

And then she saw it.

The colorful mosaic of stones that circled the court-yard—the ones they'd spent hours weeding—took on a new shape. They formed an intricate network around the fountain, the colors shifting like a rainbow from pale to bright.

"Cade—I can't believe…" Meghan swallowed. "Do you really think…" She couldn't finish a sentence.

Cade understood. "Ferris. It had to be. Mom loved her gardens—it would have been a fitting gift to cre-ate something he knew she'd treasure. But Mom never came back to Blue Key and Ferris moved to Italy at the end of the summer. He sent her one letter, explaining his sister would be taking care of him during his illness and telling her he'd left a gift for her. Mom never told him about the accusations or the divorce—she didn't want to add to his burdens." Cade's voice was husky. "You were right. What I saw that day was my mother comforting a person who'd just told her that he'd been diagnosed with cancer. They were more acquaintances than friends. Definitely not lovers."

Meghan's throat closed at the easy way Cade referred

to Genevieve as "Mom." "What about Bert? Didn't she know?"

"Bert didn't move to the island until the following summer, so she never questioned who'd created the mosaic. She was just as shocked as I was when I showed it to her."

"But how did you find it?" Meghan had spent a week in the room. She'd looked out the window several times a day and never noticed the thing she'd been searching for had been literally right under her nose.

Cade braced his fingers on the window frame and stared down at the courtyard. "The truth? I was standing right here a few days ago, praying for wisdom. Because I knew you were going to be here and I was wondering how I could ever get you to agree to be in the same room with me after I'd hurt you. When I opened my eyes, I saw it. Plain as day."

Meghan turned blindly away, rejecting the words. She couldn't read too much into them...couldn't imagine what they might mean.

Cade's voice stopped her as she reached the door.

"You told my sister that if she believed God had brought her and Justin together, she shouldn't let her fear keep them apart. Are you sure that isn't what you're doing?"

It wasn't fair, Meghan decided. He'd known she was coming and he'd gathered all his ammunition beforehand. "I'm not going to fit into your life. Maybe for a little while we could make it work, but eventually..." It would kill her if he got impatient with her. Got tired of her.

"You can leave but you aren't going to get rid of me that easily. If I have to adopt a whole litter of little puff balls to get you to spend time with me, I will."

Meghan's mouth dropped open. "Parker told you that I'm a pet photographer."

"Actually, it was Caitlin."

"Caitlin?" Meghan choked. "You talked to my sister?"

"And lived to tell about it," Cade said, a glint of humor in his eyes. "She's the one who told me you'd be here this weekend. And if I'm not mistaken, it was her way of giving us her blessing."

Her blessing…

"You don't understand." She would have explained when their eyes caught and held. What she saw in his stripped the air from her lungs.

"I understand that I said stupid things that hurt you. I understand that I need *you,* Meghan." Cade advanced slowly, crossing the distance between them until they were inches apart. "I understand that my life is a gray, boring…cubicle…without you. I have no idea what *you'd* be getting out of the relationship, but I'll make you a promise. When you need time alone, I'll guard the path to the point so no one gets past. And I'll *always* help you find your camera."

Meghan choked back a sob. "How can a girl refuse an offer like that?"

"I'm hoping it's too good to pass up." Cade brushed his thumb against a tear that ran down her cheek.

"It is."

Cade exhaled slowly, closed his eyes and drew her

against him as carefully as if she were made of glass. "What a relief," he murmured in her ear. "Because I was really hoping I wouldn't have to get those puppies."

Meghan's hiccup turned into a laugh as she breathed in the scent of him. Felt the strength of his arms around her. It felt a lot like coming home.

"Meghan?"

"Mmm?"

"If you let me kiss you, I'll let you drive the boat."

She smiled up at him. "It's a deal."

* * * * *

Dear Reader,

Eagles may be a common sight here in northern Wisconsin, but seeing one never fails to take my breath away! And they are a beautiful reminder of Isaiah 40:31. Many times in my own life, when I've felt stretched beyond what I think I can endure, I've leaned on the promise in this verse:

"But those who hope in the Lord will renew their strength. They will soar on wings like eagles..."

But in order to soar, you have to let go and leave the safety of the nest! As Meghan and Cade discovered, God sometimes nudges His children out of their comfort zones. It isn't always easy to trust in those instances, but it can result in a deeper relationship with Him...and with each other.

I hope you enjoyed getting to know Meghan.

Blessings,

Kathryn Springer

QUESTIONS FOR DISCUSSION

1. What was your first impression of Meghan? Of Cade? How did their backgrounds influence the way they viewed life?

2. Cade claimed that selling Blue Key Island was a good business decision. What was really at the root of his decision?

3. Do you have a special "retreat" where you go to think or to pray? What is it like? Where is it?

4. Both Meghan and Cade had some trust issues. What were they based on? How were they alike and how did they differ?

5. How did Parker's growing faith challenge Cade's relationship with God? What influence did Meghan's faith have on him?

6. Meghan felt as if she were out of her "comfort zone" when she helped with Parker Halloway's wedding. Have you ever been in a situation that stretched you beyond what you were comfortable with? What was it? How did you respond?

7. Isaiah 40:31 says, "Yet those who wait for the Lord will gain new strength; they will mount up with wings like eagles, they will run and not get tired,

they will walk and not become weary." Think of a
time when God strengthened you when you were
tired and weary. What were the circumstances?

8. Do you believe the saying that "opposites attract"?
   Why or why not?

9. Why did Parker doubt she was right for Justin?
   How did Meghan encourage her?

10. Meghan was attracted to Cade but afraid to let him
    get too close. Why? Has anything ever stopped you
    from allowing people to get to know the "real"
    you? What was it?

11. What was the turning point in Cade's faith jour-
    ney?

12. Meghan was looking for a "hidden treasure" on
    Blue Key Island. What do you think the "real" trea-
    sure was? Why?

Four sweet, heartfelt stories from fan-favorite
Love Inspired® Books authors!

**TIDINGS OF JOY and
HEART OF THE FAMILY**
by Margaret Daley

**LASSO HER HEART and
MISTLETOE REUNION**
by Anna Schmidt

Get two inspirational Christmas romances
for the price of one!

Available in December 2013 wherever books are sold.

REQUEST YOUR FREE BOOKS!

2 FREE INSPIRATIONAL NOVELS
PLUS 2
FREE
MYSTERY GIFTS

Love Inspired

SPECIAL EXCERPT FROM

Love Inspired

A shy bookstore employee runs into her youthful crush.

Read on for a sneak preview of
TAIL OF TWO HEARTS
by Charlotte Carter, the next book in
THE HEART OF MAIN STREET *series,*
available November 2013.

Vivian Duncan stepped out of Happy Endings Bookstore onto the sidewalk in the small Kansas town of Bygones. Watching leaves and bits of paper racing down the street, blown by a brisk breeze, she inhaled the crisp November air.

She hoped the owner of Fluff & Stuff, Chase Rollins, would help her put together a special event at the bookstore to promote books about dogs.

As she opened the door, the big green-cheeked parrot near the cash register squawked his greeting, "What's up? What's up?" He proudly bobbed his head and did a little dance on his perch.

"Hello, Pepper." Vivian smiled at Chase's recently acquired bird that was looking for a new home.

"Good birdie! Good birdie!" he vocalized.

"I'm sure you are." She looked around for Chase.

His warm brown eyes lit up when he spotted Vivian, and he produced a delighted smile. "Hey, Viv."

Smiling, he stepped toward Vivian. When she'd first met him, she'd thought he was an attractive man. She still did. At six foot two with a muscular body, he towered over her five-foot-four frame, even when she was wearing heels. His short, dark hair had a natural wave that sculpted his head. His nose was straight, his lips nicely full.

"What can I do for you?" he asked.

"I, uh…" Snapping back from her train of thought, she started over. "Allison at Happy Endings and I have realized books about dogs are particularly popular. We'd like to put on some sort of a special event and thought you could give us some guidance about where to get a dog or two for show-and-tell. I know the puppies you have are from the local shelter."

Chase ignored the bird. "The shelter is getting overcrowded, so I've started a monthly Adopt a Pet Day here at the shop. In fact I'm having one this Saturday." He handed her a flyer from the stack on the counter. "And I'd love to help you with your event."

"I'm glad." She was relieved, too, that Chase could help out.

"When you visit the shelter you'll have to be careful not to fall in love." His eyes twinkled, and his lively grin was pure temptation.

Vivian blinked. Her cheeks flushed. Had he said *fall in love?*

Pick up TAIL OF TWO HEARTS
wherever Love Inspired® books are sold.

LIEXP1013

During the Christmas season, Rebecca Yoder agrees to help
new preacher Caleb Wittner with his mischievous daughter.
Amelia's turned the community of Seven Poplars upside
down. Only Rebecca can see the pain hidden beneath the
little girl's antics—and her father's brusque manner. After
losing his wife in a fire, Caleb's physical scars may be healing,
but his emotions have not. Yet Rebecca's sweet manner soon
has him smiling and laughing with his daughter—and his
pretty housekeeper. Soon Caleb must decide whether to
invite Rebecca into his life—or lose her forever.

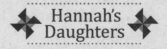

Hannah's Daughters

Rebecca's Christmas Gift

by

Emma Miller

Available November 2013
wherever Love Inspired books are sold.

Find us on Facebook at
www.Facebook.com/LoveInspiredBooks

www.Harlequin.com

LI87848